ACKNOWLEDGEMENTS

Thanks to Bedford and Luton Archives,
County Hall, Bedford
The Public Record Office, London
The Census Office, London
Flitwick Public Library Services
Toddington Public Library Services
Edinburgh Central Library
Friends Kathy and Jim Wooding, Hilda Brighton,
Thelma Spavins, Thelma Palmer, Claude and Eileen Barnes,
Richard Thompson, Reg Day, Aunt Lil, Aunt Daphne (Sally),
Aunt Barbara, and Janice Crisp, (nee Brighton and one of the
extensive Stringer clan), for encouraging me to keep going

Thanks also to the late Lynda Lee Potter, (journalist), and
Michael Brander, author of many books, for their advice
and encouragement.

This book is dedicated to the memory of my mother

ISBN
978-0-9561932

Published by: M. J. Kerr AMRSPH and Alvis Kerr
25 Haig Crescent, Bathgate EH48 1DL Scotland

PREFACE

We can trace the pedigree of princes, fill up catalogues of towns besieged and provinces desolated, but we cannot recover the genuine history of mankind. (Henry Hallam 1777-1859)

If you are genuinely interested in 19th and 20th century history, and the 1940s in particular, then this book may interest you.

The 1940s were not just a decade of war and austerity. It was a different way of life, for me, and countless others.

Around 1998, in between filming scenes for a well known detective series for television, on location in a rough housing area of Glasgow, we stopped to have a break. The chuck wagon was set up in the bowels of a bleak sky scraper block of flats. A boy, around ten years of age, approached me and asked if I was famous. I said, 'Of course,' as he thrust an autograph book under my nose, handed me his pen, and told me to sign 'there.'

I am not famous, but didn't want to disappoint the wee lad. My agent landed me parts in television plays, films, advertisements many times, but blink and you miss me. Often, my little contribution landed on the cutting room floor. That little lad in Glasgow was living in poverty, not really so very different than the poverty of the 1940s. OK! he may have a Television, mobile phone, 'Fridge, (likely empty apart from a few cans of lager,) perhaps a few modern media gadgets, but he was poor nevertheless. The flats looked in a bad state of repair, all concrete with no gardens, litter and rubbish lying around. Poorer families still live in bad housing conditions, women still suffer violence from their partners, families still struggle with woefully inadequate incomes. Can anything change it?

3

A NEW LIFE BECKONS

It was Christmas Eve 1953. The train was full, the passengers happy, singing, they were on their way home for Hogmanay, a peculiar Scottish tradition. My small suitcase held all my worldy possessions, my boats burned, I didn't look back. Next stop for me was Edinburgh, a new adventure beckoned. There was no guarantee of happiness or prosperity, but I had a job to go to and a place to live, and most of all, I had hope. This story is of the life and times, and family, I left behind in rural Bedfordshire.

Ernie and Mum at the wedding of younger sister Pat to Winston Woodcock at Ampthill, 1970, Mum is completely blind.
Pat died in 1997 at same time as Princess Diana.
The country mourned a Princess, I mourned my youngest sister.

CONTENTS

Acknowledgements, Preface, Preamble

CHAPTER/PAGE

ILLUSTRATIONS

PREAMBLE:
"Let them eat cake"

After retiring from the Inland Revenue at the grand old age
of 60, I decided against putting my feet up and knitting oversize
sweaters for my grandchildren. I took on a part-time job and more
filming assignments. The price of cigarettes increased in the next
budget, reminiscent of Sir Stafford Cripps who hiked the price up by
a shilling in the 1940s. I apologised to a man for the increase, his
reply was, 'It's OK, I can afford it.'

Well, when I was a child in the 1940s, we could not afford
them. There were other things we could not afford. A kitchen sink,
an indoor bathroom, carpets for the floor, linen for the beds, etc, etc.
We had to go without a great many things which would have made
life that bit sweeter. Come hell or high water, Ernie had to have his
cigarettes, ten to twenty per day, or we were in trouble.

Gravel Pit Road, in the village of Flitwick, Bedfordshire,
where I spent most of my early years, had been known as the Alley
for many years. The Alley provided a short cut to the school and
Hornes End via a dirt path and a cutting under the railway.

All the old cottages were knocked down to allow
a through road to Elmwood Crescent around the 1960's/70s , and
replaced by new comfortable homes. Only the thatched cottage at
corner of Station Road, and the four terraced homes nearby remain
from the days when I lived in the Alley. Children no longer pass
that way to school. I took that dirt track in the 1940s, along with
many friends. In a few years time, there will be no-one left to tell
how difficult life was for the very poor during those years, or what
they suffered to retain and build on the freedoms you and I enjoy
today. For those families going through difficult times, we have the

8

Social Security system to soften the effects. Life for most of us is not as bad as it was for the poor in the 19thcentury, where I begin.

When the Houses of Parliament were built, most of Britain's population were disenfranchised. Flitwick's population of around 400 were mostly engaged in agriculture with no right to vote. Not because of apathy, but because they were considered ignorant, not fit enough, not rich enough, or clever enough to vote.
The right to vote was hard fought for.

In the 19th century, during those apparently affluent years for some, millions died young from diseases caused by lack of good food, decent medical care, and dire poverty, but above all, from ignorance, they knew little else. Except for a few reformers, the people in power did not seem to be in too much of a hurry to make things better. The country was class riven. Ordinary men and women were more oft to doff the cap and curtsy to their so called betters, accepting their station in life with respect, humiliation, and without question, than you or I would do today. It was thought that people were poor because of a weakness in their character, they were lazy, drunkards, not very intelligent. Charitable deeds, perhaps distributing food hampers or coal at Christmas, raising funds for a charitable hospital for example, was all very fine, but what was needed, was a change of attitude.

According to the history books, Britain in the 19th century was the most powerful and richest nation on earth. We had the power, glory, liberty, and prosperity, undoubtedly true for the ruling classes and social elite, but for too many, there was starvation and the Workhouse. Large families in cramped accomodation. Victorian slums without decent sanitation spread diseases, the poor blamed for bringing their tragic circumstances upon themselves.
1900, at least a third of Britain's population lived in abject poverty.

My forebears were among those most desperate people.
On the subject of sanitation, Sidney Wood, (1850-1879) wrote in his book, "The Welfare State,"

"I see little glory in an empire which can rule the waves, but is unable to flush its own sewers."

Liberal MP (1906-1918) Leo Money, issued a report in 1909 on incomes. 1,250,000 had annual incomes of over £700
3,750,000 had an income of between £160 and £700 per annum, but the vast majority, 38,000,000 existed on annual poverty incomes of less than £160.

My Stringer and Randall forebears were among those lowest paid, my grandfather was lucky if he earned £60 per year. Poverty was my mother's inheritance, from way before Victoria's reign, right through to the 1940s and into the 1950s. Even in 1936, although the average wage is reported as being £2-12 shillings per week, step-father Ernie was earning no more than half that sum.

Few Labourers and Artisans working on those magnificent buildings in Victorian times could read, write, or vote. Low wages, no paid holidays, or sick pay if they became ill. No compensation culture for them. Death of the family breadwinner often left a poor widow not only bereft, but homeless and penniless too. There are no wealthy ancestors in my family tree.

Greatgrandmother, age 31, died giving birth to my grandmother, who became an orphan when her father died a short while later. Death in childbirth, and babies dying before they were a year old, was as common here in those years as in some of the poorest parts of the world today. In 1877, Bedfordshire Times carried a report of a child, naked, being sold for a pint of beer.

I do not believe that was an isolated incident. Rubbish thrown on to the streets, no proper drainage, several families sharing one lavatory.

In Flitwick, poor children were set to work to help family finances, making lace, plaiting straw, or setting out early dawn to work until late evening for local farmers and gentry. Honest toil with grudging rewards. To ask for a raise was tantamount to rebellion, and could brand a man a troublemaker, or worse, he could become blacklisted and unemployable. To join one of the early trade unions was risky.

Men arrived home from some far flung corner of the empire, (that is if they survived at all), weary, perhaps with the loss of a limb and maybe their sight too, from foreign skirmishes.

Adequate shelter, together with nutritious food, safe water to drink, and clean air to breathe, are basic human needs. Even today, it is an ideal we are still attempting live up to.

Before the Education Act of 1870 and compulsory education, many men and women could not read or write, not even their name. They made their mark, which was usually a cross on the paper.
Meg Abbot knew all there was to know about herbs, but when she wed Alfred Stringer she was unable to write her name. In the 19th century there were plenty of poor parents who knew education was a way out of poverty, (as it still is today), but were desperate for the children to leave school and help out. Boys were needed at harvest time, girls as young as 10/11 years of age went into domestic service.

The notion was, what good would educating a girl do? for she would soon marry and have babies. Much better that she learn how to take care of a home. Boys fared little better. What would a farm lad need with book learning. Would it build a hayrick? Follow a horse at the plough? This perception persisted right into the 1940s as you will read later about the 11 Plus. The image of poor children

11

being educated by some rich neighbour or wealthy philanthropist happened only in story books, seldom if ever in real life. As has been mis-quoted from Alexander Pope (1688-1744), many times,

"A little knowledge is a dangerous thing,"
(Pope's Essay on Criticism 1711)
Does this imply the working classes should not have higher desires?

"A little learning is a dangerous thing, drink deep, or taste not the Pierian Spring, There, shallow draughts intoxicate the brain, and drinking largely sobers us again,"

For example, Ernie's grandfather, George Stringer, enrolled at Flitwick School on 16th March 1873, age 9. He left a year later to go to work. The Education Act of 1880 required children attend school only until they were ten years old.

Fortunately, it wasn't all doom and gloom, because arising out of the poverty and grime came intelligent, self educated men and women, encouraged in their youth by enlightened parents who saw a brighter cleaner future, helped by the emergence of public libraries, museums and galleries.

I have often laid this work to one side, thinking to myself that times have changed since those long ago days, no child need go hungry or be unloved, or uncared for. However, the N.S.P.C.C. tell us differently. Intellectuals have written about poverty, but often, they have not experienced it, or the writer waxes lyrical about being 'poor and happy.' I was poor, and not happy about it.

Some have capital to fall back on. My mother and her family had no capital, no savings, not because they were wastrals, but because their income was insufficient to begin with. Today, every pressure group in the land cries out to Government and Joe Public,

'Please give us more money to do the job we'd like to do.'

Why are there so many charities? Do we need them all? Why? Happiness is an individual feeling and condition we all aspire to. Money in itself we know doesn't ensure happiness, one has only to look at newspapers to read of another wealthy couple splitting up. However, without money, the happy feeling is fleeting when the stomach is empty, children are cold, and there is no secure roof overhead. Luke Ch. 6,

'Blessed are the poor, for yours is the kingdom of heaven.'

Another quote is very forthright, Mathew ch. 19, verse 21,

'If thou wilt be perfect, go and sell all that thou hast and give to the poor, and thou shalt have treasure in heaven.'

It is no heaven being poor. Given the choice, how many would opt for poor? Really poor. When it is a choice of paying the rent, (or mortgage), or eating. Why do so many buy lottery tickets. As a contribution to charity? I think not. How many, on winning that pot of gold would give every penny away? I have not heard of one. Even those who say that winning the lottery has brought them nothing but misery don't have the gumption to do that.

Beveridge, in 1942, identified 5 evils threatening society. Idleness, Want, Disease, Ignorance, and Squalor. Living in the Alley, experiencing the squalor, deprivation, the unhappiness, was not something to be aspired to. Squalid housing, and the poverty Mum endured all those years was not for me,

The 20th century spawned many books, abounding with the lives of the rich and famous, of notable events, but we glean little about those on the bottom rung of society's ladder, living day to day. Ordinary decent people, surviving as best they could.   Is it any wonder, that, when credit cards became available, and every finance company in the land was offering the wherewithal to buy now and pay later, that so many took them up on their offer.

Mum had nothing when she married her second cousin Ernie Bland. No inheritance, no expensive wedding presents, in fact, very little more than the clothes she wore. She died in 1981, age 64, after a lifetime of hardship and denial.

FOOTNOTES

In 1834 six farm labourers from Tolpuddle in Dorset were sentenced to 7 years transportation for attempting to start up a union, (they were known as the Tolpuddle Martyrs), but before that, in 1830, William Barnes of Flitwick was one of the men instigating a strike for more wages for farm labourers. On December 6th 1830, 21 Special Constables, (paid one shilling each), quelled the mob at Flitwick. About 100 men were charged with,

'Not being content to work for their usual wages, and trying to extort great sums of money from the masters who employed them.'

William got 14 days, ringleader William Mitchell, received 6 months hard labour. Needless to say the labourers families were no better off.

You could say they were lucky. A few years before, in 1819, a rally at St Peter's field Manchester, gathered to petition for repeal of the Corn Laws, and votes for the people, was dispersed and crushed by brutal military intervention.   11 people were killed, hundreds injured, including women and children.

It became known as the Peterloo Massacre.

14

Chapter 1
1935 SATURDAY'S CHILD

It is Saturday May 4th 1935, and Mum has added to the statistics of teenage girls having a baby out of wedlock. Lonely, with no family around to support her, she cradles the baby in her arms as she lies in a hospital charity bed in the county of Kent, tired physically, and emotionally having to come to terms with her situation. She is far away from relatives she has on the Stringer family line in Flitwick and Maulden, and contact with the Randall side of the family has long been lost. They do not know of her plight. The deaths of her parents happened at a crucial time in the life of a girl, a time when she needs her mother especially.

In 1935 there are no mobile phones, no fax machines, no email. Her older half-sisters and her half brother have long gone their own way. Her younger brother Billy, now 15 years old, is living in London, working in a factory, but she doesn't know that. Another relative, her uncle John Randall, is living in Garfield Road Bedford, unknown to her.

This baby in her arms is the only person she can call her own, but she is now facing an agonising choice. The steely bond she has already formed with the baby is making the decision even more difficult. All the advice she receives is to give this baby up for adoption, it would be the most sensible solution. There are married couples out there desperate to adopt a bonny healthy baby. Does she accept the advice, or find a way of bringing up baby herself? Unmarried, age 18, wait a minute. It will be extremely hard going. Little or no money, no sympathy. It isn't until 1948 and the introduction of the National Assistance Act that unmarried mothers can apply for state aid. Mum made an emotional decision, not a level headed one, when she decided to keep me. She did tell me I had been fostered for the first few months after she left hospital, until obtaining employment where I could be with her.

Mum was born Florence Margaret Randall in December 1916, daughter of farm labourer Joseph Randall and his second wife Elizabeth Stringer, then living at the Warren, on the outskirts of Flitwick. She was baptized at the Church of St Peter and St Paul in June 1917. A few months later, he moved his family to a small cottage in Magpie Row Maulden. They are long ago demolished. Mum joined her older half sister Fanny (Stringer, but known as Fanny Randall), at Maulden school before her fourth birthday. There are new modern homes in Magpie Row today.

Although Joseph gave his age as 59 when he married Gran, he was in fact 65. Grandma was 34 and the mother of three illegitimate children. Charlotte May, known as May, born 1906, Leslie Thomas, born 1910, and Fanny, born 1913. The older children did not join their mother in the matrimonial home. Mum recalled they lived in the Braiche area of Maulden.

Joseph described himself as a widower, Grandma a domestic servant and spinster. Delving into the past, I tried to find details of Grandpa's first marriage, without success, until the release of the 1901 census, when I learned I had been on a wild goose chase trying to find him in Bedfordshire. In 1901, he is living in Sutton, near East Retford, working as a Shepherd. In the 1891 census, he is unmarried and working as a farm servant near Clayworth. Not until 1895 did he marry the widow Mary Ogley, who had daughters Henrietta and Lizzie. They adopted the name Randall. Despite further searches, I do not know what happened to the family. There is a gap in my information between 1901 and 1908, when I find Grandpa Randall destitute and ill in Ampthill Cedars workhouse.

Another mystery is why did Maulden people know him as Captain Randall? Gran died in 1930 of Meningitis, at the Cedars, age 45. Grandpa died of old age, 82, also in the Cedars.

Both are buried in the old Churchyard at Maulden.

1929 saw the end of the old workhouses. Such places became Council run hospitals for the poor. Mum's brother Billy joined the Royal Marines at Chatham when he was 17, later moving to Plymouth, where he wed Barbara in 1941. They had two sons.

Britain in 1935 was, on the surface, a very wealthy and privilidged country, for the upper classes and ruling elite. However, the poor were indeed poor. Poverty and degrading living conditions suffered along with the lack of even the most basic of utilities we so take for granted today. Financial assistance was available, but it was means tested. All but the most essentials, such as bed, table, had to be sold off before help would be considered. Many a family had to sell the piano, or some precious heirloom, perhaps for much less than it was worth, in order to eat and pay the rent when the breadwinner became unemployed or ill. It is well recorded by others, that in the depression years of the 1930s many families relied on charitable soup kitchens for a daily meal. Mum was destitute, she had no home, a baby, and no means of support. A baby layette at 39/6 was around 4 or 5 months wages for a domestic servant. She could not approach a Bank or Finance house for a loan. The sort of finance available to you and me should we require it wasn't available then for those without tangible assets to pledge. A layette consisted of 2 Daygowns, 2 Nightgowns, 2 Flannel Barries (long sleeve vests), 2 Flannel Pilches, (wrappers), 2 cream vests, 12 Terry Nappies, one Flannel Headsquare. Unless St Faith's provided them for me.

It was usual for the cot to be in the parents room, even for baby to sleep in the marital bed, as Joyce and Pat did later.

17

Now Mum had a baby, no wage, no live in position, she must have rued the day I was conceived. Yet she still clung this little scrap of humanity to her bosom, because I was hers.

1935 was the year of King George V's Jubilee, with all its pomp and ceremony. Although war was on the horizon, for a brief moment in time, those of wealth and priviledge could take their ermine robes out of mothballs, and dust off their coronets. Kings and Queens from many countries, some to lose their thrones, and perhaps a few heads, brought their flunkeys with them. They made a splendid colourful spectacle, while the rural poor were living in conditions none of us would tolerate today, and little barefoot urchins with raggedy clothes ran about the streets. Flitwick mothers were not the only ones struggling to keep their family clothed, fed and warm on very low incomes.

Salesmen went round the doors selling vacuum cleaners. Wasn't much point trying to sell one to an agricultural labourer's wife, she had no carpets and couldn't afford the instalments.

Cinemas sprung up everywhere for the masses, and dancehalls were packed with young people as the wireless churned out the music they wanted to listen to. In the Alley the wireless ran on batteries, valves, and accumulator, (more about that later).

1935 was the year when Hitler tightened his grip on Germany, and polished up his expanding territorial ambitions.
He introduced conscription, and legislated agains the Jews. Franco was pitting Spaniard against Spaniard. It was a year when pinkish red dominated the World map, depicting the British Dominions, Empire, and Dependencies.

Imperial Airways and Quantas introduced an airline service between Britain and Australia, taking 12 days each way, each trip costing £195, massively out of reach for an ordinary working man.

1935 was also a year when homes of the rural poor had no indoor sanitation or fresh water on tap. The lavatory was a bucket in a shed, or an outhouse next to the main house. In the cities, many families shared one lavatory.

From 1897 to as late as 1928, schemes to bring Electricity, Mains water, and Mains sewerage to Flitwick were rejected by the then Flitwick Parish Council as too costly. Were Councillors among the great unwashed? Farm labourers, as well as Miners and other workers, washed the grime and dirt of the workplace off in a tin bath in front of the fireplace in homes all over the country. Once each week, seldom more frequently, the family ritual of bathnight took place. The youngest dunked in first, then the rest of the children, and lastly, Mum and Dad, all in the same water. The tin bath was brought to the warm spot in front of the fire. Water had to be physically put in from jug and kettle, which was heated on the open cooking range. Dirty water baled out and disposed of into a drain if one was nearby, or on to the garden, or as we did, on to some handy nearby stretch of waste ground.   No wonder the poor were called the great unwashed.   Yes!   1935 was a good year for some, but in this wealthy very class riven country of ours there were also millions dying or leading miserable lives for want of proper medical attention, decent living conditions, and nourishing sustenance.   They could not afford the best, and the worst was often fatal. (see Medical Notes).

Bread cost approximately 9d for two loaves, milk 2d per gallon, 20 cigarettes 1/1 (5p), (Woodbine cigarettes or loose tobacco such as Golden Virginia slightly less).   Petrol for those fortunate enough to own a car, 1/9 per gallon.   Petrol sold in gallons. As can be seen above, the price of a packet of cigarettes would buy 6 gallons of milk.   The exchange rate for the dollar was 5.15 dollars to the £1. Holidays, when they were allowed by the employer, were unpaid.

Almost all agricultural workers lived in tied houses, that is to say, a house went with the job. Raising a deposit for a mortgage was well nigh impossible on such a low wage. New homes did not include central heating, carpets, double glazing, or a prepared garden. These were all extras, even as late as 1958 when Alvis and I wed and contracted for our first bungalow.

For those with a car, 1935 saw the introduction of driving tests. My father in law never sat a test, as he acquired his driving licence in 1929. In 1935 a new Austin car cost £100, a new Hillman Minx £159, and the first Jaguar rolled out on September 24th, cost £385. Just a dream to a working man. That year, a farm labourer's wage was little above £1 per week, with no state help to feed his family. In the depression years, average wages fell below £1.16shillings per week.

A bicycle could be bought for a shilling or two weekly. For those out of work, or working casually a few days at a time, life was even more difficult. Footwork or pedal power got a man to and from work, or for greater distances, he took the bus or train. Flitwick was a commuter village long before the word became common usage, with workers commuting to Luton and Bedford, to the factories, where they could earn more money than being a land worker, even though the work was tedious and repetitive.

Little of all this, and what was going on in the world that day could have been of much interest to Mum as she cradled me and pondered what to do.

St Faith's Home did all they could for Mum, but they could not provide a husband and a stable home. Returning to Readham Orphanage, where she had been since her father died, wasn't an option. Bad example to the other girls. Having an illegitimate child in 1935 was considered such a disgrace, such a serious lapse of moral standards, that some unfortunate girls found themselves incarcerated in a Lunatic Asylum, an awful place. The notion was put rationally that, because they had allowed themselves to become pregnant, they were short on sense, that in fact, their minds were unhinged. (Where was the guilty man in all this?) An abortion was expensive and risky. Legislation had made abortions illegal in 1803, and further legislation in 1861 made it a criminal act even if it could be life saving for the woman. Little had changed. A servant girl with no money wouldn't know where to turn. For the lower classes, abortions were usually performed in seedy back street premises, private houses, carried out by unqualified people with little or no medical skills, and primitive equipment.

A film shown in 1947, title Brighton Rock. starring Richard Attenborough as father of the child, also starring Hemoine Baddeley and William Hartnell, (the first Doctor Who) was controversial and caused a stir. Some local authorities banned it altogether because of the harrowing abortion scenes. For a man to sow his wild oats was considered normal, often encouraged, but for a girl to do the same thing then, she was called loose, fallen, immoral, disgraceful. Mum was neither loose, fallen or a disgrace. She was just a very young vulnerable girl who fell in love with the wrong guy. I have a theory that my father was a young man belonging to one of the many families who descended on Kent for the Hop picking season. I was conceived in the autumn of 1934. He had his fun with her, then returned to London without giving a thought to the damage he had done. I emphasise this is only a theory, because as I grew up and asked for details of my real father, Mum became upset and   cried. I gave up eventually, deciding he wasn't worth it. He should have been there for her and wasn't. Without me, she could have had the chance of a better life. Some unmarried mothers were more   ·

21

fortunate. They had supportive parents or perhaps a friend willing to help look after baby while Mum returned to work. In many cases, the man did the 'honourable thing', as they called it then, and married the girl, even if they had to set up home with one or other set of parents until they got a home of their own. (this was called a shotgun wedding). Mum was out on her own. Mum had no supportive network of family or friends. Pressure to have me adopted must have been tremendous, given the circumstances. St Faith's provided for me, but we could not stay there forever.

Mum eventually found herself a live in position as Housekeeper in a farmhouse near Radwell, a hamlet north of Bedford. On one of her days off, she visited Flitwick. In the home of her mother's cousin Charles Stringer and his wife Flo, at 17 Hornes End, she met Ernest Bland, who was to become her husband. Charles was Ernie's uncle. Ernie's grandfather George, and my great grandfather John Stringer, were brothers. Although Mum was poor, she did make me look nice for her Flitwick trips, because Aunt Daphne mentioned,

'you were a pretty little thing, in your pink coat and bonnet.'

Ernie was a good looking fellow. Although not tall, barely 5ft 2 inches, he was slim, dark haired, sinewy, and tanned from working outdoors as a Nursery man in a local market garden. Mum about the same height, plump, even pretty I'm told, wearing no make up. Her hair in a short bob.

It wasn't long before Ernie and Mum were courting steadily. Six weeks before my second birthday, on March 27th 1937, they married at Luton Registry Office, witnessed by his brother George and his mother.

It was a marriage of convenience in my opinion, (mariage de covenance). He was looking for a housekeeper and free bedmate, she

22

was looking for a settled homelife for me. Ernie proved to be jealous possessive, domineering, and violent. Three days before they wed, he struck her hard on her face. (Aunt Lil related that to me). He became someone to fear, not to love. I'd be almost five years old when an incident occurred which stuck in my mind for a long time. Just why he was angry I don't know. Mum was answering back and he didn't like that. It enraged him even more, and he struck her so hard she fell down the few steps between the living room and lean to kitchen of the cottage in Gas Street Toddington where we were living. She toppled into the gas cooker. Blood spurted from a wound to her head. I cowered in a corner, terrified. I thought I'd be next at the end of his fists. He shouted at me to stop bawling or he'd give me something to bawl for. His usual phrase was 'It's yer own bloody fault.' His violent and abusive behaviour was a continuing pattern throughout my childhood years, his bullying temper often on display. The physical violence stopped after Diabetes took its hold on Mum's health in 1954, but the verbal and mental cruelty continued until she died.   (below: old fashioned dolls pram.)

Station Square Flitwick, around 1949

Same scene 50 odd years later, former
grocery shop is now an Estate Agents

Old recreation ground, around 1949

The Avenue, around 1949, note the lack of traffic, the grass verges

Dunstable Road school around 1991, a school no longer.
This entrance (facing the road), was to boys cloakroom.

Eastmoor, Maulden Rd 1993

The Mill in Greenfield Rd, still working 1988

The Smithy before demolition 2003, and a rough illustration of how it looked in 1945 when horses came to be shod.

Vicarage hill shops (2001), built on site of village pond.
School in view has lost its boundary wall.

Crown Inn 1993, the old barns removed to provide a car park

13 Dunstable Rd 1953, entrance   17 Hornes End 1993
has been widened since then.

Ernie, Pat and Joyce on Rec 1958

High St Flitwick around 1949, note lack of traffic

Number 5 Water Lane, Aunt Meg's cottage, note washhouse at side

Little Arch 1988   Peg rug in friend's house 1988

Infant School, Station Rd, being used as a factory 1988

Flitwick Station 1988

Not a good copy, but included for illustration. Women and girls on the peasing field around 1940. They wear old clothes and overalls. Two male workers on hand to weigh the bags of peas.

Pat on Peasing field 1953
woman in check coat is Mum

Tad's Theatre, Conger Lane
Toddington 1988

Reg Day and Aunt Daphne
at Pat's funeral in Maulden 1997

myself with uncle Billy and
Aunt Barbara on holiday at Plymouth

this is how stooks were
were stacked
ready to be collected for
the rick

Running Waters around 1900. Buildings in background in spot where 101 garage was developed.

Running Waters around 100 years later, looking towards Ampthill, 101 garage, now modernised, on left.

May Watson (nee Stringer), and Millie Barnes
(nee Line) having fun in borrowed uniforms 1919

Meg Stringer, and her Granddaughter Kath Watson (age 17)

In the 1940s, this was view of the Alley from back door of No 28.
No cars parked up then, or telegraph and electricity poles of course.
The brick wall on the right marks the spot of our bucket lavatories.

The Alley in 1988, view from Station Road.
Number 26-30 straddled the road at the end, approximately where
you see my old Jaguar car double parked. On the left is the
overgrown hedge boundary of what used to be the Orchard.

Church hill, around 1901 Teacher Miss Carr lived opposite, the old barn of her house is just visible

No		Name of Member	maureen Randall.				
Date of Deposit or Withdrawal	Amount of Deposit £ s. d.	Amount of Withdrawal £ s. d.	Signature	Date of Deposit or Withdrawal	Amount of Deposit £ s. d.	Amount of Withdrawal £ s. d.	Signature
Balance ... £		/ /		Balance ... £	11 6	— — —	
5.1.48	9		J.M.S.	15.3.48.	1 0		J.M.S.
12.1.48	2 6		J.M.S.	7.4.48.	1 6		J.M.S.
9.2.48	1 6		J.M.S.	12.4.48.	1 0		J.M.S.
16.2.48	6		J.M.S.	19.4.48.	9		J.M.S.
23.2.48	1 6		J.M.S.	3.5.48	1 0		J.M.S.
1.3.48	2 6		J.M.S.	24.5.48	16 9 / 15 0 / 1 9	15 0	
8.3.48	2 3		J.M.S.	12.7.48	1 0		J.M.S.
TOTALS ... £	11 6			TOTALS ... £	2 9		

School Penny Bank 1948

Chapter 2
A WEDDING

The wedding of Ernie and Mum in 1937 wasn't exactly the wedding of the year, month or day. Compared to that other wedding in 1937, that of Edward V111 and Mrs Simpson, who wore the latest fashion, honeymooned in luxurious surroundings, attendants bowing to their every whim, Mum and Ernie's nuptials were frugal indeed.

Mum was no different than any other young woman. She had dreamt of walking down the aisle in beautiful finery to marry her Mr Right. Her dreams were shattered, as they were to be shattered throughout her life. On her wedding day there were no fabulous clothes, no mother to give her a last minute hug, no photographers fussing around, no grand shiny cars, (she travelled by bus), no wedding breakfast in a swanky hotel. When Aunt Lil married Bob Bland, they returned to their little house in Toddington, and Bob promptly went back to work. He could not afford to take a whole day off. It is likely Mum and Ernie did the same. Mum and Ernie moved into the upper part of a cottage in a lane off the north side of the High Street to begin married life, moving briefly to a flat in one of the Georgian buildings near the pond. In 1938 we moved to 33 Gas Street, a small one bedroomed cottage, the last one before Gas Street petered out into a lane leading to the Bridleway and village of Fancott. The cottage was knocked down some time ago and replaced by a bungalow.

Toddington at that time was a lovely old town. The Green is still the centre, although the pump where Gran Bland queued to obtain her water supplies is no longer used. The small garage which repaired cars and dispensed petrol to local motorists, is now a dental practice. The Fish and Chip shop behind the Green is now a Chinese

Takeaway. Gran Bland was Ellen Stringer before she married Robert Bland senior. He died. She then married Albert Gordon and they had one daughter, Betty. They moved into number 2/4 Gas Street, which was originally two cottages, and part of a terrace. Two rooms down two bedrooms up, two sets of stairs, one of them blocked off, unused. Entry into the house was through the door of number 2, direct from the street. Number 4 door never used. Access to that room, which Gran Bland used as a parlour, was through a gap in the wall from the living room.

Furnishings in the house were kept very clean. Wooden square table in the centre of the living room, covered almost all the time with oilcloth. Four or five kitchen style chairs and a sideboard, Granpa Gordon had his own red velvety covered armchair away from the window, Gran sat in a Windsor style wooden chair with her back to the window. On the wall just inside the door was a photo' of me as a schoolgirl, but when Gran died in 1954, the photo was lost in the house clearout.

A home made rag rug in front of the hearth of the old black range. Gran didn't need to cook on the range as she had a gas cooker. Each side of the fireplace, on the wall at head height, were gas mantles. I often went to the Ironmongers on the High St to purchase replacement mantles. To the rear of the living room, the small kitchen had no cupboards except the one under the stairs. There was a gas cooker, and a small wooden table placed against the opposite wall, a bucket of water on the table, and two slop buckets underneath for waste water. No other furnishings except perhaps a kitchen chair.

The parlour was well furnished. A polished oval shape dining table took up the centre of the room, with balloon back chairs tucked tidily into it. A plant pot sitting on the long lace table runner. A sideboard, I cannot recall the details, against the wall. Maybe two armchairs. Couple of pictures on the walls, window to the street. Heavy brass fenders surrounded the hearth in the living room and the parlour. The old black range had been removed and replaced with a cast iron firegrate, and like the living room, a red chenille fringed runner was fixed to the mantleshelf with real brass drawing pins.

Over the fireplace was a fine mirror, but I cannot recall if it was gilded or wooden framed. Sitting on the hearth were two spaniel type porcelain dogs. Through a door to the rear of the parlour was the laundry room. In one corner the copper boiler. Gran rose early to set a fire beneath it to heat the water before making her way to the pump on the Green to get more supplies. There was no sink, electric kettle, tumble dryer or any of the other things we are used to today.

On the wall hung the family bathtub, taken down once per week for the ritual bath night. On the window sill, soap powder and other paraphanalia. As I got older, I helped Gran fetch water.

The back door opened on to a grassy patch, with path to a barn. Next to the barn the lavatory. A bucket under a wooden seat. A hole cut into the seat, bucket emptied weekly by the Council. (Under the beds upstairs were the obligatory chamber pots, Po we called them, for use during the night). Along the ground outside the kitchen and laundry room was a gully with a grill across, where Gran emptied all her waste water. It whooshed along the gully to a gully drain in the street. A lane passed along the back of the barns to take beer barrels to the cellars of the Oddfellows pub. What was once a storeyard is now a beer garden. The floors in the house were stone.

As a younger child, I was puzzled why Gran's second staircase was inaccessible. My imagination ran riot. I figured one day, someone would open the door into the long since closed off stairwell, to find among the cobwebs and dust, a skeleton of someone who'd been murdered many years before, for revenge or money.

Or perhaps a ghost prowled. It couldn't be just a dry dusty old stairwell, could it? Surely there was a mystery to be solved, as in Enid Blyton books. I couldn't accept they were closed off simply because Gran didn't need two flights of stairs.

I recall the 13th century church near the green chimed on the hour and every quarter hour. A lot of people relied on the church clock for the right time. Dr Fawcett lived in an Ivy clad house, the first in Gas Street, to the rear of the church. Gas Street is now called Conger Lane.

Across from Gran's, cows chomped at the lush grass in a field next to the lane leading to Griffin Farm. Children, and there were plenty of us, were not afraid of the cows as we climbed the stile and made our way over the field to Conger hill. The cows stood nose to tail, swishing flies away from each other with their tails, some lay down, contented, chewing the cud, as we excitedly ran up and down the hill. Conger hill is a man made mound, with deep moat like surrounding ditch. Gorse and other bushes bordered well worn tracks made by children and animals over the years. Gran often referred to Conger hill as the Devil's kitchen, and told us a few strange tales which I have unfortunately forgotten.

Every year, on Shrove Tuesday, I caught the bus to Toddington, just in time to hear the Pancake Bell. I ran across to Conger hill with other children and put my ear to the side of the hill, listening for the Witches frying their pancakes. I was convinced there were old crones below, couldn't I hear the sizzling, imagine the smell? On other days, we ran up and down the hill playing chasing games. One game we played was Jumping on the Witches, as we furiously bounced around. A marvellous place to play.

Some say it was a Roman Fort, others that it was a Norman Motte, but if there ever was a castle on top, there is no trace left.

39

In my opinion the history of Conger hill is older. Toddington library has books and information on the hill. Icknield Way runs close. It is well known that prehistoric traders used this route to and from such places as Salisbury, the religious site of Avebury, and the east coast.

The old fire station in Gas Street has long ago been converted to two Mews flats. A little further down is the chapel, then a plainly built structure which used to be a little cinema but is now a local theatre. I fear soon, someone will snap it up and build houses on the site. Before it became a cinema in 1925 it was a Guide hall.

This marvellous little 140 seat cinema was named the Picturedrome when it opened, later it became the Cozy, then the Rex before finally closing its doors in 1958. As a cinema, it was run by a family who lived next door in the first terraced cottage. Those cottages have been replaced by new housing.

It was in that little cinema I saw Charlie Chaplin in his role as the captivating little tramp, Jimmy Cagney as a gangster, Ginger Rogers and Fred Astaire dancing, brooding cowboy Randolph Scott, singing cowboy Roy Rogers with his horse Trigger, comics Laurel and Hardy, Abbot and Costello, the Marx Brothers. Harold Lloyd doing precarious stunts, and I saw Judy Garland tripping the light fantastic down the yellow brick road.

Also the never to be forgotten Shirley Temple.

Just to the right of the screen, a woman played piano to add emphasis to the silent movies, which were still being shown, although they were years old. I went to the afternoon matinees with Aunt Betty, who was five years older than me. A short silent movie, then maybe a serial, tempting us to return next week, a trailer for the next big film, Pathe or Movietone News, then the main film as usually advertised. The projector often broke down. We children stamped our feet and hollored loudly in protest, causing uproar in the small auditorium. After a few minutes the film juddered back into life again, and peace reigned, until the next time.

I always wanted curls and ringlets like Shirley Temple, never got them of course. Aunt Betty always met me off the bus from Flitwick. Being a penny or two short for the entrance money had Betty wheedling her Dad, 'have you got another penny for Maureen?' Digging in his pockets, the penny materialized, 'Git yer Mum ter give yer enough next time,' he'd grumble, pretending to be annoyed.

When the war ended, I was 10 years old. It was at that little cinema I saw the horrors of the Concentration camps unfold on screen. We were not sheltered from that kind of information, it was all there, on the screen. Naked bodies, piled lifeless and skeletal into large pits, walking skeletons of survivors, it was worse than watching a Frankenstein horror movie. There were sad scenes of people begging and queueing for a slice of bread in the streets of towns and cities blown apart by war, rubble strewn. But when we saw our soldiers advancing on the remnants of Hitler's army, we cheered. The awful scenes were repeated a few months later when we witnessed what our servicement had to endure at the hands of the Japanese in the Far East. Man's inhumanity to man throughout history, the havoc, poverty, deaths of innocent children, is truly harrowing, absolutely dreadful, and still goes on, and on and on. It is always the poor that suffer most. Wars, hatred of another religion or country, cause so much misery and devastation. Revenge breeding revenge, children caught in the middle. For what? For political ideology? religious dogma? territorial ambitions?

The garden of our old cottage in Toddington's Gas Street was a paradise for children. Three or four brick steps and a wicket gate led directly into the garden. Ernie was a good gardener. He had been working with plants from before he left school. We had rows

41

of Beans, Onions, Cabbages, and shaws of Potatoes upright and gleaming green under blue skies.

The cottage itself was small and quaint, a bit of dull brick, some patched up wattle and daub, gable end on to the street. Pantile roof, small windows, and to the side, a lean to extension Mum used as a kitchen. It was small and held only a gas cooker and a table. No cupboards, no sink, none of the things we take for granted in our modern kitchens. The mangle sat outside the kitchen door because it maybe would not fit indoors. A narrow path led up between the rows of vegetables to the outside lavatory, in a hut at the end of the path.

A rough hawthorn hedge surrounded the garden, with gaps here and there, the occasional Holly bush. Bits of old fencing, all shapes, filled gaps to prevent the cattle from Griffin Farm intruding.

The garden had old gnarled Crab Apple trees, lovely blossom in Spring. I had plenty of kids coming in to the garden to play with me. Sometimes we'd venture a short way outside the gate into the lane, but eight foot or more hedgerows, and trees waving in the breeze, obscuring sunlight, creating shadows, fired our imagination. We thought monsters lurked there, ready to pounce on us, and we'd scoot back to the security of the garden. It must have been years later before I ventured the full length, to gather Blackberries.

Opposite our cottage was the Gas works, now demolished, replaced by housing. Toddington was just one of the towns and cities with its own Gas works. A Scotsman from Ayrshire gave Gas lighting to the world in 1792. He moved to Cornwall in 1779, and his house was the first to be lit by Gas. A cottage nearby, painted pink, flowers filled the garden, over walls, climbing the house.

Ernie fertilized the garden with the contents of the lavatory bucket when it was in danger of overflowing before the Council lorry turned up to empty it. He dug a hole in the garden, tipped the

42

contents in, and built a compost heap over it, ready for next season's crops. Water butts collected water from the roof of house and barn. It watered the garden, and Mum washed my hair in it. There may have been a Well in the garden, I cannot recall, but if not, she would have to fetch buckets of water from the pump on the Green, or use the standpipe at the rear of Aunt Lil's house at number 25.

Close by the house, in the garden, we had the remains of an old van, providing hours of fun. It had no wheels, no engine, and the back doors hung loose on rusty hinges, it was marvellous. The steering wheel was still in position, and we fought over whose turn it was to drive, especially the boys. I cultivated the friendship of one little girl in particular. Can't recall her name, it may have been my cousin Pat, a year younger than myself She always brought her dolls ancient pram with her, unceremoniously dragging it up the two or three steps from the lane into the garden. It had a cavernous body made of wood and metal, with a lining of imitation leather. A flat wooden board placed half way down the inside made a base for a bit of cloth which served as a mattress. The doll, placed gently in the sleeping position, was covered with whatever came to hand, an old jumper, bit of blanket, a raggedy towel. I paraded up and down the garden path in my role as mother.

In the deep bowels of the pram, underneath the board, was a veritable treasure of small toys with a few cast off baby clothes. Poor parents could not afford shop bought dolls clothes, these were usually made at home from worn out clothing. I'd be disappointed if it started to rain, for that meant my little friend had to go home.

Living at 33 Gas Street was great fun for me, but Mum hated it. She had a yearning to move to Maulden, where she had spent her childhood, but it wasn't to be. We moved to Flitwick in 1940. Ernie's widowed maternal Gran had been admitted to St George's

43

hospital at Ampthill, where she died in 1942 age 81. We took over her house and some of the furniture left behind.

I wept buckets when we left Toddington. Now who was I going to play with? Why couldn't we live in Toddington forever? with all my friends. Especially the one with the pram. I was happy in Toddington, except when Ernie lost his temper, making me afraid.

The town doesn't seem to have changed quite so dramatically as Flitwick has. Times of course, have to change. Would anyone want to return to bucket lavatories, to health problems such as Diptheria, Scarlet Fever, rampant Tuberculosis, or Polio, to children leaving school at 11 or 12 to work 9 hours or more daily in industry? To oil lamps, Gas lighting? To homes without the comfort and convenience of electricity? To women giving birth annually because any form of birth control other than abstinence was frowned upon, or illegal? (A woman trying to say No to a forceful partner could legally be raped by him, until the law was changed in 1991) Do we want a return to the Workhouse? the Lunatic Asylum? high infant mortality? We have came a long way since all of those were consigned to the dustbin of history. Unfortunately, in these so called enlightened times, when everyone should have enough to eat, and live in decent habitable homes, where children should feel safe, there are those who treat their offspring appallingly. I'd lock the perpetrators up and throw away the key.

I visited Toddington regularly, played in the lane and on Conger hill, so memories remained and were reinforced all the time.

I cannot recall how we got our few belongings to Flitwick, but would hazard a guess that it was with a friend, a horse, a cart.

During those first few years of my life, I was unaware of what was going on in the big bad wide world. Even when war started in 1939, nothing seemed to change. Gas masks were distributed to civilians in 1938. I must have been given one, because I can recall taking the small square box containing it to school after we moved to Flitwick, and being shown how to put it on.

Before Social Security for those out of work or ill, there was Parish relief. 15 shillings for a man, 3 shillings for each child, and 12 shillings for his wife, which I think was too generous. It was not timeless or limitless. If he had saleable assets, they had to be sold. Shoes were expensive compared to today. They were repaired over and over again. A bottle of whisky would set you back 6/5 (33p). A few bottles of beer would drown out life's agonies just as well. Women were at last given the right to divorce on grounds of adultery without having to prove desertion or violence too. Amy Johnson made the first solo flight from Gravesend to Cape Town in 1936, and the Spanish civil war began in July the same year. Minister of Transport Hor Belisha, of Belisha Beacon fame, turned down another request for a Forth road bridge. In 1936 Hitler upped the stakes when he marched into Rhineland, declaring he was restoring national honour. Coloured Jesse Owens won a Gold Medal at the Berlin Olympics, it did not please Herr Hitler one little bit. A new miracle of communications began in 1936 in Britain when the BBC broadcast a limited Television service from Olympia in London. In 1938 Neville Chamberlain became the first Prime Minister to appear on Television. Other events included Hitler's troops marching into Austria, and the signing of the Munich agreement in 1938.

The Cozy Cinema screened Shirley Temple in Sunnybrook Farm. Bing Crosby in Pennies from Heaven, (he sold millions of records of the theme tune). Broadway Melody, a wonderful musical. Dance halls offered music and romance, entrance fees modest at around 2 shillings. Going to Russia was a doddle if you could rustle up the necessary £1 per day inclusive of food, travel, and accomodation, by Intourist. A man's Sports coat around a week's wage, pair of Flannels around 15 shillings. An agricultural labourer's wage was little more than £1 per week. In 1937 boys wore short Flannel trousers to just above the knee. They cost around 5 shillings. For the home, a 6 ft high kitchen cabinet, cost around £4. A new Hoover around 23 guineas, (£24 and 3 shillings). Lux beauty soap 3d, and women emulated the screen goddesses by wearing the same kind of make up, Max Factor being favourite. Some paid a shilling or two per week to a catalogue company for new clothes.

Dinner Dances were popular. I saw one advertised for the grand sum of 10/6 (52p) per head. Fabulous gowns, wine flowed, but not for Mum. 10/6 would purchase a whole basket of groceries.

Conscription was introduced in April 1939, and war declared on September 3rd The Germans wasted no time. A Uboat sank the SS Athenia (a civilian liner) the same day. Ernie's Woodbine fags went up to 9d for 20 in the Spring budget, up 10d in Autumn, the price of 3 loaves of bread.

A popular song was Hang out the washing on the Seigfried Line, and petrol rationing began. Women were called up for the Land Army.

What would we do without Polythene? invented in 1939.

Coins not to scale

Top row: Sixpence, Silver Threepence, Farthing, Halfpenny, and Penny. Inscribed with a Robin on the reverse, a Farthing was legal tender until 1960. Silver threepennies were inserted into Christmas puddings, the finder said to be lucky. Sixpence was called a tanner, the shilling called a bob, a penny was called a copper.

Second row: Bronze Threepence, Half Crown, Florin, One Shilling.

12 pennies =1 shilling   20 shillings =£1   240 pennies = £1
960 Farthings = £1   48 farthings = 1 shilling
480 Halfpennies = £1
4 Threepennies = 1 shilling   80 Threepennies =£1
40 Sixpennies = £1   2 Sixpennies = 1 shilling
1 half crown = 2 shillings and 6 pence (2/6) 8 half crowns =£1
A Florin = 2 shillings   10 Florins = £1
Ten shilling note was ten bob, (=120 pennies),   a £1 was a quid.
Two pennies was tuppence, three was thruppence.

Chapter 3
THE ALLEY

Flitwick: Translation: Dairy Farm on the Stream, the village of Flit

28 Gravel Pit Road 1940.

I was transported from the comparitive tranquility and gentility of Toddington to the roughness of the Alley in Flitwick.

I had to make new friends. The house had only a dirt yard outside the back door. There were no Crab Apple trees to climb over, or an interesting old van to play in. The garden was several yards away, at the end of a narrow path, past the Hawthorn hedge boundary of the orchard belonging to the Crown Inn.

The dirt yard, shared by all three cottages, (numbers 26, 28 and 30), became my playground. Ernie dug the neglected garden over almost immediately to prepare it for productivity again. He now had a job with George Woodcraft, a market gardener of Maulden.

Gravel Pit Road had been known as the Alley for many years. Percy Stringer, born 1903, started school 25th September 1911, left in 1915 age 12. His address is given as The Alley. An old map shows the Alley as being part land known as Townfield. Owner of the Mill Richard Goodman received this parcel of land when the new enclosure bill became law in the 19th century. In the 1860s came the railway, slicing Townfield in two.

A map of 1800 refers to Gravel Pit Furlong, and Gravel Pit cottage, piece, garden, occupied by Thos Lane (or Line). George Brooks of the Manor also owned land in the vicinity. Ernie's grandfather George, known as Ecky Stringer, worked as a labourer at the gravel pits, but by the time we moved there in 1940, the pits were exhausted. The one behind the Crown Inn became an orchard.

According to another old map, numbers 8-14 Gravel Pit Road occupy the site of another former gravel pit.

The remains of an old sand pit between the Alley and Wilson's farm in Water Lane served as a shelter during the war. More sand pits and substantial gravel pits were situated off Maulden Road, now an Industrial Estate. Anyone walking through Gravel Pit Road today may find it hard to imagine how it once was. Modern homes have replaced the older 19th century houses, and the road is extended to provide access to Elmwood Crescent. The green fields which surrounded the Alley have been built over. The Alley as it was is gone, it wasn't worth the keeping.

George and Rosalyn Hester occupied number 8, Bernard (known as Ron) and Eugenie Abbott in number 10. A little later it became the home of the Carr family. Number 12 must have been a bit crowded, occupied by the Thompson family plus Alex and Annie Fraser. Later the Frasers moved out, Eric and Isobel Joy moved in. Number 14 occupied by Doris Wakefield, Ida Bunyan, and for a short while, Ivy Cuthbert. Number 16 was a rather run down single cottage set back a bit from the road, large barn to the front, surrounded by untidy privet hedge. A gate in the hedge large enough to let a handcart through. It had been the home of Daniel Line. I cannot recall him, but I know he was a Chimney Sweep, Tinker, Grinder, General Handyman. A Grinder sharpened Scythes, Scissors, Knives, Tools. A Tinker repaired items such as putting handles back on kettles, patching up holes in metalwork and old iron. His son Ebeneezer, (Ebber), who lived at number 30, next door to us, learnt the trades from his father. Ebber's wife Caroline was the sister of Lawrence Cox, known as Double Cox. In 1946 he moved from living with his sister at number 30 to lodge with Ebber's mother at number 16. Ebber died before 1950, he'd be around 70 then, so Carr

49

and son Fred moved into number 16 with Double Cox. Soot bagged bagged from the chimneys was put to good use, keeping some for their own use, selling some to gardeners. Soot is rich in calcium, iron, potash, magnesium, and potassium, all good nutrients, perfect for repelling slugs and snails.

There were no mobile phones, no land lines to the houses in the Alley, so you might wonder how they found customers, but there was always a demand for Chimney Sweeps. When they turned up in a road to sweep one chimney, women came out of their homes and asked when could they get theirs swept. Word spread that the sweep was in the area, plus they had plenty of regulars. Daniel and Ebber were old fashioned Sweeps, with brushes, different sizes, the soot all coming down in the hearth. Housewives had the chimney swept before doing the Spring cleaning.

Numbers 18 and 20 came next. Millie Barnes and her family in number 18 and her daughter Norah, with husband Percival Pearson, known as Pussah Pearson, at number 20. He could talk the hind leg off the proverbial donkey. Norah and Pussah eventually divorced. Millie's sons Alfie and Claude cultivated their garden, plus the small patch of ground further on in the Alley, opposite our house. One year they grew a successful crop of Lettuce, cut them with the dew on, (early dawn), and George Woodcraft's brother took them to Covent Garden market with George's Vegetables.

In the terraced cottages at the end of the Alley, the Watson's were in number 26, we at 28, Eberneezer and Caroline Line at 30. Our house was a hovel in the 40s, the only way I can describe it.

"Next to the Inn was a lane leading to a stile and path which went under the railway and came out top of Hornes End, and over this path came children to school. There were several cottages up this lane, all squalid," end of quote.

The above quotation comes from his book 'Boyhood Memories' to be found in Flitwick Library. I agree with him. When he lived in Flitwick, these cottages at the top end of the Alley, if squalid then, you can imagine how much worse they must have been by the time we moved in. All those old slum houses are dead and buried now, replaced by nice tidy new homes.

Across the dirt yard, at right angle to the houses were the three barns all under the one pantiled roof. Each barn, big enough to take a car if we'd had one, were in good condition, providing dry shelter and storage. Sturdy beams supported the roof. The outer walls and the inner dividing walls were clapboard, on brick foundations, and dirt floor. The ground at the back of the barns fell away sharply a few feet to where the gravel pit workings had been. Doors heavy, never locked. Each barn had a water butt and a metal dustbin situated outside the door. Two or three feet separated the barns from the lavatories, which were in a wooden hut style building, the three lavatories under the one corrugated tin roof. Dirt floor. The doors had a gap top and bottom, no locks. The lavatory doors faced away from the road, to the fence boundary of the orchard. The cubicles were narrow, no windows, noisy when it rained. Soft toilet tissue not available. Our toilet paper was old newspaper torn into small squares, stuck on a nail on the doorpost. The few occasions we had toilet paper it was the stiff waxy feeling Izal or Bronco in single sheets in a box, or the same make on a roll. Mum strung string through the roll and hung it from a nail on the doorpost.

If the buckets became in danger of overflowing before the Council lorry came around to empty them, a hole was dug in the garden and the contents formed the base of another compost heap, many homes doing the same.

A long washing line fixed to a nail beside the kitchen door

crossed the yard to another nail hammered in under the eaves of the barn. May Watson did the same, although her line was longer. Mum and May became very annoyed when we children ran in and out of the washing. The droop caused by wet washing hanging heavy was remedied by the use of two or three long clothes poles, shoved strongly into the ground, the notch at the top pushing the line upwards, so nothing swished against the dirty ground.

Three garden plots, surrounded on three sides by hedging, and the fourth side by the orchard, were situated between our houses and Wilson's farm in Water Lane. Reached by a narrow path past the orchard boundary, each plot was approximately 20 metres long and 6 metres wide. Elmwood homes occupy the site of those gardens today. During the war, we were urged to use every scrap of ground possible to grow vegetables.

The corner of Ash Close is built on the ground where Millie Barnes had her Well. There are still scraps of the Hawthorn hedge surviving along one side of Gravel Pit Road, but the Orchard has long gone. From a friend, I heard that some residents wanted to change the name. The road has a history, admittedly not a very illustrious history, but history same as Denel End, Church End, Hornes End and all the other ends, nothing to be ashamed of. We have to look forward, but in so doing, we cannot ignore the past. Yesterday and today shapes our tomorrows.

Around 1964 the old cottages were demolished. When we moved out in 1950, electricity and indoor plumbing were installed. Claude Barnes and family moved in to 30. The Well became redundant and was filled in, the rubble now lies under the roadway.

From the outside, numbers 26/28/30 Gravel Pit Road looked the same as all the other two up two down houses in East Anglia Built of local brick around the middle of the 19th century to house workers at the gravel pits. Slate roof, small casement with 6 or 8 panes of glass. A heavy wooden door opened into the kitchen from the dirt yard, it was the only useable entrance door. It was sturdy, with supporting crossbars and heavy bolts, pushed home each night at bedtime. There was a step of sorts, stone and shallow, a cast iron boot scraper next to the step. The front door, on the other side of the house, would have given access directly into the living room, but it was unusable. The wooden supports were rotten. One good push and the door could fall in.

The house had no cellar, no solum, no drains, no electricity or gas, no indoor sanitary provision. The red tile floor in the kitchen, and the slate floor in the living room sat directly on dirt, cracks in the flooring letting the dirt through. Coats hung on nails on the back of the door, as did Ernie's oilskins. On entering the house, on the right were three wooden doors, the first giving access to the steep windowless stairs. The second half size door accessed the coalhole under the stairs, where wood and coal was stored. The coalman called most weeks with the one bag of coal Mum could afford, tipping it into the coalhole, sending explosions of dust throughout the house. A third door gave access to the glory hole as we called it, where the shelves held all sorts of household items and our clothing, in a jumbled heap. On the floor was a shoe last which Ernie used to hammer segs into the toes and heels of our shoes, to mend our shoes occasionally. On the back of the door were Ernie's oilskin Chaps, he used these in winter when Hedging and Ditching, or Brusseling in winter. Hedging and ditching were terms used for cutting back or layering hedges, and cleaning out the many ditches around Woodcrafts fields. Machines do the work today. There were no other cupboards in the kitchen. Let me explain Chaps for those who are unfamiliar with what they are. We have all seen cowboy films where the hero straps on a pair of long leather leggings around his jeans right up to his thighs, to keep water off. They are called Chaps, from the Mexican word Chaparajos.

The kitchen was sparsely furnished. Two tables, one kitchen chair, and a floor standing mangle. On the table by the window stood two pails of fresh water drawn from the Well that morning, and an all purpose enamel basin used for washing up, cleaning vegetables, for washing our hair, for the laundry, and for Ernie when he shaved. Under the table was the slop bucket for all the waste water, which was then taken outside, around to the side of the Watson's house, and thrown away on to a patch of spare ground which was growing only weeds and grass. There was clutter on the other table in the kitchen, with a half sack of potatoes and other vegetables underneath.

Hanging from a nail hammered into each side of the window frame, and strung by a length of tape hooked over the nails, a pair of net curtains hung forlornly. During the wartime blackout restrictions, Mum hooked an old army blanket from one nail to the other to cover the window. It developed holes through being hooked and unhooked. The blanket was sufficient, because the only illumination in the dark was a six inch candle stuck on to a saucer.

I believe we were a lot better off than most people living in overcrowded homes in larger towns and cities, in slums with no green spaces. At least we had a garden of fresh vegetables.

Ernie occasionally used distemper (a kind of watery wall paint) on the kitchen and living room walls, but dust from the coal hole, and the smoky air soon made the walls grimy again. Distemper was not as convenient or good as modern emulsion paints.

Mum fixed pot menders into the holes in the cooking pots. Copper bottom saucepans were too expensive, and hard to come by, so she had no choice but to buy the cheaper tin pots, keeping them going as long as she could. Gypsies came round the village from time to time selling their wares, which included pot menders. We could also buy them in the local shops. Little round pieces of metal with a hole in the centre. One piece placed on the outside of the pot, another on the inside, and the two held together by a screw through the hole, fastened tight with nut and bolt.

We had to wear our shoes indoors as well as outdoors, as we had no slippers. It was too cold underfoot to leave our shoes off. I often went shoeless outdoors in summer.

A door led through into the living room. A small room, with dining table covered with oilcloth in centre, two old armchairs either side of the ancient black cast iron cooking range. A chaise longue with faded reddish/pink soft but threadbare cover and lightly curved woodwork, sat under the small casement window. Between window and fireplace was a dresser which had lost its upper shelves. Other furniture included four or five dining chairs and two sideboards. One rather plain 1930s style which blocked the useless front door, the other really splendid. Clumsily large for the small room, it was rather ornate, maybe baroque in style, at least Victorian. The base had a central carved panel, flanked by two cupboards. The whole was ornately carved with swirls and fancy leaves, very hard to polish up. I am not sure of the wood it was made from, if it had been new and not smoke stained, I'd say it was Rosewood or light Mahogany, an antique dealers dream had it survived. The back panel reached the ceiling. It had a central mirror flanked by three smaller mirrors each side. The smaller mirrors were fronted by shelves supported on barley twist spindles, the bottom ones more chunky. The top of the mirror was curved, following the line of the top of the wood backing. Glass in the main mirror was slightly damaged, some mercury showing through. Mum kept food in that sideboard, saying it was the only place in the house where the mice could not get in. We had colonies of mice. Many a mouse lost its life in a trap. Whack!! I became quite adept at emptying and re-setting the traps. Also, on entering the living room from the kitchen, on the right, was a rather grand looking little Whatnot. Three shelves graduating from large at the bottom to a small top one, the type of thing we'd put plant pots on today. Made of Walnut, strong, barley sugar spindles holding up each shelf.

During the war, Mum hooked an army blanket on to nails over the window for the blackout. The room was smoky. Ernie smoked, the fire smoked, the oil lamp sitting on the table in the centre of the room smoked. The lamp was traditional shape, brass vessel, rather bulbous, containing the paraffin oil, a spur wheel in the crown for controlling the length of the wick, with a glass chimney to protect the flame. Smoke from the lamp made a small round blackish mark on the ceiling. Wicks, oil lamps, paraffin, glass chimneys for the lamps, all could be bought at most shops in the village. There were a lot of homes lit by oil lamps in the 1940s. Electricity only reached Flitwick in 1930.

The wireless sat on the dresser beside Mum's armchair. An aerial wire led from the wireless, through the window, and hooked over a nail on the wall beside the upstairs bedroom window. Mum had a few ornaments on display, and also on the dresser were bits of cloth cut up to make peg rugs. In the drawers , such small things as a pad of lined writing paper, a bottle of ink, and a pen, a pencil or two, marriage certificate, wireless licence, and a host of other minutia such as drawing pins, elastic, reels of thread. Bits of bandage, used over and over again, washed in between usage. Small bottle of Iodine, bottle of Camphorated oil for my earache. Pins.

In front of the hearth, a rag rug, made by Mum, usually during the long winter evenings as she listened to the wireless. The stone hearth is framed by a brass fender, which comes up shining when cleaned with Brasso. Around the fire is a fireguard. Not one of those small ones just big enough to cover the flames, but large enough to go round the hearth like railings. Mum hung wet washing over that fireguard. Steam rising, gloomy atmosphere.

She placed pots of vegetables and the pot containing the clanger over the top of the flames. Mum had no cauldron. There was an oven in the range, but unusable due to a crack in the framework. On the left hand side of the range was a boiler, with tap, small, enough to hold a basinful of water, but that was also unusable, due to a crack. In between the oven and the boiler, Mum placed bricks at the back of the grate, to lessen the space needed to be filled with fuel. Often I took a turn to clean the range with black leading. The ashes, cleaned out daily, occasionally spread on the garden when the soil was heavy. Wood ash contains potash, a good fertilizer.

The mantleshelf, as we called it, over the range, had a fringed red chenille runner attached to it with brass pins, (a little larger and stronger than modern drawing pins). A mirror on the chimney breast. Art deco style, unframed, with a small motif of flowers in one corner. On the mantlepiece shelf were two fine first world war mortar shells, the conical ends flattened to make two vases. Real brass, heavily etched with the most decorative delicate patterns, similar to Paisley pattern. The vases contained all sorts of minutia, from hair grips, to pencils, erasers, spare pen nibs, spare buttons, collar studs, ribbons, darning wool, never flowers.

Our midday meal was dinner at 1pm, the main meal of the day. Saturdays it was noon, but Sunday dinner could be later, maybe 2 or 3pm, if Ernie was working in the garden. I came home from school for dinner at 12.15, but had to wait until Ernie arrived home to sit down to eat. He would be very annoyed if Mum fed Joyce and I before him, working himself up into a rage.

Because Mum had to have a fire in the old range every day for heating water and cooking, the living room was too hot in summer. It was also the only room which had a fireplace, so in winter, that room was cosy and warm, the rest of the house very cold.

We had no piano or gramaphone. There was the wireless for entertainment, the News, and Government announcements. Three or four framed pictures decorated the walls, not valuable works of art you will understand, just prints of famous works. Mum had her favourite. It was of a religious nature. A woman wearing a long classical gown wended her way along a path through a forest. The verse apt for her circumstances,

"Lead kindly light, amid the encircling gloom, lead thou me on, The night is dark, and I am far from home, lead thou me on, Keep thou my feet, I do not ask to see, the distant scene, One step enough for me," (from Pillar of the Cloud, by John Henry, Cardinal Newman, 1801-1890)

Ernie did not like me relaxing indoors, often making me go out. When the weather was fine, he didn't need to order me outdoors, as I would be outside already, but in winter, it was different. It could be snowing, freezing cold, and all my friends wisely playing boardgames indoors, such as Ludo, Snakes and Ladders, or perhaps listening to the gramaphone, annoying their mothers, but Mum told me to do as he says, to go out to play, 'To keep the peace,' I took shelter in the barn, climbing up into the rafters, resting on the safe secure beams, dreaming of better days and staying dry as I got older, but when I was only five, six, seven years old, I lay on sacks in the corner. Claude Barnes told me Ernie used to lock me in the barn.

Two bedrooms upstairs, the front bedroom slightly larger than the back bedroom. Front bedroom faced the railway, the back bedroom faced the Alley.

Until around 1947/48 Joyce and I shared the front bedroom with Mum and Ernie. We children slept top to tail in a small iron framed bed. Ernie and Mum's bed had brass head and foot rails.

The back bedroom was occupied early in the 40s by Uncle George and Aunt Daphne, until they moved into Army quarters. Then Renee, eldest daughter of our neighbour May Watson, moved into our back bedroom after she married Jack Hymus. She slept there, but spent daytime in her mother's house. When Renee moved into one of the Council houses being built on the new estate around 1947, Aunt Daphne and Uncle George moved in again. They had been living with Aunt Millie in Leagrave, but thought they'd have a better chance of a Council house if they moved in with us at Flitwick. However, they never did move into a Council house, as George got a job on a farm at Haynes West End. A house went with the job. He was very glad to get that job, because after he was demobbed, he had been working for the local Council on what was known as the shit lorry, which came weekly to empty the outside lavatory buckets. George would do any kind of work, he could not abide being idle.

The bed Joyce and I slept in had a thin lumpy mattress, filled with flock, which is waste wool and rags. I cannot imagine they are still being made. Of tick covering, the mattress was not strong and supportive, anything but comfortable. After that experience, I can sleep just about anywhere, anytime. The floorboards bare and unpolished, the bare walls sadly in need of a coat of paint. No carpets, no rugs. The only other furnishings in the room was an

59

ordinary kitchen style chair beside the marital bed, and a washstand with ewer and basin beside the window. Bedlinen was scarce and expensive. As sheets wore out, Mum cut them in half through the worn bit, then sewed them back together again, sides to middle. Very often Joyce and I slept without sheets, or had only a sheet on the mattress, with thin blankets, coats and jackets for cover. Often we slept on pillows without pillow cases, especially in winter when getting washing dried was a problem. I have found out since, that we were not the only family making up for the lack of bedlinen by piling on coats. Mum and Ernie's bed was covered by a faded but adequate quilt, and blankets.

On cold nights, Mum slept in her day clothes, and Ernie kept his combinations on, (long sleeve vest and long leg pants in one garment, buttoned through from neck to scrotum). There were no wardrobes in the bedroom, only a nail on the back of the door for hanging clothes on. No coathangers as far as I can recall. A nice cosy toy filled bedroom wasn't something I ever had. Bedtime was early, certainly before dark in summer, and not long after teatime in winter. I'd watch the clouds flitting across the sky, making up images as they changed form, before drifting into sleep. The curtains were seldom drawn, they did not meet in the middle. When the moon shone, the sky became navy blue, or dark velvety royal blue, the stars twinkling, like hundreds and thousands of chandeliers.

"Twinkle twinkle, little star, how I wonder what you are."

During the war years the sky was frequently lit by searchlights, and on quiet nights the ack ack guns aiming for the German planes sounded so close. Occasionally, on clear nights, we heard and saw planes going over. No blackout upstairs, there was no need, never a light on. We lit our way by candle, then blew it out when we got there. I'd never heard of a duvet.

I can recall going in to the Watson's house one day, where Renee was changing Ginger's nappy. (Alan Hymus, born 1942). Took one look at his different 'bits' and promptly declared if that was what boys looked like with no trousers on, then I wasn't going to get married when I grew up. I was only seven. Naturally, ten years later I had changed my mind. Viva la difference.

As you will read later, Mum and Ernie were in prison in 1942, Joyce and I away to a childrens home for most of the year. Renee used our whole house as her own while we were away. Later, after Renee had moved into one of the new houses on the Council Estate, and George and Daphne had moved to Haynes, Mum and Ernie moved into the back bedroom in a new (second hand) bed with wooden headboard and footboard, while Joyce and I remained in the front bedroom, taking over Mum and Ernie's brass bedstead. Ernie got rid of the single bed we'd slept in for so long. The double bed sat high off the ground. It had two mattresses, and it was like climbing Mount Everest to get into it. Brass bedsteads are so fashionable today, but I thought it old fashioned then.

Mum had an accident in that bedroom one day. The floorboards were weak in parts, the skirting boards shot with mouse holes. Mum trod on a weak floorboard. Her right leg went through the floor, and through the living room ceiling up to her thigh. Yelling and crying in pain, splinters of wood digging into her flesh, she cried out to me to fetch May Watson. I was sent for a wide bandage which May wrapped around Mum's bruised and bleeding thigh. Iodine cleaned the wound. No doctor was sent for, and Mum did not go to hospital, despite the pain.

Conditions in that old cottage were appalling. Mum tried her best, but the lack of money meant she could not afford the many things which might have made life easier for her. Even a kitchen sink and pull chain lavatory would have been an improvement. Everyone suffered shortages, either because so much was not available, or because, like us, their income too low.

Mum rummaged around at Jumble sales, kind people gave her cast offs, which she was never too proud to accept. Occasionally, the Tally man informed her his supplier had delivered sheets or pillow cases. She bought the cheapest available when she could, to be paid up shilling or two per week. By the time we moved out of the Alley in 1950, I was about to start working. Mum and I came to an agreement that I would contribute half my wage each week to the household income for my keep. That way, Mum would be able to pay the weekly rent of the Dunstable Rd house of 13/6 (67p) and still have change. Another old quilt was bought at the jumble sales, for the bed Joyce and I shared, so in the Dunstable Road house, we no longer needed coats and jumpers spread over the bed for warmth. Suddenly everything was a lot cleaner.

Starting work at 15 I really was very naive and had a lot to learn. In the Alley when we were younger, Joyce and I had slept in our dayclothes for warmth, we went to school next day in the same clothes over and over again. We had no soft clean nightwear, and personal hygiene wasn't high on the agenda. All that had to change. I had to teach myself. I was jolted into doing things for myself, such as using deodorants and being well groomed.

In the 1940s, the houses in the Alley were not the only ones without indoor sanitation. The lavatory was usually in a shed in the garden, or an outhouse attached to the main house. A chamber pot, or Po as we called it, kept under the bed for nighttime use. Some families used a commode, or had their po in a pot cupboard.

Those pots could be very ornate, some made of glazed pottery, painted with flowers, leaves or scenery, like delicate china tableware. The pottie Joyce and I shared was a basic white enamelled tin one. Families bathed once per week, or even less frequently, in the galvanised tin bath brought in from a shed, or scullery, and placed in front of the fire where it was warm, filled with water boiled up in kettles and pots. No central heating, and often no other way of getting hot water. Mum bathed Joyce and I once per week, on Sunday evenings, in the half size galvanised washtub she boiled whites in over the fire during the week. She rubbed us over with soap from head to toe, then rinsed us down. No refinements.

One Sunday evening, when I was around 13 years old, and filling out in all the right places as a young girl should, with the first fluff of pubic hair appearing, I noticed Ernie looking at my body. It made me feel distinctly uncomfortable. The following week I asked Mum to help me bath upstairs, although I knew it would be cold. Mum never did explain anything of a sexual nature to me, those kind of questions were taboo. From then on, I had a very quick wash down as I stood in a basin of warm water upst in my bedroom. Mum washed my hair in the basin in the kitchen and dried it off in front of the fire after I dressed. Monday mornings Joyce and I were clean.

One day, around the same time, I was on my way upstairs, when I noticed Ernie on the landing, his trousers unbuttoned, revealing his penis. Shocked, I quickly retraced my steps. I'd never seen anything like it. He must have heard the door at the bottom of the stairs scrape open, yet did nothing to protect me from such a shocking sight. He never apologised. We had the lavatory outside, we didn't do it in bucket or po indoors during daytime. Then something even more sinister took place. I'd wake up during the night and find him feeling me between my thighs, sometimes he'd place his whatsit there, but make no attempt at penetration. He was a violent man, and might hit me. I feigned sleep, I didn't know what to do. I always turned and tucked my bottom into Joyce's lap.

I am sure he realised he had disturbed me, and he went back to his room. I am sure if Joyce had not been there, he'd have done worse. Now always afraid of going to sleep, I used Joyce as protection, she usually slept soundly. One night, after it had happened for the 6th or 7th time, I decided enough was enough. Courage came from somewhere as I screamed for Mum, who came to see what was wrong, but only garble came from my mouth. I never did tell Mum the real reason for my outburst. Ernie pretended he'd heard me shouting in my sleep and came to see what was wrong.

Horrible little pervert. After that, he never came in again, but it took me months to recover my confidence enough to sleep properly.

I didn't clean my teeth regularly. When I did have a tooth brush, I used some odd methods of cleaning my teeth in the absence of toothpaste. Salt, or sticking the toothbrush up the chimney to gather some soot are two examples. Once, I bought Gibb's Dentifrice, a small tin of pink tooth cleaning powder.

For years, until I was 11 or 12 years old, I wet the bed fairly often, particularly if I had a nightmare. Must have caused Mum much angst and hard work. Rubber was in short supply due to the troubles in the Far East so perhaps she could not find a rubber sheet to put on the bed. No doctor was consulted, no visits to child Psychiatrists, to find the cause.

As well as big changes for me, 1940 was the first full year of the war. When it started in 1939, plenty were of the opinion that it would all be over by Christmas, but as we know, it wasn't. On the continent, Hitler was getting it all his own way. He must have been rubbing his hands with glee to know that he was better prepared for the conflict than we were. When our fleeing Army had to board all those little boats off Dunkirk, leaving behind many killed or captured, there must have been some who were of the same mind as Lord Halifax, who urged the Government to do a deal with Hitler. Hitler would have laughed in our faces if we'd tried that one, and be thinking what a lot of easy to squash wimps we were. Winston Churchill sorted out Lord Halifax, who had been Foreign Secretary under Neville Chamberlain between 1939 and 1940, and had implemented the appeasement policy, by sending him off across the Atlantic as Britain's Ambassador to the United States, (1941-46).

Holland fell to the Germans on 14th May 1940, and the British Forces withdrew from Flanders. In 1941, home on leave, Reg Day married his sweetheart Marge Stringer, (Mum's second cousin). He told me he had been the only soldier of the Beds and Herts regiment to be uplifted from Dunkirk. He'd been fighting in Belgium, even venturing into Germany briefly before being told to make his way to Dunkirk quickly, as best he could. Italy joined in the conflict on the side of Germany on June 10th 1940, and on July 1st the Channel Islands fell to the Germans, staying that way for the duration. November 14th saw the destruction of Coventry Cathedral by the Luftwaffe, and the Germans were successfully bombing other cities. 1940 was not a good year.

When the Germans marched through the Arc de Triumph in Paris on June 14th there were many here who feared they'd be marching through the streets of London next, but the mood of the country was that we were not going to be so easy to overcome as the French. That August we fought back when our little Spitfires saw off the Luftwaffe in the Battle of Britain, well documented in all the history records.

The Government issued ration books, containing coupons

65

needed to get supplies of essential foods, clothing, and household items. Buff colour for adults, green for children, plus a third ration book for general items. A pound of butter cost 1 shilling and threepence, a ton of coal around £1/14 shillings, and the price of Ernie's Woodbine cigarettes went up to 1 shilling in April, rising another penny in July. Ladies shoes from 16 shillings upwards.

Had Ernie been a non-smoker, there is no doubt we would have been substantially better off. A few more nappies, some decent bed linen, maybe even some savings. Mum really struggled to feed and clothe us. All that money going up in smoke. His answer to anyone impertinent enough to question his smoking habit was to reply that he worked hard, and it was his only pleasure. If only Mum could have had some pleasure.

By the end of our first year in the Alley, the war was well under way. Too many pilots had been shot down. Himmler ordered the construction of the infamous Auschwitz concentration camp in Poland, and Germans parachuted into Norway and Denmark. Hitler's troops marched into Belgium, Luxembourg, the Netherlands, and bombing raids over Britain were stepped up. 1940, it cost twopence halfpenny (1p) to post a letter.

The first nylon stockings went on sale in New York on 15th May 1940, and 72000 pairs were sold that day. We sang all the songs we heard on the wireless. Vera Lynn, We'll meet again, Glen Millar played to packed audiences with When you wish upon a star. All efforts were directed to defeating Hitler but entertainment was important too. Young people getting married had no homes to go to, and had to squeeze in with one or other of their in-laws. Many homes had to make a little nest in the parlour for the newly weds. Or children had to give up a bedroom. Often, within a few days, the groom had to return to his unit.

House building had come to almost a standstill.   Mortgages to buy were hard to come by, the deposit needed took a long time to save.

Nearly all the males in the Stringer clan had nicknames. Pottle and Pigeon lived with their mother Meg Stringer in Water Lane, she had another son Horace, nicknamed Bugle. Her brother in law George had been called Ecky, another brother in law, James was known as Ginger.   June Stringer's father Leslie was known as Sausage. Ernie was called Enock, but didn't like it much, his younger brother George was Bubbles. Bubbles wife Daphne was Sally or Sal. Bubbles and Sally made a lovely couple. Some thought they married too young, but they had a happy life together. She was a lovely woman, cheerful, nice natured, good looking, with her hair up into one of those hair rolls fashionable at the time. Our house was happy when they were around. Bubbles was fond of telling jokes.
Had I been older I might have remembered some.

Sometimes he and Ernie made music. George played the spoons, (two dessert spoons held in a certain way and tapped rapidly together on a thigh). He could make music using a comb too, by wrapping a thin sheet of paper over it and blowing through. Ernie made mouth music on the Jews harp, (now called a Jaw harp). Someone else with a Harmonica would be in the house, and there'd be laughter and music. Those few times were quite magical, as Daphne always made sure I was included. In 1941 she lived with us briefly, pregnant, but the baby boy lived only 4 days. Shortly after that tragedy she moved into Army married quarters with George. They went on to have David and Michael, Susan, Carol and Linda. George died of cancer of the Pancreas, and a few years later, November 2002, after suffering a long illness, Daphne died. Both had smoked and she told me shortly before she died that she wished she'd never set eyes on a packet of cigarettes. This poem reminds me

of her. She called everyone my love,
'Come in my love, 'ow are yer today,'

"Little deeds of kindness, little words of love
Help to make us happy, like the heaven above."
(Julie A. Fletcher Carney 1823-1908)

There were plenty of people in Flitwick who helped me with their deeds of kindness, although at the time, I probably did not appreciate it as much as I should.

It is not surprising that electricity had not reached us in the top end of the Alley by the 1940s. No-one in Flitwick had mains electricity before 1930, and the Alley would be one of the last places to have the connection installed. Goodman of the Mill, who owned our old hovels, would certainly not think it worth while laying out the expense. Charles and Ellen Stringer, who had lived in the Thinnings, moved to our old house not long after we moved out. It had a small bathroom by that time, the Well filled in, and electricity installed.

A report in the Ampthill Times dated July 1930 goes into great detail about difficulties encountered by the Electricity supply company in their efforts to obtain a small piece of land, approximately 2 poles, to erect a transformer station. Apparently, once the purpose was known for the request, landowners were asking an exhorbitant amount of money. 70 premises were wired up ready. They could not be switched on until the transformer was working.

The Luton supply company needed land near the railway station, for that was where all the necessary cables were to meet. The report that practically everyone approached for land had not applied for an electricity supply, adding 'It is extremely unfortunate that, although on the one hand your council have pressed for supply, on the other hand inhabitants and landowners in the area raised many objections.' Would anyone today object to the installation of electricity where none existed before. Eventually as we know, the electricity company did manage to procure land near the station, next to the Victory Hall on the Rec, off Steppingly Road.

Distemper, a watery whitewash for walls

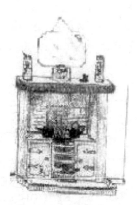 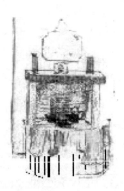

Mum draped wet washing over the fireguard to dry in wet weather.

Chapter 4
DOLLS

As they were growing up, my granddaughters had a great many dolls. Barbie dolls, Cindy dolls, baby dolls, dolls that walked and talked, some even did wee wees, and they all had enormous quantities of outfits. As a little girl, I played with dolls, but they were not mine. I was never given a doll for myself. Coming to terms with that was difficult, as each birthday and Christmas came and went without my wish being granted.

Dolls have kept little girls happy and occupied for centuries, but the first all plastic dolls did not appear until around 1939, when introduced by the Ideal Toy Corporation. They also made a Shirley Temple version, desirable because of the popularityof her films, in the same manner as today's children pressure parents into buying the must have merchandise peddled along with the latest blockbuster movie or television series. (or Children's popular books).

Some of the most favourite dolls of the 18th and 19th centuries were made of wax, in moulds, the finished product looking very lifelike, dressed in laces and flounces, with curled false hair. Children of poor families were more apt to own rag dolls, perhaps with bisque face and hands stuck on or sewn in. Wool scraps for hair. They could be made at home with stuffing of floss or straw. In the absence of money to buy a new doll, parents made tiny wooden dolls, using a dolly peg, drawing a face on it.

I doubt if you will find those in any museum, they were played with, lost, disposed of in the fire. A bit of wool served for hair, and a scrap of cloth quickly sewn on to serve as a dress. Dads whittled shafts of wood to shape into a doll for their offspring, even going to such lengths as attaching wooden arms and legs. Shops sold wooden dolls, rag dolls, real fancy dressed dolls, unclothed dolls to be dressed at home. Dads made little boxy cradles, using whatever came to hand, Mums lined a shoe box with scraps of delicate materials. Ernie was never inclined to make anything like that for Joyce or me. As recorded in previous chapters, my earliest recollection of playing with dolls was in the garden of our Toddington house. When we moved to Flitwick, it seemed so unfair. I did a bit of weeping, greatly missing my little friends, especially the one who let me play with her dolls pram.

I wanted a doll, but got a baby sister instead. I'm not so sure Mum even noticed how upset I was. She had plenty of other things going on. Joyce was due to be born, the war was raging, rationing was introduced, and she was always short of money. Joyce was born on 26th April and it became immediately apparent that she was to be treated more fondly. Ernie looked upon her and loved her, she was his own. I was extremely jealous when Joyce was given her first doll. I wanted to play with it. She screamed to be given it back.

The first black doll I ever saw belonged to one of the Watson girls. The face, hands and feet were either black vinyl, or black porcelain. The doll wore a bright red dress, and had short black beautifully curled hair. Oh how I envied its owner. A beautiful doll.

Children were given Golliwogs, usually dressed in red and white candy striped trousers, and a black or red jacket. A sprout of thick woolly curly hair went over the head from ear to ear. The Golly wore white gloves, sewn on. Golliwogs are not available in most shops today, because they are considered offensive to people of Afro-Caribbean origin. We children certainly never had any offensive prejudices to grind, to us they were just dolls. Robertson's preserves carried a Golliwog logo for many years until phased out around 1991.

71

Making pin cushion dolls was a past-time for women of the 19th century. A full skirt was stuffed to make a thick cushion, with small head and arms sewn in, some crocheted, some knitted. There are local craft fairs I visit, and they have toilet roll covers crocheted made a doll in a similar fashion to the old pin cushions. The designs are lovely, with coloured wools, delicate lace, bright ribbons.

As I got older, dolls played a less important role in my wish list. One incident, when I was about 13 or 14 pretty well put the lid on any hopes lingering that I might be given a doll of my own. Later in this tale I tell of two German prisoners of war we had to tea before they were repatriated. The older of the two had to return to what was then East Germany, the Russian sector, where Stalin held an iron grip. Our visitor was returning to Dresden, the town which was razed to the ground byAllied bombing in early part of 1945.

He said some of his family made toys. That German sent me a parcel, containing a home made wooden dolls house. It arrived broken into several untidy bits. I was so excited. The parcel was addressed to me, nothing like that had happened before.

Opening it on the living room table, you can imagine my disappointment as I tried to cobble the bits together. Hand made, hand painted, with wallpaper pasted on the outside to resemble brickwork. Our former visitor had gone to a lot of trouble to please me. Undoubtedly he would parcel it up carefully, but such were the strict censorship rules of both East Germany and this country, that it had been opened for inspection and reparcelled clumsily. Most fathers would have re-made the dolls house, using the broken pieces, pins, patching, glueing, and doing whatever it took to make it resemble something near to what was originally intended, but Ernie and Mum saw it as unnecessary and just a pile of rubbish.

I never did get to keep my dolls house, even in its broken

condition. In later years, I did acquire a Doll. It was the Gala Day, (Fete day) in the village where Alvis and I had a shop. The Doll, dressed in baby clothes, sat in the centre of the window, surrounded by flowers and coloured drapes, the window on the outside dressed in Spruce and paper flowers as was the custom on Gala days. The Doll brought plenty of business into the shop. I still have the Doll. Our dog has chewed the fingers, it has a wonky eye, but it amuses young visitors, who carefully change its clothing, choosing something from a box I keep nearby.

Ernie said I was too old for dolls at 14,

BAH!! Humbug.

Chapter 5
ARRIVAL OF A SISTER

One or two things come to mind about the day Joyce was born. It was during the daytime on Friday 26th April 1940.

It was a week before my 5th birthday, and I was in the yard next to the barns when I heard Mum yelling and screaming, the noise coming from our back bedroom. I ran to the kitchen door, and made to open the stairs door. Ernie stopped me. I began to cry, but he tapped my ear fairly hard and told me to go out to play, and stop 'ollerin,' she'd be alright in a minute. Two or three others were in the yard with me, and we were distracted by the yelling. Frantic with anxiety I had to wait. I can only assume Ernie was either home for his Bever, (morning break at 9.30), or perhaps he was home for dinner when Mum went into labour. Mum usually sent me out of the house when he was due home, 'goo out ter play, 'eel be 'ome soon.'

Eventually the noise and commotion coming from our back bedroom subsided, to be replaced by the sound of a baby crying. May Watson, and Millie Barnes, who was a sort of unofficial midwife, (every village had women like her), were helping Mum, with lots of running up and downstairs. I can't recall seeing the doctor. He maybe turned up later, when all the fuss was over. Millie also helped with the laying out, when others came to the end of their lives. Hatches and Despatches.

May Watson came into the yard and said, 'would you like to see your new sister.' Would I ? My little legs couldn't climb those stairs quick enough. Joyce had thick black curly hair and a little red wrinkly face. Ugh! Is this what Mum had been yelling about?

May and Millie were still boiling water on the range downstairs, and using the ewer and basin on the old washstand. I saw blood on a sheet on the floor. Joyce was wrapped in a clean piece of blanket, fine shawl she did not have. I'd not seen a new born baby before. After a few minutes, Mum told me to go out and play. Suddenly I was going to have to share Mum with someone else. I'd already gone through having to share her with Ernie, now I was going to have to share her with a baby as well. I was too young to analyse my feelings, bewilderment is perhaps a good word. In those days, women like Mum, who had no money to pay servants and nurses, were up and about next day doing household chores. I ran errands to the shop.

Joyce had no cot, she slept in the marital bed at night, and in her pram during the daytime. She wasn't breast fed. Bottles were made up using National Dried Milk, obtained from the welfare clinic in Ampthill. If Mum ran out of supplies, Joyce was fed Fossil's tinned condensed milk, or Carnation milk, or Mum used some of the fresh milk delivered by the milkman.

The pram was old fashioned, anything from 2nd to 10th hand, either given to Mum by someone who knew her circumstances, or bought cheap through an acquaintance. Friends gave her cast off clothing, and nappies were bought from the Tally man.

If the weather was kind, the pram stood outside the back door. In bad weather, it was in the living room, between door and Ernie's chair by the fire.

Babies wore terry towelling nappies, with a muslin barrier between nappie and skin, doused with plenty of zinc and castor oil cream, perhaps Vaseline, to try and prevent nappie rash. The nappy was square. To put it on baby, it is folded over to make a triangle shape, baby is laid on it, sides folded to tummy, and the third corner of the nappy is brought through baby's legs and secured to the rest of the nappy with a pin. Nappies hung out on the clothes line dried nice

75

and soft, but if dried indoors in front of the fire they could feel rough, like sandpaper.

Mum soaked soiled nappies in a bucket of cold water and soda. Home births were common in the 40s. Older children looked after younger ones, and neighbours rallied round. Attending clinics and surgeries cost money, so Mum did not have all the necessary pre-natal check-ups. Hospitals raised funds from local businesses, from charities, from bequests, from grants, from sponsored beds and other fundraising activities. Mum had more pregnancies after Joyce, but each baby was stillborn. She seldom attended the doctors more than once, to confirm the pregnancy, expecting to have a natural home birth, and leave the rest up to nature. Nature, however, wasn't playing ball. She was rushed to Bedford Hospital each time.

Pat, my youngest half sister, born December 1948, survived because of the NHS. Mum attended Ampthill clinic as she should, and also Bedford hospital, with no fears of being presented with an account to pay. The clinic and the hospital took blood tests, found there was a problem, and prepared for it.

More about Pat's birth later.

Chapter 6
THE RAILWAY

Those faraway places with the strange sounding names. A line from a song, sang somewhere, at some time,

The railway, running as it does through the spine of Flitwick, from London to the North and Scotland, had a magic about it. It was very much part of my life. It was on the route to and from school.

We raced there, dawdled home, stopping to climb the wire boundary fence to watch the passenger trains as they slowed down to halt at the station. Perhaps the engine driver gave a couple of whistles on the hooter as we waved frantically at the passengers looking out of the windows. To our delight, a few waved back. Where were they going? and where from? We watched the goods trains, wagon after wagon, clickety clack, clickety clack, clickerty clacking along, smoke from the engine streaming way behind.

Toddington has no railway passing through, we used the bus to get there, but if visiting Auntie Millie in Leagrave, we used the train.   Until a school outing to St Albans around 1947, I never travelled further north or south than Bedford and Luton.

Crossing station bridge at the same time as a steam train was passing underneath was to be enveloped in clouds of choking smoke, the bridge being only half the width it is today.

Before the coming of the railway to Flitwick in 1868, only fields stretched between the Alley and Hornes End. At first, it was one up line, one down line, with another two lines added later. An up and down line for goods trains, up and down lines for passenger traffic. Today, passenger trains use all the lines.

In the 1940s, before Nationalisation on 1st January 1948, the

77

engines and carriages were emblazoned with L M S on the side. London Midland Scottish. Very few people, especially from the east end of the village, owned a car. No local bus serviced the village, so we walked or cycled, through a gap in the hedge between fields, along a field boundary, through the kiss gates at the little arch, over another field full of crops, past the pond and Smithy, to Church or School, or visiting Aunt Nance in Hornes End.

The railway has three cuttings south of the station, before the Westoning bridge. The little arch, the big arch, where the brook also runs under the railway, and another arch at Worthy End farm. I found it quite appalling when on a recent visit to Flitwick to find the path beside the brook from Hornes End to Water Lane blocked by fencing and a gate. It appears that Worthy End farm have taken the liberty of blocking that route.

It is a long established right of way, but in the field between two gates, (Hornes end side of the railway), were horses. I continued my journey. However, there are people who are afraid of cows and horses. That path should have free unfettered access to it as it did when I was a child. Perhaps Flitwick residents don't bother any more about such things, maybe the local Councillors don't use their powers to investigate. Does anybody walk anywhere any more?

Both sides of the railway in the 1940s had fields of crops, and also busy allotments on the moor between the railway and Water Lane, south of the brook. In a meadow by the railway a herd of cattle from Wilson's farm grazed contentedly on the lush green grass and meadow flowers, dropping cow pats every few feet. They didn't seem to mind when noisy children invaded their quiet little world. They glanced up, as if to say, 'Oh its you lot again,' while they chewed the cud, or stood nose to tail swishing flies off each other with their tails. They always seemed to know when it was milking time, as slowly, they ambled down to the five bar gate at the bottom of the field, and waited patiently for whoever was fetching them in.

A pastoral scene long forgotten in Flitwick.

The allotments were always busy, as men spent many hours growing their own produce. Narrow paths, peaty yellow watery ditches stretched this way and that in a grid pattern, the plots of good ground yielding plenty to eat. Phyllis Watson slipped into one of the ditches one day and almost drowned, but her brother Philip (or it was Derek) grabbed her hair and pulled her out. I was always careful when I went near those ditches.

Most of those gardeners were getting old and are now in that other great garden, the allotments are gone, the ground no longer feeding families. It seems easier, cheaper, and quicker for us to buy vegetables from the supermarket these days, although in my opinion home grown tastes better.

On the Hornes End side of the railway, fields of corn ripened until golden. We kids ran through the corn and stooks, playing hide and seek. Heads popping up to see where the others were, shrieks of delight, back down on hands and knees, along a bit, more shrieks. No one ever chided us for making such noise. In the winter, snow crowned rows and rows of Brussel Sprouts, like icing sugar. Homes in Townfield Road now occupy what used to be that field. The field had a rotation of crops, from Brussel Sprouts to Corn, Potatoes, to Cabbage etc. I helped at the harvest from the age of 6 or 7.

In the Spring, after a dry spell, when the undergrowth on the embankment was tinder dry, sparks flying in all directions from the smoky steam engines set it ablaze, burning away all that deadwood and rubbish. A couple of weeks later, after a few showers, new green shoots of grass appeared, and as the summer came in, clumps of wild flowers bloomed. The Bramble bushes sprouted, blossomed by autumn heaved with luscious Blackberries. Women and children went along to fill bowls and dishes to the brim, taking the fruit home for jam, or to eat as they were, or to make a steam pudding, with custard. It cost us nothing but a few scratches.

We didn't drop empty drinks cans or plastic wrappers everywhere, for we simply did not have them to drop. Glass bottles were worth money if we took them back to the shop, to recover the deposit, usually about 1d or 2d per bottle. Enough to buy some sherbet, and even a stick of Liquorice to dip into it. Seldom did we come across broken glass, or any other unsightly litter. I do recall once, when trekking through the long grass with others, on the embankment near the little arch, coming across a used condom. French letters, or Johnnies as they were called. I had never seen anything like it, but one of our group seemed to know what it was. We were all around 14 or 15, and had a little giggle over the discovery, which we did not touch. We looked, and walked on, still giggling, speculating which one of the older girls we knew had been on the embankment with a Yank. What little we had heard of such things, as inquisitive ears listened to grown ups talk, we imagined the only people using them were the Yanks.

Boys carried a notebook and pencil in their trouser pockets. When a train came up or down the line, they ran to the wire fence and eagerly noted the engine number, the name of the engine, (engines usually had a name blazoned on the side), and what type of engine if they knew it, everything possible was noted. I can recall keeping a note book for the same reason, but girls did not have handy pockets in their clothes. I was never as serious about the hobby. Packets of tea, cigarettes, carried little cards with pictures of railway engines. A picture on one side, and details about the engine on the reverse. There were similar cards depicting Sports personalities,

Film stars, Radio performers, Castles, Bridges, Ships, Aeroplanes, the Armed Forces, battles fought, types of uniform. We could play alone or in groups in the fields around the Alley, with no fears of being attacked or plied with drugs. Going through the kissgates of the little arch, or climbing the stile next to it, we made for the buttresses supporting the arch, to run up and down. The accoustics inside were fantastic, we shouted and bellowed, our voices echoed and carried as far away as Station Road. We scrawled graffiti on the walls with chalk we dug up from the embankment. It all washed off in the next rainstorm.

Except when we went coaling, (more about that later), we didn't usually go on to the railway lines. The 1901 census shows many Flitwick men were railway workers. There is still a short cut from the east end to Hornes end. Sandwiched between Willow Way and Lime Close, the path is rubbish strewn. It is a dogs latrine, certainly not a good place for children to play.

In the latter half of the 19th century, because the railway brought much better and faster communication opportunities, the village expanded. Since the second world war it has grown even more, so much that it is no longer a village, but a town. Add to this the nearby M1 motorway, and Flitwick is ideally suited for communters to work in a wider area than was possible in earlier times. New schools have been built. A very efficient small library is sited near to where the old Victory hall used to be, and there is also a Community Centre and Leisure Centre, plus the Rufus complex.

Most change in Flitwick began directly after the war, as we kids played on the embankment and in the fields which were soon to disappear under tarmac and bricks, having little or no knowledge, or imagination, to realise just how massive the growth would be, and how it would affect us.

81

Off Station Road was Ellis and Everard's busy coal yard, and off Steppingly Road was Franklin's, an equally busy coal yard with the railway shunting yards. Fewer homes now have coal fired heating, it being replaced by central heating, which is more efficient, less dirty, and keeps the whole house warm instead of only the few feet around the fireplace. Not many new homes have a chimney stack

The deisel trains are much quicker, getting from Flitwick to St Pancras in half the time. Early morning and evenings, the Avenue was a hive of activity as many walked or cycled to and from the station. Today of course, cars have taken over, and the Avenue has to cope with the traffic.

Last train from Bedford to Flitwick was just after 10pm, from Luton a little after 11pm.

At Flitwick, the tickets were scrutinized by a railway clerk at the top of the steps on Station Bridge, and by another clerk on the gate at the end of the platform. Railway stations had a ticket machine, which. when two pennies were inserted, issued a platform ticket for those who were not intending to board, but who wanted access to meet a passenger, or see someone off. Flitwick station is little altered from the 40s, the buildings look similar to how they have always been. Passengers still have to trek up and down stairs to get to platforms, although today, they have four platforms instead of two. The two lines which used to be reserved for freight traffic now take all traffic. The safety barrier against the traffic wasn't needed in the 1940s. There are changes planned for the station, and by the time this book is printed the station may well not look the same.

The growth of Flitwick and the surrounding areas have had a huge impact on how the station can cope.

Chapter 7
STARTING SCHOOL

It is 1940 and the war is hotting up. Churchill, who became Prime Minister on May 10th, later made his famous speech, 'Never have so many owed so much to so few,' as we sent the Lufftwaffe packing at the Battle of Britain. The Italians come in on the side of Germany on June 10th, and Hitler's troops march into Paris on 14th June. I've mentioned Dunkirk in another chapter, and the history books go into great detail about the event, so I will not mention any more of it here.

Flitwick was considered a safe haven for evacuees from blitzed London, and the Alley was a safe place to play. It was an event to see a private car venture there. Only the milk cart, the coal wagon, and bread van came up the Alley as far as numbers 26/28/30.

During the war, coal carts and milk carts were horse drawn.
I had no fear of traffic. There was so little of it, and slower than today. I can guess the authorities raised little or no money on speeding or illegal parking fines. Traffic calming measures were unnecessary, and in any case, never heard of, (bliss!!), no green lanes, no sleeping policemen humps to give us the hump, and the zebras and pelicans were in the zoo. No traffic islands, no traffic lights. If there were any roundabouts anywhere, they were not in Flitwick. These were all for the future, when cars were for us ordinary folk, for when most of us wanted the means to get from A to B without having to stand freezing or being blown away at a bus stop, or squashed up like Sardines in overcrowd trains.

There were very few street lights in Flitwick, all switched off during the war. The edge of pavements, where there were pavements, were painted white, to assist drivers in the dark, because headlamps had to have hoods fitted, leaving only a sliver of light. A white mark was painted on to the rear of vehicles, so that following vehicles would not do a bumpety bump in the dark.

At 5 years of age, I had no idea what was going on in the big bad world. I paid little attention to the wireless, didn't know how to read a newspaper, but I do know times were tough for most everyone, not least of all Mum, who found herself not knowing which way to turn, for she was so poor. Quite apart from the fact that some of his wages went up in smoke, Ernie's job as an agricultural labourer paid miserable wages, less than half the average for the period. If it had not been for the vegetables he grew in the garden, we could have been very hungry.

In 1940, the armed forces had an insatiable appetite. Anyone fit enough, young enough, but unwilling to sign up, or if they objected to call-up, were considered cowards. Workers in certain trades and occupations were exempt, they were vital for the war effort on the home front.

Agricultural workers were not called up, but Ernie's younger brother George volunteered. In 1940, everyone had their ear glued to the wireless to hear news of the war, and to listen to Churchill's speeches. News bulletins at the cinema gave a pictorial version.
1940 was also a momentous year for this little girl, as I embarked on the first steps of an unknown journey through formal education. Flitwick had no pre-school playgroups, no pre-school nurseries. We 5 year olds were flung in at the deep end and expected to get on with it. We were to become literate and numerate, if it was the last thing the teachers did, war or no war. I'm afraid the picture of a sweet little girl in smart new school uniform, carrying a satchel of books, is not the picture I made, nor many of my school chums. No uniform, no satchel. On that first day, it is likely I wore a floral dress and the

84

cleanest cardigan I owned. Perhaps Mum may have been able to get me a cast off school skirt from one of the jumble sales. As we did not own a camera, I have no pictorial record of that first day of school. I can be sure my short hair was combed straight, and a bunch of it tied to one side of my head with a ribbon. My hair was always parted on the left side, so the ribbon would be on the right side.

For this occasion I am sure Mum would have gone to some effort to see that I was clean and presentable. On my feet, a pair of brown sandals, as it was August. Perhaps with socks, perhaps not. In September Mum bought me a pair of black lace up school shoes, and they were expected to last me through the winter, along with Wellingtons, and plimsolls for school physical exercises. Few children in the school wore uniform, other parents in Flitwick were on low incomes too. I never visited a hairdresser. Mum cut my hair.

Ernie had his short back and sides haircut at Fossey's on Station Square, but May Watson used to cut Mum's hair. (until about 1950 when Madge Day took over the task).

The Infant School in 1940 was situated in Station Road, opposite Sabey's Paddock, which has disappeared to become Oak Road. The school consisted of two classrooms, in a green painted wooden structure like a large shed, under a corrugated tin roof. When it rained, the noise was such that the teacher's voice was hardly audible. We had to turn up on time, there were no excuses accepted. The teacher did not repeat any part of the lesson which had gone before, the hapless late pupil would have to catch up as best as he/she could.

At the start of the school day, and on return from lunch, when the school bell rang, we lined up in classroom order, boys in the rear playground, girls in the playground to the front, nearest the street. The sexes were kept well apart, (what did they think we 5 years old would get up to?). It suited us fine. We girls had our games, the boys had their games, usually very different.

In orderly fashion, we marched into the small cloakroom, hung our coats up, then washed our hands in small sinks which had only cold taps, the teacher moving us along. Some children from the other end of the village brought sandwiches with them and had their dinner break in the classroom with one of the teachers supervising. Some, if they had a bike for example, went home for their dinner same as myself, although I had only a short way to walk. From January 1943, dinners were provided in the Victory hall on the Rec.

Vegetables for the dinners provided by boys of Dunstable Road school working on the school garden.

We had no convenient buses, certainly no school buses, and Mums didn't turn up with the family car, even if they were lucky enough to have a serviceable one to use. No Ice Cream vans, or chip vans waiting outside the school gates. Children, especially from poor homes, had no spending money for such things.

Inside the classroom, pupils sat in pairs, on the bench seats of the double seated desks. All lined up in neat rows, facing the teacher. The desk frame was wrought iron, painted black, with wooden seats and desk top. Penknives had carved initials into the wood, ink splodges had dried in. Under the desk top, was a shelf or cavity, where exercise books, pencils, chalk, a rubber, ruler, perhaps a skipping rope. An Apple for the teacher? No, not in my memory, no one wanted to be known as teacher's pet. Anyway, the Apple would be eaten long before the teacher saw it.

We did not tote bags of books back and forth every day. We did no homework. We sat in the same desk every day, the same teacher taught us all subjects. On the desk were two inkwells, one for each pupil, slots to fit pencils and a pen. Sheet of blotting paper handy, to dab ink dry on the written page. A splodge of ink on the paper lost us marks for good work.

A monitor appointed by the teacher filled the inkwells daily. We used pencils the first year, later being introduced to pen and ink We had no ballpoint pens. A chap named Lazlo Biro, a Hungarian journalist, invented the Biro around 1943, and it is reported British bomber crews were the first to use them. When they first hit the civilian market, they were very expensive and not always reliable. We had to supply our own pens, pencils, erasers, sharpeners, but our exercise books were provided. The teacher cut them in half horizontally, making supplies spread further.

Pen: Replaceable nib, fitted into metal neck, attached to wooden stalk.

Pen nibs could be bought in most village shops. Cousins shop had a card of them hanging on a nail on the wall near the counter, along with cards of pencils, rubbers, and other small items such as hair grips and hair nets. Nibs were about 3d each. Pencils were used and sharpened over and over, until worn down to tiny stumps. Rulers were wooden, marked out in imperial measurements. We began by learning to write our own name, and write the Alphabet. A for Apple, B for Ball, writing each letter in lower case script before going on to capitals, each page devoted to one letter at a time, practice practice, diligently following the teacher's written instructions on the blackboard, which sat on a large easel. When we went on to whole words, we spelt rough as rough, not ruff. Parrot fashion, in unison, we chorused the alphabet, Ay, bee, cee, dee, eee, eff, gee and so on until teacher was satisfied most of us had it right. Those who played truant regularly missed out on those lessons, as the teacher wasn't going to repeat anything for their benefit, so they learned nothing, left to catch up best as they could. How can a child learn to read and write even basically if they are never at school?

Teacher used white chalk on the blackboard, rubbed off with a felt covered wood block before she went on to the next lesson. (my husband tells me that when he started in one of Edinburgh's suburban schools, he was issued with a framed slate and chalk instead of notebook and pencil).

As far as I can recall, there were only two teachers at the Infant School in Station Road. Miss Coddington, and Miss Minney. These two women expected respect and obedience. I believe they got it most of the time. In return, they gave us love and affection, and discipline in a rather old fashioned way.

When a teacher married, she was expected to resign. One of those women taught me how to knit. One day, the teacher distributed knitting needles to the girls, along with balls of twine, and announced we were going to make a contribution to the war effort, and learn to knit at the same time. The gauge were large, a bit cumbersome for our small fingers, but the teacher was very patient, going round each girl in turn, so that we soon got the hang of this knitting lark, making a duster in plain stitch, approximately quarter metre square. With such a large gauge, and our inexperience, the mesh was loose, but there must have been many a soldier out there using our little knitted squares to clean a rifle or polish up a bit of kit. In those days there were girl tasks and boy tasks. How the boys made their contribution, I don't know, but boys didn't do knitting.

We learned our times-tables by rote, the teacher leading us in chorus, 'Two threes are six, three threes are nine' progressing up the

88

scale to 'three nines are twenty seven, twelve threes are thirty six' and so on. Those who did not try to learn, or were not paying attention, were left behind, could find themselves sitting or standing in a corner facing the wall as punishment. There wasn't anything painful such as having to put on a dunce's cap, but shameful all the same. Disobedience wasn't tolerated. Many a boy felt the cane slapped across his backside, (not bare backside, that was not allowed.) Girls were whacked across the knuckles with a ruler, or slapped on the palm of the hand with the cane.

Thrice times twelve is thirty six, we droned on. By the time we were due to go to the big school, as we called the Dunstable Road school, we were expected to know our ABC, do simple arithmetic, have a reasonable vocabulary, and spell most simple words.

An embarrassing moment happened during my first term. At the time it was a bit distressing. As I have already mentioned, we were desperately poor in 1940, although by no means unique. Other parents struggled in the same way, each household having to cope best they could. Sometimes Mum couldn't cope. If the rains came, the washing had to compete with Ernie's working clothes, draped over the fireguard railing to dry. A modern dryer would have helped, had we electricity for it.

One day there were no clean knickers for me, and I must have soiled my last pair. I went to school knickerless, with Mum assuring me no-one would notice. I was a boisterous girl, running around at playtime, climbing the perimeter ranch style fencing. That was my undoing. Someone did notice my bare rump and a chant soon erupted, 'Blandies got no knickers on, Blandies got no knickers on.' Most knew me as Maureen Bland, although my name was actually Maureen Randall. 'Ha Ha Ha,' they all laughed. Someone reported it to the teacher, who promptly ordered me to go home and come back

89

properly dressed. Until starting school, I had often run around without knickers. No socks, sometimes no shoes.

Joyce lay in her pram without a nappie on, having a good old kick, which was very healthy for her if the weather was kind, but occasionally, she'd do a whoopsie and her feet would kick into it before Mum noticed. More cleaning up to do. Perhaps simply because Mum couldn't get her nappies dried quickly enough. Disposable nappies were unknown.

Many people have memories of embarrassing moments when they wished the ground would open up and swallow them. One girl could not wait, and a puddle formed on the floor as we were in full swing with 'Ten green bottles, standing on the wall,' a popular group song. In winter I can recall my feet often so very cold because I did not have socks to wear. In summer I wore buckled brown sandals, seldom with socks.

For P.E. at school, I wore plimsolls, Mum could not afford proper specially made sports shoes. For the physical exercises we girls tucked our clothes into our black flannelette knickers which had elastic round the hem of the legs, to just above knee level.
No girl wore trousers to school. Boys wore short grey flannel trousers until they were in their early teens. Sometimes a boy would arrive at school wearing his new short trousers. Mum's always bought them a size too big, and many a young lad was embarrassed because he had to wear his braces high and tuck a belt around tight. Otherwise the trousers hung half mast, baggy. Baggy trousers were not in fashion then. There was also the lad growing so fast his Mum could not afford to replace his trousers too often. Short trousers really short, to hardly an inch or two below his rump, and he'd struggle to button them up. Trousers then did not have zips, flies were buttoned. Lads had patches on their trousers, covering a tear in

90

the rump, or at the side. Funny how the older we get, we can recall much of what happened many years ago, but get home with the shopping to find we have forgotten half of what we went for. I have a habit of losing things and finding them when I am looking for something else entirely.

One warm sunny day, must have been some time in 1941, those of us living in the Alley or down Water Lane, could not cross the road to get home for dinner. Nothing dramatic such as a bomb falling. Tanks, seemed like hundreds of them to us little ones, rumbled slowly down Station Road, past the school, one close behind the other, then another and another. The noise was deafening, and in between some tanks were camouflage covered trucks full of soldiers. We cheered and cheered, and the soldiers waved back to us. People gathered in the road to watch. I was awestruck, had never seen a sight like it before, (or since). I speculate they were on their way to the Moor for exercises.

We had three schools in Flitwick at that time. The Infant School as described above, the Mixed School at the bottom of Dunstable Road, next to the Smithy, and a private school run by Miss Hetley, who lived at Bedford. Her school took pupils up to the age of 13 to prepare for them going on to Bedford Grammar, and Public schools. Her school was situated at the end of a long drive off the High Street. It has long ago been demolished and replaced by the Croft and Highland Roads. Thelma Palmer, (nee Beale), attended Miss Hetley's school for a while, until her parents took over the Crown Inn. Miss Hetley considered the daughter of a publican not quite the kind of pupil she wanted, and asked Thelma's parents to take her out of school. Image problem methinks? Or was Thelma a bit of a rebel?

Chapter 8
THE IRON ROOM and THE MILL

The Mission room in Station Road was another very important thread woven into our lives. Named the iron room by the locals because of its corrugated iron construction, it was built in 1884 by the Reverend Ashpitel at his own expense, as a reading and recreation building for the young men of the village, for educational evening classes, and adaptable to other uses. Built on a piece of land in Station Road, at the entrance to the allotments there, it was 30ft long, and 15 ft wide, the land rented to the Parish by the Brookes family for one shilling per year. It cost £90 to build, plus extra for foundations, and the Duke of Bedford helped by donating funds towards furnishings and fitting out.

Mum and I attended many a jumble sale in the Iron Room. Around the hall were placed tables carrying donated clothing and other items for whatever cause the money was being raised for. Some of the jumble sales were in aid of the Forces funds. Mum looked around for items of clothing to fit us, a penny or two would buy a skirt. Woollens were not so easy to come by. Women would look for woollens in any condition, bad or good, because they could unravel the garment and use the wool to make a new one. Mum also looked around for suitable clothing in any condition that she could cut down into strips to make a rag rug. Then she'd look for a tweed or sports jacket for Ernie to wear at work

A pile of books or magazines had me rummaging. A little bundle of comics such as Film Fun or the Beano could be bought for one or two pennies, a hard back childrens book for perhaps one penny, or halfpenny. Boys looked for comics such as the Hotspur, with stories about Britain beating the Hun, a name given to German troops. A shilling could go a long way. There would be a table or two packed with home made jams, bottled fruit surplus garden produce, apples and other fresh fruit in season, all donated.

The Iron Room hosted Book Fairs and Exhibitions, such as the Electrical Exhibition of 1945, where it was advertised that five shillings (25p) per week was sufficient to pay for electric cooking, washing, ironing, lighting, and the occasional electric fire.

Along Greenfield Road we had a full working Mill. At school we were told that it was mentioned in the Domesday book. From an early age, I climbed upon the bridge parapet, the brook meandered under the road, and found it fascinating to watch the waterwheel turning steadily, splash, splash, paddles like buckets collecting water, and then on the turn, tipping the water back into the brook to continue on its way. Cattle grazed in the adjoining field, and there were all kinds of birds flying around. Horse drawn vehicles arrived daily with corn to be milled.

The Mill was strongly built of weatherboarding on massive heavy wooden uprights and supports. At that time the Goodman family lived in the Mill house. They also owned our old hovels in the Alley.

The waterwheel now stands silent and still, the paddles choked with weeds and debris, the Mill closed up, the hustle bustle noise and industry just another memory, outbuildings and storage sheds no longer needed, falling into disrepair.
How long will the building stand?

Chapter 9
1941 GOING FROM BAD TO WORSE

Three wheel tricycle, built in 1932, used for selling Ice Cream, Owner David Visocchi (of Kirriemuir in Scotland) gave me permission to photograph it.

I liked school. Miss Minney and Miss Coddington were strict, but also kind and fair. They helped me as much as they could, but things were going from bad to worse at home. Ernie hit Mum with his fists when in a temper, which was often, he also slapped me across the side of my head and in the middle of my back. If Mum placed herself between him and me she got more blows. Aunt Daphne told me that one day, Mum and Ernie were having another of their noisy rows, and neighbour Carr Line came into our house to tell them not to make such a racket, just in time to see Ernie threatening Mum with the poker. Daphne told me Mum suffered that kind of abuse for years.

At school I made a lot of new friends, and on good sunny days, the Alley rang with the sound of children playing noisy games. They came to the Alley from Station Road, Maulden Road, Water Lane, and even further afield. We had no notion of the anxieties our elders were suffering, wondering how their loved ones were, or how they coped with wartime rationing and restrictions. Mum must have worried about her brothers. At night I was reminded there was a war raging, as bombers flew overhead, and the searchlight beams criss crossed, lighting up the night sky, blocking out the stars. I heard the sound of the ack ack guns as they popped shots at the Lufftwaffe.

Luton suffered most in Bedfordshire. 107 deaths, and at least 500 injured. Compared to London, Plymouth, Coventry, it doesn't sound a lot, but bad enough for those involved. In 1941, Hitler invaded Russia, and got thrown out later, causing much suffering to his own troops. December 1941, the Japanese bombed Pearl Harbour, bringing the United States into the conflict as they saw this country's plight in a different light. After that the Yanks came over, Over here, overpaid, and oversexed.

Clothes rationing began on June 2nd 1941. Made little difference to us, Mum seldom bought new clothes. Government posters appeared all over the place, urging the nation to Dig for Victory, to use all available ground to grow vegetables. People were encouraged to keep livestock in their back gardens. We were urged to save paper, even used bus tickets. Buses had a little box on the platform for us to dump our used tickets into when alighting. Walls have Ears posters appeared at railway stations warning that spies were everywhere, passing on snippets of information they thought useful back to Hitler. Single women over age 19 were directed towards war work, were expected to be mobile, and work 10 hour shifts as needed.

Magazines were fairly cheap to buy, but thin. Woman magazine for example was only 3d. It contained recipes for meatless dishes, the best way to make old clothes look new, using trimmings from old clothes. There were fiction stories of heroism, of people being apart, letters, some sad, some uplifting.

1941 brought new songs, some romantic, I don't want to set the world on fire, I just want to set a flame in your heart sung by The Ink Spots, a group of American coloured singers. Billy Cotton cheered us up with an old song, I've got sixpence, jolly jolly sixpence. Noel Coward sang London Pride while Hitler's bombers were trying their best to annihilate the place. Both Vera Lynn and Sidney Burchell recorded There'll always be an England. Ann Shelton and Vera Lynn both recorded Wish me luck as you wave me goodbye, a troopship song for the soldiers embarking for overseas. Gracie Fields sang the same song. The Glen Miller Orchestra was in full swing with the famous Tuxedo Junction. Many many songs, on the wireless, on those old shellac 78s records. Whistled on the street and in the workplace, and danced to. Dance halls were packed with soldiers home on leave, factory workers letting off steam, shop girls forgot their tired feet. Queues at the cinema to see the latest film. Very often those films had a war theme. Mrs Miniver for example, starring Greer Garson. 1942 saw the debut of a new young actor named Richard Attenborough, in the film In which we serve, about dramatic happenings to sailors.

The Corn Exchange in Bedford advertised a crazy night ball for 14th July, music by the Beds and Herts Regimental Dance Orchestra.

However, for Mum, there were no such delights, only the drudgery of that hovel in the Alley, caring for us, taking abuse from Ernie, and struggling with a woefully inadequate income.

Chapter 10
MY FIRST VIEW OF DEATH

Number 17 Hornes End was a very sad place in April 1941. Aunt Flo, as she was known to us, was dead after suffering the ravages of breast cancer. Mum, Joyce, and I visited her often. It was in her house Mum first set eyes on Ernie, Flo's nephew.

Rain lashed down as we made our way over the fields to Hornes End. Miserably cold I was, Joyce in her pushchair, Mum had no umbrella, only a headscarf for protection. Mum grieved, for Flo had been a sympathetic friend. Flo's large family were in attendance. We warmed ourselves beside the fire in the kitchen cum living room. Most were strangers to me.

Tears were shed, men wore black armbands over their best, or only, decent suit. However, my most vivid memory of that day is of Flo lying in her coffin. It was placed across two chairs in the front room, (parlour), the curtains were closed. The top half lay open, revealing Flo, dressed as in her nightie, her eyes closed as in sleep, now free of the dreadful pain. I don't believe I cried until someone told me to kiss Flo's forehead. I resisted, but was raised high enough so I could lean over to her face. I felt her forehead smooth and cold as marble as my lips made contact. I've never forgotten it, her cold cold brow. That memory is etched forever. Others took their turn to kiss a much loved woman goodbye for the last time. Mum muttered something about being haunted if I didn't kiss her. Later the coffin was closed, placed on a bier, and pushed along Hornes End to Church Road cemetery. I did not go to the cemetery. Some families followed a hearse drawn by two wonderfully groomed black horses sporting dancing black plumes, the coffin visible inside a glass case, but that was too expensive for Flo's family. Most of the men present could not afford to take a full (unpaid) day off, and had to go back to work, leaving the women drinking tea and talking.   Neighbours and friends brought sugar, bread, a little tea, to help out. When I asked Aunt Daphne if Ernie was at the funeral, she said no, as Aunt Flo hadn't liked him. It was still raining as we headed back home.

Shortly after the funeral, Flo's family scattered, some to London. Charles married again two years later. His daughters didn't like that one little bit. Aunt Daphne lived with us briefly, before joining George in army married quarters.

There was a tradition in many parts of the country, including Flitwick, of hanging a black sheet out of a window to indicate the family had suffered a bereavement. Whether this was the case at number 17 Hornes End that day or not I cannot recall.

Chapter 11
THE REC

The old recreation ground, 3 acres in extent, was situated on the corner between Dunstable Road and Steppingly Road. It has been taken over for a Supermarket, Petrol Station, shops and car park. Opened publicly in 1889 by Lord Charles Russell, with over 1000 people attending the opening evening, the idea was first mooted by a wood draughtsman named Alfred Pearse. He became secretary of the group who undertook to organize it, and Major Brooks of the Manor let the piece of ground to the Parish at a rent of £3 per year.

In the 1940s, the Rec consisted of a few swings, a chute, the very basic cricket pitch in the centre, Victory hall and Electricity sub-station. The Victory hall, (some called it the village hall), was erected in 1919, the first non-denominational public building in Flitwick. It had a one room extension to the rear, built of corrugated iron, with its own entrance door. This was a Snooker room for young men, they did not let girls in. The girls scrambled up to the windows, but that was as near as they got.

The Rec hosted a few Fetes. Volunteers busied themselves in the hall, providing revellers with refreshments. Other plump women wearing aprons washed up the crockery in the kitchen, for there were no plastic or paper cups then. Out on the Rec, other volunteers organized childrens races such as the three legged race which was great fun, praise showered on winners. Later in the day there was all the fun of a small Fair. After we moved to Dunstable Road, I could watch the cricket being played from my bedroom window, our house was directly opposite. When the area was redeveloped, the Victory hall had to be demolished. The Rec was moved to ground which had been the School sports field, a Community hall built, and Flitwick

99

got its much needed public Library.

Kingsmoor school took over ground where schoolboys of the old Dunstable Road School had once grown vegetables.

From Church Road, to Steppingly Road, from the Station to edge of town, there is so little public green space. Provision of open public spaces for relaxation, games, play, and most importantly FREE, was little appreciated by previous Flitwick town planners. The present Rec can hardly be called a park. The Moor and the Wood are not handy and are not places I'd like to see my grandchildren go unescorted. If I close my eyes, I can see the old Rec, just as it was. Cricket ball against willow, children sliding down the chute, bouncing balls, playing chasing games, skipping. Happy Days?

I'm almost forgetting to mention the public lavatory on the Rec. It had to be seen to be believed.

The facility was in the left hand top corner of the Rec, and consisted of some sheets of corrugated iron fixed upright, about 6ft high, and box shape, no roof, with a gap on one side to allow entry. No pan, not even an old bucket. Anyone needing to do a pee or anything else let it go into the ground. All it was, was a shelter, the entrance gap facing the hedge, for privacy.

But to go inside was to be assailed by foul smells, and you had to watch where you stood. I never needed to use it when I lived in Dunstable Road. There may have been an official public lavatory elsewhere, but I never knew of it. Times were tough.

This is a school report we sat an exam for each year. This is 1949.(age 14) Mostly B and C, the previous year I'd had mostly A and B, so my standards had slipped.

Chapter 12
COBBLERS

Flitwick in the 1940s had two Cobblers. Sammy Wiles small workshop at rear of his house at 21 Station Road. On entering the wooden building, there was a marvellous smell of shoe polish, beaten leather, and another indecipherable heady atmosphere I am not able to explain very well. Shoes, all sizes, boots, his last, and paraphanalia of his trade, filled up that little workspace.

On shelves, on hooks around the walls, were odd shoes, pairs of shoes, working boots, childrens sandals, the buckles sewn on more securely, low heels, high heels, mostly black or brown.

Another Cobbler occupied what had once been a railway carriage, at corner of Thinnings, near the Blackbirds. Around 1948 it became a Greengrocery business. There is now a house on the site.

New shoes were bought from the Tally man, or from Inskip's drapery shop, a low bungalow style wooden building opposite the Blackbirds. I usually went there for Plimsolls, used for school physical exercise. Mum was not allowed credit, I had to take cash with me. There was no ShoeZone or any other alternative shoe shop selling imported shoes at discounted prices. Our shoes were made in Britain, likely in the shoe factories at Northampton. Shoes, and Ernie's working boots took a big chunk out of our income. They could not be bought for pennies at the Jumble sales.

Ernie obtained a four different size feet shoe last, the kind that Cobblers used. He'd also found some leather from somewhere, and said he'd mend our shoes from then on. Segs were hammered into toes and heels of shoes, little pieces of metal which helped to make the shoes last a little longer. If no leather available, a piece of cardboard had to suffice to cover a hole temporarily.

Chapter 13
SUPERSTITION and RELIGION

"The mind of man is subject to unaccountable terrors and apprehensions, proceeding from the unhappy situation of private or public affairs, from ill health, from a gloomy or melancholy disposition, or from a concurrence of all these circumstances.

In such a state of mind, infinite unknown evils are dreaded from unknown agents, and where real objects or terror are wanting, the soul finds imaginary ones. Weakness, fear, melancholy, together with ignorance, are therefore the true source of Superstition"..................

(David Hume, Political Writer, in 1741)
An Essay, Moral and Political, of Superstition and Enthusiasm

I was never in the Parish Church of St Peter and St Paul. The Vicar never came to our house. Yet Mum and Ernie thought of themselves as Christian. Ernie would remark, 'Yer don't need ter goo ter church ter be a Christian,'

History lessons at school included the Reformation and Crusades. Eastertime had us singing hymns about the Crucifixtion, and at Christmas we sang Carols. Onward Christian Soldiers was sung regularly, especially during the War. Each morning, headmaster Charlie Allen took Assembly, which included a short sermon as well as a reading from the Bible, and a couple of hymns. Prayers for the armed forces and Royal Family were said. We stood throughout. Lastly, there were intimations on school matters.

We had no dividing lines between Catholic or Methodist, Baptist or Church of England. Assembly was conducted in the main part of the building, which was two classrooms divided by a huge curtain. This curtain was drawn back by two older boys for Assembly, and dropped back in place when it was all over.

Christmas and Easter, a few pupils marched to Church. Others, including myself, went home instead. During the time I spent in Kempston Childrens Home I went to Church every Sunday, but it was many years later, after moving to Edinburgh, before I attended Church regularly again.

When I was around 11 or 12 years old, I had the idea I'd like to be a good Christian, and attended the Baptist Chapel in Kings Road, for all of three or four Sundays with Kathy Wooding, (nee See). Other demands on my time weakened my commitment.
Mum and Ernie thought there were more important things for me to do. Fetch food for the Rabbits, clean their hutches out, help Mum in the house, fetch wood from the Moor, help Ernie in the garden.

I married in a Church of Scotland Presbyterian ceremony in 1958, and remained a Christian until around 1961 when something happened which changed my views drastically.

In Flitwick we had five places of worship that recall. The Baptist Chapel in Kings Road, it has been rebuilt since. The Wesleyan Chapel in Chapel Road. The Church of St Andrew in Windmill Road, (150 seater). Then there was the parish church, the Church of St Peter and St Paul in Church Road, and a small strict Baptist chapel at the bottom of Kings Road, erected in 1660, situated to the rear of Cousins shop. Catholics had to cross into Ampthill to attend Mass.

All through my childhood I listened and believed, that whatever our position in life, poor or rich, that was ordained for us by God, and who were we to question the Almighty? Blessed are the poor, for they are always with us, but it was never explained why. If God was providing, why were some provided with so much, and the rest of us so little? In a country which boasted freedoms, had won a war for that concept, with a Monarch at the head of a deeply religious realm, Commonwealth and Empire, why oh why were so many living in poverty, suffering disease and deprivation, while others lived off the fat of the land?

All religions should respect each other, and recognise the rights of those like me who belong to no faith. There are enough examples throughout history of one religion dominating others, using the law and the name of God as a battering ram, and if that didn't work, using fear and torture along with cruel inhumane punishments in order that we ordinary peasants should do their bidding and conform. The 15th 16th, and 17th centuries saw much conflict over which religion or brand of Christianity we should follow, and Witch hunting was pursued as a career. A report in the Glamis register of June 1697 reads, 'No preaching this Lord's day, the Minister being at Cortachy burning a Witch.'

There are one or two things about religion which disturb me today, for example,

Has criticism of religion or officialdom got us to the stage that we are afraid to open our mouths and say what we think, afraid that we will land in court, be thrown into prison, perhaps even lose our life. An Atheist or Agnostic, what am I ? does it matter?

Is our freedom of speech being eroded? I believe it is, drip drip, chip, chip, political correctness has gone potty. I have nothing but contempt for those who use their faith as an excuse to kill others, in 'the name of God,' because their sect decrees their God is the only true God, therefore the rest of us are infidels and have no right to life. Should I turn the other cheek, ignore the carnage, the loss of life?

Like many others I am superstitious, not rational I know. As David Hume says, it stems from ignorance and fear. I won't walk under a ladder if I can help it. How many of us cross our fingers if we want a positive outcome to a problem? Shoes on the table, No No, it is unlucky, shoes are for the floor, we eat at the table. Mum had plenty of superstitions. Black cat crossing her path, good luck on the way, and by jove, she needed hope for that.

Thirteen should not sit down together for dinner, reminiscences of Christ's last supper, and Judas' betrayal. Trying to sit 13 around the table in our small living room was impossible.

Break a mirror and bad luck will dog you for 7 years.
I wouldn't give anyone a present of scissors or knives, the exception being a cutlery set for a wedding present. Mum always threw a little salt over her left shoulder if she spilt any. Taking a spade or axe in the house is a no no.

She was particularly afraid of Friday 13th No cutting our fingernails that day, she said the Witches would take the clippings and cause mischief. If I had a raggedy fingernail on a Sunday, she bit the offending nail to smooth it, she would not use scissors on our nails on a Sunday.

Ernie went around with a Rabbits foot in his pocket, bad luck for the Rabbit, not much better luck for him. Give a baby a silver coin, however small, to bring the baby riches all its life.

'There's a hole in the fire,' Mum exclaimed. The coals had settled. Surrounded by red flame, appeared a black hole. Grabbing the poker, Mum rattled it through the bars of the grate to shake the coals. The black hole disappeared, she breathed a sigh of relief.

Mum looked for symbols in how the coals settled. A bird or star shape were lucky signs, a bell shape celebrations, but a clock wasn't welcome, it could mean a death pending.

If a Bee came into the house, Mum said it brought illness, but I have heard another version, that it brings news of a visitor. I was advised many years ago by some older friends to talk to a Bee, it could enhance my chances of good luck. Is it a load of b.........ks?

All Souls Eve, or Halloween as we know it, has spawned many poems and stories. One I quite like because it is very descriptive, is by George McDonald, a Scottish poet. I have a reprint of his little book, dated 1905. The poem is too long to quote in full.

"Sweep up the floor Janet, put on another peat,
it is a low and starry night Janet, but neither cold nor wet.
It's the night betwen saints and souls, when the bodiless go about,
it's open house we keep tonight, for any that be about.
Set the chairs back from the wall Janet, get ready for quiet folk,
have all things clean as a linen sheet, for those that will soon be about"

When a thunderstorm raged, Mum opened windows and doors, for a thunderbolt should it come down the chimney. I took Hawthorn blossom one day into the house, intending to display it on the table. Mum immediately threw the bunch into the yard, yelling at me it was very unlucky to bring Hawthorn indoors.

We made use of large Turnips or Swedes, to cut a face into, as we had no Pumpkins at Halloween time.

We had bonfire night too, on November 5th. During the war, we had no fireworks, and no after dark bonfires. After the war, we built a bonfire and flew off a few fireworks on the spare ground beside the Watsons house. Health and Safety officials would go into spasms if they witnessed a bonfire such as we had. There was no formality, and it could be dangerous, even with Catherine Wheels and Rockets. Some children stuffed old clothes with straw and rags, making a facsimile of Hitler as the Guy.   Penny for the Guy was heard in Flitwick streets as boys, with a few girls, pushed the Guy around in an old pram or a go-kart, or even a flat board on some old wheels. Remember remember the 5th of November, Gunpowder, Treason and Plot we shouted. We'd gather pennies at the doors of homes in Station Road, Maulden Road, Water Lane, Kings Road, towards a collection which we shared out amongst us. When we burned the Guy on the bonfire, we were sending Hitler up in flames. We didn't do trick or treat, although we did dress up in whatever we could scrounge from cupboards. We streaked our faces with soot and purloined old hats, enjoying ourselves immensely.

Sharpe's shop, behind the petrol pumps opposite the station, was the place to go for fireworks once they came on sale. (The shop is now Autostores).

Each year, the Supermarkets devote whole sections to Halloween, black hats, sweets, masks, witches brooms, balloons, costumes, face painting kits to name a few products. The local shops had none of those in the 1940s.

We hadn't much money but we did have fun.

Chapter 14
LACE MAKING and STRAW PLAITING

In the 19th century, many women of the Stringer and Randall families in Bedfordshire were lace makers, or straw plaiters. They also helped to bring the harvest in, looked after children, often while expecting another child, and tended to their domestic chores without all the labour saving equipment we have today. Water had to be drawn from a Well, or perhaps the village pump. The men worked from dawn to dusk.

Babies were born at home, usually with one or two neighbours to help. The women attended to each other at these times. Life in 1880 was hard, with little or no leisure time for the poor. Agricultural workers put in 52 weeks of the year, 12 and more hours per day for a pittance. The wealthy had the money and the time to indulge in leisure pursuits, and travel, their servants taking care of the mundane chores. I doubt if my greatgrandparents ever saw the sea, never mind enjoy a leisurely stroll along the prom.

Mayday was one celebration they could enjoy, it was fun as children danced around the Maypole, (on the old Rec for instance, or Maulden Green) It was a chance to dress up in their best finery. The women spent many hours prior to the day sewing the lovely dresses the little girls wore. Pennies were saved each week to afford them a new pair of shoes.

Doing the European tour to see Italy's fabulous buildings and art galleries, to France, to the Louvre or the grand new Eiffel Tower, or to some foreign beach to lay on the sand for a fortnight wasn't an option. The few pennies they earned making lace or plaiting straw helped to keep starvation from the door. Bales of straw for the hat making industry in Luton arrived on the train at Flitwick Station, collected, distributed, plaited, then returned to the factories.

Lace making was a cottage industry. Bedforshire lace, although not as famous as Nottingham or Honiton lace, was nevertheless in great demand. Made from silk, linen or cheaper cotton, many families produced their own distinctive patterns. Flowers, Ferns, Scallops, Feathers, the lace became trimmings on table linen, anitmacassars, pillow slips, collars, caps, cuffs, handkerchiefs. Fine lace for shawls. I can imagine Bedfordshire lace being worn by gentry of the 16th century, for the Charles 1st and 2nd periods, then later, in Victorian times, maybe even for Victoria Regina herself. It is said that Queen Catherine of Aragon taught Bedfordshire women the art of making pillow lace.

Into the late 19th century, in Bedfordshire, girls from around age 3, their eyes straining to see in fading daylight or candlelight, worked from dawn to late, learning this highly skilled craft.

The children attended lace making school, or straw plaiting school, where they were supposed to do academic lessons in the forenoon, and learn the crafts in the afternoon, but too often, they missed out on the morning lessons, as many mistresses were illiterate. They had quotas to fill and acted more as overseers.

An early record of Flitwick School describes children being taught straw plaiting in the classroom, until about 1880, when it was stopped. Not because the children were supposed to be learning the three R's, but because the straw was making a mess.

Great, great grandma Charlotte Stringer was a straw plaiter. Her son John Stringer (my great grandfather,) age 9 in the 1861 census is described as a straw plaiter, not a scholar. 1901, James Stringer's daughters Rosetta, age 21, and Lizzie age 16, are described as home straw hat sewers. My great grandmother Jane Randall, (nee Cherry), was a lace maker.

Chapter 15
THE WELL

Many people associate a Well with somewhere to throw pennies into and make a wish while so doing. For us, the Well was vital. At the top end of the Alley, our three cottages shared one, which was situated outside the door of number 26. When the cottages were built in the middle of the 19th century, the village had no piped water supply, no mains sewerage, no gas, and of course, no electricity. We were still living in Victorian conditions. Even as late as the 1940s many homes in Flitwick still relied on a Well or Pump, usually shared with others.

For instance, and to my surprise, I found out the Crown Inn did not have indoor mains water until after 1949/50. Thelma Palmer, same age as myself, and a school friend, told me she helped her parents, Horace and Ida Beale, draw water from a pump out back of the pub. Waste water went into a soakaway, was thrown on to the garden, or in homes with indoor plumbing, it could be flushed into a cesspit the Council emptied.

From the outside, a village cottage could look very quaint and respectable, if perhaps a little ramshackle, but it was extremely hard work for the housewife. Her spouse worked hard too, if he didn't go on the ale too often.

Life was not so tranquil for those who had no time to stand and stare, for their lives were often filled with too much care.

Our Well was round, brick lined, measuring a little more than one metre in diameter, shaft at least 6 metres deep under a wooden lid. The spring water was fresh and cool, filtered as it was through chalk lined channels unpolluted by industrial chemicals. It never dried up completely, sometimes the water trickled through slowly.

111

Mum used two or three galvanised pails for hauling up the daily needs. When the water was low as it frustrated Mum, only a half bucketful coming up.

Covering the Well was the gallows. From this simple wooden structure, a heavy chain and hook for lowering and raising the pails was wound around a large metal roller which had an iron spindle with winding handle. We respected the Well. We played around it, over it, but not when the lid was up. It was a steep drop.

Some old folks can go on a bit about the good old days, how the summers were all sunny, with everything just lovely, but I can recall helping Mum draw water when it was blowing a gale, freezing cold, the lid covered in snow, or getting soaked with rain. Wrapped in coats and scarves, we lowered the buckets, trying hard not to get blown in beside them. There were times when the bucket parted company from the hook, and lay languishing at the bottom.

We had no grappling hook of our own, so borrowed one from neighbour Carr Line. It had four hooks attached to a free swinging chain. We waggled the chain to and fro until one of the hooks made contact with the errant bucket. Then it was hauled up like anglers taking in fish.

People wending their way past our houses on foot or bike passed a cheery greeting or juicy bit of gossip to Mum or May if they were at the Well. When mains water came to the Alley, the Well was filled in with rubble.

Chapter 16
THE SIEGE 1942

The year started off much the same as usual. Nothing to indicate an upheaval in my life was about to happen. We went to bed early to conserve fuel, and because Ernie had to rise early for work. If the weather was good or bad, made no difference, Ernie did not like me staying indoors, I had to go out to play. On dry summer days, I liked it out of doors, playing ball with my friends, skipping, chasing games, but in bad weather, it was different, as wind and wet cut through me. Cold, I took shelter in the barn. No friends wanted to come out to play in the awful weather, unless it was snow and we could throw snowballs. Claude Barnes told me Ernie used to lock me in the barn, although I cannot recall it. That would have been quite terrifying. When younger, I'd lay resting on sacks in a corner, miserable and resentful. When older, I climbed up on to the sturdy beams and dreamed of better days.

One day in late 1941, Lil Stringer was passing by the end of the Alley and heard me yelling, holloring and screaming in revolt as Mum gave me a whacking on my backside.. The back door being open, anyone glancing up the Alley could see and hear all that was happening. Whatever I had done to deserve the smacking is long forgotten, but it was surely something which really upset Mum.

Lil reported Mum to the Cruelty as the N.S.P.C.C. was known. Mum told me this many years ago. Lil, of Water Lane, was a fearless little woman and told Mum what she had done. Lil did me a good turn, for she got me out of that hellhole of a house, even if only for a few months.

A week or two before my 7th birthday, and Joyce about to have her 2nd birthday the event unfolded. Ernie and Mum were sent to prison, not for smacking me, but for neglect, and because the N.S.P.C.C. Inspectors believed Joyce and I were in danger of suffering an injury to our health. The court report said there had been 16 visits by the Inspectors. Dr Macklin visited our house on the 15th April 1942, found the house filthy, Joyce and I dirty, ill clad, undernourished, and neglected.

He signed a certificate authorising Joyce and I be removed to a place of safety for health reasons. I have to agree to the court report. Some might say Mum was idle or lazy. She did not smoke or hit the shops to spend money on expensive clothes. She didn't drink, except for a tipple of Stout at Christmas. Other women in Flitwick were also poor, and lived in homes without decent sanitation, but none that I knew of lived in such squalor. So what made Mum reach the stage where she (and Ernie) were summoned to court and sent to prison? Was I such a troublesome child? Did she suffer from depression? How did she let Joyce and I, and herself, down so badly? Was it the war, the rationing, the fear? She wasn't a feckless or stupid woman, but she did suffer indifferent health. Inspectors Brewer and Brymer did the only thing they could do, prosecute Mum and Ernie.

(See chapter nine for how bad things were for Mum in 1941). When I came downstairs in the morning, Ernie was barricading us in. He'd bolted and locked the door, put the large sideboard across the inner door between kitchen and living room, after shuffling us all in there. I didn't like to ask too many questions for I could see he was very angry. The previous evening he cleaned his rifle, there was nothing unusual in that. He was in the home guard and it was his duty to keep his rifle in tip top condition. For a change, he hadn't ordered me out of the house. Mum gave me the task of cleaning the brass fender, and ornaments.

114

Ernie ordered us to be quiet, his voice angry.

Holding the rifle close, he ranted on something about us being taken away over his dead body, in fact, he'd see us all dead first. All dead, now I was even more afraid, hadn't I seen Rabbits drop dead when shot at. Mum screamed and yelled at him to put the rifle away, they were coming for us. Who "they" were wasn't explained. Mum seldom explained anything to us.

I didn't understand all the commotion. Joyce was barely 2 years old, she clung to Mum, even more bewildered than I was. Standing by the table, Ernie kept checking the rifle over, his finger on the trigger. Mum told him not to be a silly bugger, his reply was to shout, 'It's all your bloody fault,'adding, 'Shut yer gob or I'll shut it for yer.'

P.C. Upchurch's voice boomed out, 'Open up Mr Bland, open up I say.' The copper was a big man, and bore his authority well. Ernie swore back and refused to open the door. He repeated his threat to kill us, he was spitting with rage. The constable replied he'd force his way in if he had to. Mum tried to take the gun away, he butted her in the face with it. She sank to the floor, trying to comfort Joyce and I as we took refuge under the table.

Ernie was in a right lather, shouting, raving. The rifle was loaded, lethal, and dreadful. Ernie's rages often frightened me, he had hit me many times, and I had seen Mum suffering at the end of his fists, but this was more than that fear. He lowered himself to the floor beside us, cursing and mumbling. I looked directly along the barrel of the rifle as he stuck it against my nose, I will never forget it. I squeezed my eyes shut tight. He did the same to Mum and Joyce.

Upchurch warned him again that he was about to force his way in. Ernie shouted back 'You do an' I'll blast yer ter kingdom come, an' I'll take 'em ter 'ell wi me.'

Upchurch spoke to someone else, the other voice hardly audible. Ernie remained defiant as Mum screamed abuse at him, and we children cried. If anyone looked in the window, Ernie threatened to shoot them, they quickly ducked out of sight.
Eventually Upchurch cleared his way in.

The back door was heavy and like a fortress, but the windows were the weak points. Lack of paint, and panes just about hanging in there made it easy for someone to get in that way, and open the door from the inside. Then the door between kitchen and living room could be forced, even with the heavy sideboard on the other side. How Upchurch entered, I can only guess, but he found himself on the business end of Ernie's rifle.

I have had a few ordeals in my life, but none quite like that. If Upchurch raised his hands in surrender position I do not recall, but he did say something like, 'Now Mr Bland, things are black enough for you, do you want to add murder to your troubles?' The man who came in with him spoke with a plum accent, 'Good God man, are you mad?' Ernie perhaps was a little mad at the time.
'They're not gooin away, not if I can 'elp it, ye can bury us first,' he replied.

I thought it was all my fault, asking Mum what I had done wrong, had I been a bad girl, is that why we were going away? I was confused, the situation was fearful. Mum struggled vainly to hold on to us as a woman came into the house to collect Joyce and me. Meantime, Upchurch had managed to remove the rifle from Ernie, and he was likely arrested, although I cannot recall that part. Mum sobbed, Joyce and I sobbed.

Out we went into the yard, under the gaze of the Watsons and several others who had turned up to gawp. Seated in the back of what seemed a large black car to my 7 years, Joyce and I either side of the woman as she tried to soothe and calm us. It was the first time I had been in a car, and I was most impressed. As the tears subsided, I looked around at the shiny interior with its fresh polished leathery smell. I still like the smellof freshly polished leather.

Looking out as the man driving the car turned it around, and began to journey down the Alley, I noticed May Watson, wearing her pinny, and a turban over her curlers, a fag as usual in her mouth, waving to us as if we were going on holiday. Later, I learned Mum and Ernie had received sentences of six months each for the neglect and cruelty. Mum served four months in Holloway, where they put her to work in the laundry. Ernie served his time in Bedford Gaol, where his skills in agriculture were put to good use.

Joyce and I were taken to the public institution at Ampthill, known as the Cedars in Dunstable Street. The Cedars had been the old Ampthill Union, or Poor Law institution, the Workhouse, accommodating up to 469 inmates, the buildings in red brick.

In 1929, Workhouses ceased to exist. It became a hospital, then later and old folks home and Day centre, but today, the buildings are private residential apartments. My grandmother, who married Joseph Randall in 1916, had been a regular inmate, giving birth there to three illegitimate children. Elizabeth and Joseph were poverty stricken, Joseph often ill, often destitute, and both died there. Gran of Meningitis, Granpa of old age.

Joyce and I remained at the Cedars for approximately three weeks before I was sent to Kempston Childrens Home. I don't know where Joyce went.

I loved the gardens at the Cedars, where I could walk and explore. (presumably accompanied by a nurse.) It was late Spring, the air fresh, I could touch the flowers and shrubs. There was the bath with lashings of warm water and soap, bliss!!Clean, with a clean

117

nightie, in a clean bed, sheer luxury for a little girl who normally had to make do with standing in a small tin bath of tepid water once per week if she was lucky, and who normally slept in the same clothes she had worn all day. Deloused, cleaned up, fed well, heaven.

Mum wasn't ever a criminal, just a worn out woman with immense problems she couldn't cope with. Many women have experienced extreme poverty, many women have suffered, still do, at the hands of cruel husbands or partners. A survey revealed that one in five women in Britain suffer at the hands of a violent partner, so Mum's situation was hardly unique. I believe she was deeply traumatized by her poor life, by the grinding poverty, that she stopped trying. Many women in the village all through the 40s gave her clothes for Joyce and I, maybe something for herself, but what she could have done with most was a helpful and loving husband, and more income. Ernie was vile to her. He sapped her esteem, her health, confidence, and energy.

Chapter 17
KEMPSTON CHILDRENS HOME

Three weeks after the siege, I was taken from the Cedars to Kempston. Mr W. Basford, the probation officer attached to my case, told the Court that the Bedfordshire Education Authority was prepared to take care of me. Kempston Home is still there. It is now in poor repair, and the discipline of the 1940s seems to have gone. On a recent visit, it appeared to me that chaos reigned. The children were being looked after by a young woman barely out of nappies herself. She looked harassed and overworked.

Much of the grounds surrounding the home was sold off many years ago to builders. The décor looked depressing.

The Lodge as it was known, was acquired by the Bedford Guardians in 1912. A mansion belonging to the Beaumont family, residence of Colonel E.R. Green. Refurbished and refurnished, it was taken over in response to pressure to remove children from the workhouse environment. Children adopted by the Board of Guardians were fostered out, but others had to be in the workhouse with their parents. This led to the provision of the Home for all children over three years old who were destitute, as Joyce and I was.

In 1912 the Home had lawns surrounded by fence and wall. There was greenery of Box, Yew, Hawthorn, Roses, Honeysuckle, Holly, Lilac, Ilex and Cypress. A gravel play area for the boys, and a laundry for teaching the girls the fine art of washing clothes and starching linen. A swing where the girls may pass sunny hours in maiden meditation fancy free, (WOW!). What? they could perhaps have some time off from washing all that linen? I did not do any washing when I was in the Home. The home had a day room for boys, with a bench to use for making things. It had been the Butler's pantry. Boys also took up gardening. The children attended local schools. In 1942 children were kept strictly within bounds, except when attending school.

I was admitted to Up-End School on 8th June 1942, my address given as the Lodge, with Matron named as my guardian. Other girls arriving around the same time were Vera Harris, Pauline Harris, Evelyn Dear, Irene Crawley, with Eileen Rayment. Ray Mercer joined us in August. I wouldn't go so far as to say I liked being away from home, but it certainly taught me a lot, and certain aspects of that short time were pleasant. For example. Bedding linen was always fresh and crisp, as if the sheets were slightly starched, certainly pressed, which was something I really appreciated. At the Cedars, getting into a clean bed became very acceptable, this continued at Kempston. Anyone who has always worn clean nightwear, slept in clean bedlinen, in a nice bedroom, could find it hard to understand how I felt.

On arrival at Kempston from Ampthill, we drove through large wrought iron gates, likely one of the few places left in Britain where such gates were still intact. In 1942, iron railings, gates etc, were requisitioned for the war effort. The car stopped at the front porch. My female escort took me into a small office on the left, which I now know was the Matron's office. Muted, quiet, I watched as papers were handed over, and conversation took place between Matron and my escort. A member of staff, in uniform like a nurse, all the staff wore some sort of uniform, came into the room and then took me upstairs, where I was issued with a change of clothes, and a protective pinny. Shown to a dormitory, I was told, 'This is where you will sleep.' It was airy and light. I'd not been used to such space and cleanliness. I imagine certain rules of behaviour were emphasised. Five or six single beds, hospital like, lined the walls on each side, a large window at the end. No lockers,

I had no possessions with me, not even a toy. No chairs beside the beds, no bed lights, only two distant overhead lights, the room painted white or a very light cream. Polished wooden floors. We changed into our bedclothes at night, the dormitory mistress taking our day clothes to a dayroom along the corridor, each article having our name on a tag sewn into some unobtrusive place. Boys and girls in separate wings of the building, each with its own staircase. We were not allowed to use the front stairs.

Of weekdays I have little recollection, except for sitting down at a long refectory table for meals. Meals were served to us at the tables, then the plates cleared away by staff. We had to eat all our meal, which was no trouble for me, I had a good appetite and cannot recall having to eat anything I didn't like. Probably the only punishment for a picky child was to be denied pudding, (dessert). An older girl sat at head of the table, to keep order and help the staff.

Of Sundays I do have recollections. It was the best day. That was the day I wore a special dress. Worn every Sunday. It was my dress. Although only 7 years old, I knew if I looked pretty or not, and I felt beautiful in that dress. I had longed for nice clothes, pretty little dresses, patent shoes, snow white socks, and my hair done up in ringlets like Shirley Temple. Each Sunday, apart from my hair which remained stubbornly straight, I was so pleased.

In crisp cotton, with little white daisies dancing all over the blue background, the dress was really special. Compared to anything I had at home, that dress was the bees knees for me. Buttoning from neck to waist at the back, the half belt tied at the back, little short puff sleeves, and small round collar.

We girls lined up outside one of the rooms on the first floor, where the wardrobe mistress, helped by older girls, issued each of us with her very own Sunday best. Over the dress I wore a white cardigan, the cardigan really white, unlike at home when white quickly became dull grey. For Church, we wore a grey or navy overcoat in winter, with a felt hat. I'm not sure what we wore to go to Church in summer, probably a blazer style jacket, with brimmed straw hat.

Crossing the road from the home, we marched crocodile fashion, supervised by staff, along the pavements to Church. In the afternoon, if the weather was fine we played outdoors. The garden had swings and chutes, but the lawns were dug up in response to the Government urge for people to Dig for Victory, to provide the Home with fresh vegetables. On rainy Sundays, activities were arranged for us indoors, from simple board games such as Ludo, Snakes and Ladders, to drawing and reading. Despite wartime restrictions and rationing, we had Ye Olde English Roast Beef and Yorkshire pudding with gravy and vegetables for dinner.

Regularly, we had a lovely warm bath, nails cut, hair inspection, fresh nightwear, crisp and clean. Daily we were supervised to see that we washed ourselves properly and cleaned our teeth. The beds had sheets and blankets, not duvets. Over that was a coverlet which was turned down at night, the whole bedclothes turned down in the morning for the bed to air. The curtains on the large windows were heavily lined, providing blackout.

Routine was everything, all sitting down together for meals, girls at one end of the dining room, boys at the other. We were in bed early, after supper. The dormitory mistress made sure we were all tucked in, despite protests for another five minutes.

At Aunt Daphne's, if we stayed overnight, several children slept in the one bed, with Mum tucked in beside us. Mum and two children at top of bed, two or three children at foot of the double bed.

At home, I slept in same single bed as Joyce, me at the top, Joyce at the foot. Here at Kempston, I had a bed to myself, I liked that.

We were not always well behaved. I could stand up for myself. If another girl hit me, I hit back, and the mistresses had to break up many a scrap. It wasn't quite the same as in the Alley, where we fought one day and were bosom buddies the next. Here at Kempston I was among strangers, some of them from worse homes than mine. Pillow fights I could handle, but sometimes the fun got out of hand. Someone would throw a pottie down the room, and then another one was thrown the other way, even perhaps one that had been used. I pulled the covers over my head. A pillow fight was one thing, a pottie throwing contest was quite another. Each bed had a small plain white pottie under the bed for use during the night, as there were no en-suite facility, and we were not allowed out of the dormitory unless to go to the air raid shelter.

Although I wet the bed frequently at home, it became less of a problem at Kempston. The beds were prepared for children like me. Each bed had a rubber sheet below a draw sheet. The draw sheet could be changed without upsetting the whole bed.

There were punishments. Once, I was punished for something I had not done. The girls from our dormitory were lined up in the corridor outside the mistresses room, where we were asked to name the culprit of whatever misdemeanor had been perpetrated. None of us were willing to name her. The punishment was a hard slap with the back of a hair brush on to the palms of our hands. It stung for a few minutes, but was quick and decisive. Some say physical punishment is barbaric, but children will test their parents or carers quite severely, and without some sort of punishment, not necessarily physical, mayhem will ensue.

When the air-raid siren sounded, we had to slip our coats and

123

shoes on over our nightwear and troop outside to the shelters, half asleep. The sky lit up by searchlights, ack ack guns taking a pop at the enemy planes. Then back to bed when the all-clear siren sounded.

I wondered when Mum was coming to take me home. I did not know she was in prison. Eventually she did visit, but nothing was explained to me. I must have had questions, but if she gave me a half hearted answer, or even an untruthful reply, I had to leave it at that. Just before Christmas, she visited again, and this time I was allowed to go home with her. One of the staff took me down the front stairs to where Mum was waiting just outside Matron's office. She didn't hug me, she seldom gave any outward show of affection. Matron spoke, 'Maureen, you are going home today.' I didn't know whether to be glad or sorry. There would be no more warm baths in a real bath, no more comfortable single bed to myself.

How we got home, I can only guess. Bus to Bedford, change to a bus for Flitwick.

While we were all away, Renee Hymus, eldest daughter of neighbour May Watson, used our house as her own. She continued to use our back bedroom at night, and daytime in her mother's house.

It was back to earth with a bump. The beatings started again, the bitter rows between Mum and Ernie, and I had to go back to school, where fortunately, the hoo hah about the siege, Mum in prison, and my absence for months soon faded away.

As you have read, Joyce and I spent most of 1942 away from home, and I didn't see or hear much of what was happening in the big bad wide world out there. I doubt if I would have understood most of it anyway. At least for a few months, Mum did not have to worry how she was going to manage financially, or what the price of Ernie's cigarettes was, or that coal had gone on ration on 17th March. Woodbine cigarettes went up to 1/6 (7.5p) for 20 in April.

Our soldiers were fighting in North Africa, where Rommel's Afrika Corp captured Tobruk on June 20th. We recaptured it in November. Photographs appeared in the papers of soldiers becoming prisoners of war, of soldiers missing in action. Families were informed by telegram or letter.

The British, under Montgomery, regained El Alamein in October 1942. We were fighting back and winning. 13000 German prisoners of war taken. Hitler wasn't doing so well in Russia either, as Stalingrad halted the German advance on September 6th. Convoys of British ships, laden with supplies for Russia that we could ill afford to spare, struggled through icy northern waters. Singapore surrendered to the Japanese, who went on to treat their captives appallingly. Many were soldiers of the Beds and Herts Regiment, with some reported missing. Many a heart was aching for news, but dreaded the worst. Many a sailor never made it home. Tons of merchant shipping and too many Royal Naval vessels were sent to the bottom of the ocean by Uboats.

Imagine going to the Supermarket today, to be told that half the expected food due to arrive in the ports from foreign countries was now at the bottom of the Atlantic, and everything was to be rationed. What would you do? Especially if you joined the queues at the checkout and was told what you could or couldn't buy.

New ration books were issued in May. Ministry of Food issued leaflets of recipes, such as the one for Mock Goose, without the Goose. Magazines, newspapers also included the meatless recipes. OXO was a regular favourite drink, or to use as stock. It was advertised heavily. United Canneries and the Government urged us to grow Peas.

'When you're tired and working late, Oxo helps you pull your weight.'

People were even exhorted to save matches. Confetti was thrown at a wedding in Bedford, and wrapping thrown away, (an offence), contrary to an order which prohibited paper wastage. Bedford Sessions also dealt with driving offences and blackout offences. A bus driver prosecuted for failing to immobilise his car when left at midnight near Market hall. A man received a three month sentence for beating a 6 year old evacuee so severely the child needed hospital attention. (the sentence should have been longer.)

On November 18th 1942, the Ministry of Supply decreed there would be a census of all laid up cars and tyres, due to the serious shortage of rubber, the information needed so the Ministry would know where and how many vehicles and tyres were stored. Blackout times were advertised daily.

A film starring Carmen Miranda included her singing a Latin American ditty, I yi yi yiyi like you very much, while wearing what looked like a large bowl full of fruit for a hat, Bananas on top. Bing Crosby recorded White Christmas, for the film Holiday Inn. He also recorded Silent Night, which was also a popular Carol with the Germans. Vera Lynn sang The White Cliffs of Dover, and British actors played heroes in countless war films, to keep our spirits up.

The black market flourished. If anyone had the money, they could still get almost anything they wanted. Someone, somewhere, legally, or illegally, would supply it, but in the Alley, especially for us, getting enough food on the table took priority. Perhaps a few extra sausages, or a few pennies extra of meat could be obtained. None of us was wealthy enough to have a well stocked larder full of meat, fish and dairy products, or be able to dine in a fine restaurant. r

If you wanted to start a new business, you couldn't. The Board of Trade decreed that opening a new business was illegal. I've never been able to understand that one. February 1942, soap was

126

rationed, except but not shaving soap or scourers. and it stayed rationed until 1950. Soap did not come pre-wrapped. We had to be happy with whatever soap was available. Usually White Windsor, Carbolic or Coal Tar.

Millie Barnes son Frank gave her some trouble. She was prosecuted for not sending him to school. When she did not appear in court, she was arrested.

What makes someone commit suicide? For Joe Line, son of Ebber Line, who lived next door to us, it was the extreme pain he felt over the death of his sister. On May 26th 1942 Joe took his own life, which at the time was a criminal offence, so the poor demented man was a criminal in the eyes of the law. He was partially blind and shot himself in the stomach. No one in the Alley had a 'phone, so someone had to go to the public box next to the White Horse to summon ambulance and police. Constable Upchurch cycled to the Alley. Joe was taken to Bedford hospital, but died two days later. The Coroner recorded "Death from a gunshot wound, self-inflicted, while of unsound mind"

Chapter 18
HITLER GIVES US ANOTHER WEEK's HOLIDAY

1943, and it was time for me to leave the cosiness and familiarity of the Infant School in Station Road and move on to the Big School, as we called it, in Dunstable Road. The big school, as we called it, meant a walk across the fields, through the little arch, over another field, past the pond and Smithy. I was to make the same journey there and back four times each schoolday. I came home for dinner, the main meal of the day in our house

We'd had our usual 5 weeks holidays when Hitler's Lufftwaffe gave us another few days off. His bombers scampering back to base on the continent, after presumably bombing Midland cities, jettisoned another, into Glebe land behind the Vicarage. The school wasn't directly hit, but the explosion, when it hit the ground, formed a crater, and shattered a few windows. It also sent a chimney crashing through the roof. "Hooray," another week off school. We didn't fully comprehend the seriousness of such an event. Bombs did not usually drop on Flitwick. We gave no thought to it that the bomber had been sent over to cripple our industry, and ruin homes. We made our way to view the crater. As far as we were concerned, repairs to the school could take forever, in reality it took one week.

We knew the difference between the Jerries planes and ours by the sound. The enemy planes hummed, paused, hummed, paused, hummed, like someone trying to draw breath, whereas our planes had a more continuous level hum. We had no Anderson shelters at the school. Kathy Wooding reminded me that sandbags were placed around the windows in Miss Sharpe's classroom, where we had to go when the air raid siren sounded off. A bomb dropping on the school directly would have killed us all.

At home, we donned our coats when the siren went off, and trooped down to the sand pit between the Alley and Wilson's farm.

Flitwick Mixed School was built in 1852, and taken over by the school board in 1872. It started off as one main room, 22ft x 55ft, height 18ft 9inches, no ceiling, just pitched up to the roof. Wooden floors, large windows intended to let a great deal of light in. No electricity supply when the school was built of course. It was later extended to provide two further classrooms in 1873 and 1893, and could accomodate 200. In the log book, John Abbott, the first headmaster, wrote in 1860,

> 'The school is having to contend against all the hindrances of straw plaiting, but will I hope succeed.'

By 1864 there is no mention of straw plaiting.

When the school was built, parents were expected to pay for their child's education, but there were plenty of temptations to spend the school penny or two elsewhere. Fathers drank ale, mothers nursed a sick baby. An agricultural labourer's wage was pitifully low, and when it came to paying for little Jimmy to attend school, it came well down the list, with few exceptions. Sometimes Sweets on display in a nearby shop too much of a temptation for young Jimmy.

The fees for elementary schoolchildren were abolished in 1891 when the fee grant was introduced. Children left school at 10 years of age. Looking over the 1861 census, I noted one of the Randall men had 6 children, three of them girls. From the youngest Ellen, to the oldest Elizabeth age 12, they are described as straw plaiters, not scholars. What would a farm boy want with book learning when he spent his days from dawn to dusk in the fields. At harvest time all hands were needed, including whole families with

129

toddlers in tow. Flitwick school pupils needed free books, writing materials and time. The poorest children lacked time most of all. At the end of their school day, girls helped Mum around the house, looked after younger siblings, boys were called upon to help Dad. Sitting down to quietly read or write without distractions was seldom enjoyed by poorer children in their overcrowded homes.
A child's potential seldom nurtured, or recognised.

In 1818, the population of Flitwick was 413, but no school. (Digest of returns to circular letter from the Select Committee of Education of the poor). It was also reported that no poor children were being educated, but that the poor would embrace any means of educating their children. Flitwick's population rose to 1639 by 1921. By 1851, a few Flitwick children were being educated at Westoning, and in 1852 Flitwick Mixed School opened at last. The 1902 Education Act ended the School Boards, and the County Council took over the school in 1903.

Mr Abbott, the first headmaster, warmed to his (uphill) task,

Many parents among the poor wanted their children to start working and earning a living as soon as possible. What good was all that education to a straw plaiter or lacemaker who would soon be married and producing babies. Some took a lot of convincing that children were required to attend school. In 1875, Joseph Stringer was fined five shillings, (about half a week's wage), or 7 days in jail jail for not sending his 10 year old son Fred to school. Joe could neither afford the fine, or be in jail.

1853, shift work for children was abolished, but they could still be putting in an 11 hour day. The Shop Hours Act of 1892 forbid employers to work young persons for more than 74 hours per week. When did they get time for schooling?

January 1899 the school roll was 126. October 23rd 1913,

'Frosty and Foggy, fires to keep the school warm commenced.' Diptheria was a scourge: November 3rd 1925, 'Rhoda Daniels died from the effects of Diptheria.' January 28th 1924, 'Two cases of Diptheria, Violet Willy and Alfred Line.' December 1913, 'Violet Line must continue at school.' February 14th 1903, 'Two Stringer lads playing truant.' February 1924, 'Eight year old Ronald Stringer fired a small haystack on way home from school. ' (Ronald was son of Albert and Elizabeth Stringer). 1908,'Two weeks off for Christmas, beginning 24th December, returning 5th January.' Stringer names litter the school records.

Next to the school stood the caretaker's house, built in 1869 for the headmaster. Demolished, now new homes built on the site. Old it may have been, it is a pity it wasn't repaired and put in good order, but like so many others in the village, it fell on the altar of so called progress.

Our school was set back slightly from the road. During the war, the grassy strip along the front was dug up to grow vegetables. The school also had a garden plot further up Dunstable Road. Flitwick Lower School was later built on the site. Many boys, especially Stringer lads, were destined to become agricultural workers like their fathers and grandfathers, although, by 1950, many were going into factories instead.

Classrooms were numbered 1- 4 until around 1947 when two prefabricated classrooms were added in the school ground to the rear Two classrooms were provided by the use of a dividing curtain, in the main hall, and there were two side classrooms. Just four teachers until the two extra classrooms were built. Miss Carr, Miss Chatterton, Miss Sharp, and lastly, Charlie Allen, who doubled up as the Headmaster.

In 1947, the Government raised the school leaving age from

14 to 15. Along with the raising of the school leaving age, the local council were building new homes off the Avenue. The Education Authority had to introduce more classrooms, and better sanitation.

The old dry bucket lavatories separating the girls and boys playgrounds were the first to go. The girls lavatories consisted of several cubicles with wooden doors which had a gap top and bottom. If there were any locks they were useless, for I cannot recall locking a door. The front of the building had a portico, colonade, along its length, supported on round wooden columns. To wash our hands we had to go into the cloakrooms, where sinks were lined up against the wall opposite the windows. No hot water taps. A brick wall separated the playgrounds from the pond and the Smithy. Each cubicle had a wooden bench with a strategic hole cut into it, and underneath, a galvanised bucket to pee and pooh into. The council lorry came along (probably weekly), to empty it. The school had not altered much since it was built in the 19th century. When the old lavatories were demolished, the two playgrounds merged.

Four large windows to the front of the school, large window at gable end, overlooking the boys playground. Electricity installed many years before, electric lights on high, in the ceiling void.

Between school and Dunstable Road were iron railings, a dirt path, a stretch of scraggy grass.

Most of the hymns sung at morning Assembly were favourites and we sung loudly and lustily if we knew the words. If we were thrown a new one, it confused us. We even sang the hymn 'Glorious things of thee are spoken,' (John Newton 1725-1807) to the tune of Uber Alles, the German anthem.

There were around 40 pupils in each class, desks in neat rows facing the Teacher. We were bursting at the seams. Without some drastic changes, Flitwick wasn't going to be able to educate all the children. Radiators kept the school reasonably warm. I have a vague recollection of there being a fire in the fireplace in Miss Sharpe's classroom and her standing with her back to it. A small room was accessed from Class 4, for the sole use of the Teachers.

Ernie lost his temper when they raised the school leaving age to 15, swearing at Mum as if it was her fault, remarking 'That means I've got ter keep that bastard for another year,' (Me). Mum was also disappointed, she wanted me to leave soonest and get a job.

From the beginning, I was in awe of the headmaster, he was God, he who was to be obeyed. Charlie Allen took over after Thomas Strickland retired in 1938. I spent one year in his classroom, where I found him not so fearsome as I had expected. My last year or two was spent in the prefab' Annexe, in new teacher Mr Markham's class. At the same time as the prefab' buildings went up, a new lavatory block was built, to the rear of the playground. Hooray!! we were going to be able to flush, WOW! no more smelly buckets, we even had toilet paper. Sinks too, but still no hot water. A row of cycle racks was provided, used daily by boys and girls who came from the other end of the village.

A lifelong friend of mine progressed through the school at the same pace as I did. Kathy See, as she was then, later married Jim Wooding, a classmate. Kathy and I sat together most of the time, and we have kept in touch. We share the same birthday.

The school bell rang, we formed columns according to class order, marched into the cloakroom under supervision of a teacher, to hang coats, scarves, etc on numbered hooks along the walls and centre island rack. She made sure we also washed our hands. Running down Vicarage hill from the fields, past the pond, I often rushed headlong through the gate as the bell stopped dinging. The teacher glanced disapprovingly as I hastily joined the end of my

133

class line up. Many a child came panting through the cloakroom door at the last minute, gasping for air, making some lame excuse. Mum always had something for me to do. Draw water from the Well, fetch some wood, take the ashes out, run to the shop, sometimes my time wasn't my own. Dinner time I had to wait for Ernie to arrive home before sitting down to eat. Mum always timed the cooking of the dumpling (Bedfordshire Clanger) to his expected dinner time of 1pm. If we ate before him he went bonkers and there would be another row, which could often turn to violence. I almost always had to run all the way to school after dinner. I wasn't skinny, but never a fat child. I did too much running, burning off those stodgy dumpling calories.

I was fairly good at English, Arithmetic was a doddle, History and Geography particularly enjoyable. I loved finding out about other parts of the world, the wildlife, the way the people lived. Eventually, later in life, I was able to visit some of the places I had only been able to read about while at school. One term we attempted the French language. I recall a few lines from a couple of French Canadian songs, but that's about it. Music was mostly enjoyed, but sometimes it was heavy going. What we really wanted was more of the popular songs being sung on the wireless, or on records, by the famous singers of the time, not some ancient song such as Who is Sylvia, from a Shakespeare play we'd never heard of. We didn't care who Sylvia was, and did not appreciate the teacher was only trying to introduce a little culture into our simple rural little lives. We did read Shakespeare many times, but great though the bard undoubtedly is, I was never particularly interested.

We had no Gym. Physical exercise we did in the boys playground, on coir mats. We donned our black lace up plimsolls, tucked our dresses into our black cotton knickers which had elastic around the hem of the knee length legs. We ran around to warm up, we stretched, we lay flat on those mats, stood up, bent over, played leap frog, and joined up for team efforts. In very cold weather, we started off the session, shivering, but soon warmed up as long as we kept on the move. Miss Chatterton came up and down the line of girls, 'Chin up, tummy in, rear tucked in,'as she put one hand on tummies, the other on bums, jerking us up straight. Were we to become model fodder? We were heading for shop, factory or domestic bliss. not model fodder. 'Posture, posture, stand up straight, don't slouch,'she was a paragon. Today, there are too many children with appalling posture.

At the end of our P.E we returned the coir mats to the boys cloakroom, where they were stored under the coat racks. Most of us had no proper sports outfits until we were around 13-14 years old, and made our own in sewing class, (more about that later).

After the new prefab' buildings were erected, a little patch of rough ground remained, which Mr Allen thought would make a nice garden. Older girls and boys, including myself, dug and planted under the supervision of Mr Markham. I enjoyed it, it was something different. The boys thought it great too, for while working outside, they were not doing lessons in class. We put in bushes and flowers, a very nice garden when finished. I don't know how long it lasted, it certainly is not there now. The School in Dunstable Road was sold to Flitwick and District Youth Association by Bedfordshire County Council in 1982 for a mere £20,000. After being left in bad repair for a long time, I notice that the cloakrooms have been demolished, and there is a porch structure built to the front of the main part of the building. What is to become of the school?

Mr Markham presented me with a book, "Little Women", by Louise M. Alcott, on the day I left school. I still have the book.

Chapter 19
SNIPPETS of 1943

The old Duke of Bedford made a speech in 1943 which seemed to indicate support for Hitler's attacks on Checkoslovakia, Poland and France. People in Flitwick called him a Quisling, after Norwegian Vidkun Quisling who aided Hitler's invasion of Norway in 1940, being made Prime Minister of that country in 1942.

Mussolini was overthrown on July 25th and Italy surrendered September 7th. Women were admitted to the home guard, and school dinners were provided in the Victory hall from January 11th. Many of the vegetables for the dinners were provided by Flitwick schoolboys, from the school gardens. Those schoolboys could teach some of those fancy television gardening presenters a thing or two about growing vegetables.

The Rural Food Control Committee Executive Food Officer, (cor! what a mouthful), issued a directive to Council employees to give him information on who was putting bread in dustbins. We could never afford to produce such waste as cutting crusts off a loaf to make dainty crustless sandwiches. We used every slice, including crusts. Food rationing had been in operation for three years, with the exception of bread. Price controlled by the Government.

Dance halls opened every night except Sunday. Entrance about one shilling and nine pence Monday to Thursday, increased to around two shillings or half a crown Friday and Saturday. Patrons arriving early, say before 8pm got in for a little less. Because very often, young men went to the pub first, to pluck up Dutch courage to ask the girls to dance. Few dance halls had a drinks licence.

By 1943, the Yanks were over here, reputedly overpaid and oversexed, so local young men had rivals. Many a young man who

136

escorted a girl home, found himself without transport to get him back to barracks or billet, or his own home. Parents did not take kindly to young men jumping into their daughter's bed. They might let him stretch out on sofa or easy chair in the living room. Should a squeaky floorboard be heard in the night, Mum or Dad were out of bed like a bullit to prevent misbehaviour.

Sulsky Rubber Works in Luton advertised New Wellingtons for old, repaired, soled and heeled. Rubber was in short supply due to the loss of rubber plantations to the Japanese. Can you imagine Wellingtons being repaired today?   Rubber was a precious commodity. Bennet's in Ampthill offered the same service.

Soap was rationed and not a scrap wasted. Little end bits were kept and packed together to form another bar. Soap cost around two pennies, plus two coupons. Tea was fairly expensive at around two shillings and tenpence or three shillings per lb. Solidox toothpaste one shilling. Beer one shilling and one penny per pint. In 1943, one of the Bedford Schools raffled a Banana, (can you imagine it?), raising £3 for the aid to China fund. I am puzzled as to where did they get the Banana from? All shipments had been stopped in 1940 to free up ships for the war effort.

A radio licence cost £1 in 1943, increased to £2 after the war. Radios could be rented for one shilling and elevenpence per week. That could buy about 7 or 8 loaves of bread. The main grocery shop in Flitwick was Ideal Stores on Station Square, later it became Dudeney and Johnston. Utility furniture at an affordable price could be obtained using form UFD/1 from the Fuel Office, and sent to the District Officer at the Assistance Board in Cambridge.

Cinemas were showing old films of the 1930s, as well as new ones. The indomitable James Cagney sang and danced his way through the film Yankee Doodle Dandy at the Plaze in Bedford.

Other films included Holiday Inn, starring Bing Crosby. Walt Disney's Bambi. The Zonita in Ampthill screened Zeigfield Girl, starring James Stewart and Judy Garland. Sadly, the art-deco building which was the Zonita is no more, gone, gone, gone.

The original Thirty Nine Steps, made in 1935 but still going the rounds, starring Robert Donat, was on at the Zonita on 6th July. Too many to mention them all. Age only 8 in 1943 I would be more interested in Keystone Kops being shown at that little cinema in Gas Street Toddington.

I often travelled to Toddington on the bus on my own, Mum came now and again, to visit Gran Bland. Aunt Betty met me by pre-arrangement. She was Ernie's younger half-sister, daughter of Albert Gordon. On the music front, Billy Cotton belted out This is The Army Mr Jones, Anne Shelton sang I'll Be Seeing You in All the Old Familiar Places. A popular pub song was Roll out the Barrel. Vera Lynn sang another appropriate song of the time, When the Lights Go On Again, All Over the Town.

Sadness there was too. People scoured the papers for those killed in action, telegrams were sent and received, loved ones lost. The sight of the Telegram boy put dread into the hearts of many, but it wasn't all bad news. Very few private homes had a telephone installed, and to send an urgent message, such as 'arriving 3pm,' or 'Pauline had a baby boy,' a telegram was sent.

The first telegrams were transmitted in 1870, and soon became popular. They were sent from a Post Office at first, but later they could also be sent from a public telephone box, if you had enough coins to put in the slot. If using the public box, you lifted the receiver and dialled O. An operator in the local exchange took the message, helping with the wording if necessary. Not to make it dearer, but to make it clearer, cheaper, and easier to understand.

The advice given freely. Enquiries cost nothing.

The money box was fitted with two push buttons. A and B. A local call cost two pennies, deposited in the coin slot. Most local calls could be dialled direct, and you could talk for a very long time for tuppence. Telephoning long distance, you had to go through the operator, from Flitwick to Plymouth for example. That cost extra. As well as numbers, the dial had letters too, and each area, Shillington for example, had their own sequence of three letters. If there was an answer at the other end, you pressed button A and the coins dropped into the money box, but if no answer, you pressed the B button to retrieve your pennies.

The telegram boy came to the house on a red bike. The bike had a pouch fixed to rear of saddle, the pouch holding an emergency repair kit, and cape for bad weather. His uniform was usually red jacket, grey trousers with red piping down sides, grey hat, white gloves, and black belt with pouch containing his telegrams and forms forms for an answer if there was one. He stood at the door while the telegram was read, and asked if there was a reply. The call box near the White Horse pub was the nearest one for us in the Alley.

Those few who were lucky enough to have a telephone in the house found themselves having to pass on messages to nearby neighbours, or there would be a request, 'Can I speak to Nellie please?' Nellie may well be living three or four doors away. Or it was, 'June, your brother's on the phone, says can you hurry, something about your Dad.'

If we had seen people walking along, holding their ear, and talking into thin air, we'd have thought them crackers.

During the war years, the Government introduced Zoning for the movement of goods. Transport of flour for instance, could not go from Bedford to Newcastle, a different zone, without a certificate.

139

Something made in one part of the country wasn't necessarily available in another part. Edinburgh Shortbread needed a certificate to send it to Slough. A certificate was needed for Mars bars to be sent from Slough to Edinburgh.

Free vitamins, free milk, and free concentrated orange juice was made available for children. Mum had to register at Ampthill Clinic for for them. Cod Liver Oil, horrible stuff in a bottle, Mum forced Joyce and I take the daily dose of a dessert spoonful.

Leather for making and repairing shoes was in short supply. Sometimes a child wore shoes with wooden soles. I was given a pair of clogs once, so uncomfortable.

Foster parents received ten shillings and sixpence per week for each evacuee child they took in. Most did a good job, but it is also true that there were others who were only interested in the money. Millie Barnes fostered an evacuee, his name John Humphrey. She was a very good substitute Mum for him. Millie was a round cuddly woman who made sure he had his fair share of food and plenty of motherly love.

Mum visited Aunt Nance frequently at Hornes End. She was daughter of James and Priscilla Stringer Mum always got a warm welcome. Nance had four sons, Wilf, Ken, and Les, who everyone knew as Sausage Stringer, and also Maurice who was killed in Palestine in 1947. Les was father of June Stringer, a school friend.

In 1943, emergency water tanks appeared. Surrounded by fencing, they had strong wire mesh around top, presumably to deter sabateurs. I never saw a biro pen before 1950. First patented in 1943 by a chap named Lazlo Biro. Very expensive to begin with, often leaking, unreliable, we couldn't afford to buy the early ones. We continued using our old pen nibs fixed to a wooden stalk, and ink

Chapter 20
THE BROOK

Clear water rippling over grit and shingle, ankle deep mostly, a beautiful hot sunny day, and we were a noisy crowd. Fish, shoals of little tiddlers, not even half inch long, hurrying and scurrying in and out of the reed beds, trying to avoid home made fishing nets made from the foot of an old stocking and a bit of stick. Frogs on the embankment, Lizards on the brick wall near the arch, sunning themselves before slipping back into the water to frolic. Green foliage, wild flowers in the meadow, cows grazing contentedly before ambling along the farm track to be milked. Children laugh and splash each other, laugh, shout, sit on the wall, jump into the water, splash. The water ripples along under the big railway arch which carries the L.M.S rail traffic north and south. Ducks, below the footbridge near Hornes End, their plumage bright and colourful, are schooling their young in the art of scooping up a meal, and fish shoot to the surface for flies. Long thick grass and weeds line the muddy banks, providing cover for plenty of little creatures we seldom see, such as voles, fieldmice and water rats, insects, scurrying around on their special business. We were so lucky.

You will not see any of that in Flitwick brook now. The water is so polluted I would not let my dog paddle in it. The embankment is untidily overgrown, the flower bedecked meadows of yesteryear built over. Gates have been erected by Worthy End farm, blocking the freedom, (an illegal act I am sure, and so frustrating), of a path by the brook, established for centuries.

Most of Flitwick's population do not go near the brook, and it is likely if I lived in Flitwick today, I wouldn't go near it. It has lost the charms it had in the 1940s.

The water authorities do make an attempt occasionally to clean it up, but it has never flowed so clear as in those heady days of my youth, when we could see the shingle below our toes as we paddled. I despair when I walk along its banks and see rubbish thrown in by thoughtless morons, their vandalism spoiling what little natural amenity is left.

I had none of the modern wizardry which children enjoy today, and yes, had I come from a wealthy family with all the financial benefits that come with it, then I too may not have spent so much time out of doors or enjoyed so much freedom.

I'm glad I experienced those halcyon days with likewise friends in Flitwick. Magic, beautiful, and so so precious.

Chapter 21
THE SMITHY and THE POND

There are fewer people around to remember the pond, with its muddy banks, behind the Smithy and School, at the junction of Hornes End and Dunstable Road. The pond was filled in many years ago, and replaced by Vicarage hill shops for the population at that end of the village. Although Flitwick is now a town, you will find me throughout this story referring to it as a village, for that is what it was in the 1940s.

Times change. The pond, along with the Fir Tree Inn on the corner of Westoning Road and Hornes End, the tumbledown barns, and the long silent Smithy are gone. Horses no longer wait patiently for new shoes, frogspawn no longer collected in jam jars by inquisitive schoolboys. I found that a bit too messy for me.

Separated from a field to the rear, where the bomb dropped in 1943, the pond had Lime, Sycamore, and lovely White Birch trees bordering the rear bank, and on one side, a large weatherboard barn which was home to barn owls.

In Glebe land behind the School and Pond, there could have been an Oak or two. In the autumn the leaves on the trees were so colourful, browns, yellows, oranges, wonderful. I wouldn't go so far as to say the pond was beautiful, because it wasn't. Weeds and scraggy grass grew around the edge of its muddy banks, the water very muddy, especially in autumn when the leaves fell into it. Its saving grace was as a watering hole for the native wildlife. The insects attracted the birds, and many times I had to stop to watch Swallows ducking and diving, scooping up a feast in mid-air. Other birds making their homes around the pond, as well as the Barn Owls, we had Chaffinches, a Skylark or two, a lot of squabbling

143

Starlings, plus the cheerful little Sparrows. Housemartins too. Occasionally we caught sight of the elusive Woodpecker. Just once in a while, we caught sight of the blues and greens of the Kingfisher, so perhaps there were fish in the muddy waters, or he flew to the brook to raid the shallows.

In the winter of 1944 it rained through October, then it snowed over Christmas, with plenty of fog, and the pond froze over. We skated on the ice. Not one of us had a proper pair of ice skates, we slid around in our shoes, (leather soles). We gingerly ventured out on to the surface, the boys a bit more daring, showing off. No-one wanted to be thought of as a softy. The first crack sent us darting back to the bank, jumping over loose chunks of ice.

There was always something to make us stop and watch and waste time over as we made our way home from school. Mum wasn't pleased, she always had errands for me to run.

The Smithy was an old barn like building where Roland (Ron)Carr, Blacksmith and Farrier, sweated over the anvil. I loved to stop and look over the half open stable door. A chimney at one end from which smoke spiralled up to the sky. I'd watch him work, lifting one leg of the horse, steam rising, then another shoe to fit, another horse waiting outside for its turn. Flitwick had a lot of working horses at that time. Large Shire horses, maybe a Suffolk Punch, beautiful glossy brown, tail flapping flies away, gentle eyes, long lashes. Strong, able to plough an acre or more each day. There were also one or two black horses. Those big animals were built for hard work. One, two, or more horses were used for the plough and other farm machinery, side by side, or one behind the other.

We often crowded around the door of the Smithy to watch Ron at work, he never minded as long as we didn't cause trouble.

The coalman delivered the coal by horse and cart. I had just

144

came out of Cousins shop one day when I saw the coalman with his horse and cart near the White Horse. Something spooked the horse, for he suddenly took off, on his own, galloping as fast as he was able, considering he was still attached to a heavily laden cart, down towards Greenfield Road, with the coalman and other men in pursuit. The horse was caught, with no more damage than a few lumps of coal scattered over the road. The coal did not remain there for long. I had Mum's large shopping bag with me. I quickly picked up two or three lumps and scarpered home.

Across the road from the Smithy lived a wheelwright by the name of Bunker. A wheelwright made and repaired cart wheels. He must have been kept very busy when horses and carts trundled everywhere. The cottages where he lived were picturesque, set back a little from the road, with tidy front gardens, but a few years after the war, they were replaced by new homes.

It is generally recognised that the Celts and Gauls were the first to nail iron shoes to their horses feet around 50bc. Mum believed in lucky horseshoes, one was pinned up outside our kitchen door in the Alley. She always had faith and hope for things to become better.

Chapter 22
THE SOUND OF MUSIC

As already mentioned, Italy surrendered in 1943. Many Italian prisoners of war were ensconced in Nissan huts at Chimney Corner, Kempston Hardwick, and remained there for the time being.

One day, I believe it was 1944, because I was around 9 years of age, we heard singing coming from the direction of the railway.

It was a quiet day, one of those days when sound travels very well over a distance. A few of us, children and women, gathered at the side of the Watson's house to look over where the sound was coming from. Just beyond the big arch, spread out along the railway line, were workers moving steadily towards Flitwick Station. We quickly established from someone that the workers were Italians, "Eyeties" as we called them, doing maintainance work on the line. It is difficult to remember how many there were that day, I'd estimate more than fifty. Accompanying the singing was the tap tap of hammers or any other tool they were using on metal. The sound was incredible. We recognised the tunes, what could be called the most popular of Italian Opera music.

If I close my eyes, I can still picture the scene, the progress they made, singing with such emotion and strength in their voices.

Years later, I believe I was about 20 before I went to an Opera for the first time.

Many Italians settled in and around Bedford after the conflict, bringing their families over to be with them. Some married local girls. Kempston Hardwick Camp was not the ideal home, but the former prisoners of war had little choice. Love in a Nissan hut was better than being hundreds of miles apart.

It was to be June 5th 1944 before our men marched into

Rome, pushing the Germans northwards. There never seemed to be the same animosity towards the Italians as there was against the Germans, who we called Jerries, Bosch, or Huns, (said with some venom). We already had a large Italian community in Bedford before the war. They were as everyone knows, famed for their Ice Cream Parlours, as well as their latin good looks. Some Italian families had been here since the 19th century.

I've never forgotten it. It is love and love alone the world is seeking. A line from an old song, and if sung in Italian, WOW! Wonderful.

This is the last verse of a Robert Burns song,
some words translated from the Scottish prose.

"Then let us pray, that come it may,
        (as come it will for all that),
    That sense and worth over all the earth,
    Shall bear and win and all that,
    For all that, and all that,
    It's coming yet , and all that,
    That man to man, the world over,
    Shall brothers be, for all that."

Chapter 23
AUGUST

When Adam delved and Eve span, who was then the Gentleman?

August is truly a wonderful month. Despite the war and all the shortages, the austerity of the years after the war, it was a month when life seemed a little bit better. Mum managed to earn a few extra shillings by going Peasing and Potato lifting. It all helped to add a little to the household income.

We had fields of crops to be harvested. Childrens voices, unhindered and unsilenced, were heard everywhere. After the war, Church bells rang again, joyfully for weddings, or on Sundays summoning the faithful to prayer. We always knew when a funeral was taking place as a solitary bell tolled.

Steam trains, smoke billowing, were the delight of schoolboys as they jotted down engine details. The brook ran clear and clean through rushes and reeds which sheltered tiny fish. Townfield Road now occupies land where once the wonderful golden corn stood in stooks ready for collection, to be hauled away by horse and cart to a rick. Fields had Potatoes, perhaps Cabbage in another field, Cauliflower in another. Fields around Flitwick heaved with splendid produce. Men were furiously trying to catch up on all the work to be done on their allotment or in the garden.

From the Moor, the Moorhen gave vent to that chk chk throated sound, and the Willowherb (another name for it is fireweed), went into full purple hue as it spread out over any spare ground it could get rooting. The breeze spread the seeds of Thistles and Dandelions profusely, ensuring more or the same next year.

The birds added to all this August activity. Chirpy Sparrows balanced precariously on twigs sticking out of hedges, and voracious groups of Starlings fought each other as usual. Blackbirds, tails jerking, made little clk clk noises, foraging the bottom of Hawthorn hedges, and the Thrush made song. The Swallow, soon to depart south, gave us acrobatic displays, swooping and diving, feasting on plentiful insects, catching them in flight. It's a month of thunderstorms, rolling noisily through the heavens, accompanied by flashes of lightening. Mum opened doors and windows. Mum said God was angry about something and was up there stomping around, clapping his hands together, to make all that noise, the lightening the flash of his anger.

I'm always fascinated by flashes of lightening, followed by the pause, before suddenly, with a loud rumble like an iron clad wagon wheel rolling out of control over uneven cobbles, the thunder bangs the big drum. Mum perspires a lot, 'Ooh, it's so 'ot gal, aint it,' as she passes the time of day with May. It rained occasionally.

The orchard groaned under the weight of a bumper crop of delicious Apples, which we children of the Alley happily scrumped, to the annoyance of Horace Beale.

That was the 1940s. Does anyone bother any more? as they sun themselves on a Greek Island, go clubbing in Benidorm, or view the wonders of Disneyland?

Everywhere, roads, bricks, and concrete cover the land where once grew crops to feed the nation. Most of the lovely orchards have gone, traffic clogs the roads, and children seem to prefer virtual reality on a computer screen to real life.

A beautifully manicured lawn may look splendid, but we also need habitats like meadows and hedges to provide a food chain for wildlife. The lush meadows, full of wild flowers and grassy seed heads, are hard to find now. Cowslip, Poppy, Buttercup, Daisy,

149

Celandine, Nettle, Bellflower, the tufted blue flowered Vetch which winds itself everywhere, Saxifrage, Clover pink and white, Coltsfoot, Primrose, Oxslip, St John'sWort, Wild Marigold, Sowthistle, to name a few. All found in Flitwick in the 1940s, in the fields, the hedgerows, the Moor, railway embankment. Even the chickweed, which our Rabbits devoured by the sackful, had a lovely little white flower. Thickets of Gorse, Hawthorn, and trees such as Larch, Beech, Birch, Elm Sycamore, Oak and Lime were all there in Flitwick. Perhaps some survive.

We import most of our fruit and vegetables today, pay our taxes in order that the government then hands over huge sums of money to the the European Parliament in Brussels, who in turn pay Farmers and Market Gardeners to leave good ground either untilled and idle, or to grow Maize. It's crazy.

Many old paths which once took villagers over fields are now gone, blocked by buildings or unusable because of neglect.

Cropspraying of the few crops now grown in the area is another hazard for the fauna and flora to contend with, destroying many native plants which once afforded shelter and food for the wildlife. The brook, where I spent many happy hours, is a muddy yellow gungy fetid water course, the sticklebacks and tiddlers gone, and I believe it would be impossible to enjoy a splash today.

Chapter 24
HITLER IS ON THE RUN

1944, and a couple of years on from my time in Kempston Home, things were pretty well much the same as usual at home. Ernie was as belligerent as ever, and Mum continued with her humdrum hard life.

I shared a desk with Kathy See at school, we were both 9 years old, and we got on very well together. During daytime, at school, and playing with friends, life wasn't too bad for me. In the summer months I helped Mum at the Peasing and went Potato lifting too. The air raid sirens didn't sound off so often, and Mum ceased to decant Joyce and I out of bed in the middle of the night to go to the shelter. News filtered through that our Lancaster bombers, and the Yanks B49s were doing lots of damage over Germany. Because this country had suffered so much, we had little sympathy for them.

One of our favourite little ditties was this one, sung to the same tune as in the film Snow White and the Seven Dwarfs,

Whistle while you work, Hitler is a twerp, Hitler's barmy, so's his army
Whistle while you work

Anne Shelton recorded Coming in on a Wing and a Prayer, true for many pilots and bomber crews returning from a raid. Bing Crosby got us into Christmas mood with Jingle Bells.

There were a lot of patriotic songs being sung on the wireless. The first V1 rocket fell on London on 12th June. They became known as Doodle Bugs, followed by the more deadly V2 rockets on 8th September. Whoosh!!, straight down they dived, smash, but they soon stopped altogether as our forces dealt with their launching sites.

151

We were getting stronger as Germany weakened, but there was still some way to go. Hitler must have been getting desperate as 1944 came to a close. It wasn't until I read history later that I learned there had been an attempt on Hitler's life by his own Generals.

June 6th the D Day landings, then Paris liberated on 25th August. September 17th brought the lifting of some blackout restrictions, to allow buses and trains to have their lights on, and the lights went back on at railway stations. Made little difference to us in the Alley, for we had no street lights.

Fields in and around Flitwick groaned under the weight of corn and wheat. We children went along to witness the activity one evening when the reaping machine cut the corn on the field where Townfield Road now curves. Up and down, round and round, went the machine, from the edge of the field to the centre. Men busily bound bundles of corn and placed them in neat rows of stooks. We crawled through the stooks, having a whale of a time. Some men positioned around the field were on serious business, like the old hunters. The blades of the machine kept turning, getting nearer and nearer the centre of the field, until only a small area remained to be cut. The Rabbits sheltering therein were by now terrified. Get cut down or make a run for it. Did they have any alternative?

Suddenly the air was rent with the sound of gunshot. Bang Bang!! Ernie pulled a length of string from his belt, wrapping it around the back legs of another dead Rabbit. More fell to the guns, the meat destined for the pot, and the pelt a pair of fur gloves. Plenty made it to the safety of hedges, to live for another day. Finally, from a field full of stooks and stubble under our feet, we dispersed.

A few older women descended on the field as the men left, for gleaning was still going on at that time. These women were keeping a tradition alive, although Mum did not join in the activity.

The practice of gleaning in Flitwick is now dead. Five or six dead Rabbits hung on the back of the barn door that night. Ernie sold the skins, we feasted on the meat. Rabbit meat is tasty, cooks like chicken, but a little darker in colour. I liked Rabbit stew.

Some might be horrified at the scene above, there is no need. Rabbits are destructive to crops. The shooting served many purposes, it wasn't done just for pleasure. It helped to keep the Rabbit population down, was a supplement to the meat rations, and provided target practice for men like Ernie who were in the home guard.

In 1944 most babies, rich or poor, were still being born at home. Something was wrong and Mum was rushed to hospital in Bedford, where her baby was stillborn. The hospital disposed of the dead baby girl, I don't know how, but Mum never brought the body home. She lost another two or three babies over the next two or three years, before giving birth to Pat at the end of 1948. See Medical Notes later.

The weather wasn't so good in the autumn. It rained through October. The winter was bad, with frozen ponds, plenty of fog, and snow over Christmas into January. Mum struggled to keep the home fire burning.

A bag of coal cost around 4 shillings, but the one weekly bag was not enough, and she could not afford to buy any more. Even presuming the coalman could supply her with more. Coal was rationed. Saving fuel during the summer months was not an option as Mum had to have a fire on all the time. It was our only source of heat for cooking and hot water.

Chapter 25
THE GHOST

I'm a bit of an old cynic. I would like to say I don't believe in Ghosts, but that is contrary to something which happened to me when I was around 9 or 10 years of age. Is it a trick of the mind? Vivid dream? Or as Mum tried to explain to me, a reflection of the moon on the mirror of the old washstand? Joyce was asleep at the foot of the single bed we shared.

I am as certain today as I was then, that I saw a ghostly figure, an apparition. Our old house was built in the middle of the 19th century, which could explain the kind of clothes the ghost appeared to wear. The moon shone in the window, and the bedroom door was ajar as usual. The sound of the wireless floated up from the living room below and for once Mum and Ernie were not arguing. It must have been around 9.30pm to 10pm, a clear winter evening.

Something made me look towards the door. I saw a woman, watching me, silently. Her apparel was strange to my eyes. She wore a light coloured shawl, with a straw bonnet framing her youthful face. The bonnet was the most striking thing. It had a large rounded brim, the type of bonnet tied with a bow of ribbon under the chin. Within seconds I began screaming and yelling for Mum, and the apparition vanished.

Mum came upstairs to see what all the fuss was about, and told me there was no such thing as ghosts as I gasped, 'I saw her Mum, it was a ghost, she was there, at the door.' While awake, I kept looking towards the door, but the ghost did not reappear. In the years since, I have sometimes wondered, who was she, did I really see her?

Strangely, many years later, in a play I was filming, my historical costume included an almost identical bonnet.

Chapter 26
1945 THE WAR IS OVER

I was 10 years old when Germany surrendered on 8th May 1945. The end of the war had been expected for months as Hitler became increasingly isolated. Blackouts were taken down, and the air raid wardens knew they would soon be out of a job. In towns, cities, villages, all the lights were turned on again.

The wireless spread the news, the war was at an end, everyone went mad with delight. Bells rang out, people cheered, everyone was chatty and sociable, songs were sung, crowds danced in the streets. Bonfires were lit, and some street parties were hastily organised. We had a bonfire on the spare ground beside our houses, but the Alley didn't hold a street party. A village bonfire was built on the Rec. Although the war was over in Europe, Many a mother, wife, families, were still worried about their menfolk fighting in the Far East, or in a P.O.W. camp.

Heartache there was for others, who would never see the return of loved ones who lay silent in overseas graves.

A day or two after the end of the war, Ida Beale, wife of Horace Beale, proprietor of the Crown Inn, organised sports for us in Sabey's field. Great excitement as we competed in the sack race, three legged race, sprinted, and the egg and spoon race. How did we get the eggs. Perhaps we used pebbles instead of eggs. Perhaps someone with a few laying hens made a donation.

Some luxuries, such as Peaches, began to arrive in Britain, the first ones cost seven shillings and sixpence each. Large ones eighteen shillings each. Now that was indeed luxury, if you could afford it. You can be sure I never got to taste any.

In June, Ampthill Rural Council at last approved a scheme

costing in the region of £100,000 to provide Flitwick, Westoning, Harlington, Steppingly with mains sewerage. The scheme provided for main sewers, and pumping stations at selected points, sewage finally making its way to works at rough lands near Folly Farm.

Earlier in the year, on the nights of 13th and 14th February, Dresden was carpet bombed. Some said it was in retaliation for the devastation suffered by Coventry on the night of 14th November 1941. 70,000 died in the firestorms. We did not know many were refugees fleeing the Russian soldiers who were raping women.

Before the war, Dresden was famous for its delicate porcelain and fine buildings, it was called the Florence of Germany. In the 19th century, those with some cash to spare did the European tour, often to include Dresden. In 1945, at the start of Lent, the city of Dresden lay in ruins. Was revenge sweet? We believed the Germans deserved all they got, after what they had done to cities like Plymouth, Coventry and London. We did not know the truth about the fleeing refugees. Bomber Harris and the RAF were heroes to us. War is horrendously cruel, there is no doubt about that.

April 28th, Mussolini was shot, but to make sure, the Italian partisans hung him upside down as well. 2nd May, the German army in Italy surrendered, and on the 8th it was all over. The American forces liberated Buchenwald concentration camp on 13th April. 20,000 prisoners were released, their bodies emaciated and skeletal. Hitler killed himself on 1st May, the day after he'd married his long time mistress Eva Braun. Eve took cyanide, and Hitler shot himself, UGH!! We felt no sympathy.

I saw grown ups getting drunk, said prayers of thanksgiving at school, and life went on. Rationing and shortages of everything in the shops remained, and sometimes got worse. The cinema showed soldiers returning to civilian life, but scenes of the goings on in

Germany made me gasp. We hadn't heard the word Holocaust.

On September 5th we re-occupied Singapore, and in November the Nuremburg trials began.

Perhaps Mum visited the kitchen planning exhibition held in the Iron Room in Station Road in March, and marvelled at the displays of new cookers and other electrical wonders. In many kitchens, if there was an electricity supply, a geyser was fitted next to the sink to provide instant hot water, and in those homes lucky enough to have an indoor bathroom, a geyser was situated to provide hot water to sink and bath.

All over the country, families were experiencing the joy of loved ones returning home. Demobbed soldiers were given a demob suit. Trousers, jacket, waistcoat, 2 shirts, socks and a pair of shoes, to help restart their lives in civvy street. Many a wedding took place with the groom proudly wearing his demob suit.

In June we had the general election. Churchill had seen us through the war, and lots of people thought he would win, but Clement Attlee and the Labour Party won, with a majority in the House of Commons of 146. They were thrust into responsibility for rebuilding the country. It was firmly believed that the Labour Party won because they promised to introduce the National Health Service.

Poorer people recalled the 1930s, chronic unemployment, miserable wages, soup kitchens, unhealthy social conditions too many suffered when the Tories were in power. Memories still vivid of the crushing of the General Strike in the 1920s. The Conservatives got the blame for all and anything that the poor had to suffer through those years. Churchill had been a brilliant war leader, but he was not to be trusted with the peace. Mid-Bedfordshire returned a Conservative M.P. Lennox Boyd, which pleased Ernie, who had voted for him. Ernie didn't trust the Labour Party.

His opinion was that the Tories came from good families who were educated to rule us. Prefabs and new Council housing were hastily erected all over, to house the homeless, the overcrowded.

Japan signed surrender documents on the warship Missouri on 2nd September, after the Yanks had chucked a couple of atomic bombs at Hiroshima and Nagasaki. Barbed wire was removed from beaches. On the home front, Mum struggled on, looking after us as best she could. From 1945 the Avenue in Flitwick became a hive of activity as lorries full of building materials passed up and down, turning it from a quiet cul-de-sac of gentle middle class homes into through road to the new estate. Flitwick was on the move.

On the lighter side of life, more new songs came through. Don't Fence Me In, crooned by Bing Crosby with the Andrews Sisters. Tommy Dorsey and Orchestra recorded On the Sunny Side of the Street, and Judy Garland gave vent to the Trolley Song. The Andrews Sisters gave us Money is the Root of All Evil, and that Cockney duo Flannigan and Allen strolled along to Dreaming. Young Doris Day sang My Dreams are Getting Better All the Time.

A pint of beer cost around one shilling and three pence, Gallon of petrol two shillings, pound of tea around three shillings. Nylon stockings became available, if you could afford them.

An Acme wringer for fixing to the side of the sink was on sale. Shipyard workers were given a rise of four shillings and sixpence per week. Johnnie Walker Whisky red label cost twenty five shillings and ninepence, black label two shillings dearer. The cost well out of reach of an Agricultural labourer's income, unless he substituted whisky for food and didn't provide for his family. No coupons were needed for Bournville Cocoa, and Mum bought that in small canisters costing about sixpence.

Chapter 27
MEDICAL NOTES

'Here, have some of this,' Mum said, taking the lid off a bottle of Ipecac Cough Mixture bought from Cousins shop. I was crooping. Little did she realise she was dosing me with a liberal amount of alcohol at the same time as trying to ease my cough. It wasn't until many years later I learned some people enjoyed drinking the Ipecac mixture even when they had no cough, they were hooked on the taste. Vapour Rub, from a small squat jar, heated and smeared across my chest and back, really did ease a stuffed up nose.

How on earth would anyone want to revert to Victorian and Edwardian times. Even those living in affluence could not avoid the terrible diseases of the time, as was proven with the death of Prince Albert. Flitwick women, many were poor, had to cope with insanitary conditions, and risked dying in childbirth. My great grandmother died, age 32, the day she gave birth to my grandmother. To survive beyond the first birthday was quite an achievement. Today we are so sanitized, so smug, that we give the impression to the young that it is alright to abuse yourself with drink, drugs, promiscuous sex, and tobacco, because there is always some miracle cure available. It aint necessarily so.

Reformers in the 19th century knew that health care, hygiene, and living standards could be improved, must be improved. Eventually in 1911 the Government introduced a limited form of National Insurance, available to regularly employed workers. Those taken on casually, agricultural workers like Ernie, and the unemployed did not enjoy this advantage.

After the Poor Law was abolished in 1929, a new scheme was introduced to help the poor and sick. It was called the Panel, and was means tested. Proof of real need was required to qualify for help from the Panel. It wasn't paid automatically, and not for any lengthy period. Poor families found themselves having to sell off almost everything they owned, and that was usually little enough, when the breadwinner became ill or unemployed, before assistance was doled out. Free health care for all did not become available until National Health Service came in 1948.

Many years ago, a brilliant surgeon, working under extremely difficult conditions in an old hospital, not only saved my life, but also gave me years of a better quality life. That old hospital, with its Florence Nightingale wards, has long gone, we have a modern replacement, but the care I received would be hard to beat.

I am old enough to recall the days before the introduction of the N.H.S, when visiting the doctor's surgery was undertaken only after careful thought, in desperation, and very often too late, because of the cost. If a hospital stay could not be avoided, it was to a charity bed, with no frills such as choice of meals or listening to the radio. God forbid the day when the Government consigns the N.H.S to the dustbin, to be replaced by a health service funded by Insurance Companies , because, like my family in my youth, there are those on low incomes who would be unable to keep up with the premiums. We really should be grateful to all those early pioneers who fought hard and long, often to the detriment of their own health, to bring us the Social Benefits we now enjoy.

Family allowance began on June 15th 1945. Five shillings for each child under school leaving age, except the oldest one. For Mum it meant she had five shillings for Joyce, but nothing for me. Later, when Pat was born, Mum was given family allowance for Joyce and Pat, but still nothing for me. When I left school, she lost the family allowance for Joyce.

In 1946 or 47 I fell and sprained my ankle. Doctor Howe called, told Mum how to look after me, and I lay resting on the chaise longue by the window. When well enough, and able to walk again, I had to go weekly with a shilling or so to the surgery until the seven shillings and sixpence fee was paid in full.

Mum took an attack of pleurisy around 1948. A serious chest infection usually caused by a germ, it can also follow a blow to the chest. Mum took plenty of blows from Ernie. I stayed off school to look after her, with a little help from May Watson. Those whimsical scenes of the doctor being paid by the gift of a home made bottle of wine, of bottled fruit, as seemed to happen in all those old TV series Doctor Finlay's casebook, did not happen in Flitwick to my knowledge. Dr Howe, knowledgeable, and not without compassion, even though Mum did not like him, also had to earn a living.

A few months later, the doctor had to be called out again. Mum had an attack of Quinsy, a really sore throat condition. As usual, I had to stay off school to help around the house. Quinsy can cut off air to the windpipe, so Mum was in serious danger of losing her life. Dr Howe told her to take warm drinks, and Aspirin. Medical science has moved on since then. Mum was ill for three weeks, very ill, so much that at times I panicked because I thought she was going to die. She could not stand up. May Watson calmed me down. I still do not make a good nurse.

I put the ingredients for the Clanger in a mixing bowl, and Mum mixed it while resting on the chaise longue. I rolled the dough out on the table, then helped her cut up the meat and vegetables for the filling. All the while she was exhausted and had to lay back on the pillows often. I didn't understand how ill she was, how very painful for her to talk. The N.H.S had came into being, there was no medical bill to pay.

161

In 1946 Ernie had an accident at work. An industrial accident it would be called today, he would be advised for free by a Solicitor to sue for damages, but in the 1940s we had not quite got the hang of this compensation lark. He was knocked off balance when he came too close to a Threshing machine. (most of the information given to me by Claud Barnes.) Unable to walk, he came home on the back of a lorry. Dr Howe came, Ernie was in agony, but there was no therapy, no help at all except Aspirin. If the Doctor gave him a pain killing injection I don't know, but if he did, it would certainly be added to his bill. Ernie was off work for little over a week, then painfully, he got on his bike and slowly cycled back to work. How Mum managed financially I don't know. Ernie would not be paid for his absence, she had no savings to fall back on, and he still could not get by without his fags, in fact he smoked more than ever to help him cope with the pain. We never had a full larder, no reserves of food, except the garden vegetables.

Mum never worked in the garden, that was Ernie's domain, but if he was ill for any length of time, then he'd not be able to dig and plant, or keep it weed free. It is likely Mum was allowed a little extra credit at Cousins shop, the Milkman would be put off for another week, the coalman too, and she'd have to forget about getting a little meat from the butcher for the dumpling. Once Ernie was back at work and getting paid again, then it would take her weeks to try and catch up.

Tuberculosis was a scourge in the 1940s. Some older people called it Consumption. Isolation hospitals were dotted all over the country, for other infectious diseases like Scarlet Fever and Diptheria. I recall one event, when men in white suits arrived at number 26, to seal off the Watson's house. They fumigated the house with Sulphur, (I didn't know of Sulpher at the time, I learned

162

of that later), they pasted strips of paper around the doors and windows, covering the entrance door with white sheeting which looked like billowing white clouds, the sheets were so large. One of the children was taken away to the isolation hospital, although which one I cannot recall.

Mum did not have a first aid box or a medicine chest. Her first aid consisted of a few items kept in one of the drawers of the dresser which sat between the fireplace and the window. A couple of bandages, one slightly wider than the other, used over and over again, washed between uses.

If stung by a wasp, or bitten by another insect, Mum sucked the wound, then rubbed blue bag over it, or sometimes Iodine, OUCH! I don't know which was worse, the sting from the wasp, or the sting of the Iodine. (Blue bag was a rinsing cube used in laundry). If I fell and grazed my knees, she spit on her hanky and rubbed the blood off, leaving it to scab over. Vaseline was rubbed on sore spots. Should a wound continue to bleed, it was wrapped in a bandage or a torn off scrap of the cleanest rag she had. Splinters were removed by the use of a sharp needle passed through the steam of the kettle. She never rushed me off to the doctor if a mishap occurred. It had to be really serious before he was contacted.

Ernie had a habit of slapping me on the side of my head, causing me earache which always seemed worse through the night. Mum used Camphorated oil, warmed up before pouring a few drops in my ear. She then stuffed a little warm cotton wool into my ear, and that usually soothed it enough to allow me back to sleep. I did some wailing.

Joyce had pneumonia when she was only about three years old. Mum nursed her through it. We had a picture of a collie type dog on the wall, and Mum knew she had recovered when Joyce

163

looked up at the picture, pointed to it, and murmured 'Doggie.' That picture went with us when we moved to Dunstable Rd.

When Joyce suffered Measles, the curtains were drawn to keep out the daylight. We had little medical help. Dr Howe called, told Mum to give her plenty of liquids and to watch out for the fever pitch, when she was to cool her down with cold water sponges. Mum mixed a Beecham's powder with water if we caught a cold, or if no powders in the house, she gave us Aspro or Aspirin. Beecham's powders could be bought singly at Cousins shop, at one penny or one and half penny each. Mum gave us laxatives to ease constipation. Squares of bitter chocolate, or she'd open a bottle of Syrup of Figs.

The word Depression wasn't used. Mum said to May one day, 'Ooh Gawd, I feel a bit run down terday Gal,' May rummaged in a drawer to produce a bottle of magical pink pills. Dr Williams little pink pills. Cost, a shilling and threepence.
'There yer are Gal, these'll make yer feel better.'
No one, absolutely no one in the village wanted to have a mental breakdown, or admit to having ever spent time in a mental institution. The stigma was so great. Stories abounded of those that did find themselves taken to these places and the horrors they endured. If a box of pink pills allowed you to get on with your work, then that would do for now. We'd never heard of Penicillin, discovered by Alexander Fleming in 1928. Our antiseptics consisted of a small bottle of Dettol or Izal, Germolene cream in a tin, a small bottle of Iodine, presuming we used anything at all most of the time. When Joyce and Pat were babies, Mum smeared Zinc and Castor Oil cream , or sometimes Vaseline, in an attempt to prevent nappy rash.

Home remedies were normal. Because of my fair hair and freckles, I suffered sunburn. Cold water was a temporary relief, or Mum would rub a little Vinegar over my face and arms.

Talcum powder was seldom in our house, it was scarce and expensive. Calamine lotion I had not heard of.

At school I drank a daily bottle of milk, approximately one third pint. Despite our poverty, we got through those hard times, but the effects of that hardship, deprivation, poverty, was not good for Mum's health. By the time we left the Alley, it was too late for her to recover, she had suffered and suffered, and ill health continued to ride her for the rest of her life. At age 38 she went into a Diabetic coma, and although she recovered from the coma, she lost her sight.

She had been a strong woman. Hauling pails of water up from the Well, day in day out. Bringing sacks of coal home from the railway, harvesting crops for local growers, lifting the heavy washtub off the fire in the range, while all the time suffering mental and physical abuse from an uncaring and brutal husband.

After Joyce was born in 1940, Mum little suspected she would not be able to give birth at home again. Home births were normal for the time, but risky if complicated. Mum became pregnant several times. Each time the baby was due, she was rushed to Bedford Hospital for emergency medical help. Nobody could or would tell her what was wrong. She seldom attended the doctor's surgery. There was no financial help with bus fares to the clinic or to the Bedford hospital .

To have the baby in hospital cost money Mum did not have. £2 per day plus expenses.

I am not sure what year it was, maybe just after the war, and once more, I was sent to the 'phone box beside the White Horse to summon the doctor. The baby had gone full term, then overdue, and Mum became very ill. Mum was once again rushed away to Bedford. I learned later, the baby's body was in bits and had been dead for a while. Mum escaped with her own life. Sounds awful, but that was life then. At home, I had no idea the trauma she'd gone through. May Watson had to cook the Clanger for me. I could put pots of potatoes on the range, but getting the pot off without scalding myself was quite a problem. Again I needed help, and May sent her daughter Phyllis in. Without Phyllis, who was only 16 or 17 at the time, there was a problem. I don't know how I could have managed. Even if there had been handy Takeaways near the Alley, we could not afford to buy them anyway.

When Mum arrived home, I didn't understand what she had gone through. She had to get on with everything just as if she had never been ill. There was no sympathy from Ernie, who was, within days, demanding she satisfy his conjugal rights. (Debitum conjugale, the mutual right of partners in marriage to each other's bodies). Rape within marriage was still legal until 1991. Police were reluctant to become involved in what they perceived to be a Domestic, leaving the couple to work it out for themselves. Horrible little man.

Ernie was still living in Victorian times. In 1854, Barbara Leigh Smith wrote,

"A man and wife are one person in law, the wife loses all her rights as a single woman and her existence is entirely absorbed in that of her husband. A woman's body belongs to her husband and he can enforce his right."

Joyce and I slept in the same room as Mum and Ernie. He muttered over and over again, 'I know my rights,' as Mum protested she was tired.   Pat, we called her Trish, who was born December 1st 1948, had a better chance of survival thanks to the N.H.S. Mum attended the Doctor's surgery and other clinics as necessary, because she knew it was all free. Had she gone on as before, there would have been another stillbirth. The Gynaecology unit at Bedford were prepared.

She was admitted a few days before the birth. They explained that Pat was a Rhesus baby, and the problems encountered already. The first baby of a couple with that problem can be unaffected, hence the safe delivery of Joyce at home in 1940, but pregnancies after that can go disastrously wrong, as Mum had experienced. As far as I am aware, it is a problem for mothers with Rhesus positive, and baby being Rhesus negative, and the two bloods mixing with each other. I don't know the modern procedures, but for Pat, it meant a blood transfusion immediately she was born.

Mum lay on one operating table, baby lay on another. As Pat's blood drained away through one ankle, Mum's blood was being pumped in through the other. Someone referred to Pat as a Blue Baby, but she wasn't. However, the dangerous procedure that ensured she lived was similar. The baby's circulatory system is connected to that of father or mother whilst baby's heart is out of action, the donor's heart and lungs taking over. Blue baby is a description given to those babies born with heart defects. Mum and Pat remained in hospital for approximately two weeks. It was all free now under the NHS. Ernie had grumbled about National Insurance off his wages, but no grumbles after that. Pat had a small scar on each ankle all her life, until her tragic death from a blood related problem near to the time Princess Diana died.

After arriving home from hospital, Pat slept in the marital bed at night, as Joyce had done. She had jet black hair, and big dark eyes. I took her long walks in her pram, which I kept clean. Mum didn't breast feed her. She fed her bottles made up of National Dried Milk, obtained from the clinic in Ampthill. If she had none left, Pat was fed Carnation Milk, or Fossil's Condensed milk, watered down.

By now I was almost 14 years old and beginning to be interested in boys, although, except for one, they were not interested

167

in me. Ernie had became friendly with a family who had moved from Fife to settle in Ridgemont. On one of our family visits to Ridgemont. One Sunday I trekked all the way to Ridgemont, which is a long walk. The boy was indifferent to me. I walked home very tired, the pram heavier than when I set out. Ernie was out looking for me, angry. He found me as I neared Hornes End, and I got an earbashing for my troubles. He said he was giving me another half hour and then calling the police.

Pat had been marvellous all day. She was about 8 months old. I took milk in a bottle, the boy's mother rustled up something for her. I paid for my sins with sore feet and Ernie's nagging.

I had regular medical inspections at school. In 1907 a law was passed requiring the medical inspection of all schoolchildren.

In 1912 the Board of Education set up a Medical Department, leading to the introduction of school clinics. I recall some of those inspections. Screens were erected at the far end of the main building, in part of Miss Carr's classroom. Boys and Girls were lined up separately in class order. One by one we were taken to the doctor by a nurse. He was behind a screen. Boys were stripped down to waist, we girls were stripped down to vest and knickers. A nurse checked our weight and height, and we had to lift our feet up for inspection.

The doctor looked in my mouth, Say Ahh, as he probed with a spatula. He checked my ears, using a probe with a light at the end of it. I had to cough as the cold stethoscope came into contact with my chest and back. Lastly, for some reason known only to him, he pulled my knickers away from my waist and peered down to my privacy. It annoyed me immensely. Did he think we were boys masquerading as girls? I squirmed but could do nothing.

Chapter 28
SHOPS, CLOTHING, and CHARITY

'I've got a few things put aside for you Florrie, call in when you've time.' Mum did indeed call on Esther Stringer, wife of William, (Bill?), to collect a bundle of hand me down clothing.

I thought Esther's house at 44 Kings Road very posh. She had a proper kitchen with sink and cooker. There was a geyser providing hot water. The lavatory was inside the house, the cistern half way up the wall. Pulling the chain which hung from it flushed the gunge away from the toilet pan, to go into a cesspit somewhere out of view. I am not sure if the lavatory was upstairs or downstairs.

They gossiped for a bit, exchanging news, views, and opinions before we went home, for me to scrabble in the bundle to see what Esther had given us. A couple of grey skirts for school, perhaps a cardigan or two. A couple of cotton dresses, all washed and clean. In the bundle were a pair of patent leather shoes, a strap across the instep, fastened to a buckle at the side. I shrieked with delight. Slightly tight, I mentioned it to Mum, 'They'll stretch, wear'em fer a bit, see ow they do.' I don't know if it was vanity, as the shoes looked new, and I had desired a patent pair, or because my old shoes were letting in water, but I wore them for almost three weeks before giving in. A hammer toe developed on my left foot and has been a source of discomfort ever since. When one pair wore out I got another, sandals in summer, black lace up school shoes in winter, with plimsolls for physical excercise and sports, wellingtons when the weather was wet. Shoes were repaired over and over again. Plimsolls were usually bought from Inskips, a small general Drapers shop in a low dark painted bungalow style wooden building opposite the Blackbirds Inn.

Mum told me I'd have to withdraw my savings from the school penny bank and go to Inskips to buy a new pair of shoes, as she had no money. Inskip's sold knitting wools, womens and mens underwear, blouses and skirts, and they had a haberdashery selection, all behind the counter, in boxes, a few samples of their wares displayed in the window. I went into the shop and stood at the counter to await someone to serve me. It was either Mrs Inskip or an assistant who went through to the back storeroom to fetch the shoes. There was no choice of styles. They fitted, I paid the money, price thirteen shillings and sixpence, (68p). Mum shoved the patent pair to the back of the glory hole, remarking they would do for Joyce, but I believe she never wore them.

The school caretaker's wife Mrs Lowe, a plump pleasant woman, occasionally stood at the school gates waiting for me at home time, to hand me a bundle of clothes her own daughter had outgrown. All hand me downs were gratefully welcomed, otherwise matters could have been even worse for Mum. Although my clothes were not new, at least they were not rags. On the income of an agricultural labourer, very few wives could afford a lot of new clothes. Dress patterns were bought, and they made their own clothes, using whatever materials they could lay their hands on. They knitted and they adapted old clothes by adding trimmings, taking in seams, or inserting extra material where necessary. Mum did none of that for us, yet she could darn so very neatly.

Shopping is so different today. We are not restricted by ration coupons. We go from aisle to aisle in the Supermarket, selecting this and that from the shelves, buying what we need, and plenty that we could do without. We can examine racks of clothing without necessarily intending to buy. We are bamboozled by everything on offer at the Deli counter, we can even buy our

Televisions in these places. If it is being made somewhere, we can purchase it. The cost added to our overloaded credit cards. To be paid next year, sometime, never.
On our personal computers at home, a site for selling and buying second hand goods cheaply. In the 1940s, if you did not have the cash, then you could buy nothing. Those in the middle classes had accounts at favoured stores, but that facility wasn't available to the lower paid, most did not have a bank account.

Shopping by computer is today becoming more and more popular. There are more cookbooks today than there ever has been, yet no-one needs to know how to cook, only how to work the microwave. (I've had two and blown them both up).
Vegetables are already cleaned before they reach the Supermarket shelves, and the bread department is piled high with so many different varieties, sliced if I wish. Queues stretch out from the Checkouts, and we wait impatiently to empty our trolley and get our goods home, but it is nothing to the queues families had to contend with in the 40s.

Considering the rationing restrictions, shops in Flitwick and Ampthill managed to keep families supplied most of the time, within the boundaries of supply and demand. We were not used to luxuries, or great choice. Food was bought in smaller quantities, fresh, daily, home cooking being cheaper and healthier than ready meals prepared in some distant factory. Going from Butcher to Baker, Baker to Greengrocer, Greengrocer to Grocer, and perhaps a visit to the Ironmonger and the Cobbler too, all took time, queues at every one, and no capacious car boot to stack everything into.

Shopping for a month's food at one time was out of the question. There was either a lack of money, lack of enough coupons, not enough goods in the shops, but mostly, there wasn't enough arms to carry it all. Behind the counter, (no self service), were shelves carrying the goods the shop had to offer, with gaps here and there where stock had run out. In the back store were large paper or hessian sacks holding loose commodities such as sugar, Rice, Lentils, Dried Fruit when available, sacks of dirt covered potatoes, and other vegetables, along with Firelighters, soap powders, bleach. Nicholson's shop on Station Square, at the corner of Kings Road, had two long counters to left and right as you entered. On each counter was a set of scales, not digital or electric, but balanced with little brass weights from a fraction of an ounce upwards. Staff wore white coat style overalls with either a green or white apron on front. Wooden chairs were placed conveniently for customers use while staff assembled their requirements, taking a tin from one shelf, packet from another, going through to the storeroom for something else. Apologies for goods out of stock. Once it was all assembled, then it was totted up and the customer paid for it, or signed for it if she had an account. Some Flitwick housewives were registered at Lipton's in Ampthill. They stocked a greater variety of foods. During petrol shortages, home deliveries were curtailed, or even stopped.

Mum did not take us from shop to shop, to come out laden with designer label clothes in large glossy see where I've been shopping bags. The household budget hardly stretched to feeding us properly. Occasionally, something was bought, very cheaply, from the Tally man, or a friend's Littlewoods catalogue.

Mum always wore a coat when going further than the end of the Alley. Even if the weather was warm, she still put on her coat, declaring it hid her fat, which it didn't.

Children seldom had a say in the way they were dressed. It made no difference whether the child was rich or poor. A revolution in childrens and teenage fashions was about to take place, and today, children are firmly in charge of what they wear. But not then.

In 1933, after her divorce, novelist Barbara Cartland complained £500 annual income was not enough for her and Raine. (Raine later became step-mother to Princess Diana). Maybe it wasn't in the circles she was party to, but if she thought it such a paltry amount, I wonder how she would have coped had she been reduced to rummaging around at Jumble Sales.

Miss Chatterton did her best to impart a little elegance into this peasant girl, Miss Sharpe suggested I clean my own shoes, and the sewing teacher did her bit, showing me how to use needle and thread and a sewing machine. When I left school to start work, it was with a company who insisted on high standards of deportment, behaviour, and personal appearance. It wasn't long before I left that scruffy Alley kid behind me. One of my treasures is my washing machine. Mum didn't have the convenience of automatic anything.

None of us could go around with bare midriffs, it was too cold to do that, and certainly not along any High Street. Bikinis had not arrived, and belly buttons were definitely covered up. Most homes had no central heating, only one fire burning in either kitchen or living room. The rest of the house shivered.

A matching jacket and skirt was called a costume. Skirts were slightly flared, five flares as in Goray pleats, other skirts were straight but a straight skirt doesn't suit anyone who has the slightest bump of a belly. Shoes were stocky, cuban heel style, mended repeatedly. Blouses were shapeless. We had none of the easy wear and wash tops which can be worn today instead of a blouse.

Hats came in all shapes, from home made knitted berets, to the very fashionable, adorned with feathers, ribbons and all sorts of trimmings. A hat pin was necessary to keep the contraption on the head. Mum had no hat.

173

Walk along any street today and you find most women in trousers or jeans. We'd never heard of jeans, except to see them on Cowboys in the Western films. Trousers were called slacks. Stores and offices did not allow their female staff to wear slacks for work. Factories did allow slacks, even encouraged it because there would be no flapping skirts to come into contact with machinery. Marks and Spencer allowed only the window dressers to wear slacks. Mum wore flat heels, and lisle stockings kept up by a rubber band garter just above the knee. When she had no elastic band, she held her stockings up with a length of white tape tied round just above the knee, and the stocking rolled around it. There was a narrow puffy bare wobbly bit of flesh between stocking and the elasticised leg of her bloomers. Not a pretty sight when she bent over.

May was thinner than Mum, but she also wore garters to hold her stockings up. Both had tartan legs from sitting open legged in front of the fire. A chain smoker, May's cigarette was stuck to her bottom lip as she worked and talked, her eyes screwed up against the smoke, but she was a cheerful woman.

Two or three years after the war, Christian Dior caused a stir with his New Look. Long full flared skirts almost ankle length, slim fitting bodice and waist, emphasising the bust. As I was still at school it hardly mattered to me, but I do recall hearing older women pooh-poohing the new fashions, 'It'll never catch on, where'they goona git all the cloth?' 'And what about the coupons?' Catch on the new fashions did. When I left school, my new coat was fashionable.

Around 1949 Mum bought one of the new long length dresses from the Tally man's catalogue. It was loose fitting style, and the new softer material draped over her ample figure quite nicely. Along with the dress, she bought a new swagger coat in green check, a cheaper copy of the new styles being paraded on the catwalk. With its dolman sleeves it also hung comfortably loose for her. Clothes were not so easily washed then. Housewives wore cotton easily washed aprons and overalls to protect their clothes. Usually sleeveless, folded double over the front, with tapes going through holes under arm at waist level, tied at the back. Or it might be an overall with simple halter neck, tied with tapes of ribbon from sides of waist to back.

In 1950, it cost me a small fortune having my grey flannel skirts dry cleaned. Two shillings nearly every week. I wore an apron at home. Aunt Daphne wore her hair in the popular roll hairstyle of the period. A padded tape was fixed around the head, over the hair, hair rolled over it and pinned in. Hairpins were a girl's best friend with a hairstyle like that. She wore bright red lipstick. Cream, powder and rouge on her cheeks. I always thought her very pretty. Girls on a night out wore mascara, but it wasn't so easy to apply as it is today. It came in powder form, had to be moistened, and applied with a tiny brush. It wasn't waterproof and if it rained, well, panda eyes describes it. Many older women with long hair rolled it up into a bun on nape of their neck. Granny Bland did her hair that way.

Sometime around 1948, Ernie and Mum stopped off at Dunstable when on our way to Whipsnade Zoo. We called in on his Aunt Polly, (must have been the Bland side of the family). We entered her terraced house straight from the street, no front garden, into a long narrow hall leading to a small living room at the back of the house. She made us welcome with a cup of tea and piece of cake. While there, she took me into her front room to show me the hats she was working on. Around the room were boxes of feathers and trimmings in all the colours of the rainbow. Fabrics, silks, and satin ribbons, muslin, patterned nets for veils. Absolutely wonderful.

175

She was an outworker for one of the many Luton hat factories. They brought the basic hats to her, already blocked to shape. Polly was to make those hats into desirable fashion accessories. When I saw those hats in various stages of completion, it fired my imagination, and I decided I would be a Milliner when I left school. Fate, as it often does, took me along a different path.

Almost everyone, men and women, wore a hat if they were socialising/attending Church/ going to Wedding/Funeral/Christening. It was unthinkable for a woman to enter a Church hatless. Working men wore a cap for work, and a trilby for socialising, a la Frank Sinatra style. Ernie's trilby was size six and a quarter. Public schoolboys and girls wore straw boaters made at Luton. Straw boaters, bonnets, Wedding hats, Felt hats, plain hats, fancy hats, Luton made them all. I have a vague recollection of wearing a straw bonnet, tied in by ribbons under my chin, as a 3 or 4 years old child. Babies in prams and toddlers in pushchairs were seen wearing fine little straw bonnets to shield their face and eyes from the sun. The bonnets had ribbons or tassels, with perhaps straw flowers sewn in.

The first wedding I was ever at was my own, and my going away hat was the most expensive purchase of a hat I'd ever made.

As well as the hat factories, where the workers were mostly women, Luton was a good place for the men to find work too, at Vauxhall motor works, and Skefco Ballbearing factory, along with other factories connected to the motor industry. The shops in Luton were a magnet for the factory girls. On Saturdays, places such as Woolworths, Marks and Spencer, British Home Stores, and all the other shops in George Street were heaving with girls from the factories anxious to spend their wages on the latest fashions. At Christmastime there was hardly space to breathe in the street.

The working week was 44 hours, before 1949 it was a 48

176

hour week. The factories also required their workers to do overtime as necessary. Lingerie was a fancy name for underwear when I was younger. I had to make do with flannel or knitted cotton undies. Mum wore an underslip made of rayon material, same length as her dress from shoulder to hem. It did not have delicate stringy straps, but had sturdy shoulder supports cut in one with the garment. Those underslips of yesteryear are now being worn as evening dresses by film and TV stars. I saw a film star at a Premiere recently. I could have sworn I once owned a fine nightie just like it in the 1960s. Thin shoulder straps, lace trimmed bodice, shimmering body hug, lovely. In one of the Daily Mail fashion pages, I saw dresses very much like the petticoats I wore when in my teens, stiffened to make my summer dresses and skirts flounce out more.

Mum seldom wore a bra and corset, she hated them so much, felt very uncomfortable.

Clothes were rationed as you know throughout the 1940s and coupons had to be handed over as well as cash. Trousers 8 coupons, Jacket 13 coupons, Boots 7 coupons, Coat 14 coupons, Blouse 5 coupons, Dress 11 coupons. When the coupons ran out, that was the end of buying anything until the next coupon issue. unless some became available on the black market. Although the activity was illegal, and could land both seller and buyer in jail, poorer women like Mum used the cash to buy some necessity they otherwise could not afford. Mum sold a few of our clothing coupons to Phyllis Watson. She'd left school at 14 and was earning her own money.

As I've already written, Mum was given hand me down clothes for Joyce and I, as well as rummaging through piles of discarded clothing at the Jumble Sales. A jumper or cardigan could be bought for a penny. No coupons needed.

At the beginning of the war, the utility label CC41 was

introduced, attached to everything from clothing to household linen and furniture. The items had to conform to certain regulations on quality and fashion. For example, coats and dresses had a standard length, usually to the knee, trousers were not to have turn-ups, (who wears dust trap turn-ups today? but it was the fashion for men then). Lapels were not to be too wide, jackets have no more than three buttons, with minimal pockets, no trimmings. Frilly blouses of the 1930s had to lose their frills, to be replaced by plain rever collars.

Children today have never heard of a Liberty bodice, wouldn't even consider wearing one. (The name actually came from the company Liberty, who made good quality cotton underclothes for all ages). I wore one for most of my young life. It was another layer of clothing, and helped keep me warm. Made of white cotton, with self coloured shirt type buttons, it was like a sleeveless double breasted jacket to waist level. With a round neck, it was worn over a vest, and below a full length petticoat, then a dress over all that lot, with cardigan on top. The vest tucked into black flannel knickers with legs reaching almost to the knee. I was wearing my central heating.

Womens knickers were in various materials, from flannel to delicate silk or lace. Three basic styles. Directoire, we called them bloomers, legs with elastic inserts at knee level. Then there were panties, similar to directoire, except there was no elastic at the hem of the shorter leg. Shorter than panties were briefs, much the same as we buy today, except they covered the bum a bit better and came up fully to the waist. To pay an arm and a leg for a bit of string and an inch of cloth that has a designer label on it, makes a fortune for some, makes monkeys out of the rest of us. Call it a thong if you like, but in my opinion, anyone wearing a thong might as well go knickerless, it would be just as effective and a whole lot cheaper. (Oh! I must be getting old, I like my rump well and truly covered)

It was obligatory to have a length of elastic in the house, in order to repair those knickers, because the elastic didn't stand up to frequent washing. Holes were darned, burst seams sewn up.

Buses and trains were not heated. I've sat shivering freezing cold on many a bus.

At school, in my final year, I made some underwear in sewing class. An underslip, made of smooth rayon, pink, shoulder to hem. Another of our projects was to make a pair of cami-knickers. We girls took two shillings or half a crown to school to help cover the cost of materials which the teacher purchased. We girls thought we were grown up by this time, especially as older sisters, cousins, neighbours daughters, had left school at 14, before the raising of the leaving age, and they were now out working, earning money, and taking care of themselves. We wanted the same.

The teacher brought in the lovely silky rayon in pink. Under her supervision we cut to pattern those risque garments, fitting the crotch to have a button opening. We were well used to our crotch being covered up by those flannelette knickers, so it was somewhat revolutionary to be sewing knickers that could let the draught in. We fitted elastic into the waistband, handstitched the button holes at the crotch, hand sewed the buttons on, then finished off the article with dainty scalloped handstitching around the edges of the wide leg openings. I learned to use the hand driven sewing machine in that classroom. When the knickers were finished, we proudly took them home, expecting to wear them. I don't know what other parents thought, but Mum went into orbit. She ranted and raved about how could teacher allow us to 'make that sort of thing.' She thought they were immoral. I never understood what she was going on about, but I had to sell them to Phyllis Watson, who thought they were lovely.

I never possessed a pair of stockings until after leaving school

179

I went bare legged until October 1950, when it started to get cold travelling on the bus to Luton, so I bought a pair of flesh coloured Lisle stockings for one shilling and elevenpence. I also had to buy myself a suspender belt to hold them up. I told myself I wasn't going to be like Mum and hold them up with garters.

At the Luton branch of Marks and Spencer where I worked, staff were rationed to one pair of nylon stockings per week, two if we received extra deliveries. Thursday was delivery day, it was also pay day. Pay packets in hand, we lined up in the canteen to buy our quota. When Kathy Watson, (Kate Carr), learned I couldn't afford to buy my quota, she asked me to get them anyway and sell them to her, which I did until supplies became more plentiful. When the nylons went on display, queues stretched out of the doors, and there were near riots as customers pushed their £1 notes forward to the extra staff helping out. Prices were upwards of 15/11, fifteen shillings and elevenpence, all usually 15 denier, and to begin with, they were all flesh coloured, favourite shade was American Tan. Staff had a 33% discount on all purchases except food. After six months, the purchases were added up, and the discount paid out.

There sprang up in little shops, or in a corner of the Dry Cleaner's, a new business, for mending those nylons when they laddered, which they easily did. A woman bent over a special machine did a marvellous job. The slogan was, We'll repair your nylons to look like new. Price from one shilling upwards, (5p) depending on the damage. To preserve the stockings, most girls, including me when I eventually bought some, wore cotton gloves to don them. Nail polish was dabbed on the start of a ladder, to stop it going any further, but of course, there is only so many dabs of polish a stocking could take.

The first nylon stockings were made by Walter J Carruthers

180

in 1937, and were available in America before being made in Britain. When they went on sale in New York around 1940 70,000 pairs were sold on the first day. We didn't see nylons until after the war, although the Yanks brought some over with them when they came here, to woo the girls.

Spivs got in on the nylon trade. On street corners, pubs, around the doors, in factories. Spivs opened a suitcase full of them and proceeded to do good business, undercutting shop prices, sometimes selling them alongside other goods in short supply. The imagery of the Spiv, sharp suit, trilby hat, fast moving and talking, with possibly a cigarette hanging from his bottom lip, with watches and cigarette lighters lining his coat, and a suitcase full of contraband goods is a joke now, but at the time, he was for real. The crowd, intrigued by his patter, closed in, pushing forward, very anxious to part with their cash before the bloke sold out of whatever it was he was selling cheap. When the Spiv spotted the police, he did a runner, to another of his favourite pitches. 'Nylons, come and get 'em girls.' He was brash, cheeky, complimented the women on their shapely legs, even those who looked like stick insects or elephants, and he did a brisk trade. Customs raided the liner Franconia when it docked in Liverpool in 1950, and found about £80,000 worth of contraband nylons destined for the black market. Tights were for the future, I cannot recall seeing any nylon tights for sale in those years.

The early nylons were easily damaged. The slightest snag, and whoosh!!, a ladder went from top to toe to top. Sometime around 1951/52 a new fashion emerged. Nylon stockings adorned with patterns on the back of the ankle, and a striking black seam. The applique pattern could simply be a square shaped outline, or it could be something more decorative such as a butterfly or rose. Keeping the seam straight up the back was a devil of a problem, as they seemed to have a wayward life of their own.

Suspender belts were first produced around 1870, and always were made of finer and more decorative materials than restrictive corsets. My first suspender belt was made of cotton broderie anglaise, easily washed. With a matching bra, I had a good figure and no need for a corset.

Mum and May Watson were not the only women holding up their stockings with garters. In my opinion that is the reason so many developed varicose veins later in life. Despite standing at my job for most of my working days, I have no unsightly varicose vein knots, or any other horrible leg markings.

At school one day, Miss Sharp took me to one side and asked if I had shoe polish at home. I replied we did, for I regularly polished Ernie's best shoes for him when he prepared for his trips to Luton. Miss Sharpe said I was old enough to do it for myself. My shoes were always scruffy, a mess, and something I hadn't paid attention to. They were not so scruffy after that, and Mum had to buy more polish. (The power of a caring Teacher.)

Every Saturday the Tally man called and Mum paid him two or three shillings off his account. If she wanted to buy something, he'd open his battered suitcase of samples, and she'd place an order. If the item was in stock, he brought it the following week. If not in stock she went without. Her cotton dresses were less than ten shillings, she bought one or two per year. He supplied Ernie's shirts. Collars came separate, needed starching and were affixed to the shirt using what are called collar studs, back and front slightly different. The shirts also had a tail, that is the back of the shirt was longer than the front, the back reaching down to below his rear. Good quality smart shirts have separate collars. Usually they did not button through, but were buttoned only to about waist level. Starch powder came in a little box, had to be mixed to a paste in cold water before hot water was added, enough to cover two or three collars, Left overnight in the starch, rinsed and pressed next day. Working shirts were heavier and rougher, flannelette kind of material, check or colour striped. No tails, collar was attached, and button through.

I found something interesting in the Ampthill News of 1946. We live in a throw away society today, but in 1946, because of rationing and shortages, we threw nothing away that could be put to another use, or saved for a future need. They had a feature entitled 'How can I save his shirts to defeat braces wear?' The article went on to advise on how best to do it, by cutting some material from the shirt tail and making matching pieces to cover the worn bit of shirt. Mending and patching were a way of life. Ernie's working trousers were made of Melton, a heavy cotton sort of material, easily crushed, although that did not matter much as he always wore bib and brace overalls over them. Priced from about thirteen shillings and elevenpence. (70p)

In January 1951, after four months as temporary sales staff with Marks and Spencer, I was offered a permanent position and had to decide. Do I go to the hat factory and take up the apprenticeship to become a Milliner or do I stay put. I decided to stay with M & S and remained with them for 11 years, working in four different stores, Luton, Bedford, Falkirk and Edinburgh. I was moved to the mens wear counter, just inside the entrance of the Luton store. Goods displayed neatly on the counter. Bib and brace overalls, Boiler suits, Trousers in different materials. I had a great time flirting with the blokes. But when one of them needed to be measured, (there were no fitting rooms in M&S at that time), I had to call the male Supervisor over. Unlike today, when the newspaper headlines scream about stories of girls kissing and telling, how many

183

men they've slept with, we girls were a bit more choosy and discreet. Girls that slept around got a bad name, were reviled.

Before I began working for Marks and Spencer, I spent the three weeks after leaving School on 14th July 1950 working for George Woodcraft. Nipping the tendrils of Runner Beans, Pea picking, Potato lifting. The money I earned in those three weeks helped me to pay for a new coat, shoes, skirts, blouses. The coat was the dearest item at £6. I paid a deposit to the Tally man, afterwards giving Mum a shilling each week to pass on to him until it was fully paid. I also had enough cash by me to pay for my bus fares and dinner money at M&S for two weeks, because I'd have to wait that length of time before I received my first pay packet.

In those days at M & S , factories, office jobs, we were not paid until the end of the second week of employment. At the end of the second week, we were paid the first week's wage. We were always a week behind, they called it a lying week, and at the end of our employment with that particular company, we were given that lying week's money because usually all employers operated the same system, it kept us going until the new employer paid us. We were paid weekly, in cash. If anyone left before completing the statutory notice period, the employer would normally keep that lying week's pay as a penalty. Most workers worked their notice.

I felt good as the bus conveyed me to my first day's employment at Luton's M&S. Clean, wearing my new coat and shoes, my hair tidy, I was a very different young lady to the scruffy schoolgirl of a few weeks previous. I was apprehensive, but also joyful, and anxious to make a good impression. Just a note about the Tally man. Where he came from I don't know, I presume it was from Luton or Bedford. A travelling salesman, selling all sorts of goods from clothing to household linen.

Ernie smartened himself up after dinner on Saturdays. He worked in the morning, came home about noon to eat. I helped Mum get his things ready for him going out. I polished his shoes, Mum fiddled about inside the old shell case vases on the mantleshelf for his collar studs. A freshly starched collar for his good shirt. I pressed his suit, including the waistcoat. To press his trousers, I heated the flat iron by placing it on the trivet in front of the fire, placed brown paper over one trouser leg, then the other, heating the iron two or three times before I was finished. The brown paper prevented shine, and prevented any sooty deposit from marking the trousers. If no brown paper in the house, I used a damp cloth. Using a cloth around the handle of the iron, and wiping it with a damp cloth, I'd spit on the base to see if hot enough. Ernie put his suit on, and his fringed white artificial silk scarf, very 30s Gatsby style. I can recall once seeing him with white spats over his shoes. The trilby finished it all off. Very smart. On cold days he wore an overcoat too, my memory fades, but I believe it was brown herringbone tweed. He never wore a tie to work, but he did have two or three good ties for going out, they were not expensive silk, more likely to be rayon. His tie was fixed to his shirt by a fairly plain tie pin. He tucked his fob watch into the left hand chest pocket of his waistcoat, the watch attached by a chain to one of the button holes.

Tucking his trouser legs into bicycle clips, off he went down the Alley on his bike to Luton, sometimes to see his lady friend Mabel Flecker, often to compete in a darts match. Some men on low wages wore casual wear, such as grey flannel trousers with a navy blue blazer, or a tweedy jacket. The same jacket could be worn with any trousers. Leisure clothing of the kind we can now buy in stores for less than the hourly wage rate wasn't available then.

Patching and darning was a way of life. Families had not a lot money. A man's good suit was a major purchase, bought from places like Burton's or Fifty Shilling Tailors, paid for by hire purchase weekly instalments.

Working class men usually sent their wives/mothers/sisters to shop for them because they worked long hours. A basic 48 hour week included Saturday mornings. The last thing they wanted to do in their little spare time was to traipse around the shops with children incessantly crying I want, I want. He had little cash to spare after the bills were paid, often in debt because some bills had to wait to be paid. There was no holy dress allowance for either him or his family. Food on the table and fuel for the fire came first. The women shopped while the men attended a football or cricket match or some other sport, or tended the vegetable patch.

M & S, British Home Stores, Littlewoods Stores did not have changing rooms, where the customers could try on the clothing. Goods in the stores were displayed on counters, even shoes, all neatly lined up in colours, styles, sizes. The staff carried a tape measure to help the customer choose the right size, but customers took a chance on whether it would look right when worn. If it did not fit when they tried the garment on at home, then another trip had to be made the next week, usually having to wait until the next Saturday because the shops closed at 5.30 or 6pm and didn't open again until 9am next day. No Sunday trading. Many customers came from out of town. Ladies toilets in the town often resembled the dressing rooms at the back of theatres, as women tried on a dress or skirt they had just bought.
'What de yer think Kath? I like the sleeves, bit long.'
'Yeah, but yer cn shorten 'em.'

In the 40s we didn't have credit cards, couldn't go to a hole in the wall to withdraw cash, so if the money wasn't in the purse, the item could not be bought. Not everyone had a bank account and use of a cheque book. Poorer people had no overdraft facility either. We called in each week to whatever shop was due a weekly payment for goods which had been bought on hire purchase, such as furniture, radio, or a bicycle.

At the end of the day in M&S we covered each counter with dust sheets, and in the morning each assistant was responsible for mopping the floor under and around her counter with a bucket of soapy water and a mop usually kept in the cupboard under the stairs, where there was also a large sink. The only male staff at the time were the Managers, and Floor Walkers as we called the Supervisors, Managers of Departments, and Porters, (warehousemen). The lighting was poor, single light bulbs hanging below small white shades, high up to the ceiling, wide apart. The floor was wooden, but by the late 50s M&S were replacing the wooden floors with Terrazzo, and putting in new strip lighting. Banisters on the stairs were French polished, a chap came every year to freshen them up. Luton store for example had only the ground sales floor. The basement only for storage. The window dressers had a small workshop down there. The basement also housed huge jars of acid.

Another kind of shopping was the department store, such as E.P. Rose, at the corner of Silver Street in Bedford (Debenham's took over the site), Jenners in Edinburgh, and Harrods in London were the same. They did hang their fashions on racks as well as counters, they did provide attendant serviced fitting rooms. Customers seldom browsed on their own, there were assistants on hand to pander to every customer's whim. Garments were usually dearer and too expensive for Mum.

These stores have adapted with the times and it is more difficult to tell someone's income today. A pair of jeans is a pair of jeans, on a pauper or a millionaire, they look the same. Look along any High Street or in any Shopping Centre today, and the throngs milling there have money to burn. (the credit crunch has came, but it will go). If they have a credit card or two, or three, they spend spend

I came across on old advertisement for E P Rose of Bedford of 1942, it illustrates how women used to make do and mend.

'Your laddered stockings repaired by the famous Stelos re-knitting method. A repair service demonstration is in our hosiery department from 9th March for several weeks.' The store had Cord slacks at twenty five shillings and ninepence, Crepe shirts for fourteen shillings and threepence. The advert included a blurb for the Dig for Victory campaign. None of the stores had a central paypoint. Goods were paid for to the counter staff at the point of sale. Customers didn't gather their purchases and pay for them all at a paypoint.

Mum occasionally travelled to Luton to the Indoor Market, she felt comfortable there, or to the market on St Paul's square Bedford. I can recall she was delighted once when she managed to get half dozen plain white cups very cheap. The markets were interesting. Selling local produce from local growers, live day old chicks, live rabbits, cats, birds, including exotic species such as Parakeets, Canaries and Budgies. I even saw snakes for sale once. There were haberdashery pitches where Mum could buy threads, ribbons, buttons, elastic. Cheap jewellery stalls, a Fishmonger, clothing and footwear for the masses.

Before the age of 24 hour shopping, and before we could buy over the Internet, it is forgotten that it was difficult for shop workers to actually shop for themselves. When it was their half day, all the other shops were on half day too. Many shops also closed for lunch. When I worked in Edinburgh store, I had to take a bus to the Co-op in Picardy place during my lunch hour and hope the queue was not too long when I got there. Shops closed all day Sunday, didn't open until 9 in the morning, closing at 6 pm, or 5.30. The advent of the 5 day working week was a long time coming, but it is a boon to shop staff who can now shop wherever they like at times to suit them. Many Supermarkets open 24 hours, the staff working shifts. All the ease of shopping today was opposed by the Clergy and the Unions, who thought staff would be exploited, but these organisations were mostly run by men who did not have to fit their shopping in a rushed lunch hour or a rare weekday off.

I have the use of a car today to bung everything in the boot to get the goods home. No housewife, no shop staff, no-one would put up with what we had to put up with all those years ago. Waiting in one queue for a piece of cheese, another queue for bacon to be sliced, another queue for a pound of carrots, and another queue for something else. Newspapers, milk, bread, butcher meat, was delivered door to door if requested. Someone had to be at home to pay for it at the door, or make special arrangements with the supplier.

When I started work, shop assistants were expected to be numerate. We used paper and pencil, then rang the total into the till. Those cash registers I trained on were pre-war, so out of date, totally inadequate for the increased prices, we just had to know how to calculate, they were not equiped with all the abilities of modern cash points. $2/3+4/6+5/11 = 12/8$ or twelve shillings and eight pence in imperial coinage, and totally undecipherable to the modern assistant. Reading the above as decimal gives a different figure.
We had to handle such figures every day.

As you have read, during our childhood, Joyce and I slept in the clothes we had worn all day, for warmth. Age 13 or so I began to take better care of myself, and asked Mum to buy me a nightie, which she did, a winceyette one, probably late 1948 or into 1949.

I made another one in sewing class. Things were still far from perfect, but I certainly made an effort. Kathy and Phyllis Watson next door were interested in the fashions of the day. I admired the way they dressed and resolved that one day I'd look as good as that.

Despite the rationing, anyone who had a sewing machine could make good use of it. The Drapery and Haberdasher stores sold patterns for making up clothing, and women could make something new from something old. I made several items of clothing in my teens, sewing by hand as I had no sewing machine. I knitted jumpers and cardigans. Padded shoulders were the order of the day, but not as prominent as worn by those Dallas women in the 1980s series.

I could make errors when sent to Cousins shop by Mum. One day I forgot to get Ernie's cigarettes. Oh Woe is me!! Ernie would hit me, Mum get agitated. It was half day, Cousins shop closed at 1pm, not opening again until next morning. Oh dear. I had to go through the wooden gates into the cobbled yard between their house and the bakery. Mrs Cousins answered my knock at her door. I got the cigarettes for Ernie and peace reigned again, until the next time. Today of course, the Supermarkets and responsible shops do not sell cigarettes to children. Children still seem to be able to acquire them from somewhere, for they start smoking as early as youngsters did then. At the Cousins shop, we could buy packets of five, and she even sold them singly if that was all the customer, even children, had money for. When I asked Joyce how she was able to smoke when she was only 14, and she did not receive pocket money, she told me she took them from Ernie's packet. She got away with it, but had it been me I'd have been beaten. I did not have the urge to smoke until nearly 18 years old. Tried it for a few weeks, then I met Alvis. He didn't smoke, so I stopped, thereby saving myself a great deal of money and preserving my lungs.

Chapter 29
THE NIT NURSE

Robert Burns (1759-1796), known all over the world as Scotland's bard, wrote a poem, "To a Louse" after spotting one crawling up the neck and under the bonnet of a well to do lady sitting in front of him one Sunday morning at the Kirk. I'll have to translate it for you if you are not familiar with the Scottish dialect.

"Hey! where are ye going, ye crawling wonder, your impudence protects you sorely, I can't but say ye swagger rarely, over gauze and lace, tho, faith, I fear ye dine but sparely, on such a place. Oh would some power the gift to give us, to see ourselves as others see us, It would from many a blunder free us, and foolish notion, What airs and graces would leave us, even devotion."

Head lice are nasty little creatures and were difficult to eradicate. Mum combed my hair with a close tined nit comb. Leaning my head forward over a sheet of paper, or an old rag to catch the horrible things, she threw them in the fire where they crackled. It all seemed so normal then. Not many admitted to nits when they were children, but it was inevitable. When one child became infected, most others fell victim too. Clean or dirty hair made no difference. Mum used chemicals doled out by Nurse Groom. We'd be clear for a few weeks, then inevitably the problem rose up again.

Nurse Groom was the School's nit nurse, as we called her. She visited the school to inspect our heads for those parasites. She lived with her husband Ted at Eastmoor in Maulden Road, and worked out of a Luton Clinic. Her children were grown up. Aged somewhere in her 40s, she wore her dark hair drawn back in a bun.

Around 1947/48 Nurse Groom decided to do something about these two girls who had suffered head lice frequently for years.

191

She sent us off to the Luton clinic with Mum. We came home clean, and with special lotion to use, but the problem cropped up again. She offered Mum what she saw as a solution.

We were to go to her house every Sunday to have a proper bath, have our hair inspected, and washed with special shampoo. On arrival, we were shown through to her large kitchen. The aroma of baking, the warmth, the cosy friendly atmosphere, it was really quite heady for this 12/13 year old. So different to the Alley.

Provided with towels, Joyce and I were shown the way to the downstairs bathroom, below the stairs. Mum came with us the first two or three Sundays, but we made our own way after that. It was absolute bliss, having a lovely warm bath, in a proper bathroom, being allowed to splash, Joyce and I in the bath together. Nurse Groom washed our hair, and helped us dry off. We dressed, she brushed our hair, afterwards we went to her cosy kitchen where we had tea, and warm scones. I thought it was wonderful. Before going home, we were allowed into her side garden to play on the long lawn.

The only time I saw her husband was one day when she let us look in the library, which was the room on the right, just inside the front door. He was sitting in a leather armchair reading. A table in the middle of the room had several books lying on it. I would have liked to look at some of the books. After a few months, Ernie lost his temper over something one day and said we were not to accept Nurse Groom's charity any longer. What was wrong with us having a bath in our own house. Joyce and I protested, Mum became angry, there was a ding dong row, but he had the last word. Ernie was right, we could not go to Nurse Groom's forever. Nurse Groom's house was my idea of heaven. Two storeys plus attic, a second bathroom, and grander furnishings than we had in the Alley.

Chapter 30
THE MOOR

The Moor, or Bog as we called it, on the southern edge of Flitwick, was a mysterious and dark place to me. When much younger, I imagined monsters lurking there, ready to grab little girls to eat. I pictured St George of England riding in there on his big white charger, to kill the Dragons. Collecting firewood, it seemed right spooky when I trod on broken twigs, the birds suddenly soared noisily into the air, frightened off by the echo.

By the time I was 12 or 13 years old I felt brave enough to venture on to the bog by myself. Before that, Mum and I gathered wood together. We took a few sacks, walked down Water Lane to the path boundary of the allotments, passing men digging and planting their patch. We gingerly stepped on narrow planks spanning ditches filled with mustard coloured water.

Many stories abounded of unwary people, or a horse and other animals, being sucked down into the bog, and years later, the bog giving up its dead, but how many of them were true I couldn't say. Recently, on TV, I saw an item on a bog giving up two very well preserved bodies from the ancient Bronze period. I wasn't surprised. I used to imagine there were snakes in the undergrowth, huge ones ready to devour us, and one of those logs could be a snake, couldn't it? There were no snakes, no Anacondas, no Boa Constrictors, but that didn't stop me imagining the worst. A crack, or unusual noise, had me ready for flight. The bog could be a deceptive place. What looked like a patch of fresh green grass was not, it was wet swamp, and to be avoided. Straying from the well beaten paths was not recommended. It may well be all different now, as the bog is a managed nature reserve, but I would still not stray from paths.

In a clearing on the Moor, and a short walk from Worthy End farm, stood an old farmhouse surrounded by an acre or two of cultivated land. This was occupied by a family named Puzzles. That cultivated land was long ago taken over by an aggregates company named Dawson Wham, who obviously saw another use for it to profit them. The company revived the former gravel pit industry and has destroyed whatever Flora and Fauna was on that part of the Moor. If Flitwick residents are not careful, the Moor will be looted of what is left of its peat and natural heritage.

There were plenty of broken twigs and bits of wood lying around, we stuffed them into our sacks before heading back the way we'd come, to store the wood in our dry barn.

Now and again, fires broke out on the bog, usually small outbreaks in very warm dry weather, quite often started deliberately. In August 1950, flames rose so high that Water Lane residents became very alarmed.

The bog is mentioned in the Gore Chambers book of Bedfordshire, held by the County Archives. It says the place is, or used to be, a Botanist's dream, full of plants I never knew the names of. In the late 19th century, it was recorded that the moor was home to at least 720 rare and curious varieties. Large patches of purple Willowherb abounded in late summer, crowding out many other plants. Other wild flowers included Marsh Marigold and Forget me not. A legend I heard of springs to mind:

A knight and his love were walking along the banks of the Blue Danube. They were to be married the following day. Seeing beautiful blue flowers dislodged from the bank, being swept downstream, the lady in the story wept, begging her knight to save them. As he struggled against the current, he cried out

'Forget me not'

194

A farewell gift of Forget me nots on February 29th in a leap year is supposed to bring happiness and contentment to the giver, and a safe journey to the recipient. It is said that Waterloo was covered with masses of Forget me Nots for many years after the battle. Along the verges of the allotments, and along the embankment, were swathes of the lovely pink Campion. I'd pick bunches of it to take home, plonk in a jam jar and place proudly on the sideboard or centre table.

At the Maulden Road end, down from Folly Farm, a narrow gauge railway ran along just inside the boundary of the bog, for the peat trade, which destroyed much habitat. Before North Sea gas was introduced, peat from the bog was used in purifying the old town gas, from approximately 1910, until it closed down in 1967. This part of the Moor was also a great playground for us children.

In the 19th century, Folly Farm tenant Henry King Stevens introduced Flitwick Mineral Water. Very enterprising, selling bottles at 2d a time locally, and sending 10 gallon containers to London. An article in the Lancet of October 1891 goes into great detail over the results of their analysis. Calling it remarkable, very palatable with Lemonade, the Lancet adds,

'It oozes from a fissure in surface cutting about a foot and half deep through a layer of black peat. The crumbly peat, which readily dries, contains a high percentage of oxide of iron, alumina, and phosphoric acid. Under that is a substratum of dark sands which is reputed to belong to the Cretacean period.'

In 1885, the water won a major prize at the National Health Society's Exhibition. Henry died in 1898 age 62. The business was then sold on to soft drinks distributors R.W. White, who kept it going until 1938.

195

As well as selling Flitwick Water, Henry King Stevens was also a very good Taxidermist, his speciality being birds. I recall once, Ernie brought home a stuffed animal, (fox I think), in a glass case. Mum hated it, said it made her flesh creep, and it wasn't long before it was given away. It may well have been one of Henry's works of art, we shall never know.

In the 1901 census, Charles Short is recorded as manager of the Folly Mineral Spring.

There is a short cut through the Moor from Maulden Road to Greenfield, providing access to an area which used to be allotments for the poor of Ampthill and Flitwick. Originally the track had begun in Greenfield Road, but it is said that Richard Goodman, owner of the Mill, had the track diverted to Maulden Road in order for him to build some houses on the site. When I was younger, Mum threatened me with the Bogey man if I was misbehaving. I'd laugh, but was never too sure, for I thought it could have something to do with the bog. A child's imagination can go from the sublime to the ridiculous very easily.

Ernie sometimes related a story from the 1920s, of a man making his way home through the bog from Flitwick to Greenfield, when someone jumped him, (mugged). A fight ensued and he was killed and robbed of his week's wages.

The Moor is now a nature reserve, which means hopefully that it won't be built over.

Chapter 31
THE MANOR

Colonel Lyall took over ownership of the Manor in 1934, after the tenure of the Brookes family had lasted since it was built in 1792. Squire John Thomas Brookes was philanthropic. It is recorded that in 1815, he distributed blankets to 27 lucky poor people. This appeared to be an annual event, so over the years, there must have been quite a number of Brookes blankets in Flitwick homes. One old man broke down in tears of gratitude, saying he'd never received such a fine gift. Were some Stringers among the recipients? Had the villagers been paid better wages, they could have bought their own blankets.

Colonel Lyall, (who died in 1949), gave permission for Fetes in the grounds, especially during the war, to raise funds to provide comforts for the troops. An elderly woman sat at a trestle table just inside an entrance gate off Church hill. Entrance fee, I believe, was 6d for Mum and 3d each for Joyce and I. We walked up the avenue between the Lime trees. I became impatient for a ride on the Carousel as I heard the sound of the fairground organ. Toffee apples for sale, maybe Ice Cream too, from the pokey man on his three wheel specially fitted bicycle. A fairground is not complete without a Carousel, all the better if powered by a steam engine.

Stalls were set up to sell home baking, jams, bottled fruit, surplus garden produce. There was a story that the Manor was haunted by a woman with a strange perfume smell, but it could have came from outdoors, from any number of flowers, or Honeysuckle on a warm evening.

The last Fete I attended at the Manor was in June 1950. The British Legion to held a Rally and Fete in the grounds.

197

You will read elsewhere of the forays I and other children made into the grounds to pillage Conkers from the Horsechestnut trees. Flitwick Water, or the Lake as we knew it, was a little overgrown with pond weed during those years, the ducks and other wildlife enjoyed the environment, and so did we. We slid around on the lake when it iced over in winter.

Did Colonel Lyall have any idea of the misery Mum and others like her were going through? Did he believe the poor brought it all on themselves? It was their weak nature, they drank too much, were feckless, thriftless, behaved improperly, uneducated?

Flitwick Manor is now a hotel. I can go there, have Dinner, and so to bed, a comfortable bed, rise, shower in the en-suite, enjoy a full English breakfast, go for a walk in the grounds, without the Gamekeeper shouting at me to 'Bugger orf.'
(The grounds are now a park).

Chapter 32
DAD'S ARMY

Secretary of State for War, Anthony Eden, in 1940, spoke on the wireless, appealing to men age between 17 and 60, who could hold a rifle, to join the local Defence Force, which later, in July 1940, became the Home Guard. Women admitted to the Home Guard in 1943.

As well as working long hours in the fields for George Woodcraft, Ernie took his stint at Home Guard duty. As an Agricultural worker, he was exempt from call up to the Forces. He was issued with a rifle, and uniform. Once each week, usually Friday, he stripped the rifle down for cleaning, moveable bits spread over a sheet of paper on the living room table. Mum or I cleaned his boots. I cleaned the brass buttons on his uniform, using a metal button protector, which was a flat brass plate in a U shape. It slid between button and jacket, preventing the Brasso liquid marking the khaki cloth. The badge on his cap was cleaned in the same manner. His uniform included a khaki shirt, kept only for Home Guard duties. At the end of the war, he was allowed to keep his uniform, including the greatcoat, which he wore to work in bad weather.

Ernie's younger brother George enlisted and remained in the Army throughout the War. He related a tale about one of the nights Ernie was on duty guarding the entrance to the Ampthill railway tunnel. Appreciative of the quiet night, and despite working all day, he didn't feel particularly tired as he slowly paced back and forth. Ernie heard no giveaway noise as Tom Cat silently and stealthily did the rounds of his patch, on the lookout for a tasty morsel of mouse. When Tom Cat tired of hunting, he decided to make the acquaintance of the chap in khaki quietly smoking a cigarette by the tunnel. Tom Cat made the error of choosing a human who was disinclined to appreciate his company. Ernie jumped with fright as the cat landed deftly on his shoulder.

As Uncle George put it, 'E nearly shit 'isself, thought E were done fer, the jerries had got 'im, but it wor only a cat, tryin' ter be friendly.' The cat was cursed and sent on his way, unceremoniously knocked from Ernie's shoulder. Ernie had told the tale to George, but once George got hold of it, the incident became part of his repartee whenever he got the opportunity. No doubt there was some elaboration in the telling.

Home Guard training took place on the Firs at Ampthill, and at Flitwick Sandpit, next to the station shunting yards.

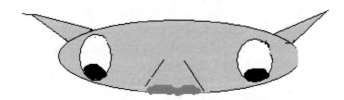

Chapter 33
CAT FOR A DAY

It was around 1947/48, I was either 12 or 13 years of age, when Ginger Tom decided to visit. We had little enough money to feed ourselves, without the responsibility of a pet. I cannot recall anyone in the Alley having a pet, not even a Goldfish.

Ernie bred Rabbits, but as I write in another chapter, we ate them, they were not pets. Beatrice Potter wrote sweet little stories about that lovely bunnikin Peter Rabbit with his fluffy white bobtail. Our big and hefty well fed bunnikins were destined for the dinner table. Mum was a little afraid of dogs, but she considered a good big cat would keep the mice at bay. Ginger Tom seemed to fit the bill. He had a heavy bull like face, and wanted affection in the short time we knew him. He ponged a bit, like all Toms do if they have not been spayed. Ginger Tom was with us too short a time to even think about neutering him. Where would Mum raise the funds for it? No!, poor thing wouldn't be so lucky as to only get a little snip. Ernie told Mum to get rid of the cat. Next day, when he came home for his dinner, Ginger Tom had ingratiated his way back into the house. Ernie grabbed the cat by the scruff of its tough neck and promptly ducked it head first into the water butt beside the barn. I yelled at him to stop, Mum cursed him, the poor cat struggled, but lost the last of his nine lives. Where it had came from I do not know, although there were plenty of strays roaming the village, living off peoples kindness and the abundant mouse population. Ginger Tom made an unfortunate choice when he decided to adopt us.

Mum continued with the mouse traps, Little Nippers, first made about 1897. Anything edible in the trap, the mouse came out of its hole, (we had plenty around the house), whack!! dead mouse!!

Chapter 34
1946 BRIEFLY

The year started off well for me with a party in the school on New Year's Day. We were fed, given the princely sum of sixpence each, and entertained by a concert group.

Each year we held a Christmas Party in school. On those occasions, each child took whatever they could to school, placing it on teacher's desk. A few sandwiches, biscuits, maybe someone's mother had baked a cake. To drink, we did not have bottles or cans of Coca Cola etc, we had the small bottles of milk which were delivered daily to the school. Carols were sung, games were played, such as Stick the tail on the Donkey. Oranges and Lemons, the Grand Old Duke of York, One Man went to Mow. Games which involved all the children in the class enjoying themselves.

In May, a new educational decree was announced. Children to attend primary school until the age of 11, then go, according to ability, to either Grammar School, Technical School, or Modern School, (some of us would stay put). Bread wasn't rationed throughout the war years, but on July 22nd 1946, the Government decided to take this retrograde unpopular step, it remaining on ration until July 1948. Morris of Ampthill, and Vass of Pulloxhill, (whose twice per week bread delivery van came to the Alley), said it would increase wastage. The first thing a newly wed housewife had to buy was a bread knife, as bread already sliced was not on sale yet.

Flitwick housewives never wasted a slice. Birds would have starved had they relied on us for crumbs. In 1946, the Education Department took over the emergency cooking depot in Dunstable Street at Ampthill. Boys to be instructed in woodwork, girls to be taught Domestic Science.

There was an air of relief as men were demobbed from the armed forces. The lack of enough housing and shortages in the shops caused concern. Queueing had became a way of life, time consuming and tiresome. Pre-fabs made their appearance in the village. Hastily began while the war was still raging, the pre-fabricated materials were put together in factories and transported to site, where they could be erected quickly. Usually they were two bedrooms, bathroom, kitchen and living room, providing temporary homes until more conventional construction caught up. Although the life span was meant to be about 20 years, I heard a snippet of news one evening in 2006 which included a report of some pre-fabs in another part of the country still in existence. The residents protesting against being re-housed, they still loved their nice little pre-fabs. Bedford Food Depot, on 12th March 1946, saw the first delivery of Bananas since the start of the war. They were sold out within minutes of hitting the shops. Another month or two and we tasted one Banana. It was shared between Mum, Joyce, and myself.

On the entertainment front, new songs were being sung. The Squadranaires, (Air Force Regiment Band), put out a song called Give me five minutes more of your kiss, very appropriate for sweethearts meeting up again after all those separations. Anne Shelton sang the Anniversary Song, and Kitty Kallen sang another appropriate song, Kiss me once and Kiss me twice, and kiss me once again, its been a long long time.

In October, Goering, one of Hitler's sidekicks, chose to commit suicide during the Nuremburg trials, other Nazis were hanged. In the Alley, Mum's life had little changed. She had never enough money, no personal comforts, Ernie was as abusive as ever.

The National Insurance Bill went through Parliament, to be put into legislation for 1948. Old Age Pensions were implemented right away. 26/- per week, plus 16/- for the man's wife. Suddenly pensioners were a lot better off. Almost as much as an Agricultural Labourer was earning for a week's work.

The Rag and Bone man continued to come in to the Alley from time to time, his horse and cart piled high with whatever he could lay his hands on, although after the war there could not have been much left to salvage, especially from the Alley. No money changed hands. He got the kids on his side by giving us balloons, to get us to look in sheds and barns and beg our Mums to give him something. Mums had to be very watchful in case little Johnnie or Betty gave away the whole contents of Dad's tool shed for a few paltry balloons. During and just after the war, balloons were a rare commodity, so there was no shortage of kids jumping about the cart trying to lay their hands on one. After a year or two, the Rag and Bone man and his cart came no more.

People started to enjoy day trips away, and seaside holidays. Also in 1946, the ban on fraternising with the Germans was lifted.

I corresponded for several years with Enid Palmer, who lived at Folly Farm during the 1940s. She told me conditions on the farm were just as bad as our hovels in the Alley. We were not the only ones still suffering such outdated Victorian conditions.

In December, the weather turned nasty and a fuel shortage existed. See the Fuel chapter for how we coped.

Chapter 35
WASHDAY BLUES

Twas on a Monday morning, that I beheld my darling
she looked so neat and charming, in every high degree
she looked so neat and charming oh, a washing of her linen oh,
dashing away with the smoothing iron, she stole my heart away

I've just completed a basketful of ironing, with my modern very good electric iron. As you will read, Mum had no easy to use laundry equipment. Quite frankly, I do not know what I would do without my automatic washing machine. I can go to work or do the chores while it happily swishes around. Mum had none of that convenience. She got up at 5.30 or 6 a.m. stepped out on to cold floorboards, put her shoes on, (she had no slippers).

The first chore was to clean out the ashpan under the firegrate. Wearing the same clothes she had worn the day before, and slept in overnight, she splashed a little cold water on her face. The cock a doodle doing at Wilson's farm in Water Lane usually woke her up.

Mum had no copper boiler or washhouse when we were living in the Alley. All over Flitwick, other housewives were also rising early to get the fires going and prepare breakfast. Mum took kindling from the coal hole under the stairs, small lumps of coal, and a firelighter or two, (little napthan soaked squares bought from Cousins shop). In the front of the grate, low down, a knob, when pulled to one side, moved part of the front grill to produce a draught under the fire, making it blaze up quicker. During the day, Mum had to keep topping the fire up, to keep a blaze going.

The old range was difficult to clean. Using Zebo or Zebrite

black leading, which Mum bought in a tube, and using a shoe brush, it was rubbed all over the grate, then shone it up with rags, usually about twice each week. I helped her clean it sometimes.

Kettle boiled, Ernie washed and shaved in the kitchen, (he did not shave every day), using the same basin as Mum used to wash laundry and the dishes. Bread an Jam for breakfast, then he came home at 9.30am for a half hour break, (called Bever time, pronounced Bavour), when he'd have toast, or occasionally, a bowl of Three Bears Porridge, quick to prepare. We never had a breakfast of bacon, eggs, black pudding etc. I have only heard the word Bever in Bedfordshire. If he was working too far away to come home for his half hour bever, he always had a breakfast of sorts before he set off, and took sandwiches with him.

Ernie worked on the Threshing machine at harvest time, perhaps at Clophill, Silsoe, Shillington. He picked Brussel Sprouts in frozen conditions. We called it Brusseling. It was hard work. Woodcraft specialised in Sprouts. Although a nasty cruel man at home, Ernie was experienced, knowledgeable and skilled in his job.

Another job in the winter months was Hedging and Ditching, done in days gone by with axe, shovel, shears and scythe, but today, it is done by machine. A dirty cold job, for which workers should have been better paid. Also, and this is not always mentioned, workers had to buy all their working clothes themselves. If off sick, they were not paid. Ernie wore bib and brace overalls over his working clothes. Many ditches which carried surplus water away have been filled in, ploughed over, or built over today, a mistake in my opinion, and could be the cause of much flooding.

After Ernie left for work on his bike, Mum roused Joyce and I for school. Breakfast for us was mainly a couple of slices of bread and jam, even perhaps a slice of bread and dripping, the dripping doused in salt. A cup of weak tea and we were on our way. If we had porridge, a little milk was added, and a sprinkling of sugar.

By the time Joyce and I were off to school, Mum had placed the tub of washing across the fire in the range. Water bubbling, she stirred the laundry around to distribute the soapiness. How she took the tin wash tub/bath off the range I can't recall. She must have always carried the risk of being scalded by the hot water.

I often helped her put rinsed items through the rollers of the mangle, which stood between the table by the kitchen window and the door to the yard. Mum soaked other laundry, such as dirty nappies, in a pail of water which had washing soda crystals added. Mum removed her cardigan, revealing strong plump arms, and proceeded to hand wash those clothes which did not need boiling, using Fairy or Sunlight bars of washing soap, always bought in small quantities. Used frugally. She did not have a scrubbing board, her hands red and sore many times. The washing was then strung on the outdoor washing line. A long enough stretch, and the weight of the wet washing made the line sag, bringing the wet things dangerously near the ground where they'd get dirty again. This was remedied by the use of a clothes pole. Simply a length of wood about 1 inch x 2 inch thick, with a slot cut into one end. With a heave, the slotted end was jammed into the washing line and lifted upwards, with the other end of the pole firmly anchored into the ground of the dirt yard.

Today, we do not see the waste water going from our automatic washing machines into our drains and away to wherever it goes. In the Alley all our waste water was taken outside and tipped onto a patch of grass situated between the Watson's house and a field of vegetables. To this day, I marvel at the way women, just like Mum, coped. She seemed to have a strength born of necessity, but after the diabetic coma she suffered, most of that strength left her.

As the whites boiled in the tub over the fire, Mum prepared the Clanger (Bedfordshire meat dumpling) for dinner. It needed at least one and half hours to steam in the cooking pot to be ready in time for Ernie coming home for dinner at 1p.m. The washing tub had to be removed from the fire by 11.30a.m. On rainy days, the laundry was draped over the fireguard rail, where scorching could occur if not careful. Some cottages had an outhouse, or scullery attached, where a copper boiler, with a little firegrate underneath, was situated. The washing on a wet day could be hung up to dry in these warm outhouses.

Kath Wooding, (nee See), told me her mother also drew water from a Well shared with neighbours same as us in the Alley. They had a sink in their small kitchen, but no taps. They put water into the sink from a pail, and added hot water from the kettle. The waste water did not go into a drain, but through a pipe from the sink to a bucket outside, then the waste water was tipped onto the garden. That was typical of cottages which had a sink, but no taps or drains. Kath's father also did the same as us when the shit bucket was in danger of overflowing, he emptied the contents into the garden.

The lack of resources was an enormous load for Mum to bear. Poverty grinds people down. Her history was one of poverty, and she was still being dealt a duff hand. No instant hot water, central heating, washing machine, electricity, gas, or labour saving devices to make life easier, so little income. Primitive sanitation.

As you will see when I discuss budgeting, a man on a good salary, although not wealthy, could provide his wife with the help of a maid. The maid did the dirty and laborious jobs around the house. WOW!! a maid to help around the house. Mum could dream on.

She went down on her knees to wash the floor, just plain water as she could not afford the cleaners then available, and soap was rationed. If it was a choice between a loaf of bread or a packet of cleaning powder, then the loaf won. Mum certainly knew that Lemon juice and Vinegar made a good cleaner and polisher, but Lemons were not usually available. I often cleaned the sideboard for her, using Vinegar and elbow grease alone.

Gypsies came round the doors selling Dolly pegs which they made themselves, they made and sold baskets too. There will still be some of those baskets and Dolly pegs being used by a few older villagers. I have Dolly pegs bought over 40 years ago.

Most of my clothes went unpressed, white cardigans looking rather grey and grubby. A year or so down the line, by the time I was around 13, I was pressing my own clothes, ironing out depressing pegmarks. I got upset when Mum disturbed my neat pile. It was more of a nuisance to try and heat the iron just right. Girls were expected to help their mothers about the house, boys expected to help their fathers with outside chores.

As well as detergents and soap powders, and the bars of washing soap, all of them rationed, Mum used little sachets of Dolly Blue, made by Reckitt and Colman. The fine blue powder, when added to the wash, were supposed to enhance the whites, in the same manner as today's modern washing powders, which have the blue subtly included, do the same job. The Dolly Blue came in a little muslin sachet, about the size of man's thumb. The little square of muslin, the blue powder placed on it, and drawn up into a pouch, had a tiny plug of wood placed in the neck of the sachet, all anchored in with a length of fine thread, preventing the powder from leaking out. When rinsing the wash, Mum placed one of these little sachets in the water, and the blue seeped out through the muslin, tinting the water. Dolly Blue could be bought in most small general stores and Ironmongers well up to the 1970s. I do like to see a man in a crisp clean shirt and his shoes polished.

Ironing was particularly awkward. We had no electric or gas iron. It was an old fashioned flat iron, made of heavy cast iron, which had to be heated against the fire. When hot enough it was taken from the heat, the handle wrapped around with a cloth to prevent our hands burning. A damp towel or piece of cloth wiped over it to remove any sooty deposit before using. Some homes had two or three of these irons, heating one while the other was being used. We had only one, so ironing took a little more time. Before ironing, I'd spit on the base of the iron, to test the heat. The spit bubbled, and how it bubbled determined how hot it was. Too hot and it could scorch, too cold and it was useless.

For Ernie's cotton shirts, the iron had to be very hot. Mum did not iron his working shirts. By the time I was 12 or 13, I was pressing Ernie's good trousers, Mum said I made a good job of it. Using a square of brown paper, the kind parcels were wrapped in, and a very hot iron, the paper placed on one leg, then the other, each side, I pressed those trousers, the paper preventing shine. If no paper, I used a damp cloth, then draped the trousers over the back of a chair to dry them off. Old flat irons are now used as doorstops.

I can now understand why Mum hated ironing. It was so tiresome, time consuming, the iron having to be heated at the fire.

An old blanket and a clean bit of sheeting laid across the living room table served as an ironing board. Ironing boards were hard to come by during the war years. Even after the war, supplying the home market was suppressed in favour of exporting. Homes where they were lucky enough to have gas or/and an electricity supply found ironing somewhat easier with a gas or electric iron. The flex was long enough to reach up to the ceiling, into the central light fitting, on a double fitting which could have the light bulb and the iron plugged in at the same time. There were one or two drawbacks, such as no safety cut outs, and mishaps could occur, such as one day when Alvis's mother had been ironing. She folded the ironing, put it away, went to bed, forgetting to unplug the flex. The family were awoken during the night by smoke. There, still hanging by the flex was the iron. It had burned through the wooden worktop in the kitchen, causing a hole in the shape of the iron, and the worktop was smouldering. An unattended iron can cause tragic accidents.

Below, flat iron, and mangle………….

Chapter 36
FUEL

1947 started off a very cold year indeed, the coldest winter since 1881. December 1946 had been extremely cold. January and February saw some of the worst snowfalls and storms in living memory, certainly some of the worst of the century, and the worst floods recorded in England happened on March 15th with the Ouse bursting its banks. No talk of Global warming those months.

Between 25th January and 16th March the snow lay unmelted, (51 days)), and March was the wettest month. Ponds and lakes froze over, and to pile misery on misery, a hurricane occurred on 16/17th March.

1st January, the coal industry was nationalized. The many power cuts didn't affect us in the Alley, as we had no electricity.

Although the coal ration was around 5 bags per week, Mum had not enough money to buy that lot, at 4/6 per bag. The one bag of coal Mum could afford was upturned into the coal hole under the stairs, clouds of dust exploded, sending coal dust all over the house.

Again, it was the lack of enough income which prevented her buying all her needs, then she would not have had to resort to the kind of activity I am about to relate to you.

Our old black range had an insatiable appetite, burning all day, every day. A lot of things were changing, but one thing did not change and that was our need for fuel, even in the height of summer on days such as June 3rd , when temperatures soared to 90f, because if there was no fire on she had no means of boiling water or cooking. The mineworkers threatened to strike for more pay. They had the strength of the union at that period in their history.

Water from the Well, fuel for the fire, were essential.

You could say life was simple, I say life was primitive, debasing, and hard work for Mum, her parents, her grandparents, and all those on poverty wages. Modern women would kick up a fuss, and even Asylum seekers coming from countries poorer than this one do not have to endure such conditions as many of the women in Flitwick did during those years. Women brought up families without financial help from the Social Services honey pot in conditions you and I would not tolerate today.

From the week in 1940, when we moved from Toddington to Flitwick, the forays on to the railway line to pick up those nuggets of black gold became a necessity, and especially so in 1947. Two or three times each week, after tea, I went with Mum, May Watson, some Stringers, Millie Barnes, and one or two others, to glean coal from the railway line. Coaling as we called it was highly illegal, and dangerous.

Caught on the railway without permission could mean a hefty fine, and/or imprisonment. Coal fell from the wagons as they swayed and wobbled round the bend in the line between Westoning and Flitwick, shaking and rattling as they approached Ellis and Everard's, and Franklin's coal yards by the station.

We were trespassing. Fortunately no one was killed or injured, apart from a few bumps and scratches, not from the trains, but by hiding from the station master (I believe his name was Victor Crawley), when he made an effort to catch us. We always made our escape easily. Arresting any of the women would have caused a riot. In those days there were no mobile phones, and the women may well have upset his dignity by removing his trousers and shoes.

Whichever way you look at it, the man was best staying put in his warm little office. Desperately poor, Mum found this source of fuel just one of the ways to keep the fire going. Ernie remained at home to look after Joyce, she was too young.

We stuffed sacks with lumps of coal, large and small, the women cracking jokes, gossiping, some grumbling about one thing and another, then we headed for home as quickly as our legs could carry us, to empty the sacks into the coal hole or barn. I was 12 years old in 1947 and quite capable of carrying a half sack of coal home. Thick jute sacks, normally used for carrying produce to market.

Trains were a hazard, but steam engines are noisy, not difficult to hear, even on windy nights. In the winter when the moon and stars were shining, our haul was heavy because we could see every shiny lump, big or small. Rainy and cloudy, it took a bit longer as we fumbled around the tracks for the treasure. I would not advise going on the railway line these days, the deisel and electric trains are faster, quieter, and the line is electrified. No more coal falls on to the line, as wagons are now covered.

Sometimes the stars shone like beautiful little diamonds of light, the moonlight so bright it was like daylight, as we worked along the tracks, sometimes going as far as Harlington. When a train approached from Westoning, we worked on until it got to within less than 50 yards, then we jumped well clear to let it pass. The engine driver, on seeing us, cursed, and May Watson, cigarette hanging from her lip as usual, cursed back. 'Come on, come on, Oh 'ees a slow bugger aint ee Flo,' and shouting at the driver to get a move on as wagon after wagon trundled by.

Coal rationing began on March 17th 1942, and was still on ration in 1947. Like many other commodities, if someone had the cash, they could get extra. There were times when the coalman called and I was sent to the door to tell the man Mum wasn't in. Mum was hiding behind the living room door, ashamed she had not enough money to pay him.

The sack of coal already on his back, he dumped it in the coal hole, saying she could pay him next week. The next time he called, he came to the door for his money before taking the sack off the cart. If Mum still could not pay him, she got no more until it was paid.

We all know money does not ensure happiness, but the lack of enough money for even very basic needs such as heat, light, and food, caused a lot of unhappiness. An empty purse is not a pretty sight, an empty belly is worse, and shivering beside an empty grate compounds the misery. Save the Children Fund are running an advertisement on TV as I write, and I agree with every word. Children living in poverty stricken homes in this wealthy country of ours today are being denied their human rights. The poverty Mum went through was etched on her face all through her life. It is easy to say she should have risen above it. With support, a less brutal husband, and better health care she might have done. If there was any way out, she didn't know of it. It never occurred to Ernie that we really could not afford his smoking habit. Mum may just have been able to manage a little better.

As well as gleaning coal from the railway line, Mum went wooding, mostly on Flitwick Moor as mentioned earlier, where fallen branches and twigs were abundant, particularly after a storm. Clearing undergrowth of debris was permitted, it encouraged new growth, and Firebote, collecting wood from common land had been a tradition for centuries among the poor. Hedges beside public footpaths and around the fields also provided firewood.

Today, many of the tracks we walked, and collected wood from, (most of them were public rights of way), have gone, are lost in the shrouds of history. In this day and age we do not use footpower to get from A to B so much. The old shortcuts, where they exist, are little used. Just about anywhere there were a copse or

215

belt of trees was good wood gathering territory for us.

It is just as well most homes are now centrally heated, I doubt very much if modern Mums would do the same as my Mum did. Modern Mums do not have to clean out ashes every morning before they can put the kettle on. We have plenty of labour saving gadgets and equipment today. Mum couldn't even flick a lightswitch on.

The allotments off Station Road is one small area not yet taken over by a developer. Wouldn't it be nice if the powers that be let it remain a green place. It is now too late to do anything about it.

It is a pity that Flitwick's early town planners did not make provision for more green space within the town, allowing for at least one substantial central park. We cannot call the present Rec a park, it is too small. The Wood, the park by the Manor, and the Moor, are not central. I'm no stick in the mud. When house building began in earnest after the war, it was welcomed with open arms. The town I now live in has two central parks, and two golf courses.

Sometimes Ernie trailed home a large branch tied to the back of his bike. He sawed it into logs, using our joiner's style wooden horse, and I chopped those logs into smaller pieces, using an axe and the chopping block in the barn. By about 1948/49 I went wooding on my own, to the Moor. If a bit of wood was too long to go in the sack I placed it on the ground, put my foot in the centre and pulled one half of the wood sharply upwards. Snap, the long piece became two smaller pieces, fitting into the sack. Spindly long lengths were snapped over my knee. Dragging the sacks, I made my way from the bog, along Water Lane to the Alley, to deposit my haul in the barn. Some women used an old pram to carry the wood home. Boys used their go-carts.

In later years, when Mum was ill and very weakened by Diabetes, I recalled how strong she used to be, carrying those heavy sacks of coal, and all the other heavy work she did. In the bitter winter at the start of 1947 there would have been no fuel in the house had Mum not gone coaling and wooding, often knee deep in snow. If down to her last lump of coal, we went out, whatever the weather, hail rain snow wind, didn't matter, to the railway line, to the bog, to gather more fuel. We just could not phone up the coalman and plead for another bag of coal, how could we pay for it?

Recently, I spent a day pruning the shrubs in the garden. The prunings went into a heap at the bottom of the garden to be shredded later, not fed on to a blazing home fire.

In the centre of the dining table in the living room stood the plain brass based oil lamp. The base tapered up, with a slight central bulge, topped by a bulbous glass chimney which needed cleaning daily to keep a clear light. A wick soaked up the Paraffin from the reservoir, (in the central bulge). Replacement wicks were easily obtained from most of the shops in Flitwick. It gave an adequate light at the table, but corners of the room were gloomy. There always was a sooty deposit on the ceiling above where the lamp was placed. We used a candle stuck on a saucer in the kitchen, and the same to make our way upstairs.

Paraffin for the lamp was bought from Cousins shop. I took a tin canister, it held about half a gallon, to be filled from a tank outside the back shop. I never saw a plastic container, I don't know if they existed. Some people put paraffin in a glass pop bottle. A law was introduced, making such practices illegal. Alvis and I owned a local small shop in the 1960s. One day a man requested I put paraffin in a Lemonade bottle. When I refused, he became so abusive, I had to call the police.

Chapter 37
BICYCLES

The 1940s was an age of the bicycle. P.C. Upchurch went about his business on a bike, not whizz about the village in a striped or chequered car. Men went to work on their bike, perhaps leaving it at the station and travelling to Luton or Bedford on the train. Women went shopping on a bike, a shopping basket strapped to the front strut. Mum could never ride a bike, but I did.

One day, I'd be around 12 years old, maybe coming up 13, and Ernie arrived home with an old bike, telling me it was mine. Ugh I looked at it aghast. It was very old fashioned, with a low curved crossbar, first built for women who wore Edwardian long skirts.
It was rusty. I was not very appreciative of it, and thought he should have been paid for taking it off someone, instead of paying them. He gave it a coat of black paint, it looked a little better.

Claude Barnes, when I was speaking to him during the course of my research for this book, told me that Ernie had retrieved the bike from the village dump along the Ridgeway. I believed him, for Ernie did rummage over the dump now and then. Ernie held the saddle for me as I wobbled up and down the Alley a couple of times, and then I went hurtling down on my own, over confident, couldn't stop, Crash!! into a bed of nettles. Stinging from head to toe, cursing the bike, and wobbling many more times, determined not to be beat.

Although I did not like the design of the bike, it was highly unlikely I'd get a better one. We had no safety helmets or any of the other safety gear which are considered required accessories today. It was just me, the bike, and dodgy brakes. Ernie fixed the brakes a day or two later, bought me a bicycle pump, and dynamo lamp.

Ernie repaired the bike along with his own when a puncture

occurred. Turning the bike upside down in the yard beside the barn, he loosened the inner tube, dunked it in water, swizzled it around until he found the leak, then marked the spot with chalk, repairing it with a rubber patch.

Most of the small shops in Flitwick, and Sharpe's store opposite the station, sold little tin boxes of puncture repair outfits.

Ernie had two bikes, and for two or three years he also owned a tandem. He and Alfie Barnes or one of the older Watson lads rode it to Luton almost every Saturday. I don't know what the lads got up to, but Ernie went to see his lady friend Mabel Flecker, and to Darts matches. Aunt Daphne told me about Mabel, who he'd met while playing darts. She also told me that while Mum was struggling to manage on the rations and whatever came out of the garden, Ernie took stuff, (her words), that means food, to Mabel Flecker, pretending he was taking it to his sister Millie who lived in Willow Way Leagrave. Even after he sold the tandem, he still smartened up on Saturdays and cycled over to Luton until around 1949.

When I was about 13, Aunt Daphne and Uncle George, (Sally and Bubbles), who had been living with us, moved to Haynes West End. Bubbles had found a job on a farm. I often cycled over to visit them. Usually I went via Maulden, but one fine summer day I used one of Ernie's bikes and rode via Flitton. On the hill leaving Flitton for Maulden, I was freewheeling when OOOPS!! I went too close to the grassy bank and flew over the handlebars. I lay dazed on the grass, fortunately my head missed a large boulder. I would not be sitting here writing this had my head made contact. I was curious to see a spring called Holli'ton basin, It was rumoured that to fall in was to disappear forever. The bike not badly damaged I carried on my way, but Ernie was less than pleased I borrowed his bike.
I never cycled to school. Some children did. A cycle rack was built

under a canopy this side of the new lavatory block. Children received new bikes as Christmas or Birthday presents, showing them off. I should have counted myself lucky to have any old bike, but still wished for a new one.

If I had been allowed to keep the money I saved in the school penny bank, (instead of buying shoes etc), I may well have eventually had enough to buy a new bike, but it wasn't to be.
I couldn't blame Mum or Ernie. He'd done his best to provide me with a bike, and Mum never had enough money for her needs. She must have wished many times that she had a nice cooker, new furnishings, nice clothes and so on. Even a kitchen sink.

Going to the shops, riding around the Alley, the old bike was OK, it was practical, and I soon got over that it wasn't a new one. Many women in Flitwick rode the same kind of bike, so it wasn't really all that strange. Mum sold my bike a few months before I left school, saying I would not need it after I started work.

Chapter 38
AN ENEMY PLANE

One day during the war, a German plane crashed into a field just off Flitwick Road, in Westoning. Children and adults together rushed to Westoning as soon as word went round about the crash. To look at it, and to see what could be salvaged before it was taken away. The pilot had gone by the time I got there, he may well have been dead. If not, he would be another Prisoner of War. Compassion is hard to feel when the only reason he was in that field in Westoning was because he'd been sent over here to bomb us. Usual remarks I overheard were, 'The only good German is a dead one.'

Whoever saw the crash must have alerted the village bobby. I felt very excited, I'd never been close to a plane before. It seemed so huge. Although damaged, it was still an impressive sight to my young eyes. Local men were already there, stripping the plane of anything remotely re-usable, including the perspex windscreen. The men shared the loot between them. Ernie fashioned some rings from his chunk of Perspex, and sold them on. He didn't make much money. I am certain that by the time the authorities arrived, there was little more than the shell to tow away.

A plane crash nearby was a rarity.

Each night, searchlights lit up the sky, shafts of light beaming out in white ribbons through the darkness, picking out the dark shapes of enemy planes. This one at Westoning had not been able to shake off the ack ack guns. Either that or the plane had ran out of fuel, because it is said they had a limited time to deliver their bombs and get back smartly to the continent before the fuel tank emptied. Later on, I will describe how two Germans came to tea with us after the war was over, and I formed a very different opinion of them.

221

Chapter 39
MONEY MATTERS

A German plane crashes in a Westoning field

In the summer months, I went with Mum, other women, other children, to the fields, to fill baskets with full green pea pods, working for George Woodcraft or other Market Gardeners.

A few pea pods in the basket, open a pod, eat some, another few pods in the basket, eat some more. The women were too intent to earn as much as they could to slow down, although a stop was made at midday for sandwiches, which they had brought with them, along with flasks of tea. Often, a field could be stripped in less time, either morning or afternoon.

Mum earned enough to put a little extra into her purse. Not for luxury, not for going from shop to shop and splurging on the latest fashions, but to have enough for everyday needs, and catch up on debts. Peasing, and Potato lifting gave her the opportunity to get ahead, have a few shillings to spare.

Eventually I started filling my own baskets, earning money for myself. I stopped fooling around and really got cracking. Not as fast as the women, but I earned a few shillings during the holidays.

Miss Sharp, one of the teachers, introduced me to the savings ethic. She ran the school penny bank. Children from around the Alley did not receive pocket money, we worked for it when we had the opportunity, otherwise we went without.

When I was around 9 or 10 years old, Ernie took me to Woodcraft's field, put a hoe in my hands and told me to 'hoe that row,' so I duly did as I was told, and hoed all the weeds from that row, the next and the next. That would be called organic farming.

Another task I learned was how to nip the tendrils on runner beans. They grew bigger and fatter if the long tendrils were nipped back. So a hoeing, and a bean nipping I went, on school holidays or in the evenings after tea during the summer months. Not every day, only when the jobs needed doing. Sitting across the crossbar on his bike, before I got my own bike, Ernie took me to whichever field was to be worked on.

I enjoyed the opportunity of having some cash of my own, and I gave some to Mum. I bought cheap books at the jumble sales, seldom sweets, they were rationed and Mum had sold most of the coupons. I only needed to be shown how to do something once, and got on with it. Summer and Autumn were potato lifting times. In the early 1940s, we followed two big shire horses, as they swayed gently up and down the field, pulling the farming equipment. Up the field, turn, and turn over another furrow. Later, the horses were replaced by tractors.

Most of the women and children at our end of the village went potato lifting. Each woman or older child such as myself, was set a certain width (a stint). When that was finished we were given another stint and paid according to our efforts. (not by the hour).

We walked or cycled to the fields, but if the field to be

223

worked was too far distant, such as Pulloxhill or Clophill, a lorry picked us up in Station Road, opposite the Crown pub. Clambering on to the back of the lorry, we joined other boisterous yelling noisy kids. The boys sat with their legs over the tailboard, ready to jump off quickly as soon as we reached the field. Health and Safety aficionados would go bananas if they saw that kind of thing today. Nattering women, wearing flowery overalls, and old coats over that, wellington boots or heavy old shoes on feet, some with gloves, some not. Mum wore old socks on her hands, finger and thumb holes roughly cut in. The women wore headscarves or an old hat, some kept their curlers in. When we reached the field, the horse and digger, or tractor was already working up and down. Boys jumped from the back of the lorry, women ran to get started.

We also lifted potatoes on Sabey's fields. (of East End Farm), and Brittain of Worthy End Farm. I never got a pay packet, just the cash put into my hand by whoever was sent to pay us.

All through the war years, the Government urged the country's farmers to grow peas and potatoes. In the peasing field, an old stool, or even an upturned bucket, served as a seat while stripping the shaws of peapods.

A driver and mate weighed each bagful as they were filled. Full bags were weighed with a weighing machine which was hand held. It had a ring at top to hold, and a hook below to hook into the sack, which, when lifted off the ground made the dial of the gadget whizz round, giving the precise weight. The contraption was made of brass and widely used in agriculture. Pea picking and potato lifting were great fun as well as hard work, but sore on the back. The women cracked jokes, and laughter was infectious. They complained of the menfolk, particularly their husbands, the price of food, the shortages, gossiped about people not present, chided the children,

224

while all the time busy hands kept moving.

Another source of income for me was running errands for Millie Barnes or anyone else who wanted something from the shops. Millie was very generous to me. She suffered arthritis, and eventually in later life, she was doubled over so badly, unable to straighten up. She gave me a threepenny bit every time I went anywhere for her, and that was at least four or five times each week. She gave birth to Sheila in 1945 and I enjoyed taking her out in her pram. Up and down the Alley, up Maulden Road, down Water Lane, up and down Station Road or Kings Road, Sheila was never any trouble as long as the pram kept moving. Millie was able to get on with her housework, and when I returned, she said, 'eres summat fer yer,' and handed me the threepence. She eventually met a Welsh man by the name of David Meyrick, and he moved in with her.

1950 and it came time for me to start my career in the retail industry. I had wanted to become a Milliner, and that part was easy. I applied to the hat factories, was accepted for an apprenticeship, to start the following January. I left school on July 21st but could not remain idle for nearly six months, so had to look for a temporary job to do me until January.

To get the clothes to look neat and tidy for interviews, I spent three weeks working most days for George Woodcraft. The Tally man brought me a very smart grey flannel coat to try on, couple of skirts, blouses, pair of shoes. A handbag bought in Ampthill. I can't recall the total cost, but the coat I do remember was £6. I paid him as much as I could from the money I had earned at Woodcraft's, the rest was to be paid 1 shilling per week. I gave Mum the shilling each week for her to pay the Tally man, as I worked on Saturdays. Jobs were easier to come by in 1950. Although I left school with no paper qualifications, I didn't need them for shop or factory work, or even for an office junior position. I did apply unsuccessfully for office jobs, but the School had not prepared me for the commercial world.

Sylvia Stringer, (Hutchins), who was one or two years older than me, told me Marks and Spencer took on temporary staff for the Christmas season, so it seemed the ideal solution. I went to Luton, saw a Supervisor, and was interviewed within the week. Got the job, as a Trainee Sales Assistant on three months trial, to start on 14th August. Pay to be £2-2s and 6d (Two pounds, two shillings and sixpence). I soon resumed the savings ethic begun by Miss Sharp and joined the National Savings scheme at work, having 2/6 (half a crown, or 12.5p decimal), taken off my wages weekly. The first two or three months were a struggle. I worked on an extremely tight budget, using the bus instead of the train to get to work for the first 9 or 10 months because bus fares were cheaper. Three course lunches in Marks and Spencer canteen were just 4d per day, a great help. It all had to be paid out of the money I had left over after paying Mum her share for my board. I was independent, even if hard up.

My hours were five days of 8 hours each day except Sunday, when the store did not open. Wednesday (4hours), the store closed at 1pm for the half day. We had 1 hour for lunch, unpaid. I had to carry a little book, for purchases (except food) to be marked in, signed by the counter assistant and the supervisor, (as a receipt to prove payment). Every six months the amounts were totalled up, and 33% discount paid to me in cash with my wages.

Every few months I sent my bank book to the Savings Department of the Post Office where they marked in the amount saved. I could then take it to the Post Office to make a withdrawal. Buy shoes, or have a hair perm.

By Christmas I'd had 3 wage increases of half a crown each time. When I was offered and accepted a position as permanent

226

staff, I received another increase, and I remained with M & S for another eleven years, not all at Luton. I moved on to Bedford, then Falkirk in Scotland. In 1957 the Edinburgh store first opened its doors. As I lived in Edinburgh, I did not need to commute to Falkirk any more. I was among the first members of staff to prepare the store for opening day. I had reached Supervisor level, now responsible for the intake of stock for the new store.

I never did become a Milliner.

The contribution I made to Mum's housekeeping in those early days, after I started working at Luton meant a great deal to her. She had my money to pay the weekly rent of the Dunstable Road house where we'd moved to in the Spring of 1950.

Ernie insisted on coming with me to the interview for the job with M & S. I felt so embarrassed.

A little incident illustrated the kindness shown to me by some Flitwick folk who knew how poor Mum was. I had to run down Kings Road to the corner of Maulden Road to get the bus to work. There was just the one bus which would get me to work on time. It came from Bedford, through Ampthill, Maulden, to Flitwick for 8 a.m. then on to Greenfield, Pulloxhill, Silsoe and so to Luton. I had to rise about 7 a.m. to have breakfast and get ready. (Mum always made me a cup of tea and some toast, even if we didn't always have cornflakes or any other cereal).

One morning, I was running down Kings Road for the bus when a woman from one of the houses called to me. It was November and the weather was taking a turn for the worse. She gave me a pair of gloves, saying she had seen me passing every morning without gloves on. I thanked her and accepted. (I would never throw a kindness back in anyone's face). I don't know if that kind of thing would happen today.

227

Chapter 40
FROST and SNOW

In the deep winter, when all the countryside is bathed in white thick frost, it makes for a pretty picture postcard. It is not so good for getting around, and it wasn't so good for us in the Alley, in our bedroom.

The bedroom I slept in faced westwards towards the railway, which appeared like a black pencil mark across a sheet of white paper. The room was freezing cold, as cold as outside. It made getting out of bed very uninviting. Joyce and I shared a bed. We had a couple of thin blankets supplemented with old coats, cardigans, and wore the clothes we'd had on all the previous day.

I lay in bed gazing at the marvellous patterns Jack Frost made on the window panes, patterns as fancy as the best cut glass, crystal, or lace. So beautiful. My imagination as usual went into overdrive. I made up pictures in the patterns. My shoes on, I went over to the window and let my warm breath create a gap in the pattern, to look out at fields awash with the same frost, like a thick dusting of icing sugar on a cake. Days went by without the window defrosting. Downstairs in the living room, the only warm room in the house, the window ran with condensation.

Each winter brought Jack Frost to the village, along with the snowman, and sheets of ice. Although we had no real skates, we still enjoyed sliding on any icy patch we could take advantage of. We made slides on the tarmac road beside our dirt yard, near the Well. Then we lengthened the slide down to Millie Barnes house, and on to a dip in the alley where it joined Station Road. If we fell over, we picked ourselves up and started all over again. We made a slide on Vicarage hill. It wasn't a proper roadway then, only a farm track.
No thought given to elders having to negotiate the treacherous surface.

Ernie had potatoes stored in a clamp. A shallow pit, laid with straw, plus a final layer of straw before the lot was covered with soil. Mum or Ernie dug into the clamp as she needed supplies, until about February or March when the store became depleted. Ernie dug the straw back into the garden. He grew Cabbage and Brussel Sprouts. They survived the frost, as did the Turnips.

I would be surprised if there was a pair of skis anywhere in Flitwick at that time. During the war, Bavarian Alps were out of bounds, as were French and Italian Alps. Many parts of Scotland were out of bounds too, being used as training grounds for the Forces. Those places were also expensive to travel to.

The pond near the school always iced over in severe weather, such as in 1947. To the rear of the pond was a narrow belt of trees, partly forming a shelter for the pond. The ice could look deceptively thick. Stepping gingerly on to the ice, we'd take the risk, but a crack or two sent us rushing for the bank, stepping on chunks of ice breaking up under our feet. Fortunately there were no serious accidents. In the yard outside my house, we threw snowballs, until our hands were too cold. Mum plunged my hangs in a bowl of warm water, it hurt, I wailed, but it did the trick.

In the winter, Ernie arrived home a little earlier for his tea, about the same time as I arrived home from school. We ate our tea, but I was not welcome indoors. Mum said, 'Let her stay in, it's snowing out there,' or 'It's raining and cold,' but Ernie always replied, 'She can goo out ter play, a bit o' rain won't 'urt er.' It could be cold, dark, (no street lights), freezing, and all my friends, even the Watson family, were indoors listening to the wireless or playing records on the gramaphone.

Yes, I did feel resentful, and wondered why I could be so excluded. Why was I pushed out? Playing with my friends in the cold was no hardship, we seldom felt cold as we chased each other around, but on my own? well that was different. Suddenly, on my own, there is too much cold, it is lonely, dark, and I felt bitterly unhappy about it. I did protest, Mum protested, but Ernie was adamant, I had to go outside. If I stood my ground and would not budge, I was physically pushed outdoors. If Mum said too much, she was hit and swore at by Ernie. He was small in stature, small minded, discourteous, ill-bred, bad tempered, a bullying control freak, ill mannered, and I grew to utterly detest him.

Claude Barnes mentioned that Ernie used to lock me in the barn, although I cannot recall it. I only remember being in there, climbing up on the the strong heavy crossbeam, wrapping my hands around my knees, feeling sore done to, but dreaming of better things as the wind and rain bounced off the tiles.

Ernie bullied Mum constantly. Selfish, self centred, and so utterly possessive right up until the day she died. When Mum reached the stage when she could do little for herself, and he was ill with Bronchitis, he would not accept a Home help, saying he did not want strangers traipsing in and out. It laid a heavy burden on Pat, his youngest daughter, who was the only one who still lived in Flitwick.

She did the shopping. He was distrustful of others.

His only redeeming feature was his skill as a gardener. The people he worked with had little clue to what he was like at home. An incident happened in 1981, just a few months before Mum died, which illustrates his utterly selfish nature. How could someone who grew such beautiful flowers and vegetables be so cruel? I was in Flitwick on one of my twice yearly visits to Mum from my home almost 400 miles away in Scotland. Her health had deteriorated rapidly from my previous visit, and she'd had two toes removed. She could not see anything, and I sensed she was feeling very low.

Ernie and Mum had moved from the house in Dunstable Road to one of those nice tidy little pensioners bungalows in Billington Close. The front garden was a profusion of Roses, some floribunda, some were large tea Roses, all in full splendid bloom, but there wasn't a flower in the house. I said to Mum, 'Where are your scissors and have you got a vase, I'll go and cut you two or three Roses, they look so wonderful and they have a scent.'
'Oooh,' she replied, 'E'll not let yer touch 'is Roses,'
I found scissors in a drawer, went outside, to ask Ernie if I could cut a few roses to bring the scent indoors. I had hardly moved two feet from the door when Ernie stopped me. I explained my purpose. Instead of replying 'Yes, we'll cut this one, this one, and there's another nice one,' he said flatly, ' If she wornt's ter smell 'em, she can come outside an' smell 'em.' How cold hearted is that? Loving husbands would be only too glad to give their wives a bunch of Roses, and be proud to display them on sideboard or table, but not Ernie. He wanted his Roses to stay put, right where they were, to show off to the neighbours, who would admire his front garden. Did they know his sick wife could not do the same? Ernie showed no shame or remorse for the way he treated her. The day she was buried

231

he stood beside the grave and said to Aunt Daphne, 'She'll haunt me she will, the way I treated 'er.' He died three months later, of pneumonia.

Lets get back to the bitter winters of the 1940s. The steam trains were better able to cope with adverse weather conditions than the buses. Lorries and cars used chains over the wheels as they skidded and slid around, it was just as well there was not so much traffic. Getting from A to B must have been a nightmare. Most vehicles in those days had no heating.

I was in Miss Sharpe's class in the early part of 1947. We had two very hot radiators to keep us warm. A couple of boys brought the crates of milk in from outside, and we lined the small bottles, (one third of a pint), along the top and sides of the radiators. The heat warmed the milk up a treat. There were 40 or more in our class. Those who wanted milk got it, those who didn't were not forced to drink it. There was always someone like me willing to drink another one. We drank the milk at playtime, pulling the sleeves of our jumpers over our hands because the bottles were by now hot to handle, but they warmed us up terrific. No one was ever scalded or burned. (Health and Safety aficionados would not let us do such a thing today if we still had free milk for our schoolchildren).

Chapter 41
THE ELEVEN PLUS

The exam in progress, I looked anxiously at the others as I bit the end of my pencil and tried to think. Just about everyone else was doing the same. We did not have calculators, or computers, or ballpoint pens. We'd never heard of a module, and we had no library. We also were seldom set any homework. All our lessons had been rattled off on a static blackboard set on a large easel, the school did not possess a rolling blackboard. I did not expect to pass.

For the exams, one of the classrooms in the main hall, usually Miss Carr's, was used. It had a platform where Mr Allen stood to conduct morning assembly.

Upon passing the 11 plus, boys were sent to either Luton Technical, or Bedford Modern, or possibly Bedford Grammar. Girls expected to go to Dame Alice Harpur's in Bedford, or Bedford Grammar for girls.

I tried very hard, under the impression that if I passed, I'd go on to higher education, because everything would be paid for by the education authorities, but that is not how it worked out. I wasn't particularly clever or knowledgeable, but I passed with fairly good marks, which surprised me, as my studies had been all in class during school time. Flitwick public library did not exist. I did enjoy reading, but all my books had been bought for pennies at the Jumble Sales. A few classics among them.

Mum and Ernie were not interested whether I passed or not, in fact, I doubt if they even knew I was sitting the important exam. If they did know, well, they maybe thought little of it. The significance of it was unimportant to them, as my following words will demonstrate.

233

It was decided by the education authority that I would be given a scholarship to attend one of the schools in Bedford, although I cannot recall exactly which one, but there were snags. Mum had to acquire a school uniform for me. I would be given a free train pass, and have free school meals. There were a few books to buy, as well as sports clothing and some equipment. The letter from the education department explained all that. Ernie raged. In his opinion, what was the point of educating girls? What could I learn at Bedford that I couldn't learn at Flitwick? He complained he wasn't working all week just so's I could swan off to Bedford. Mum said I was in danger of getting ideas above my station. A class argument.

It was extremely unlikely Ernie would give up smoking in order for me to achieve my ambitions. He spat out that they would educate me, but as soon as I left I'd marry and have kids. All that education would be wasted.

He and Mum were of the opinion that I didn't need higher education, that it was not for the likes of us, and the sooner I left school to start work the better. All valid arguments from their point of view, just as the same arguments had been used for generations by short sighted parents of girls who were quite capable of furthering their education beyond the merest trickle of the three R's.
My views and aspirations were irrelevant.

Very few older women we knew had worked after marriage. Either they were unwilling, or were pregnant, or worked in a job which didn't employ married women. Most working men of the day expected to come home to a clean house and a meal ready on the table, they did not expect or want to share domestic chores. I kept my job on when I married, and Alvis shared the chores and helped with the children when they came along. I worked all through my married life, and long after the official retirement age, only giving up age 69, because of health problems. Some women in the 1940s were lucky to have a sibling or parent who would be baby minder, but usually, to have a baby was to have to give up work.

All these arguments played a part, but the most forceful reason I was stopped from taking up my place in the school at Bedford was that I'd have to stay on until I was 16 or 18. Mum reasoned that she looked forward to me leaving school soon and earning some money. Mum had my future mapped out, and it did not include, 'going to a posh school,' (her words).

One of the teachers (I believe it was Miss Sharp), came to the house to try and persuade Ernie to change his mind. Miss Sharp even offered to buy me my first uniform out of her own pocket, adding that she would personally give all assistance she could to get me started. She sat with her back to the oilcloth covered living room table, the light from the oil lamp to her back, the firelight flickering as she outlined the benefits of higher education to a bright girl like myself. I was suitably flattered, as no-one had said anything like that about me before. Mum and Ernie sat by the fireside, I sat at the table in the centre of the room, allowed to take no part in the discussion. The teacher held my exam results, pointing out that I could train to be a teacher for example, but her arguments fell on deaf ears. Eventually she sighed and left, her mission fruitless.

I protested, badgered Mum for reasons, but at 11/12 years of age, I could not change things as they were then. It was only a year or two after the war, and the school leaving age was still 14 at the time I sat the exam. Attitudes towards the education of girls, and women in the workplace, were changing slowly, but it seemed to be taking a hell of a long time. There are still parents who do not realise or recognise that education is one way out of poverty.

In enlightened families, attitudes were changing faster, they scraped together the means to help a girl through those few years, and often on to University.

I have read a book by the late Lynda Lee Potter, the title, "CLASS ACT". It is fascinating. Before she died, she gave me permission to quote a few words from the book. She writes, (about her mother and sitting the 11 plus),

'Nothing was too good for me as far as she was concerned, no goal too out of reach. But the vital thing for me was to pass the scholarship.'

How I wish Ernie and Mum had taken that forward thinking attitude. I was 18 before I furthered my education when I enrolled at Boroughmuir School in Edinburgh for evening classes in Bookkeeping, taking the first steps in my aim to gain some commercial qualifications. I passed the exams and received my first education certificate. A few years later, I studied at West Lothian College, and Telford College in Edinburgh, at my own expense. Other commercial qualifications followed, in Personnel, Scots Law and Management, I also studied to become an Associate Member of the Royal Society of Health. When I retired from the Inland Revenue, I returned to the retail industry and worked on for a few more years, until ill health forced me to stop. I also enjoyed a few years of acting in films and Television as a support artiste.

It wasn't the school's fault that my education was limited in those early years. The teachers did what they could for me. Mum and Ernie had other plans which did not include academic achievement. I've enjoyed travel to several countries, including New Zealand, Sweden, America, Canada, seeing places I'd only read of. Like lots of women of my generation, we grasped the opportunity of a better life, and passed the torch on to our daughters.

236

Chapter 42
HIS NAME WAS JOACHIM

The second world war lasted nearly 6 years, both sides taking prisoners. Families were told their loved ones were missing, believed killed in action, some that sons, husbands, brothers had been taken prisoner, others that their worst fears were realised.

Italians were camped at Kempston Hardwick, near Chimney Corner, the Germans camped at Ampthill and Clapham. Italy surrendered in 1943, but there were still many Italians at Kempston Hardwick as late as 1952. (see chapter on the Sound of Music). In 1946 the ban on fraternising with German POWs was lifted. They wore a prison type uniform consisting of white shirt, and grey pullover under a boiler suit garment, with their German military style cap. No tie. We called the Germans 'Jerries'

The War over, and trouble brewing as Russia tightened their grip in Berlin, made West Germany an Ally instead of enemy. Animosity towards the Germans did persist here and there, but the attitude had softened by the late 1940s. Many Germans were sent to work on the land, and quickly earned the reputation for being hardworking and efficient. Curfew was 10pm with few reports of the curfew being broken. It is said that the last of the Germans were repatriated by July 1948, but many remained here, some married to local girls.

At least two Germans, working on the fields for Woodcraft, were brought to our house by Ernie for Sunday tea, around 1947/48. The first one, a very polite man in his 30s or early 40s, he was upset at having to leave Britain. He said he had no choice, because his wife and family were in the Eastern Zone, which was under Russian Communist control. They refused to allow his family to come here.

237

The second German who came was much younger. I was about thirteen then, and this typical Aryan fair haired youth must have been barely 18, almost certainly one of the boy soldiers recruited by Hitler in the dying days of the war. Very handsome, with wonderful blue eyes, bronzed from his work in the fields, he produced in me a very disturbing mixture of feelings. We had been used to hating the Germans, but I couldn't hate this one. Looking into those blue eyes melted me. He was the stuff of a young girl's dreams, and my heart beat so much faster. A glance from him had my cheeks aflame. Did I feel the first immature bubbles of passion stirring in my stomach? He pierced my very soul as he talked directly to me. I don't know what he made of this gawping schoolgirl. I had no idea how to hold a conversation with this handsome stranger, so I remained mute most of the time. He was very well mannered, especially to Mum, getting up out of his chair to help her, thanking her and Ernie profusely for their hospitality, I'd never seen anything like it.

The last time he came to our house, he asked Ernie if he could take me to the pictures. Ernie said 'No, she's too young,'
I didn't get a chance to say yea or nay to this. Oh I so wanted to go to the pictures with him. I was very disappointed and heart broken when he never returned. I have no idea if he was re-patriated or if he was allowed to stay on in England. Life takes many twists and turns. My heart has taken a few bumpy rides since then, but that was the first. Adolescence can be painful, distracting, unnerving.
We never even held hands, or stole the most chaste of kisses.
His name was Joachim

Chapter 43
FROM CONKERS to the CAKEWALK

Over the fields we went, walking, running, our step determined. It was the season of the Conker, the fruit of the Horsechestnut tree. There were games to play, winners and losers to declare. The corn had been cut, harvest gathered in, the days shortened, but we still had another thing to do before winter really took a hold.

On the road to Westoning, just before the bridge over the River Flit, and before a bend in the road, were wrought iron gates on the right hand side, the entrance to a lodge house, and one of the entrances to the Manor grounds. The house is long demolished, being in a bad way even in the 40s. Inside the gates, mature Horsechestnut trees lined what had once been an elegant drive, now reduced to a rutted track with overgrown grass verges. Leaves were turning all those wonderful autumn colours, yellows, splashes of red and russet, some purple. The track petered out into parkland and view of Flitwick Water, or the Lake as we knew it. Earlier in the year the trees had been loaded with the most wonderful blossom hanging like chandeliers.

We children set about our business, collecting as many Conkers as we could carry, then returning hurriedly to the Alley, to Water Lane, to Station Road, and Maulden Road. A hole hammered through the Conker with a nail to thread the string through, kept the boys happy for hours as they bashed away to see which Conker lasted the longest before disintegrating, even heating some to make them harder and more difficult to smash. I played Conkers too, but was never so near dedicated. I never see children playing Conkers today. It is an old fashioned game which has gone the way of many others as our Health and Safety aficionados go overboard in their efforts to stop children enjoying themselves.

A Fair set up in the field next to the Blackbirds Inn every year. The field is now a car park for the pub. Larger than the Fairs which came to the Fetes at the Manor or on the Rec, it had excitement for teenagers. Surrounded by a fence, the railway to the rear, and the road to the front, it was an ideal site. Fairly central to the village, it attracted a lot of revellers.

One of the attractions at the Blackbirds Inn Fair was the Cakewalk. This contraption was unsuitable for young children, but great fun for the older ones. I always joined in the fun of it. Described as a walk, but like no other walk, and not easy. The queues waiting to take a turn seemed to be the longest, as we all shuffled forward on to the wooden slatted platform, squashed up tight one behind the other. It shook, (shuggle is a more apt word), backwards and forwards, from side to side, violently, as we hung on to the support rails for dear life, laughing and squealing. There was noise, music, and we enjoyed ourselves immensely. The Dodgems brought more squeals of delight.

There usually was a small Switchback, a Waltzer. Sideshows aplenty, such as the Coconut Shy, Roll a Penny stall, Loop the Loop, Shooting Gallery. It was amazing how much could be packed into that small field.

The Fair was usually a summer event, but the Circus came in the winter months, perhaps nearer to Christmas, also to the field beside the Blackbirds. It was usually a one day event. As well as the traditional clowns and trapeze acts, the Circus had live performing animals such as Tigers, Lions, Elephants, Horses, Monkeys, Dogs.
The big tent went up and word spread quickly through the village that the Circus had arrived. People came from the villages around,

as well as Flitwick, until the wooden bench seats around the one ring were full. Usually an afternoon matinee for families, and then an evening performance.

Girls in spangle costume rode the Elephants and Horses. The Elephants did tricks, three or four trotted around the ring, trunk to tail. Horses pranced around the ring with acrobats, women and men in fancy colourful costume, jumping on and off, from one to the other, sometimes two horses in tandem. We gasped, we clapped, cheered. We gave no thought to the animals welfare, or if they were being ill treated in order to learn the tricks.

In a cage, in the centre of the sawdust arena, a Lion Tamer cracked his whip and brandished a chair as a lion roared, another one or two next to it. Dogs clambered through hoops, playing tricks, and there were gasps from us as one highwire act appeared to falter.
The Ringmaster, on introducing each act, went over the top in praise, and Clowns fell over themselves, making lots of noise. It was colourful, fantastic, very exciting for this young village peasant girl.

A few years later, I saw a marvellous film at the cinema. The greatest show on earth, starring Betty Hutton, Cornel Wilde and young Charlton Heston, great film. It started off with the parade, colourful and grand because they had more Elephants and other animals, more performers of course, for the film depicted a three ring Circus, whereas the Circus which came to the Blackbirds was rather small in comparison. One year, when on an errand to Station Square, I do recall seeing part of a parade, with spangle clad girls on horses near the front. Dads had to make stilts similar to the ones seen at the Circus. Dogs were confused as boys tried to teach them the tricks they'd seen at the circus. We spirited our mothers clothes lines away to make swings in the trees. My stilts were made by myself from two soup cans (thicker than those of today.and two lengths of string.

Chapter 44
CHRISTMAS

Until I was about 8 or 9 years old, I really believed in Santa Claus. If I didn't get what I wished for, then it was because Santa had not enough to go round, or some other plausible excuse Mum told me. Some say Christmas is too commercialised, but I love it, always have done. A ray of sunshine and glitz in the middle of an otherwise depressing season. Light, laughter, shops and stores doing just what we want them to do, display their wares in the best possible way. Did I have a bottomless purse, to spend and spend as I liked? Certainly not. Never have.

Some say children get too much these days, but we either indulge them or we don't, it is up to us. We should not blame the shops if foolish parents go into massive debt. The shops and supermarkets are there to provide us all with just about anything we desire, and we have the Internet too, that's their job, but it is up to us if we buy or not.

The tinsel, baubles, the brightly lit trees, the carols, the parties, the whole chebang, I love it. To go into stores and see those Christmas displays makes me feel like a kid again, my nose up against Sharpe's window in Flitwick High Street. They always had loads of toys, bikes, and other goodies on display.

I can't recall what Joyce and I got as presents during the war. Later, I do remember waking up on Christmas morning to see we each had one of Ernie's thick working socks hanging on the bedknobs. When Oranges became available again, we had one in each sock, along with a few nuts, crayons, sketch book, and a small packet of something like Liquorice cigarettes with those little red hundreds and thousands at the end, looking like a lit fag. The shops sold Liquorice Pipes just the same. I am sure that at least one Christmas we were each given one of those little clay pipes for blowing bubbles with. Mum found herself with a little less soap. One Christmas I found a small Kaliedescope in the sock. It was fascinating. Every time I put it to my eyes I saw the beautiful colourful different patterns produced as I turned it this way and that. It may seem such a simple present against the many wonderful toys in the stores today, but for me, it was magical. Beside the sock, on the floor, perhaps one or two books or a board game like Snakes and Ladders. One year, Aunt Daphne gave me a wonderfully illustrated book of Grimm's Fairy Tales, a real treasure. Cinderella, Rumpelstiltskin, The Golden Goose, Hansel and Gretel, delightful stories. Nothing has survived my childhood except the memories. That isn't to say I wouldn't have liked a new bike, or when I was younger, a Doll with pram. In many ways, Christmas was joyful enough for us. I have read of worse, of children getting nothing, or being beaten, a day like any other.

One year Joyce was given a rag Doll with porcelain head, hands and feet sewn into the rag body. Of course I was jealous and upset, it seemed so unfair. I had something else, probably a Jigsaw, or Girls Annual with stories so different to the kind of life I lived. We never saw a Turkey, dead or alive, or Chicken, that was also scarce and expensive. For our Christmas Dinner, we had stewed Rabbit served with mashed potato, sprouts and gravy. The Watson's next door killed off a hen or two.

In the run up to Christmas, I went Carol singing with other children. Calling at houses in nearby roads, we lustily sang such regulars as Oh Come all ye Faithful, Oh Little Town of Bethlehem, Come rest ye Merry Gentlemen, never quite getting all the words right. Station Road was always good for our collection, then we'd head for Kings Road. Another evening we'd do Maulden Road, then it would be Water Lane, or further afield to the Avenue. Most welcomed us and handed over a few pennies, even a sixpence. We drooled if we received a shilling. Only the occasional household sent us off empty handed. At the end of the evening, the collection was totted up and divided between us equally. I gleefully handed Mum half. We did not go Carol singing for charity, we did it for ourselves. It was to be our pocket money for Christmas.

Mum used ration coupons to buy dried fruit for mince pies. Either Vass or village baker Charlie Cousins then made mincement pies for her. They were a real treat. Towards the end of the 40s, dried fruit such as currants became more plentiful.

I'm not sure how often we had Christmas Pudding. We did have it one year at least, because I can recall finding a traditional silver threepenny piece in my share. We never had a Christmas cake. Families saved a small portion of their rations all year to either bake a small cake themselves, or get the local baker to do it, but more often it was the cardboard cake, decorated somehow to look like the real thing. Hollow, with no substance, it looked good on the table. We had neither.

Colourful paper chains we made at school, some we made at home. Cousins shop sold packets of strips of coloured paper, and a small bottle of glue with glue brush. Cutting the strips into smaller lengths, splodging a little glue on one end, folding over to join, then looping the next little strip through the first ring, repeating until the desired length of chain was achieved. Later, the shops stocked strips already cut to size, which only needed licking at one end, just like an envelope or stamp. We hung the colourful chains corner to corner across the ceiling. No tree, or fairy lights. Plenty of Holly, with berries on it, from a Holly tree in the orchard hedge. Mum decorated the mantlepiece, across the mirror and pictures on the wall with the Holly. Occasionally we had Mistletoe, likely also from the orchard.

Ernie bought bottles of beer. The bottle glass was thick, and the bottom heavy, with a concave underside, giving the impression the bottle held more than the actual pint or two inside. Empty bottles returned for the deposit. I went in the front door of the White Horse pub, along a corridor past the bar, to a little cubby hole at the rear. Knocking on a wooden hatch, I placed Ernie's money on the ledge, with his request. Within a minute or two, I'd be on my way back to the Alley with the beer. Mum liked Stout occasionally. In the 1940s it was normal to be sent for his beer.

We had a very happy Christmas one year, when Uncle George (Bubbles) and Aunt Daphne (Sally), were living with us. Ernie picked a tune out on the Jews harp, (it is now called a Jaw harp), and Bubbles played the spoons. (banging two large spoons together against his thigh, to produce a beat). Stan and May Watson came in from next door with Stanley, Kathy and Pearl. Bubbles also played a tune on paper and comb, (blowing through them by mouth), and the men became quite merry. Some jokes and stories were told, with a lot of laughs. A good day for Mum.

The Vicar came to the school to conduct a service, with all the children expected to attend. It included carol singing. We were also expected to attend a service at the Church, but I didn't go. Ernie and Mum listened to the King's Christmas speech on the wireless. Ernie thought that the Monarchy, Aristocracy, and us peasants all had our place in society, and we should not step out of our class. Had there been a vote for Monarchy or Republic, he'd have chosen Monarchy. We didn't send or receive Christmas cards. Wartime put the brakes on the activity. Sally took me to my first pantomime when I was 5 years of age. I did not go to another one until I was 15.

Chapter 45
FRIENDS and NEIGHBOURS

Millie Barnes and May Watson had been friends since childhood. Both born at the birth of the 20th century, 1900. Millie to Albert and Kate Line of Water Lane. May to Alfred and Meg Stringer also of Water Lane. Mum and Ernie were related to May Watson through the Stringer line. May's father Alfred, Mum's grandfather John, Ernie's grandfather George, were brothers. May, a little taller than Mum or Millie, had the larger family. She smoked heavily, but I never saw Millie smoke. May Stringer married Stan Watson when she was just 19 years old.

We moved into number 28, May lived at number 26, and Millie, a widow, lived at 18. May and Stan had at least 8 children. Renee, Bernard, Philip, Derek, Phyllis, Kathy, Stanley (same age as myself), and Pearl. May's husband Stan, an agricultural labourer like Ernie, was a quiet man. I knew little of him, never heard him shout at anyone, or make a fuss, but May herself could do a bit of shouting, or 'ollering as we called it, especially to her large brood. Mum and May went into each other's house quite freely, did not need an invitation. A little tale comes to mind.

Mum and I were in her small living room, watching May busily making a clanger for the family dinner. Flour at the ready, rolling out dough on the oilcloth covered table in the centre of the room, the usual cigarette dangling from her bottom lip. Talking through and over the smoke drifting up over her nose, her eyes squinted and screwed up, she smoked on. All the family, except Pearl who was then too young, smoked. Mum pointed out to May that ash from her cigarette was falling into the dough, 'A bit o ash won't do 'em any 'arm gal, it's good for 'em,' May replied, drawing on her fag as she continued to roll the dough, which by this time had absorbed quite a bit of ash. May had several 78rpm records, the old shellac type. The days of the vinyls and long play 45s and 33s, then CDs and all the other ways of listening to music was still to be discovered. The Watson's record player was wound up for each record. A wooden box like structure, with a turntable.

Attached was a large horn to enhance the sound. A record was placed on the turntable, the handle at the side wound up until tight enough, the needle arm and stylus, (heavier and thicker than a modern stylus), was placed on the record and a lever at the side of the turntable was released to allow the record to rotate. If the handle was wound up too tightly, the record spun too quickly, causing the singer's voice to go high and squeaky, but if the record wasn't wound up enough, the singer's voice sunk slowly, to low bass.

Like us, there was a wireless sitting on the dresser beside the fireplace, next to Stan's chair. They listened to the news items intently, as we did. We all heard the famous Churchill broadcasts. Sometimes the wireless and gramaphone were on at the same time, children ran in and out of doors, while Mum and May gossiped above the din. It could be bedlam in that small cottage. Bernard Watson was rather a strange fellow. He always sat with his back to the rest of the family, looking out of the window, even at mealtimes. Ignoring visitors, he'd only grunt when spoken to, even to his own mother. Philip and Derek went into the armed forces. Philip died in 1977 age only 48, Derek died 1979, too young at 55, and Stanley died in 1987, only 51. Renee's son Alan, born 1942, nicknamed Ginger Hymus, died in 1979, only 37.

Kathy married Peter Carr, whose parents had lived in the Alley. She died of heart disease, in her late 50s.   Phyllis married a French man. She died of breast cancer before she was 50.

247

Had those years of smoke in that house in the Alley have anything to do with their early deaths?

Madge Day, (nee Stringer), told me that one day, May was waiting at the bus stop near the Crown Inn for the bus to Ampthill, when she happened to notice the bus bowling along the top Westoning-Greenfield road, and knew it would soon arrive. The view is now blocked with trees and housing. There was no next bus, if she missed that one, she'd have to forget about going to Ampthill. Agitated, she had forgotten her cigarettes, and no time to go back home for them. She called out to her son Stanley, riding his bike nearby. 'Goo and git me fags Stanley, if ee sees 'em, eel smoke the bloody lot' she said, referring to her husband Stan. Stanley had to pedal furiously home to get her cigarettes and back in time to hand her them before the bus turned up. Whheww!!

Another time, when cigarettes were in short supply, she asked Fred Line to get her some. Fred was in his 40s, and people labelled him simple because he was rather mentally challenged. May knew that Carr Line, Fred's Mum, had an account at Dix's shop in Station road, and that he could get cigarettes from there on credit, so she asked him to go and get some for her. Fred duly went to Dix's, got the cigarettes, and handed them over to May, but Mrs Dix had given him Pasha, which didn't please May one little bit. It didn't stop her smoking the horrible smelly things. Mrs Dix's small general store was in the front room of 77 Station Rd. May was honest enough and would pay Carr Line for them later.

When drawing water from the Well on her bit of land opposite our houses, Millie often popped into May's for a chinwag. Sometimes Mum joined them. They'd gossip over a cup of tea. Millie was one of the kindest women there could be, but had a hard life too. Her husband, a horse dealer, left her a widow when Claude

248

and Frank were still young boys. One daughter, Gladys, spent most of the war years with her R.A.F. husband in Birmingham. Norah, lived next door number 20 with her husband Percival Pearson, who we knew as Pussah. They later divorced. Sheila came along in 1945.

As Millie got older, arthritis and spondylitis took over, making her life a misery. The last time I visited she was bent double over the copper boiler in her small kitchen, she died soon afterwards. Shortly after the War, she met Welshman David Meyrick, a short stocky man with a shock of black wavy hair. He came to live with her. Her old house was no larger than ours, just two down, two up, but somehow she still found room for one of the evacuees during the war. His name was John Humphrey, and he went to school along with Frank. Millie was a fount of knowledge about old fashioned remedies for all sorts of ailments, but her knowledge died with her, which is a pity, for some of it could be useful today. She also had a wonderful, if rather bizarre knowledge of old wives tales. I forget most of them, but one does spring to mind, relating to pregnancy. Millie bade the pregnant woman to lie down, and using the gold wedding ring at the end of a length of string, she swung it backwards and forwards like a pendulum across the bulging tummy. If it swung east to west, it would be a girl, if it swung north to south it would be a boy, (or was it the other way round?). Very unscientific. She had a 50-50 chance of being right hadn't she? No scans in those days.

May Watson's mother, Margaret Stringer, who we knew as Aunt Meg, lived at 5 Water Lane, surrounded by a well tended garden full of vegetables and herbs. Mum visited her often. Pigeon and Pottle, (her sons Herbert and Cyril) did most of the work outdoors. They came into the kitchen, taking off their boots at the door, sat down and were served their dinner. They would never say to their mother, 'You sit down and we'll wash the dishes.' Working we'll wash the dishes,' Working men just did not do that. Meg, in her late 80s, would have felt quite offended had anyone even hinted that she couldn't manage any more. The men had their work outdoors, and she had hers indoors, and that's the way she liked it.

Meg, born Margaret Abbot died in 1952, age 93. Her husband, known as Coddy Stringer, died many years earlier. Later, her cottage was demolished and the land sold off.

Millie's parents, Albert and Kate Line, lived at 45 Water Lane, in a little wooden bungalow surrounded by an orchard.

Once each week, on Saturdays, Millie and May donned their best togs and caught the bus to Ampthill, to go dancing at the Drill hall, or to the Zonita cinema. Stan did not object to May going out, he would not have dared. He was a quiet man and liked a quiet life. In later years, when Millie's arthritis and pain riddled body discouraged her from going past her front gate, perhaps she could smile at fond memories of fun times.

The routine on a Saturday afternoon was the same. May called in at Millie's house, smoking or lighting up as she went in. 'You ready yet Gal,' We children had a bit of fun as we watched them leave and proceed down the Alley to catch the bus. All dressed up in their finery they were, wearing shoes that had higher heels than normal daily wear. (Poor Millie often wore shoes with very run down heels around the house).

Tottering precariously on those heels, backsides wobbling from side to side, May and Millie reached almost the bottom of the Alley, pausing to check their stocking seams were straight. One leg up, look, damp a finger in mouth, stick leg out sideways, tweak the seam, check again, repeat with the other leg. A bit nearer the bus stop, out came powder compact from handbag, dab a little more powder on nose, more bright red lipstick on to an already overloaded mouth. Check the little mirror to see the mascara is OK. It wasn't waterproof. A little bit of hair tweaking, Millie had a lovely crop of dark curly hair, then hurry the last few steps as the bus approached.

I was one of a gaggle of children who thought this a great deal of fun as we mimicked every movement, following them all the way down the Alley. They threatened all sorts of dire action as they turned and shook their fists, shouting at us to go back home, or they would do what? Thrash us, band our heads together, give us a good walloping? Next minute they were laughing, they had a bus to catch.

Our other next door neighbour, Caroline (Carr) Line, was getting on in years when we moved into the Alley. Until then, she had Ernie's grandmother Eliza as a neighbour. Suddenly, Ernie and Mum moved in, and everything changed. Mum and Ernie had many noisy barneys, there was a 5 year old child and a baby making unwelcome noises, it was all too much for Carr. She banged on the party wall when the noise became unbearable, indicating she'd had enough. Mum's voice went down to a whisper, but her and Ernie kept the argument going. Carr banged on the wall again and again.

Ernie could keep an argument going in an empty house. If Mum replied, it encouraged him and he would say, 'And there's something else,' Poor Carr had to put up with all that until she moved out in the late 1940s. If there had been any such thing as an Anti Social Behaviour Order (ASBO) in those days, Mum and Ernie would have got one.

We didn't see much of her husband Ebeneezer, who we knew as Ebber, he was getting on in years. He swept chimneys, a family business handed down from his father Daniel Line, who had lived at number 16 Gravel Pit Road, (the Alley). They lost a daughter to illness, one son shot himself, and their son, Fred, was mentally backward. Carr had gone through a lot of heartache. Some said Fred was dangerous to women and children, but I never found it so. In fact, I think we children were often cruel to him. We mimicked his rather awkward walk, and laughed at the way he wore his cap. Fred ambled slowly back and forth to the barn for fuel, did a little work in the garden, a few rows of potatoes, the rest left to weeds. He helped his Mum draw water from the Well. He never spoke much.

Around 1948/49, Carr and Fred moved to number 16, where her brother Lawrence, who we knew as Double Cox lived. I am not sure, but believe Ebber had died.

Ivy Cuthbert who lived at number 14 was friendly towards Mum, and another friendly face was Mrs Gulliver, who lived next to Cousins bakery. She often invited Mum in for a cup of tea.

Aunt Nance Camwell at Hornes End wasn't our aunt, she was cousin to my grandmother, but Mum did enjoy friendship over a cup of tea by the warm fire in her house. Mum had little self confidence, and while most knew of her plight, they were not in a position to alleviate it.

Another family who were friendly towards Mum were the Stringers in Maulden Road. Bugle Stringer was also a cousin of my grandmother. Madge Day (nee Stringer), one of his daughters, married Reg Day, did become a close friend in Mum's later years. She kept Mum's hair trimmed, and provided a link to the outside world. Bugle's granddaughter Janice, who now lives in Maulden, has also written a book on Flitwick, a little different to this one, detailing many of the changes which have taken place over the years.

Chapter 46
PEG RUGS

Having a look around IKEA one day, I spotted rag rugs for sale. Very similar to ones my Mum made from old rags.

During the long winter evenings, while Mum still had her sight, she made those rugs as she listened to the wireless. A jute sack on her knee, cut and shaped to size, the fine mesh of the sack ideally suited for the purpose. Nearby, lay cut strips of cloth, about 4 inches x 1 inch. At the ready, a half bit of wooden dolly peg, sharpened at one end into a point, like a blunt dagger. Used to push each strip of cloth through a hole in the mesh, and back through the next hole in the mesh, creating a rag pile, like the pile on any carpet. When finished, the rough edges of the sack were tucked in underneath and sewn in tidily. The pile was trimmed down level, and the underside looked like the underside of any other wool rug. Lastly, another sack was trimmed to size and sewn over the underside to add strength. Ernie brought the jute sacks home from Woodcraft's, where they were usually filled with produce for market. I drew a pattern on the sack in chalk, and Mum pegged in the coloured strips she had to that pattern. She rummaged at jumble sales for clothes for us to wear, then rummaged for a few suitable things she could cut up for the rugs.

To make a larger fireside rug, Mum sewed two or three sacks together. Sometimes Ernie and Mum fashioned a rug between them. Ernie sitting in his chair, Mum in hers, both working from each end until they reached the centre. If this paints a cosy domestic scene, don't you believe it. He'd grumble about something or other, while Mum, her tongue sticking out one side of her mouth, listened, tried to ignore him, but he noticed, 'ere, yer listenin' ter me.'

She'd have to reply. If she didn't agree with him, maybe a row would begin, perhaps degenerating into blows, started over the most trivial of remarks. Perhaps something had been said on the Radio, or an earlier disagreement came into Ernie's head. Carr Line banged on the wall again, indicating she'd had enough of the racket,

I'd be sent outdoors, or to bed, depending on time of day, Joyce ignored it all. She had got well used to Ernie and Mum having a slanging match.

An agricultural labourer's income did not stretch to buying Wilton, Axminster, Persian, Chinese, or beautiful Indian carpets and rugs. The cost of keeping them clean well out of reach. A vacuum was also too expensive, unless he could lay his hands on a cheap second hand one. Rag rugs, cheap to make, had to be enough.

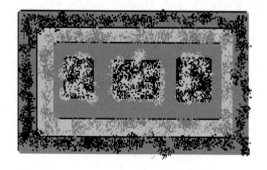

Chapter 47
A GLIMPSE AT 1948/49

The Nationalisation of the railways took place in 1948, becoming British Rail. In July the National Health Service really began. April 1st, Electricity companies were nationalised. In 1949, the National Assistance Act allowed unmarried mothers to apply for State support. When I was born in 1935, Mum was penniless, with little or no hope of being supported by the Social Services of the day.

May 1st 1949, Gas industry was nationalised, and clothes rationing ended at last on March 15th 1949. The fashion industry breathed a sigh of relief. Some items such as household linen were becoming more readily available, but not any cheaper. Income Tax was high at 40%, there were plenty of grumbles about that, but nationalisation and getting the country back on its feet had to be paid for. Boys age over 9 or 10 years old began to favour long trousers instead of the short ones their older brothers had been used to. Some boarding schools and private establishments still clothed their schoolboys in short trousers and silly little caps until they were strapping big 15 and 16 years old.

War films were popular, it was all still fresh in peoples memories. The Olympic Games were held in London in 1948, but the event was of little interest to me. It was wall to wall coverage in the newspapers, at the cinema and on radio. Few families had television. Although London was not too far distant, it was still too expensive for us to go there. We had even less chance of competing.

At school, we took an interest if the teacher brought in newspaper cuttings for discussion. The only sports activities I was involved in was school sports. I wasn't encouraged to take part in sports outside school. As far as I was aware the grown ups played cricket, and the tennis club in Kings Road was too expensive.

To enjoy swimming, children from Flitwick travelled to Stewartby or Eversholt. The school laid on a bus. Public transport between Flitwick and those places didn't exist. The boys had football and rugby teams, we girls had our hockey and netball teams. Local boys kicked a ball up and down the Alley, when they could. If a boy was given a proper real football as a birthday or Christmas present, every boy in the area wanted to kick it.

Prince Charles was born in 1948, that event got wall to wall coverage too. The succession was secured, but just to make sure, the Queen went on to have three more children.

In the Army, a Major's income was £11per week, a poor Corporal received £3 and a Private even less. On the political front, the Russians tried to blockade West Berlin into submission. America, Britain, France, supplied the city by air. The Iron Curtain descended. The Government urged the car manufacturers to export most of their output, to earn the country much needed currency.

In Flitwick, William Fowler and Richard Chibnal got the bit between the teeth and were very busy building new homes for sale. They built Oak Road and Beech Road on ground which had been the Paddock. Little space was given over to provision of car parking for the Council homes in the Avenue. Many could not afford a car.

At the cinema, some classic and not so well known films made their appearance. Ingrid Bergman in Joan of Arc. Key Largo, starring Humphrey Bogart, Lauren Bacall, and Edward G Robinson, who always looked like my idea of a gangster. Kind Hearts and Coronets, with Joan Greenwood and Alec Guinness, who portrayed eight different characters. It also starred Denis Price who seemed always to play smooth smarmy types. Other films being shown, but not new, were The Blue Lamp, starring Jack Warner and a young

256

Dora Bryan. The Blue Lagoon, starred Jean Simmons in the lead. John Wayne in Fort Apache. The Zonita also did re-runs of old films such as the 1930s Fred Astaire/Ginger Rogers musicals.

One little snippet I came across in an old newspaper was interesting. We all know how popular Butlin's holiday camps were after the war. I can recall asking Mum if we could go to Butlin's for a holiday, the answer was as expected, No. But many Flitwick children did enjoy one or more of those holidays. But how many of us knew that Billy Butlin also opened a Butlin's in the Bahamas in 1949, to cater for the Americans, at 12 dollars per day. At that time, the exchange rate for the dollar was about 5 to the £.

In Flitwick, women waited impatiently for the end of food rationing. Some were elated because they had been allocated one of the new homes being built in the Avenue. Some planned to emigrate to a Commonwealth country, or the Colonies, to a new and better life instead of struggling along here.

While all this was going on, coloured immigrants were entering Britain from the Caribbean Islands. There was plenty of work for them, albeit low paid. Many lived in poor housing conditions, just like us in the Alley. We had a lot in common, although Ernie called them unmentionable names.

257

Chapter 48
BUDGETING

"Poverty, a Study of Town Life," a book by Joseph Rowntree, included the following,

"Wages for unskilled labour in York are insufficient to provide food and shelter and clothing adequate to maintain a family in bare physical sufficiency. It means a family must not spend a penny on fares, they cannot save, they cannot join a sick club, the children have no pocket money, the wage earner must not be absent from work."

  The above observation could also apply to the agricultural labourer in Bedfordshire, well into the 20th century. He was skilled in his craft, providing food for the dining tables of the nation, but often his own children wore rags and went shoeless, and his home lacked decent sanitation. He couldn't save.

  I came across a 1942 copy of Good Housekeeping magazine. The GH magazine described a typical budget which amazed me. The budget was £11.14shillings per week, excluding mortgage, rates, savings and insurance. Where did they get the figures from?

A dream budget. One that many a factory worker, shop assistant, nurse, ambulance driver, road sweeper, canteen cook, and farm worker, all essential for the nation, would like, but didn't have. The GH budget included a clothing allowance of £2 per week, and £1.10 shillings for a maid. The average weekly wage in 1939 was almost £3.10 shillings (three pounds and ten shillings). 1940 it had risen to £4.10 shillings, and in July it had risen again to £6.4 shillings. Aunt Lil mentioned that her husband Bob, and Ernie, earned twenty five shillings per week in 1939. Less than half the national average weekly pay,and certainly nowhere near that £11 odd mentioned in the GH magazine. It is little wonder Mum had such a hard time budgeting. The old age pension, introduced around the end of the first world war, (around eight shillings) was means tested. In 1945, the Government introduced a new Pension scheme which was not means tested. Pensioners suddenly became better off.

In 1940 a kitchen maid earned in the region of £40 annually, some considerably less. Gents hairdressing paid £3 per week, but only because there was a shortage of male labour. A Telegraph messenger boy of 14 earned 12 shillings per week, a daily cleaner £1 per week.

In 1948, the United Nations adopted the declaration of Human Rights,

"Everyone has a right to a standard of living adequate for the health and well being of himself and his family, including food, clothing, housing, medical care and necessary social services, and the right to security in the event of unemployment, sickness, disability, widowhood, old age, or other lack of livlihood in circumstances beyond his control."

An ideal the world is still trying to live up to.

Children such as myself were very used to second hand clothes, or even third and fourth hand if bought at the jumble sales.

I can't remember his name, but the Tally man, (travelling salesman), came to the Alley on Saturdays to collect his weekly instalment, and to sell his wares, carrying a battered suitcase full of samples. An order placed one week would be delivered the next, or as soon as he could . Payment usually one shilling in the £1 for 20 weeks. Thus, if a garment cost £2, it would be paid at two shillings per week. As well as clothing he supplied sheets, towels, table linen etc. Many women, as did my mother in law, operated a system of putting money into several purses, or pots and vases about the house. One purse held the rent money, another held shillings for the gas meter, another purse held payments for milkman and coalman, and yet another purse or pot held money for the Insurance man.

Mum kept the rent money in a vase on the mantlepiece after we moved to Dunstable Road. The rent man called weekly to collect. Other bills were paid by calling at the office or shop where the item was bought, to pay the instalments, or a Postal Order was remitted. A £5 note in Mum's purse was a rarity and I never saw her with a tenner. Hitler tried to flood Britain with fake notes during the war, all notes over £5 were withdrawn. A metal thread was introduced, but the tenner did not re-appear until 1964, when, for the first time, notes carried the Sovereign's image. The old £5 note was white with black lettering, and almost 4 x times the size of the present fiver. The £1 coin was introduced in 1983, replacing the £1 note, except in Scotland, where the note still circulates. Scottish bank notes do not carry the Queen's image. The first penny was minted in Saxon times 765, farthings were legal tender until 1960.

We would not have been so desperately poor if Ernie had not smoked. His cigarettes burned a hole in at least 5% of his wages. To have a maid, and an income over £11 per week, what heaven. To have a husband who came home and said, 'Hello dear' followed by a kiss, WOW!! that would be a dream.

'That's four weeks you've paid me short Mrs Bland,' Pussy Cousins said. Then, with pursed lips, she continued to measure the rations as Mum stood at the counter, down at heel, and downtroddenly silent. Other people in the shop acted like the three wise monkeys, seeing nothing, saying nothing, hearing nothing. Were they in the same boat? Who knows.
Debt was a constant companion.

There wasn't a week went by without Mum having a huge struggle. The Coalman called, and knocked at the door for payment, but Mum sent me to the door to tell him she wasn't in. I told the lie while she hid behind the living room door, no money left.

The Insurance agent stopped calling, but later, when Ernie went to work in a factory, the Insurance was resumed.

Ernie handed Mum what he though fit for housekeeping, and kept the rest. Mum going out to work and getting a little independence in her own right, even if it meant a little more money coming into the house, he would have been really against. In poverty, she was his slave, his property, he was the provider for the family. It was the way it had always been. Doing some Peasing and Potato lifting was OK for her, it was seasonal, was acceptable.

He never brought coal in for the fire, or drew a bucket of water from the Well, not even when Mum was ill. He didn't clean his own shoes. He considered all that was woman's work. (Although in their latter years he had to do the house chores, because Mum was incapable of doing anything.) There was also the question of child care. Who would look after her children? He constantly questioned her, who did she speak to? what did they say? why this? why that? Putting on a splash of lipstick, longing for fashionable clothes, made her a tart, a whore. Hugh Dalton, a Government Minister said, 'To wear clothes that have been patched and darned, perhaps many times, is to show oneself a true patriot.' Mum was a patriot alright, for she did indeed patch and darn. She darned extremely neatly.

Eventually, in 1950, (I was leaving school), two things happened to improve our situation. We moved to a Dunstable Road council house, and I started work. Suddenly Mum had extra in her purse. From the first pay packet I received, I handed half to Mum. When I got a raise, she got half of that too. That little extra paid the rent of 13/6 per week, with some cash left over.

Mum was born into poverty, had lost her mother when only 13 years old, been betrayed by my father, and she married a man who was abusive and cruel to her. She wasn't equipped for the fight. She was never a feisty woman. Her nature desired a better life, but she was knocked back so many times. Those years in the Alley, and the harsh treatment from Ernie, had a very negative impact on her health and well being. In 1954, age 38 she fell into a Diabetic coma, and thereafter her health went swiftly downhill. I had moved to Scotland the year before. Twice each year I travelled down from Scotland to visit her. I saw the blindness enfolding her eyes. She always apologised for not sending presents to her grandchildren, because, as she explained to me, ' He won't give me any money.' I didn't expect any different. Ernie gave Pat money for the shopping, and remarked to Mum, 'What der yer need money fer.'

I made arrangements for her to come on holiday to Scotland, where I lived in a comfortable roomy house, but even that idea was scotched by Ernie, who was against it. He said, 'If you go up there, yer needn't come back.' Mum was not strong enough to defy him.

He bought a Television on hire purchase in 1953 from Wynne's Shop just before the Coronation.

Ernie died in December 1981, age 66, of pneumonia, unable to carry on to enjoy his retirement. Mum died September 1981, painfully, after being housebound for many years with Diabetes complications, her troubled life over. If there is a God, surely in all mercy, she deserves a place in heaven, her burden laid down at last. She always longed to return to Maulden to live, but it was death that took her back. Mum is buried in Maulden Cemetery, where Ernie joined her 3 months later, and where Pat, who died in 1997, is also buried, all together in the same grave.

Chapter 49
WHEN BUTTER WAS A SUNDAY TREAT

Litte Tommy Tucker, sang for his supper, what shall we give him, brown bread and butter.   Food, glorious food.

As a child in the 1940s, when Butter was rationed, we had bread spread with only Butter on Sundays. The rest of the week bread was spread with margarine, or a mixture of margarine, lard and left over butter all in the one dish.

In 1942 a Doctor examined Joyce and I and found we were undernourished. Mum scraped through best as she could. Joyce and I were not starving. We had eaten. So why were we undernourished and the house filthy?   Mum wasn't a shopaholic, spending the housekeeping allowance on frivolous things, she was never the height of fashion, so why did it happen? It was wartime, we had no expensive holidays, no big payments towards a car, no latest gadgets. Was she depressed? Did she have the baby blues?(Joyce was a baby). I'll never know the answer, but can guess it was because of poverty. How many times did she sit with Joyce on her knee, with not enough nappies to wrap around her bottom, her purse empty.

We were fortunate to have vegetables in the garden. After moving to Flitwick in 1940, it took Ernie several months, but gradually the garden yielded some produce. We did not eat ready meals, and seldom enjoyed sweets, crisps, chocolate, but on reflection that was no bad thing.   Although I can recall feeling hungry many times, and too often Mum had nothing in the house to eat, not even a slice of bread, the situation was only temporary.

Food rationing began on January 8th 1940, a month or two before we moved to the Alley. Rationing, coupons for almost every commodity, became a way of life. Although it wasn't legal, there was a thriving trade in selling and swapping them. Would Vegetarians need meat coupons?

By the end of 1940, 728,000 tons of food lay at the bottom of the ocean. By 1942 times were desperate as Uboats harassed shipping in the Atlantic. They sunk 11,000 ships. Hitler tried to starve us into defeat. The poor, like Mum, took the brunt of this assault. Propoganda being what it is, I don't believe the country knew the full extent of the problem until shortages became very visible. Bare shelves, and rations reduced.

From as young as 3, I ran errands to the shops for Mum. When we moved to Flitwick, Mum registered for her rations with Mrs Cousins general grocery shop at the bottom end of Station Road. (Registration with one shop for general groceries, required by law). For butcher meat, she registered with Feazey, who had a shop at 33 High Street. On Saturdays, I accompanied Mum to Cousins shop for her rations, and to pay her account. It worked like this.

First, Mum paid her bill up to date, if she could, although many times she told Mrs Cousins she'd not enough to pay the full amount, could she carry some over to next week. That done, Mrs Cousins noted the balance due at the top of a clean page in the tick book. Mum didn't buy all her rations at once, only enough to do her over the weekend, we had no refrigerator. Mrs Cousins weighed her rations and other needs, totted them up on a scrap of paper and wrote the total in the tick book.

Butter, Jam, Lard, Sugar, Tea, Cheese, Soap, Margarine, to name some, plus Salt, Vinegar, Firelighters, pot of meat Paste, tins of Soup, Beans, cold Meat such as Spam, Flour, Candles, Cigarettes for Ernie, Custard Powder, and any vegetables not in our garden. (The margarine packet bore no brand name until later, when Mum usually

264

bought Echo margarine because it was the cheapest).

Sometimes we had Dripping on a slice of bread, and sprinkled with salt. It tasted quite nice. For those of you who have never heard of Dripping, it is fat which drips off meat when it is roasted. We bought Dripping at the Butcher's.

Cousins shop was very small. No refrigerators full of different brands of dairy products stretching into infinity. The ration of Butter was cut from a large block brought through from the rear storeroom. Mrs Cousins cut a half pound of Margarine in half if Mum wanted only a quarter pound. Same with Tea. If Mum asked for only two ounces, Mrs Cousins cut a quarter pound packet in half. Almost daily, I was sent with a note to the shop for skiddly small amounts, such as two ounces of margarine, 2 slices bacon, 1 candle.

Breakfast was two slices of bread spread with the mixture of margarine and lard, and a cup of weak tea. Occasionally we had hot porridge sprinkled with a little of the sugar ration. Brands were Scott's, Three Bears, or Quaker. Recently on TV, a programme was shown which attempted to get children in a school to eat the kind of foods we ate in the 1940s. The mother of one 8 year old boy made porridge, and what a ghastly mess she made of it. She hadn't a clue. Congealed into a gooey lump, it looked inedible, the child expected to sup it. Ugh! I wouldn't have eaten it. I thought the child was going to be sick. It was nothing like a good plate of porridge. Experimenting by going back to how we ate in the 1940s is not the answer. The recipe for a decent dish of porridge is as follows, to serve two or three.

1 cup of porridge oats, 2 cups of cold water. mix the water and oats in a small saucepan, bring to boil and simmer, keep stirring, do not leave the pan, stir, stir, until oats and water well mixed to a gentle consistency, then serve with a little milk poured over.

Please yourself if you sprinkle it with salt or sugar. To do it the Scottish way, it must be salt.

Once in a while, we had the luxury of a bowl of Kellogg's Cornflakes, or a bowl of Weetabix. There were times we had jam on our two slices of bread, or maybe golden syrup, instead of margarine. There were also times when I went to school having eaten two slices of dry bread, no spread at all.

We never had a cooked breakfast of black pudding, eggs, bacon, sausages, devilled kidneys, kippers, or anything else of that kind. Eggs were strictly rationed to one per person per week.

There was dried egg, one packet every four weeks for adults, every two weeks for children. Mum used it to make Omelettes or Pancakes. May Watson threatened to wring her hens necks when they went through spells of low or no production. She loudly grumbled to Mum, 'They ain't give us no eggs fer over a week gal, if they do..oon't bloody well lay soon, 'ees gooin ter git rid of 'em, we'll 'ave 'em fer dinner instead.'
We'd sing this little ditty,

> Chick chick chick chick chicken,
> lay a little egg for me,
> Chick chick chick chick chicken,
> I want one for my tea,
> I haven't had an egg since Easter,
> and now it's half past three,
> so, Chick chick chick chick chicken,
> lay a little egg for me.

Our Dinner time was at 1pm, we did not call it Lunch time. The term lunch wasn't in our vocabulary. Dinner was the main meal of the day. Ernie started work early in the morning, came home for his bever at 9.30 am, then again at 1pm for his dinner. When Brusseling in winter, he took sandwiches and a flask of tea, working through to when darkness came down. Works canteens in factories provided subsidised meals for those who could not get home for dinner.

Meat was rationed by price, around one shilling and ten pence worth per person per week. Mum bought stewing steak, all sinewy, scraggy. I chewed and chewed, trying to swallow it, refused to eat the rest on my plate. Ernie told me to eat it or else I'd starve the rest of the week. I had to obey, or I would indeed have gone hungry. Dumpling, or Bedfordshire Clanger was our usual midday meal, along with mashed potato and a second vegetable. Cabbage, or Sprouts, Carrot, Cauliflower, depending on what we had available.

The Clanger was traditionally a dumpling with meat in one half, and jam in the other half, with a wedge of dough in the middle to separate the two. By the 1940s the Dumpling was all meat and vegetables, there was no jam at one end. As well as most weekdays, we had the Clanger and Veg on Sundays too. It was a cheap and filling meal. This is how she made it.

Mum wiped the oilcloth on the table. then proceeded to make the dough. She had no scales, it was all guesswork. Most cookbooks will give you a recipe for plain dough, however, be warned, Bedfordshire Clanger can be heavy on the digestion.

A small amount of meat is chopped up, in Mum's day it was very little. She chopped Onions, Potato, Carrot or Swede and added the chopped Veg to the meat, adding pinch salt, and pepper. Similar to the filling in Cornish Pasties. If she had no Beef, she used Sausage meat, Mutton, Pork, Bacon. The mixture is then laid along the length of the rolled out dough, (rolled into an oblong shape), the whole thing is rolled up like a Swiss Roll.

It is now ready to be wrapped in an oblong shape of clean

cloth and dusted again with flour. The cloth has to be longer than the Dumpling. Mum did not have one of those useful long shaped metal containers for steaming. Rolling the cloth all around the Dumpling, it is secured by tying twine at each end, just like a Christmas cracker, another length of twine around the middle. Mum cleared a space on top of the range. Placing the Dumpling in a large pan of boiling water, the lid placed on, she boiled it for at least one and half hours. Often, when making dough for the Clanger, she made extra, enough to make Jam Roly Poly, or Spotted Dick pudding, to be served with Custard, usually on Sundays. Clanger almost every day became a bit tedious, but if Mum tried to be adventurous, he'd turn his nose up, saying, 'What's this supposed ter be?'

Once we started to breed our own Rabbits, we had Rabbit stew for a change two or three times per month on Sundays. A man came around now and again to buy the skins. Liver was cheap to buy, and also provided a change from Clanger. I liked Liver fried with Onions, served with mashed Potato. When Mum went Peasing or Potato lifting, there was no time to cook the Clanger. She'd come home, send me to Cousins shop for a tin of Irish Stew, Spam, or Corned Beef, and while I was on the errand, she peeled the Potatoes and cut up Cabbage. Corned Beef hash, made with heated Corned Beef and mashed Potato, with Oxo mixed in, then fried was a favourite of mine. Spam is now part of computer language, but in the 1940s it was sliced, dipped in batter, (made with flour, dried egg, and milk), fried in very hot fat, and served with mashed Potato, with maybe Baked Beans, of the Heinz 57 varieties.

As you will read here, our food was basic, but nourishing and filling, and just as importantly, it was freshly cooked every day.

Mum could not afford a Joint of Beef, even if she could have used the oven in the old black range. Black Pudding was another delicacy I never had the pleasure of eating. It was more a Scottish or Northern English thing. Mum made Burgers, using Sausage meat, Onions and mashed Potato, dipped in salted Flour, and fried.

Ham or Bacon ration was 4 ounces per person per week. Mum cut the Bacon up to mix with chopped vegetables for the Clanger filling.

We made a trip one Sunday to visit Aunt Daphne and her family at Newport Pagnall, where Uncle George was the town's Gravedigger. Bus to Bedford, then another bus, eventually getting there. We arrived just as she was dishing up dinner for her brood. Suddenly, before any could start eating, she whisked the plates away, and took half the sausages from each plate, telling us to sit down, she'd plenty of Potatoes and would cook some more. Sausage and Mash coming up. Daphne and George were never wealthy, her house topsy turvy, but she had a big heart, and had love for everyone. Sausages were not rationed, had hardly any meat in them, and not always available. Gourmet food they were not, but for poor families they were tasty and filling. Mum said the Butchers swept up the sawdust from the floor to help fill out the sausages. There is no doubt they had a lot of cereal packed into them. Cheaper ones contained a lot of gristle. A splodge of HP sauce helped the taste.

Few housewives had a fridge. Before the war, housewives were used to going to the Butcher and choosing poultry or a Rabbit which hung from hooks inside and outside the shop. Poultry did not come ready plucked, although a member of staff would do the job for a little extra charge. The Butcher's block was a great big wooden slab, well worn, big enough to take a whole cow. Mum thought Barker's sausages better than Feazey's. Both shops no longer exist, they have been converted to other uses. During the war, the hooks hanging from the ceiling in the back of the shops were almost empty.

A little snippet I came across in the Edinburgh Evening News, Christmas 1943, illustrates the problems Butchers had in supplying their customers. 15 Turkeys were allocated to each Butcher with 800 registered customers. How on earth did they share 15 Turkeys between 800 people? It is no wonder I never tasted Turkey. My first tasting was 1950/51, when it was included in the menu for Christmas dinner at Marks and Spencer.

Chicken was almost impossible for us to obtain, unless someone local sold surplus from their back garden. Today we have Chicken Burgers,Chicken Korma, Chicken Curry, Chicken this and that. Mum cooked Rabbit for our Christmas dinner.

Until recently, local Butchers had vans trading door to door in housing estates and rural areas, but that is a declining operation. For many years, the housewife took a large plate or platter to the van, and the Butcher placed all her purchases on the platter instead of wrapping the meat in paper/polythene, same as he had been doing since the shortages of the 1940s.

The Ministry of Food issued leaflets and advertized recipes in magazines and newspapers, the recipes for meals containing very little meat, or none at all, such as Mock Goose that had not a trace of Goose in it. Hoarding was a criminal offence. Many risked prosecution if they hoarded important foods like Flour.

Mum had little enough money to hoard anything. Meat was salted. Salt had been used for centuries by rich and poor alike to preserve food and for making it palatable. We always had too muchsalt in our diet. Salt in the Clanger, in the cleaning water, in the cooking pot, and sprinkled over our food on the plate.

Tea time was whatever time Ernie arrived home from work. Mum did try to vary it a little, but restricted by rationing, and more importantly, by cost. We had two or three slices of bread and jam, or

270

a mixture of margarine and lard, sometimes we had peanut butter on the bread. Now and again, she toasted the bread. We had no electric toaster. The toast was made by putting the bread on a long fork and holding it against the heat of the fire. If we were really lucky, we'd have scrambled egg on the toast, (usually using up our meagre egg ration). We had beans on toast, (Heinz, first sold in Pittsburgh in 1901), or toast and marmalade. Sandwiches sometimes, instead of the above. Filling was a pot of meat paste bought from Cousins shop, or a slice or two of Spam with Spring Onion, or maybe a slice or two of Palony, a sort of meat similar to Luncheon meat. She used the cheese ration to put in Ernie's sandwiches when he did not come home for dinner, but once in a while, she made Rarebit, and we had that on toast at teatime. Salmon out of a tin, along with slices of Cucumber, made sandwiches for visitors.

The crusts were never cut off the bread, Mum could never afford that kind of waste. On a good day, perhaps I'd help by making the batter for a few pancakes, which we ate hot, straight from the pan. The batter was simply dried egg, a little milk, a little water, and salt. We sprinkled sugar on the pancakes.

Sugar was rationed fairly generously in my opinion, at around 3lb per week per family of 4. It was used up, as families liked their tea sweet. The sugar did not come in convenient 1 kg packets. Pussy Cousins had to weigh it into blue paper sugar bags. It was the same with dried fruits when they were available, she had to weigh the amount allowed from a large sack, (You could only buy amounts you had ration coupons for). Sugar rationing ended in September 1953. A customer could never be sure if the weight was correct when anything was filled into a bag in the back shop.

Thelma Palmer, (nee Beale), told me her parents, Horace and Ida Beale of the Crown Inn, kept a Pig out back, and a local Butcher did the necessary slaughter when the time came for it to provide large hams, which were cured in the pub's cellars. The local official, who was supposed to oversee the legalities of this activity, I'll not name hime, enjoyed a lovely large ham that weekend.

Mum had no larder. Groceries were kept in the only place that was dry and secure enough from the mice, and that was in one of the cupboards in the more ornate sideboard of the living room. The few pieces of crockery we had were kept in the other sideboard.

Cheese didn't come readily packed in plastic. Mrs Cousins cut the amount within the ration limit from a large Cheddar which still had the rind on it, using a wire cutter. Mum occasionally bought cheese spread in little boxes containing 6 portions. It cost between 6d and 9d, one advert read,

'Ssh! careless talk may give away secrets- Don't spread rumour, spread Velveteen, the delicious food that spreads like Butter.'

Today, we have a huge array of food choices. Supermarkets open 24hours/7days per week for our convenience. We can shop on the Internet day or night. Every High Street and Shopping Centre has Takeaway food shops, cafes, and other instant eateries. Pubs serve meals, restaurants specialize in meals from all corners of the globe. Country House restaurants charge us a fortune. A Carvery near to my home does a better job, I can see exactly what goes on my plate, and there is a fantastic choice of vegetables. Also, a little café in town serves a good lunch.

In the 1940s, we had restaurants of course, I believe five shillings was the limit anyone could spend on a meal, but it could be difficult if not impossible to find a Japanese Sushi place.

Mum could not afford to take us out to dine. She prepared

272

sandwiches and a flask of tea on the few occasions when we went on an outing. I do not recall going to a restaurant as a child, and I was never at a Dinner party.

The earliest I can recall going out to eat anywhere was after I began working for M & S in Luton, when my first boy-friend took me to a Milk Bar, (small café). We sat there, I sipped my cup of tea, I believe we held hands, some friends turned up, we sang rebel Irish songs. There was no juke box churning out inane noises from boy or girl bands. There were none. Elvis Presley unheard of.

McDonald's, Burgerking, KFC, were all for the future. The only takeaway Flitwick had was the Fish and Chip shop on the corner of Windmill Road. Fresh fish such as salted Cod costing around 9d (4p) per pound sold on two or three weekdays, Fish and Chips sold on Friday and Saturday evenings, wrapped straight into newspaper which were handed in by customers who had finished reading them. The shop did not sell Pizzas/Chinese/Chicken/Indian or Chinese meals. A Fish and Chip van stopped on Friday evenings at the foot of the Alley. Sometimes, Mum sent me for Rock Salmon and Chips. Rock Salmon was a fancy name for Wolf fish. Plaice and chips were dearer. Fish and Chips were not rationed during the war.

As for delicacies such as Escargot, No!! they were for the Frogs, as we called the French. Eat Snails, Ugh!! Ernie wouldn't accept a Salad for his dinner, remarking he wasn't eating Rabbit food. He certainly wouldn't have appreciated Mum making him foreign muck, as he called anything he considered not quite English.

Mum sold 3 out of the 4 ration books quota of Sweet coupons to the man on the Vass bread van in exchange for a reduction in her Bread account. Sweets were rationed from 1940 to February 4th 1953. In 1953 I was working in Bedford M & S store, and well recall the mad scramble and queues at the Sweet counter when rationing ended. The nation went stark raving bonkers as they scoffed ration free confectionery.

The Supervisor sent me over to the Sweet counter to help out. Queues stretched out of the side door into Harper Street and up past the Butcher's shop. I was unfamiliar with using scales, but soon learned as people frantically waved £1 and 10 shilling notes at us, 'Half a pound of those, quarter of those.' A crazy day. Sweets and chocolate were displayed in jars and boxes, not prepacked.

Fruit was plentiful and cost little or nothing to us while we lived in the Alley. I scrumped Apples. Scraped knees, scratches on my arms, and nettle stings. The orchard stretched up the left hand side of the Alley to the path which led down to our garden plots. From that path, we children went through a gap in the hedge. Horace Beale crashed through the orchard after us, but he was a big man and made so much noise that we made our escape easily. We girls gathered up our skirts into carrying cradles and scampered quick with our haul. The boys bundled Apples into their rolled up pullovers. It was a very tempting place, as we made repeated forays. Mostly windfalls, but a few shakes of the branches brought down plenty which were not attacked by worm or other insects.

Home with our catch, we cut out bruises and worm eaten bits, then tucked in until our stomachs cried out for relief. Delicious, maybe because they came straight from the tree. (and no chemicals on them).

Another favourite place for scrumping was the Vicarage orchard. Lovely Cox Pippins. The Vicar also had Plum trees. One day he came pounding through the trees, closing in on us. My companions flew through a hole in the hedge unscathed, but I got caught by an angry Bee. The sting hurt, but I kept going, with my hoard still rolled up in my dress. I'm sure the Vicar's boss, (God), forgave us, even if the Vicar didn't. To him, we were those scruffs from the east end. I rarely tasted Strawberries, they were too expensive to buy. A few allotment holders risked growing them. Inevitably some went missing, the thieves those east end scruffs again. Supermarket fruit is tasteless in comparison.

Ginger Tom spread his bulk in the sunniest spot among the Fruit and Veg in Cousins shop window. Health and Safety officials would go apoplectic if they saw such an old fashioned thing today.

The import of Bananas became illegal on November 9th 1940, to free up ships for the war effort. Lord Woolton, in charge of the Government's Food Department, said only Oranges would be allowed in, to be made into concentrated Orange juice for the country's children. Mum often mixed the Orange juice with water to make a long drink, especially on hot days. During the war, I never saw a whole orange. When they became available again, the shops operated a rationing system by price, and by allowing each family only an alloted share. The first one Mum bought, we shared it quarter each. The juice ran down my chin, round my lips. Scraping at it with my little sharp teeth, I'd have eaten the peel too but for the bitter taste. Oranges were not packed in cardboard boxes of neatly arranged fruit on fibre trays. They were packed densely, each Orange wrapped delicately in orange coloured tissue, into wooden crates secured by wire. The tissue was kept for other uses. Apples were packed similarly, but in shallow wooden boxes. Those wooden crates were eagerly sought after. They came free. People used themas storage chests, some enterprising men used the wooden slats to make temporary furniture, kennels, Rabbit hutches.

Bananas were packed in heavy long wooden crates. It was fairly common for shop assistants to find a Tarantula had smuggled itself aboard. Bananas began to arrive from Jamaica by the end of

1945. I didn't taste one until 1946. Bedford Food Depot reported their first delivery of Bananas in March of 1946, and queues quickly formed at the shops. Scuffles broke out, the Police having to be called to keep order. When Barbara Cousins had a delivery, her shop, which was on the corner of the Avenue, was crowded, queues outside. Mum sent me to join the queue, and gradually I moved forward, to be told when it was my turn that I could have just ONE Banana. Perhaps I didn't have enough money for more than one. Mum sliced it to share. I ate my slices slowly, savouring every little bite. Bananas are still a favourite of mine.

As autumn came in we gathered Blackberries, in plentiful supply along the railway embankment. Every Spring, the sparks shooting all over the place from the steam engines going up and down the line set the thick untidy dry undergrowth on the embankment alight. The fires, when they died down, left ash full of nutrients, encouraging fresh growth. Most of the Brambles were between the big arch and Worthy End farm, on the east side. With all the dead wood and rubbish removed, they grew with vigour, and by end of the summer, were heaving with luscious ripening fruit.

Picking Blackberries became an almost daily occurrence for me. Eat one, two for the bowl, eat another, more for the bowl, fill the bowl to the brim. Take it home. The vitamin C from those Blackberries undoubtedly helped to set me up for the winter. On my frequent visits to Toddington, I often gathered Blackberries in Tingrith Road for Gran Bland. The road very quiet, I barely saw two or three cars in the whole hour or so I was there. I had no fear of being on my own in such a deserted place. At the end of Gas Street, (it is now Conger Lane), a lane leads to the Bridleway and Fancott. This lane also yielded plenty of Blackberries.

Mum made Blackberry steamed pudding, in a pudding bowl,

276

served it with hot Custard. She did not add Sugar. Making a dough, same as for the Clanger, rolled out two thirds of it to form a base in the pudding bowl, filled the bowl with the fruit, rolled out the remaining dough to form a lid and laid the lid over the top of the fruit. Wrapped the pudding bowl in a cloth, closed the top of the cloth loosely using a length of twine, and steamed the pudding for around one and half hours. Custard did not come ready made. She bought a small packet of Birds Custard powder. The custard was always lovely and smooth, and she showed me how to make it to ensure it was not lumpy.

On Station Road, opposite the Alley (the house number used to be 79), there was a lovely Plum orchard. A few years later the orchard was destroyed by a scrap yard, now there are houses on the site. For a 3d coin, the woman of the house filled a paper sugar bag, or a similar size brown bag, with delicious Victoria Plums or Damsons. Sometimes I took an earthenware bowl instead of a bag. 'Can I have some Plums please.' Straight from the tree. Very generous. 'Can yer lend me a cup o' Sugar Florrie, I'll pay yer back whin I git me rations,' May Watson pleaded, hoping she was lucky Mum had some left. She had a sweet tooth.

We had Walnuts one Christmas, but Peanuts, or Monkey Nuts as we knew them, were hard to come by. We roasted Chestnuts at the fire, they were plentiful locally, as were Hazelnuts. Kathy Wooding told me that families collected Acorns and Rose hips, taking them to the Bank on Station Square, where they were weighed and paid for. Her mother received 6d each time. Acorns roasted in the oven until the shells split provided nuts for cakes and puddings. Can you imagine any bank doing that sort of thing today?

Bread wasn't rationed during the war, but in 1946 the Government decided it would be, and it stayed rationed until 1948.

277

The price was controlled, fourpence halfpenny per loaf. There were no trade names, it was called the National loaf, unsliced, unwrapped. Mum used one or more loaves per day. Asked for a'Yesterday's loaf,' because it was easier to slice, being slightly stale.

The village bakers were up early in the morning to bake bread, selling it the same day. Today, we really have no idea how long ago the bread was baked. One of the first essential items a new bride had to buy was a bread knife. Sometimes Mum spread Black Treacle, or Golden Syrup on a slice of bread for us as a snack. Deliciously sweet. Marmalade in 2 lb jars, cost around 1 shilling.

Robertson's jams carried an image of a Golly on the label. It was their trademark, but around 1991 it was removed as it was considered no longer appropriate. I removed the Golly from the label and stuck it in a scrap book. Mum bought the cheapest varieties, Mixed Fruit, Plum or Apricot.

Mum never baked tarts or pies because of our damaged oven, and seldom bought them from a shop, except for Rhubarb tart, which could be ate cold with hot custard poured over. Every Saturday, she bought 4 Rock buns from the Vass van, we ate them at teatime. In 1943, the Rural Food Control Committee Executive Officer, (what a mouthful), asked employees of the Council to give him information on any stale bread found in dustbins. No chance of breadcrumbs in our dustbin, we ate every last crumb. When Joyce and Pat were babies, Mum dipped a crust in jam for them to eat.

Biggleswade, Bedford, Luton, Ampthill all had their market days. Flitwick heaved with fields of fresh vegetables which found places on the growers stalls. Onions, Carrots, Sprouts, Runner Beans Cauliflowers, Savoy Cabbage, Spring Cabbage, Parsnips, Turnips, Potatoes, Peas, Tomatoes, to name just a few.

The formalities of serving were scant, we had no serving

platters. Vegetables were served straight from pot to plate. The Clanger was emptied on to a plate, the twine cut and the cloth wrapping removed, then it was sliced, with Ernie receiving the lions share. Mum made a gravy. Unlike lots of families today, when so many seem to eat on the trot, out of paper or plastic, we did sit down to our meals, using a knife and fork.

Ernie grew Celery every second or third year. Dipped in salt, we ate it raw with dry bread. Despite the rationing and the shortages, food was available. Perhaps not always what was needed or desired, usually for lack of cash, but nobody, not even us, actually starved, as you can see from the variety of above. The Clanger, bread, and Potatoes were our mainstay, all the other foods mentioned were not always available, or they were only bought occasionally. We never threw food away, I wasn't allowed to leave any on my plate, although that wasn't hard to do, my appetite was good. Ernie and Mum said, 'There's starving kids out there who'd gladly eat that,' if I (rarely) left anything on the plate.

When preparing food, Mum was very clean indeed. She went to great lengths to make sure our food went into the pot properly cleaned and prepared. Salt was important, to salt the water to soak the vegetables, salted to remove little beasties, bugs, slugs. Washed again in fresh salted water, then more salt in the cooking pot. As you know already, every drop of water had to be hauled up from the Well. Vegetables plainly boiled or eaten raw. Mum also bought tinned Peas as needed, Marrowfat variety as they were cheaper.

Ernie placed a few Marrow seeds in the compost heap, it acted like a hotbed and they grew into marvellous large Marrows. Mum peeled and sliced them, removed the seeds from the inside, and boiled the slices until soft. Served with Sausage meat sliced/fried.

It was taught to me at School that the humble Potato came to this country with that great adventurer Sir Walter Raleigh. Evidence found in an old gardening book I own indicates the Potato may have been here before that. A 16th century herbalist named Gervade Herriot, in a work entitled Herbal, of 1597, refers to a vegetable he grew, called, "The Potato of Virginia". He worked gardens near the site of Somerset House in London.

It wasn't until the 18th century that Potatoes became part of poor peoples diet. Ernie planted earlies in late February. Then came a succession of plantings into early summer. His favourite was King Edwards. He dug, put in Lime, manure, dug again, before planting the seed. A few good showers and sunshine did the rest.

It is said the first crisps were made when Cornelius Vanderbilt, (of that famous family), asked for thinner french fries in a hotel in Saratoga U.S.A in the late 19th century. Another report says crisps were invented in 1853 New England by an American Indian named George Crum. (An Indian with that name?) Quite frankly, I think crisps were around long before that, in Bedfordshire especially. Mothers are bombarded by children complaining they are hungry. There were no big mass produced multi-packs available.
In the 19th and early 20th century there may well have been nothing to eat in a poor cottage except Potatoes. Slicing one or two very thinly and frying in some dripping, provided something tasty for the youngsters. Mr Vanderbilt's snack that day in Saratoga Springs may not have been the first crisps.

When Carter's of London introduced crisps in 1913, Bedfordshire, and Flitwick in particular, might have been sending supplies of Potatoes by rail, which provided quick and easy transport. After the first world war, Frank Smith, who had worked for Carter, began his own crisp making business, and it was Smith's crisps I was familiar with. Smith's crisps, in individual bags slightly larger than today's, contained a little salt in a blue waxed pouch, not to be confused with the little flat containers of salt in their plain crisps today. A blue bag was simply a square of waxed paper, the salt placed on it, and the paper drawn up around the salt into a pouch, then twisted to seal.

In 1960, Golden Wonder, at their factory in Broxburn, near Edinburgh, introduced ready salted crisps. 1962, came Cheese and Onion flavoured crisps, followed a year or so later by Salt and Vinegar crisps. Sadly, Golden Wonder closed their doors a few years ago. During the War, the Government put up posters urging the nation, "Dig for Victory" We dug for survival.

In the autumn, Ernie made a clamp in the garden for the surplus potato crop. Dug a shallow trench, lined it with straw, laid the Potatoes on the straw, covered with more straw, a layer of earth, with a funnel or two in top for air. Mum dug into the clamp as she needed supplies. The manure for the garden was delivered by horse and cart and dumped next to the barn. When Ernie came home from work he barrowed it down to the garden. Between the manure and the smelly buckets in the lavatories, you can imagine the pong but it did wonders for the vegetables. One day, the cart horse which pulled the coal wagon, dropped a load of dung as it made its way down Station Road. The horses which drew the wagons were strong and sturdy, but when they needed to relieve themselves, they did it wherever they were at the time. Women rushed from nearby houses with shovels to clear the road and put the good stuff on their vegetable patches. Children, home from school were ordered to, 'Hurry up, get that dung in here quick, before it's all gone.' Flitwick residents never wasted a thing, recycling was second nature.

There are houses now on the green fields which at one time surrounded the Alley. One season around 1948/49 the field next to

281

the railway had the most delicious looking small white Turnips. On our way home from school, we kids pulled some, wiped the dirt off on our clothes, ate them just as they were, straight from the ground. They tasted scrumptious, and especially fresh. Our sharp teeth scraped the fine skin off, to spit out, and we devoured the rest. The farmer found a few missing when he came to harvest the crop, and didn't have far to look for the culprits. I can imagine some readers today may be quite aghast, 'Eat raw Turnips, Ugh!' but believe me, we took pleasure in such simple activities.

We were luckier than most children in inner city slums. At least we had the fields to enjoy the fresh air and had plenty of vegetables to eat. Getting little John or Susan to eat up all their greens was a bit easier when they hadn't been stuffing their face all morning with junk food and cans of fizzy drinks. Children were used to eating vegetables from the day they were weaned. Most were also breast fed, which was another advantage. For babies, Mums mashed down to eatable softness a portion of the same meal adults were eating. I knew little else except vegetables and fruit.

Jam jars were useful. Undamaged and clean, they were returned to the shops, worth a penny each. They came in handy when fishing for tiddlers in the brook. The foot of an old stocking tied to a bit of stick by wire or string, and we had a fishing net to scoop the water. We made a carrying handle for the jam jar by tying a length of string around the neck of it. The little fish needed flowing fresh water, but at home, cooped up in a jar, not fed properly, it was inevitable they'd die. The brook teemed with these Minnows darting hither and thither in and out of the reed beds. Fishing for them was so easy, and a most enjoyable activity. Around tuppence bought a fishing cane and net from Cousins shop.

When Mum ran out of cups we drank our tea from a jam jar

until she could afford to buy replacements. Cups were not thrown out when they became chipped or lost a handle. We used them until such time as they fell to bits or the tea leaked out. We used a jam jar as a water tumbler. Cups were not cheap to buy, shops ran out of stock. Tea at 4pm, with silver or best china tea service, delicate cakes on a pretty stand, how nice. Mum had no best tea service, silver or otherwise, and no fancy cakes. Even if the oven had been usable, I doubt very much if she would have baked cakes.

Jam jars were useful to plonk a bunch of wild flowers into. We caught Wasps in jam jars, smearing the inside with a scraping of jam and half filling with water, the Wasps fell into the water and could not get out. Mum caught flies with flycatcher strips. Hanging from the ceiling in the living room, with another in the kitchen, were strips of sweet smelling sticky tape, about an inch wide and 7 or 8 inches long. Costing around 6d, the strips lasted about a week.

Shops in the village sold glass bottles of Tizer, Lemonade, Corona. A returnable deposit paid. I never saw any plastic bottles or cans of fizzy drinks. Pussy Cousins sold Lemonade Crystals which, when mixed with cold water made a refreshing drink. Sherbet too, measuring it out from the jar on to a square of white paper and twisting it into a cone. We dipped liquorice sticks into it, or a finger to suck on the Sherbet. Price, just a penny or two, or even a smaller amount for halfpenny or three farthings. A real treat.

Few varieties of Biscuits were available. Many factories were turned over to munitions. Pussy Cousins had just 12 tin boxes with glass lids on a stand just inside the door, the glass lids allowing the customer a glimpse of the contents without having to open the lid up. On choosing one of the boxes, the customer handed the box to Mrs Cousins. The amount taken from the box by hand, weighed, placed in a paper bag, usually the customer brought a bag with her.

Mrs Cousins may have been weighing Potatoes or handling firelighters before weighing the biscuits, but no hand washing took place. Her hands were given a cursory wipe on her apron. We must have been immune to all those germs. Now and again I was sent to the shop to ask for a bag of broken biscuits. There were always broken ones at the bottom of those boxes. For around thruppence I'd go home with a bagful, roughly sugar bag size. I savoured every last crumb of each broken bit Mum gave me.

As a child I was never privvy to a cup of Coffee. Mum had no Coffee percolator, no dainty coffee cups, and I never saw coffee beans in our house. In Mum's words, it was only Toffs who drank Coffee, they were the only people who could afford to. Instant Coffee of the kind we now see on Supermarket shelves wasn't available. The only Coffee I recall, was Camp Coffee, a mixture of Coffee and Chicory essence, sold in glass bottles carrying an image of an Indian Army Officer complete with turban.

Ice Cream was a treat. None of us had a Freezer, and it would have melted before we got it home from the shop. Cousins shop had no Ice Cream Freezer at that time. When the Pokey man came into the Alley we whooped with joy and asked our Mum's for a penny or two to buy a cone or ice cream in a wafer. Vanilla only. If a housewife was feeding many children, she took a bowl out to the Ice Cream vendor and asked for scoops. It worked out cheaper that way. The tricycle the Ice Cream vendor came on was very ingenious. Inside the cavernous storage box fitted to the front of the three wheeler were two drums of Ice Cream, the Ice Cream kept cold by insulation and dry ice, (solidified carbon dioxide). One drum for selling first, one in reserve. We children watched in fascination and anticipation as a drum was opened up.

The salesman may well have came from one of the many

Italian families around Bedford. By 1949/50 the Pokey man on his tricycle came no more. Shops and Cafes were installing vending freezers, and Wall's Ice Cream for example replaced their three wheelers with motorized vehicles.

Milk was delivered daily except Sunday. The Milkman came to the Alley with a horse drawn cart, to be replaced later in the 1940s by a small open backed pick up truck. Mum took her white enamel milk jug out to him. He measured the pint or two, using a deep long stemmed ladle hanging from the lip of the churn. The ladle had measurement marks. Milk was rationed at 3 pints, (sometimes 2 pints) per person per week. Watering down the milk to make a pint go further was normal for us. The milkman was paid on Saturdays, but if Mum hadn't enough money to pay him, she sent me out with the jug for the supply, and I was to tell him she wasn't in, she would pay him the following week.

Carrier bags at that time were made of thick paper, with string or cane handles. Notorious for the bottom dropping out, the contents scattered over the street. No use on a wet day. Most of the time we used our own shopping bag, made of cloth, or part cloth part leather, like a small holdall. Most things were put in the bag unwrapped, heavier items at the bottom, in no particular order, smells all mixed.

People saved paper, used it over and over again. To waste paper was a criminal offence. We did not have plastic bags and wrappers. Plastic carrier bags were not around until about 1960, when a Swedish shoe company began to use them. The Irish thought of a good money spinning idea by introducing a tax on them in 2002.

Across the yard at the side of Cousins shop was the bakery, Charlie Cousins the Baker. Both he and Mrs Cousins were getting on in years, but he still got up early to work in the large barn like

building, baking bread and cakes for villagers. Access to the yard was through large wooden gates, swung open when supplies arrived. Set into the large gates was a smaller gate, for access when the large gates were closed. Many times I went through that small gate to knock on the side door of the Cousins house when the shop was closed. 'Mum says can she have some firelighters please,' or 'Can I 'ave some bread please,' Perhaps it could be margarine, a baby's dummy, or 2 ounces of tea. Pussy Cousins never said much, but her sister Rose, (Hartwell), was displeased and showed it.
'This won't do you know, you should come when the shop is open.'

Opening hours were 9am to 5.30pm with hour and half for lunch, (1pm to 2-30pm). Half day closing at 1pm on Wednesdays, and closed all day Sundays. Other shops in the village operated the same hours. Ampthill had a different half day closing. The yard has since been built over. A Newsagents and a Video lending library took over shop and yard.

Opening the shop door rang a bell fixed near the top, ting ting, and Mrs Cousins or Rose was alerted that someone needed serving. Customers came in, and sat on a chair beside the counter. Mrs Cousins or Rose got this tin from that shelf, stretched up to lift down a jar of sweets, under the counter for the shoe box which held a few Birthday cards, weighed a few Biscuits, and went through to the back shop for Firelighters. Took a card of shoe laces down from a nail on the wall. Nothing was wrapped in plastic. It was all placed on the counter in front of the customer, the cost totalled up on a scrap of paper, the final total being written up in the tick book, for almost all her customers paid at the end of the week, after the menfolk brought home their wages. While I was being served, another two or three children followed in with shopping notes. Children did not sit on the chair beside the counter, some had to stand on tiptoe to hand their errand note to Mrs Cousins.

Nothing was wrapped that did not have to be wrapped. I still think it daft to wrap Bananas, Oranges in plastic. I buy them loose.

There were several grocery shops in Flitwick. Dudeney and Johnson, which used to be Ideal Stores before that. Nicholson's beside Wynne's Radio shop. These were two of the better grocery shops. Some Flitwick women registered with Lipton's shop in Bedford Road Ampthill for their rations, for the more varied range of foodstuffs, and because Lipton's would also deliver to Flitwick.

At 77 Station Road, Mrs Dix ran a smallgrocery shop in the front room of her house.

From around 1947/48, the old railway carriage on the corner of the Thinnings and the High Street, had once been a Cobbler's workshop, became a Greengrocery store. There were three Butchers in the village that I know of, also a Dairy in Windmill Road. I think it was Leemings.

On the High Street, next to Dudeney and Johnson, opposite the Station, we had Sharpe's Bicycle and Toy Shop, and repair garage They sold spares for cycles/cars, as well as Paraffin and Candles.

The Post Office did sell a variety of goods, including Newspapers, but not quite such a variety as it does today. The public Telephone box and the Post box are still in the same spot. Other shops were the Chemist, a Bank, Hairdresser Fossey.

Up to around 1948, there was a small Tearoom next to the Post Office, but the Co-op then took over the front garden. They built a shop there. Down the High Street were two shops opposite the Thinnings, one of them was Inskip's Ironmongery shop. An Aladdin's cave. Galvanized pails and dustbins, floor tiles, wall tiles, wallpaper chosen from a book of patterns, paint, screws, nails, chicken wire, string, planks of wood, pots and pans, bottles for

287

bottling fruit, garden tools, too many things to name here, although there were times it was hit or miss if the shop had what the customer needed in stock. Next door was another Grocery shop. Further along, opposite the Blackbirds was Inskip's drapery shop in a dark low bungalow style building set back a few feet from the pavement. Mum sent me there for my plimsolls for P.E at school. 19 Station Road there was another Ironmongery shop. At the back of the shop was a long bench like counter where the customers were served. Like Inskip's Ironmongery shop at the other end of the village it was an Alladin's cave for the handyman and housewife. Some items such as Carbolic Soap and Reckitt's Dolly Blue are no longer available. They probably do not have much call for Zebo blacking for grates today. We knew the shop as Dillingham's but later it became Short's.

Shop owners had to put up with all sorts of restrictions, regulations, and often had empty spaces on the shelves where stock should be. Ernie bought his garden seeds at Dillingham's. Small galvanized pails cost 3/4 (17p), aluminium saucepans were 5/6 for size 6 inch, 7/6 for 7 inch, 9/5 for 8 inch. An electric iron could set you back 38/6, not cheap.

At the other end of the village, on the Ampthill Road, next to the One O One garage, just before Running Waters, was a little sweet shop, in the front room of the house. Mrs Monk sold home made Chocolates. She was a miniature Thornton style Chocolate heaven. They were expensive, but Uncle George and Aunt Daphne paid most of the cost, we'd use the coupons from the one ration book Mum had not sold the sweet coupons from, although I cannot recall handing over any coupons. It was the only shop I knew to open on Sunday.

On my 14th birthday, Ernie took me into the chemist's to choose something, (or it may have been a Christmas present). Overwhelmed by this sudden and unexpected show of generosity,

288

and choice, I chose a little gift of Blue Velvet soaps and Talcum Powder. At least I would smell nice for a change.

A year or so before the end of the war, Ernie cobbled some Rabbit hutches together and built a Rabbit run at the top end of our garden plot. Rabbit meat for us to eat, skins to sell. Rabbits breed profusely, can have up to ten litters each year, of anything up to eight young at a time. It made good sense for him to set about breeding them. Myxomotosis was unheard of. Traps were set for wild Rabbits, but damaged skins were not so valuable. Some sent Ferrets down Rabbit holes, some used small Terriers to get at the Rabbits.

Ernie scavenged planks of wood and fence posts, bought chicken wire and nails, making an enclosure for 20 or 30 hutches. Hutches I've seen in Pet Stores have not changed significantly since then. He brought straw home from Woodcrafts, the Rabbits leading a comfortable life. Starting off with only 3 or 4 Rabbits, it wasn't long before they were breeding and the hutches filled up. I did most of the gathering of food for them.

Not to a Pet shop, there wasn't one in the village, but out into the fields. They ate almost anything. Carrots, Carrot tops, bits of Cabbage, Apples and other fruits. Allotments between Water Lane and the railway provided loads of Chickweed which the Rabbits loved. I filled a couple of sacks in minutes. The allotment holders were glad to have the troublesome weed removed. I gathered Grass, Dandelions, Clover, and a Fern which I am not sure of the name, but it was probably the leaves of Wild Parsley, growing in abundance along the edge of the brook, railway embankment, roadway verges.

Forget Beatrix Potter and her lovely little Bunnikins Peter Rabbit & Co. Our Rabbits could be vicious great big lumps of fur and fury. Many times I had my fingers nipped, or they'd kick out their back feet to land a whacking thump as I cleaned the hutches and moved them around. Our Rabbits were definitely not pets, they thought anything coming within an inch of their teeth was edible. As for their rampant sex lives, I had little idea what that meant, not in detail anyway. I knew if a Doe and Buck were left together, and she didn't try to kill him, baby Rabbits were born shortly after. The Buck wasn't left with the Doe after mating. Sometimes there were 30 or more Rabbits in the enclosure. Ernie killed them by breaking their necks when we required one for our dinner. I will not describe the action to you, it wasn't nice, just quick. The dead Rabbit was then hung by the back legs tied together with string from a nail on the back of the barn door. Ernie skinned it and we ate the meat. Every few weeks a man came round the village to collect skins. I am not too sure how much Ernie was paid, but it gave him funds to take us on excursions to the Zoo and seaside.

Neighbour Carr Line was helpful to Mum when it came to preparing a Rabbit for the pot. Mum became nauseous if she tried to do it. Mum provided the salty water and next morning Carr returned the Rabbit, cut into suitable pieces, legs off, saddle all clean, ready for cooking. The basin was red with blood. Now and again, Carr was given a Rabbit for herself as a way of thanks.

Ernie used a Whetstone to keep his knives and tools sharp. Rabbit fur was acceptable to the makers of fur gloves. I spent a short time on the gloves counter in Luton M&S, selling gloves made of Rabbit fur, although it was not described as such. Cheaper fur coats and hats were Rabbit fur given a fancy name. A few months before we moved to Dunstable Road, we ate the last of the Rabbits, and he sold the hutches.

Truffles, or Pignuts as we knew them, are mostly thought of as food Pigs sniff out in France, and sold for fantastically high prices, prized and graded according to quality. I will tell you about one old

Oak tree in Flitwick, where in its spreadeagled raggedy roots, Pignuts could be found. Opposite the Infant School in Station Road was a Paddock where East End farmer Sabey kept a shire horse when it wasn't working on the farm. We rushed out of school, crossed the road, where the horse waited by the five bar gate to get his nose patted and fed grass we gathered from the roadside verge. Flicking his tail, he liked to trot around the field, head held high, mane bouncing. On a hot day, he sheltered under the widespread branches of the solitary Oak in the centre of the Paddock.

The Paddock was another playground for us when the horse was absent. We did handstands against the tree, ran around it playing Tig, and we dug for those Pignuts, using any old spoon or knife, or anything which would sift the earth away. Very rough in shape, knobbly, maybe a little larger than the size of an adult thumb, tasting nutty, we ate them as they were, wiping surplus dirt off on our clothes, a bit of dirt didn't bother us. Whitish/grey in colour under the dirt. The Paddock and the Oak tree are long gone.

Tea didn't come in handy little bags, ready for pot or cup. Tealeaves were sold loose, in packets from quarter pound upwards.

Brooke Bond Dividend Tea carried a penny stamp on the quarter pound packet, two stamps on the half pound packet. The stamps to be stuck on a card and when full the card exchanged for five shillings, (60 stamps). Dividend Tea cost 1/3 per quarter. Tea rationing and Government controlled until October 1952. Packets of Tea, (and Cigarettes), contained a small card, same size as a playing card, prized by Collectors. Schoolboys swapped cards. On the front of the card was an illustration/photo, on the reverse, the details. If the card were of Footballer, the details were his age, what team he played for, previous teams etc. If the illustration was of a soldier of the Crimea, or Boer War, details explained his uniform, regiment,

291

battles fought and so on. There were cards detailing animals, birds, castles and famous landmarks, radio stars, steam engines, motors, such a variety.

Mum and May gossiped over a cup of tea, usually in May's house, with Millie reading the tea leaves when the cup was empty. They had no elaborate ceremony. Kettle boiled, water poured over tealeaves in pot, pot left to stand for a minute or so, tea poured into cups, without a strainer if the tealeaves were to be read, (Tasseography). They had no delicate china teasets. Tea was drunk from plain cups, chipped cups, cups with broken handles, tin mugs, bakelite beakers, or even a jam jar. The cup was drank almost dry, tealeaves swirled around before the last of the liquid was carefully drunk. Millie looked inside each cup, pondering over the shapes of the wet tealeaves. Where I only saw soggy tealeaves, Millie saw images, which could be anything from an aeroplane to dogs, cats, cars, birds houses, all representing a message she said. A little ditty comes to mind,

'One two three, mother caught a flea, she put it in the teapot to make a cup of tea, when she put the milk in the flea came to the top, when she put the sugar in the flea went pop.'

With the remaining ration book of sweet coupons we bought favourites such as Liquorice Allsorts, Jelly Babies, Winter Mixture, a Fry's Choccy Bar.

Pizza, Curry, Pasta, Thai cooking, Mexican dishes, Chinese Stir Fry, even had we heard of them, Ernie would not eat what he called 'Foreign muck.' We now import many foods we could so easily grow ourselves, given encouraging government support.

Chapter 50
HE's A   BLACK MAN

A Robertson's Golly from Marmalade jar

One warm sunny day, some time in 1947/48, when playing in the yard with other children, a man carrying a rather heavy looking suitcase made his way up the Alley towards Millie Barnes house. We had seen Pedlars before, but none quite like this one. We must have been a nuisance as we gawped at him in a distasteful manner. Until the late 1940s, even into 1950, we were unused to foreigners, as we called anyone who didn't appear to be English, in the Alley. This man wasn't only a stranger, he was a dark skinned Stranger, wearing a turban and an illfitting suit. Only women wore turbans in our village, to keep their hair curlers hidden. We gazed in awe at the contents of his case when he opened it on Millie Barne's doorstep. She wouldn't let him over the threshold. All sorts of trimmings, ribbons, beads, buttons, reels of thread, it was a miniature haberdashery shop. Collar studs, pretty hair slides.

I wanted one. 'Mum, mum, can I 'ave an 'air slide.'

When he reached our door, Mum was courteous towards him, but spoke too loudly, as if the poor man was deaf. He showed her his wares, spoke softly in pidgin English. Her purse would certainly be near empty, but I got my hair slide, Joyce a ribbon, and she may have bought a reel of thread too.

As that poor Indian Pedlar ambled slowly back down the Alley with his battered suitcase, to try his luck in another street, he must have been very tired, and certainly not much richer. I cannot imagine he made a lot of profit in the Alley, or even in the other streets at our end of the village. Slowly and wearily he'd make his way from street to street, trying to earn a bob or two, all the time having to suffer gawping kids like me.

Ernie and others miscalled dark skinned people. Wogs if they were Arabs, Chinks if Chinese, the Japanese were Nips, Africans and Americans of African origin were Niggers. Germans were Jerries/Huns Bosch, sometimes a more genial Fritz. I tell it as it was then. In the shops, a dark shade of brown was still known as Nigger brown. I'd seen black actors on the screen where they were either musicians or servants.

In this so called free country of ours, as we had suffered a war in which many coloured men had died, there were adverts in the papers with a tag on the end, 'Coloureds need not apply' or 'Not for sale to Niggers.' Neighbours were worried that a coloured family moving in would depress property prices. I once asked the Manager of the store in Luton where I worked, 'Why don't we have any West Indians working here,'? and he replied, 'Because the customers would refuse to be served by them.' It could have been true in Luton at that time. Stores would not dare to discriminate in such a fashion today. In some shops, if a coloured person was waiting to be served, they were ignored. As a child I was often ignored in shops, or put to the back of the queue, so we had something in common.

Where racism exists, it is not all one-sided. Doesn't matter what the colour of skin, we have good and bad in all societies. An obnoxious or cruel person is the same whatever the skin colour. What good to the world did those suicide bombers achieve when they blew themselves up. Did the destruction of the twin towers in New York change anything for the better? Did the killing of those people on the bus and tube in London change the government? Did it bring more understanding? No!!. Are we not all brothers and sisters, with every right to life and liberty?

We all bleed the same colour of blood.

Chapter 51
GETTING AROUND

Much has been written by others about transport, but I'll add some words and views of my own. The school run didn't exist. It was a long walk from Denel End to Dunstable Road school, many cycled there.. In Flitwick, perhaps only a dozen or so women knew how to drive. The few private cars in the village were nearly all driven by men. It was the man's toy, his pride and joy. No one in the Alley owned a car.

Most took the bus or train to work, or cycled. Working class men had Saturday afternoon off to watch sport or potter in the garden or allotment. They did not go shopping in their droves, they left that to their wives and mothers. Sundays were for the Church or allotment, but sometimes a man worked overtime on Sunday to top up his wages. George Woodcraft did not work his men on Sundays, so Ernie spent the day in the garden if the weather was amenable.

When the Council built the houses on the new estate in the late 40s, no provision was made for cars. People with little enough income to buy a house, were considered too poor to own a car. Look down any road in those years, few cars could be seen.

Between 1940 and 1945, cars were used for voluntary work or laid up for the duration. In 1940 for example, the private motorist was restricted to 6 gallons of petrol per month. In 1942 even that small allowance was withdrawn. After the war, the allowance was gradually increased, until petrol rationing ended on 26th May 1950, after motorists kicked up a fuss because Germany had already ended rationing. Motor manufacturers introduced new models, updated versions of pre-war cars. They were required to export 50% of production in 1945, rising to 75% in 1947. Waiting lists for new cars were long, maybe even two years. Hire purchase being the normal way of borrowing the finance, if you could afford it. Banks and Finance houses did not trip over themselves to lend out money for new cars, it was hard enough for couples to get a mortgage. The finance company lent the money to the dealer, a deposit of 25% was required to purchase the car. (one year it went up to 40%).).

The car belonging to the supplier until the last instalment had cleared. To go into a showroom, choose a car, arrange payment, and drive straight out with it, or wait a few days only, was just a dream. Because of the export drive, second hand cars, many of them over 10 years old, were fetching fancy prices. Second hand car lots sprang up everywhere, sometimes selling old bangers fit only for the scrap heap. On the road and legal, the M.O.T had not yet arrived.

Petrol pumps had no brand names, there was no self service. It was called Pool Petrol, petrol companies pooling their resources to supply the motorist, but things were looking up. More cars began to appear on the roads, and by 1950/51 brand names began to appear again. Petrol was paid for by cash or cheque, unless the customer had an account at any particular garage, in which case he would sign a docket, and pay it after he'd had the account sent to him. The driver drew up at the pump, but did not leave the driving seat. If smoking, he often continued to puff away. At Sharpe's garage for instance, cars came in off the road and stopped at one of the two pumps, between road and shop front. Someone appeared from the shop, perhaps an elderly man or a woman assistant, and they proceeded to fill the car's tank with the required amount of fuel. The attendant took the payment into the shop, where the cashier at the till issued change and a manually written receipt if a receipt was asked for. There was no V.A.T. The service included the attendant checking the water and oil, and wiping the windscreen if required.

Neither Sharpe's, nor the One O One garage opened late in the evenings, Sundays, or all night. Forecourt shops of the nature we are now used to didn't exist, not around Flitwick at least. Little kiosks, or shops, perhaps the front office of the garage, stocked such items as tyres, batteries, wipers, spare plugs, oils, inner tubes, lamp bulbs, but not food and drink or fags, certainly no booze. You could not buy a pint of milk, box of chocolates or bottle of Wine at midnight in Flitwick, Ampthill, or anywhere else that I know of. Sharpe's shop sold toys, bicycles, repairs outfits, batteries, as well as car spares. They did booming business at Christmas.

During the war, after Singapore fell to the Japanese, flogging car tyres was forbidden for private motorists. It became a criminal offence. The car had to be sold along with the tyres. In February 1942, the Government issued a decree which meant only people on essential work could buy tyres, after applying to the Divisional Petroleum Officer. Essential services included lifts for service personnel, for hospital visits, helping evacuees to their destination, for ambulance purposes, and for those in rural areas if there was no alternative transport. Driving little Susie to school was not acceptable, she'd have to walk or cycle.

Some drivers converted to Gas, but it had its problems, such as the Gas bag flapping about. The few cars on the roads had white painted running boards and bumpers, to help drivers see each other in the dark. Light fittings had to have hooded black covers, with only a small slit aiming a sliver of light a few feet in front. For a while, a lightbulb had to be removed from one of the headlamps. The police had few speeding problems. Cheaper cars could not go too fast, even long after the end of the war.

Any car appearing in the Alley was surrounded within seconds by hordes of kids asking questions of the driver. There was no need for yellow lines up and down the streets, with so few cars around. If a driver needed to pop into Flitwick Post Office, he parked right outside, no fear of receiving a parking ticket.

As for multi-storey car parks, we'd never heard of them. Traffic lights, roundabouts, 1940s Flitwick had none of those. No Pelican or Zebra crossings, no bleeping pedestrian crossings. The railway bridge linking the two halves of the village was narrow and difficult for lorries to negotiate. It soon became apparent that it would have to be widened as lorries became larger. Even today, it can still be a bottleneck.

During the war, drivers were stopped by police and asked their business. If they had no good and acceptable reason for using their car, they could be fined, or even imprisoned. The Ampthill news ran many stories in their Court columns of motorists flouting the law and paying the penalty. Kerbstones and Bollards were painted white, streets were unlit, and most roadsigns removed.

It was to be another decade before the first motorway was opened. I passed the driving test a couple of years after we were wed. He bought a Morris Minor traveller from one of his friends who was emigrating. It was an easy car to drive and I used it to travel down to visit Mum, instead of going by bus. The car gave us much more freedom of movement.

On our honeymoon in 1958, on visiting Mum, we borrowed a couple of bikes from Joy and Pam French who lived at number 11 Dunstable Road. We rode up Church hill, past Priestley Plantations until we reached a bridge. Underneath the bridge was a straight road with no traffic on it. Alvis said it looked like an airfield, similar to where he had installed a top secret facility a few years earlier. We rode the bikes down the slipway, on to the roadway, and cycled a fair distance before leaving it and returning to usual roads. We saw one or two bulldozers and other road machinery, but no workers. We later learned we had cycled on the as yet unopened M1, (opened 1959). We were witness to, and part of, history in the making.

In subsequent years, the M1 was a great help in shortening the long journey on my almost 800 mile round trip to visit Mum. Oh how she would have loved to have the freedom I had, to hop on planes, travel on Ferries, put the groceries in the boot of the car, drive to and from work, live in a house with all mod cons.

In the 40s and 50s, workers stood at bus stops getting drookit, the wind ruined umbrellas, women wrapped headscarves over their head to keep a hairstyle in place, men wore a flat cap to work. Everyone had to wear warm clothing. Is it any wonder that drivers are unwilling to forsake their warm cars?

Ernie went to work in a factory around 1960, swapping his bicycle for a moped. It has not been so very many years since the only mode of transport in villages like Flitwick was horse and cart. Not everyone could afford a fancy carriage, or an early motor car.
Mum mentioned that her father walked five miles to and from work. I am informed by a former Maulden resident, who was at school with Mum, that Grandpa Randall had a Fish and Chip van in the 1920s.
I have no way of checking this out, but if true, he likely was able to drive a vehicle. Driving licences were not compulsory until 1935.

Mum boarded a bus if she went to Ampthill or Toddington, going by train if to Luton, Leagrave (where Aunt Millie lived), or Bedford. She was a poor traveller, having sickness bouts on a bus after only a short ride. On a train she always sat with her back to the engine, she said she felt better that way. In those old carriages with no corridor, there was no lavatory either. Opening the window, she felt the cool breeze cooling her down.

Flitwick had four garages. Billington's in Kings Road, large, very busy, the garage on ground through from Kings Road to Station Road. It is now a Masterfit and Vauxhall dealership. The One O One garage at Running Waters then owned by the Vass family. On the High Street was Sharpe's, already mentioned. They had one Diesel pump, down the side towards the repair garages.

Another garage was behind the Fir Tree inn at Church End, on the corner of the road to Westoning. Flitwick Oils, supplying oil to businesses and households locally, did so from their premises on the corner of Kings Road and Maulden Road. The company was eventually swallowed up by a larger company and the site of their business was sold off to provide flats at Kings and Dukes Courts.

In 1948, the Red Petrol Act came into being. Only commercial vehicles were allowed this cheaper fuel. A motorist found with red petrol in the tank could have his licence suspended, be fined £1000, even imprisoned. A retailer dispensing the wrong fuel could lose his licence to operate. Cheaper cars had only three gears, no heaters, no power steering, no automatic direction indicators, (hand signals for left, right etc used). Radio was a luxury.

When I took my driving test all those years ago, I had to indicate the direction I intended to take manually by hand signals as well as using the car's automatic indicator. After a law was passed requiring all cars to have automatic indicators, older cars still on the roads had to have little red signal arms fitted to the bodywork. Earlier cars carried a starting handle, which, when placed and turned in a fitting to the front of the car, below the radiator, cranked up the engine with a sudden surge. It was used when there was difficulties getting the car started through ignition failure, a frosty morning, or a low battery. Turning the ignition key looks so romantic and easy in some of the old films, but believe me, many times it wasn't so easy. The drawback of only three gears and reverse was when decreasing speed, to change down gear, we had to double de clutch. It was done swiftly, and I learned to do that in my father in law's car.

When I first started work at Luton, I could not afford the train fares, so travelled by bus. The first one through Flitwick in the morning came from Bedford, through Ampthill and Maulden, stopped at the corner of Maulden Road and Greenfield Road, the route continuing to Greenfield, Pulloxhill, Silsoe, Barton and on to Luton, getting me there on time. In the evening, I caught a bus from Luton, (it was either Bute Street or Silver Street), the bus leaving at 6 pm except Saturdays, when it didn't leave Luton until 7 pm, coming home the same route in reverse. When my wages were increased, I started travelling by train, it was more convenient. There were other buses to Luton, Bedford, Dunstable, coming through the village, two or three per day to each of these places. The Dunstable-Bedford bus did not go to Greenfield, it came direct from Westoning and up Dunstable Road, over the bridge and on to Ampthill-Bedford. All the buses to Bedford went via Houghton Conquest and Chimney Corner. The Ampthill-Luton bus went through Flitwick via Station Road to Greenfield and Pulloxhill before doubling back to Westoning and on to Luton via Harlington and Toddington.

Recently, on a visit south, I had cause to use the bus to get from Bedford to Milton Keynes. I'd travelled down by train, but wish I'd had my car with me instead. The bus station at Bedford was a disgrace. People were standing around in rubbish that had been there all day, bins overflowing, no cleaners in sight. The building itself was a disgrace. It either needed to be pulled down or given at least a coat of fresh paint. I wrote to the Town Council about the condition of the Bus Station and the reply was very unsatisfactory. They disclaimed all responsibility, saying that the Bus Company Stagecoach operated the station, and I should write to them.

I gave up, just glad I don't have to use it every day. Bedford Town Council, and the Bus Company should be ashamed of themselves for the foul and stinking place it is.

In 1948, Aunt Daphne, (Sally), and Uncle George, (Bubbles), moved to a tied cottage at Haynes West End. It was in the middle of a wood, very reminiscent of the Hansel and Gretel story. Bubbles had got a job on a local farm. Mum wrote to Daphne to let her know we would visit the following Sunday.

We had to be at Station Bridge for the 11.30 am bus to Bedford, where we caught another bus to Haynes. Leaving the house, Mum had the things we were taking with us in a shopping bag. Although not an old lady, she couldn't run, so we hurried as fast as we could up Station Road. Passing Billington's garage, we saw the bus about the pass the Swan Inn. I ran on, telling Mum I'd hold the bus up for her. In my haste I dropped the bag of hair curlers I was carrying, (what was I doing with a bag of curlers?), leaving Mum to pick them up, which slowed her down, but somehow I had to reach the bus stop before the bus drew away. Missing it meant having to turn around and go home, with no way of letting Sally know we were not coming. There was no next bus. I put my foot on the platform as the last person boarded, begging the Conductor, 'Please wait fer me Mum.' He was impatient, said he had a timetable to keep to. One foot on the platform, one foot on the ground, I persisted. Very puffed out, Mum, with Joyce in tow, climbed aboard, sank with relief into a seat. The bus was a double decker, with platform that had a pole to hold on to when boarding or alighting.

Bus drivers were in a little cabin, sealed off from the passengers, as can be seen in the buses at transport museums. The old red London buses are a good example. The driver had a little window at the back of his seat. He slid this window to one side when he or the Conductor wished to speak to each other. Many of the Conductors were women Clippies, drivers always men, I never saw a woman driver. Buses were heavy to steer.

Fares were paid to the Conductor, who paced up and down the aisles, issuing tickets from a ticket machine fixed to a leather belt around his/her waist. The machine did not hold a roll of paper, the stiff cardboard tickets were on a sort of clipboard, different colours for different fares. The appropriate ticket was taken off the clipboard, and another machine punched the boarding stage and date on it, then a hole was punched in so the ticket could not be used on another route. The money collected went into a leather bag which hung from the Conductors neck and shoulder.

Tickets available for weekly journeys of six days. A hole punched in the left hand side for each day on the morning journey, and a hole in the right hand side for the return journey. From time to time the company's Inspectors came aboard to check we'd paid our fare. Schoolchildren paid half fare, under fives free. No concessionary fares for the elderly. My first weekly ticket to work cost me 5/6, (Five shillings and sixpence, or 27.5p) in 1950. When the bus filled up, people stood all along between the seats, (except upstairs), jammed in just like the London tube trains, the Conductor calling out, 'Move along there, move up.' If no seats left, and no more standing room inside, people stood on the platform, hanging on to the pole for dear life. They ran for the bus and jumped on the platform as it drew rattling and swaying from the stop. Out of breath, they always claimed the bus was early. The Conductor was supposed to have only eight standing, but God help him if he left anyone at the stop that could possibly be squeezed in. Single deckers were entered from a door at the side.

I didn't think too much about planes. We never thought we'd

ever have enough money to go on a plane. When the Comet, (first jet passenger plane), came on stream, I took little notice. It wasn't for the likes of us in the Alley. As a child I never went on holiday, and neither did many of the adults I knew. They could not afford it.

The 1940s was an age when there were no cheap package holidays to places like Benidorm, Athens, Tenerife, Barbados. Strange places to us. I don't believe anyone envisaged that a week's holiday in Spain could ever be bought for less than a week's wage. Working families went to Butlin's for a week, or to a boarding house at the seaside, putting a few shillings away every week into a Post Office account to pay for it. Factories ran a holiday club that the workers could put away a weekly sum into.

As the Council built new homes off the Avenue, and sewerage mains were laid, working lorries carrying construction materials made the village a noisy hive of activity. At 13 and 14 we were witnessing the beginnings of Flitwick's rapid rise from rural village, to commuter land. Flitwick was growing out of its old clothes, putting on a new face. Not a very handsome face, many would agree. It perhaps needs another face lift now, some tender loving care, for a prettier future.

Oh I do like to be beside the seaside

Chapter 52
FAGS and BOOZE

No Government would have dared to introduce a smoking ban anywhere, except perhaps in Hospital wards. A few years ago, when I was in hospital, smoking was permitted. A patient, going through the same operation as myself, smoked right up to the evening before her op. I recovered within hours of the op, she was ill, sick, for three days. People were not prohibited from smoking in restaurants, or at work. A friend of mine smokes, loves her two children, but she still inflicts nicotine poisoning on them. She says she has no money for good food, yet finds the money for tobacco.

The cinema auditorium was usually a haze of smoke. Advertizements in papers newspapers and on hoardings depicted good looking men and beautiful women smoking a Particular brand. My sister Joyce smoked while still at school. I asked her how she obtained them. She said she dipped her dad's packet.
Joyce died aged only 65. I am sure it was smoke related.

Small groups of children disappeared behind the lavatory block or some other discreet distance to have a surreptitious puff, little realising the threat to their financial well being as well as their long term health. Later, I worked beside girls who lit up as soon as they entered the canteen, before getting a cup of tea.

We were all unaware of the serious health risks of smoking. I'm glad I was too hard up, skint, broke, to buy a packet. If my purse was empty through the week I had no one to borrow from, unlike my friends who always seemed to be able to cadge the price of a packet of fags off someone. One of my friends paid her board money to her mother on pay day, borrowed it back the following Tuesday for ciggies, she seldom repaid it.

In many families, the Watson's who lived next door to us in the Alley for example, almost all the family smoked. Although there were more pay packets going into the house, in essence, they were hardly any better off than us. The smoke wafting up to the ceiling made for an expensive yellow stain. May Watson and many other women smoked all through their pregnancies, when cooking for the family, while relaxing. All the family except one died far too young.

In 1942, cigarettes went up to 1/6 (7.5p) for twenty. Mum and Ernie were imprisoned for neglect and cruelty to Joyce and me, when the house was filthy and the doctor said we were undernourished. His fags money could have purchased many a small necessity to make life more bearable. I am sure Mum lost heart.

Will's Wild Woodbine was Ernie's favourite brand. Often he rolled his own, using Sun Valley or Golden Virginia tobacco. He only smoked plain brands. He said filter tipped cigarettes were for women, poofters, fairies, or nancy boys, derogatory terms for any man with an effeminate style.

Shopkeepers split a packet of 20 into 10 or even 5 if that is all the customer could afford. Sometimes I couldn't get his cigarettes at the shops, Cousins shop was the only one which would allow us cigarettes on tick. I'd go home empty handed, then there was trouble. Ernie did some cursing, Mum worried he'd stay off work, and she searched down the back of the chairs, in the old artillery ornaments, in pockets, deep into her purse, in the vain hope of finding enough coins to send me out to try other shops. Having a tantrum, he struck out at her, accusing her of frittering money away, (a verbis ad verbera, from words to blows). Mum had too little to fritter it away.

'That's four weeks you've paid me short Mrs Bland,' Pussy Cousins remarked. Then, with pursed lips, she continued to measure the rations as Mum stood at the counter, down at heel, and downtrodden silent. Other people in the shop acted like the three wise monkeys, seeing nothing, saying nothing, hearing nothing. Were they in the same boat? Who knows. Debt was a constant companion.

If May Watson heard what was going on, she came in to rescue Mum by lending Ernie two or three fags. At other times, Mum pleaded with friends until someone helped her out. There wasn't a week went by that Mum didn't have a huge struggle. Without a fag, Ernie didn't know what to do with himself. He would not tend the garden, or go to work. Mum who suffered the shortfall when he lost earnings. The shop account was not paid in full, she hid from the coalman and the milkman, the Tally man was not paid his full dues. I was sent to the door to tell them she wasn't in.

My father in law was a smoker. Sir Stafford Cripps, Chancellor of the Exchequer when the Labour Party were in power after the war, put another shilling tax on cigarettes in one of his budgets. That was quite a price hike, and father in law uttered cries of dismay,
'The Labour Government is supposed to be for the working man, and this is how they treat us.' He was so angry he threw his last packet of fags in the fire. He must have had an awful night. He had to wait until the paper shop opened next morning to buy more, the extra shilling forgotten. Another time, father in law almost died from the effects of smoke, almost setting the house on fire. In those days thefilling in armchairs was sometimes horsehair, sometimes kapok. His cigarette, alight, had slipped down into the chair as he dozed.
The chair began to smoulder, smoke filling the room. Alvis and mother in law came across this when they arrived home. Father in law was doused with a bowl of water, he did some swearing, but at least he lived.

Ernie went twice weekly usually to the Crown Inn where he was in a darts team. He took a tin mug with him, because often the pub was short of glasses. Whereas some men become unpleasant or mindlessly vicious after they've had a drink, Ernie was the opposite. He never drank a lot, and I never saw him drunk. When he did imbibe a little extra beer, he could be jovial and friendly. A practice dart board hung on the rear of the kitchen door. In winter, he sat at the living room table, fag in mouth, sorting and repairing the flights.

Bubbles and Sally visited, Ernie sent me to the pub for beer. It came in large brown bottles holding two or three pints. Beer and fags were not rationed, but pubs and shops ran out of supplies occasionally. Mum liked bottle of Stout now and again.   At the Crown Inn I passed through the lounge where women sat talking, to the serving shelf near the bar. Not many women drank in the bar then. If I went to the White Horse, I entered and walked along the corridor to a little hatch at the far end, and knocked. Mrs Ellis took my note and served me. Next day I took the empty bottles back for return of the deposit.

Chapter 53
MUM REBELS

'If her husband is so cruel, why doesn't Flo Bland leave him?' Where would she go? How would she support herself? No money, no roof, two children in tow, only desperation must have made her leave the twice that I recall. In the 1940s there was no social security net for women who abandoned their home, however cruelly beaten down they were. The police did not respond well to domestic violence cases, the couple had to sort it out for themselves. There was no place of refuge, unless a sympathetic friend or relative took it upon themselves to help. With additional mouths to feed, and the prospect of a violent husband arriving on their doorstep, anyone could be forgiven for not taking the risk.   Neighbours knew how cruel Ernie was, Aunt Daphne knew him to be a 'bad un,' but to the world at large, he put on a different face.   Some said he was odd. Josie Stapleton's husband, Maulden, who worked with him for a few years, told me, 'eee were at the threshin' an ee jist cleared orf, ooh, ee were a funny sort a bloke. Left us all wunnderin' what ee'd took the 'uff about.' Ernie was a key worker when Threshing time came around, but Mum was the chaff he stomped all over.

Packing a shopping bag with a few things, we went to Millie Barnes parents at 45 Water Lane. Mum would help Kate Line around the house in exchange for food and a bed. Kate wasn't well, and the old man wasn't up to much either. Cuddling up that night in the spare room, Mum in the middle, Joyce and I either side, I felt bewildered. I clung to Mum's skirts when Ernie turned up next day, very contrite. Very penitent, agreed he treated her badly, professed his love, and promised to mend his ways. After much pleading, he won Mum over. What else could she do?

310

It wasn't long before he was back to his bad old ways.

Aunt Daphne said he became agitated at Mum's funeral, murmuring, 'She'll haunt me she will, the way I treated 'er,' in his broad Bedfordshire accent.

I believe every time he looked at me he saw my own father, the man who'd been Mum's first lover, and he couldn't handle his emotions. He was consumed by a jealousy burning like a fire inside him, and the way he dealt with it was to use Mum as a punchbag, and me as if I was something brought in on somebody's shoe.

Chapter 54
MUM's JOY IS UNBOUNDED

One fine day, must have been 1946, we kids were playing around the yard. We became aware of a man in uniform making his way up the Alley from Station Road. He was waving to us, as if we knew him, which we didn't. Strangers in the Alley were few, 'Somebody's coming,' we called out to Mum.

She came to the back door and looked down the Alley to see who it was, and as the man drew nearer, he removed his cap. Mum gasped, 'It's Billy, ... Billy.'

I thought she was going to fall down as she mopped her face with the hem of her overall, leaning against the door jamb for support. The shock, joy, emotion that swelled up in her can only be imagined. As he drew nearer, she moved towards him, tears flowing freely down her well worn face.

Something extraordinary was taking place. I'd never seen her like this. Billy ran the last few yards. She had spoken of a younger brother Billy. She had not seen him since the loss of their mother and father in 1932. They embraced, holding each other so tightly.

She always said she had no family, although she must have meant on the Randall side, because there were plenty of Stringer relatives in and around Flitwick. Billy wiped her tears with his white hankie. He embraced Joyce and me, his uniform smelling smoky,. Seeing khaki clad soldiers in Flitwick was normal, but Billy wasn't dressed as a soldier. His uniform was navy, the trousers were not bell bottoms as worn by sailors. The buttons of his jacket shone, his white belt sparkled, and he was so handsome. I thought he looked like a film star. I felt proud when Mum told me he was my uncle.

He must have carried a kit bag or suitcase, but the description doesn't come to mind. I had seen naval uniforms on the screen, in some of those war films where the yanks and British heroically defeated the cunning of Germany's Uboats, I'd never seen one so close.

Amid great excitement, I began to think Mum had gone crazy. Billy had gone to a lot of trouble to find her. There was no computers to use for information, he had to slog manually through Church records, Marriage Registers, Voters rolls. He told Mum he was married, living in Plymouth with his wife and family, and serving in the Royal Marines. Mum took him into our old hovel, where he sat down in Ernie's chair. She fussed over him as she made a pot of tea, I did nothing but gawp, as I stood close.

This man was nice, he wasn't at all like Ernie, this man had made Mum very happy. Her cup of happiness was overflowing, bubbling and fizzing like Champagne when the cork pops.

Ernie was none too pleased when he arrived home from work to find Billy ensconced in his chair by the fire, I could tell by the look on his face, but he did not say anything at the time. He and Billy went to the pub for a drink or two or three, and Ernie was jovial and friendly towards his brother in law. After Billy left to return to Plymouth, Ernie started on Mum, using foul language.

She had made too much fuss, 'You'd think he was the bloody King of England' he complained. He scoffed at his smart uniform, complained of what he had eaten, scathing of the way he spoke, was there anything good he could say? He complained of the way Billy had expressed affection for Joyce, Mum and me, complained of the money Billy gave Mum to buy something nice, (it went on food), he scoffed and ridiculed Mum for being so excited. 'Ee needn't come back, 'e aint welcome.' Billy did come back, several times, sleeping overnight on the old chaise longue. What Billy thought of our old hovel I can only guess.

313

Mum of course wasn't the only one delighted about the return of a loved one. Some from German P.O.W camps.

For example: Mrs Cuthbert, who lived further down the Alley, had a really lovely surprise in May 45 when her long absent husband, Sgt Cuthbert, arrived home unexpectedly, from a German P. O. W. camp. Sadly and distressingly, some didn't make it home, their names engraved on War memorials lest we forget they fought not only for our freedom, but also for our European neighbours.

Television documentaries about 1945 tend to show us little more than the hordes of people crowding around the gates of Buckingham Palace when the war finally came to an end, but Flitwick residents were just as relieved, and showed it by building bonfires, Church bells rang, and pubs filled up until the beer ran out. There were tears for those who had lost loved ones, tears of joy for those returning. Mum and Mrs Cuthbert had a lot more in common than either realised.

Mum thought Billy could do no wrong, but Ernie was jealous. Jealous of the attention Mum gave her brother, unnerved by Mum's super boost of confidence, she was stronger, more resiliant, he could not control her in his normal belligerent manner, something had came over her that he'd never seen before, and he didn't like it. The bitter and angry words exchanged after a visit often turned to physical violence, but Mum would have stood in the very furnace of hell for her brother. Sometimes I'd get angry, summon up some courage from somewhere, and tell him to shut up, then wallop, he'd thump me, on my back, shoulder, head. It hurt.

When I was 11 years old, Ernie was still a young man, 31/32 years old, fit, tanned, and like all Stringers, good looking. He was also jealous of Uncle Billy because of Phyllis Watson, one of the girls next door, she was around 18 years old. She had helped to look

314

after Ernie, Joyce and me sometimes when Mum had gone into Bedford hospital through pregnancies going wrong. Aunt Daphne said she did much more than cook and clean.

Billy had been through horrors and terrible wartime skirmishes, involved in campaigns in Ceylon, (Sri-Lanka), Aden, and plenty of other places, but now, Ernie thought Phyllis paid Billy too much attention. Ernie fretted. Phyllis later married a French man, going to live in France, dying of breast Cancer while still in her 40s.

Aunt Barbara informed me that he remained a Private in the Marines, although she told me little else. I wanted more information, but decided not to press it because by that time she was an old lady over 80 years of age. On my visits to Plymouth, I noted he smoked heavily, and drank rather too much beer. Retired from the Marines, he became batman to a Senior Officer. Someone found him slumped in a chair, duster in hand, a heart attack the cause of death. Age only 54. I firmly believe had he never smoked, or drank so much, he may have lived well into old age.

Barbara, petite, very tidy and clean, came up from Plymouth two or three times. It must have been quite a culture shock for her when she arrived. I know she was appalled at the conditions we lived in. Mum tried to find her other brother and sisters, Thomas Leslie Stringer born 1910, May (first name Charlotte) born 1906, and Frances, known as Fanny, born 1913, all in the Workhouse.

I found May, but no trace of her family. She married William Lockley, a furnace man, around 1932 and lived in Luton. It is so sad to think of Mum trying to trace her through the Salvation Army, who usually were successful tracing families, but for Mum, the trail went cold. If Mum had been able to make contact with May, she'd have been very happy. It is sad that May was so close, living in Luton, yet Mum had no idea where she was.

315

Chapter 55
MIS-SPENT YOUTH?

"Lets play Rabbits"

Did I have a mis-spent youth? No, not really. I didn't drink, smoke, have sex, take drugs, if that is what is meant by a mis-spent anything. I didn't need any of those things to enjoy myself.

In my opinion, teenagers today are under a lot more pressure than ever my friends and I were, despite our lack of riches and fine things. They are pressurized to obtain good exam grades, experience pressure of a different kind to keep up to date in the race to have the best and latest in technological development, pressure from the insidious drug trade, and pressure to begin sexual activity too young.

Unlike today's children, most poor families in the 1940s did not own a camera, or if they did they took fewer photographs. There was no 'phone in the house, so we could not annoy our parents by its constant use.

I did have a few school photographs taken, but Mum sent them back to the school, she could not afford to buy them. The cost was 2/6 (half a crown), each, equal to about 4 or 5 loaves of bread. Gran Bland was the only person who had one of the school photographs. Lost when Gran died and the house cleared.

Until I was 11 or 12 I wore my hair short, bobbed straight, cut by Mum, with a small bunch pulled to the right side and tied with ribbon. See photo of Pat and you could be looking at me. Pat had dark hair, my hair was very fair, and I had freckles on my face.

On reaching my teens, Mum let me grow my hair longer, kept back from my face various ways. With a hairgrip or hairslide, severely fixed on the right hand side of my head. When it was longer

I wore my hair in two bunches on the nape of my neck.

Although I knew a little about sex, I hadn't much of a clue. Mum told me nothing. I picked up snippets of information here and there, gossip amongst my friends, giggling sometimes. I slept in the same bedroom as Ernie and Mum most of my childhood, so I did know something, yet nothing. What was sex? Mum and Ernie thought the school taught us about the birds and the bees, although lessons designed to enlighten us were absent.

I was beyond the bit where Mum had me believing babies came from under Cabbages, beyond believing kissing a boy meant I'd be pregnant. I had plenty of friends who were boys, but no boyfriends. I saw romance on the cinema screen, that was grown up romance. Maybe Mickey Rooney and Judy Garland in the Hardy films were the ideal, but the dirt yard outside Mum's kitchen door was hardly the stuff of romance. We were all as poor as church mice, none of us had cash to flash, and you might well ask what did we have to talk about? But talk we did, aplenty.

One summer day, in the meadow by the railway embankment, I pounced on Stanley Watson, demanding he kiss me. We were both 14 years old, alone, rolling around on the grass, having a laugh and scramble. My hormones were buzzing and I was curious. I'd known Stanley since we were 5 years old, and I felt safe with him, although when we were younger I didn't like him. He had a habit of thumping me in the middle of my back and then running away. At 7 years of age I'd had enough and hatched a plan to get my own back. I trapped him against the door jamb between the living room door and the glory hole in our kitchen. He did not have a chance to escape. Mum had to haul me off him as I attacked him ferociously. He never thumped me again. We became friends. Now here I was, 7 years on, he was trapped again, except this time I didn't want to kill him.

317

I wanted him to kiss me. Reluctantly he did. Our lips touched, but there was no magic to it. Stars didn't flash before my eyes, my heart didn't thump, what was I expecting? It was quite farcical in a way. Kissing wasn't something that happened to us, we knew nothing about tonsil licking. Stanley was more bemused than eager. Any other boy wouldn't have hesitated, especially if there was even the slightest inkling that it could lead to further developments. However, by hesitating, Stanley lost his chance, because we were both saved from doing something we most certainly would have regretted later by the appearance of Richard Thompson.

Richard, a year older than Stanley and I, lived with his parents at number 12 in the Alley. I am of the opinion that his mother did not approve of him mucking in with the riff raff at our end of the Alley. I saw him coming along the path by the next field. 'Oh crikey!' I cried, as I pushed Stanley away. We ran down the meadow to the brook. We never spoke of or repeated the incident again. Perhaps it is a little dramatic to say that Richard altered the course of my life that day, but if he hadn't happened along, my life might have been so different. My guardian angel took on the guise of Richard Thompson.

We had not seen graphic sex scenes at the cinema, and had no TV, unlike today, when some films and plays leave little to the imagination. In the 1940s, the camera seldom ventured beyond the bedroom door.

On warm summer days, school holidays, weekends, when we were not potato lifting, peasing, or doing chores and running errands for our parents, we got together for excitement, companionship and games. The brook was a favourite place. Swimming costumes were very rudimentary home made efforts, made from old jumpers and vests. I cannot recall one of us having what could be called a shop

The boys wore old pants, perhaps something cut down and made from old vests or bits of material and some elastic. Mine for example was one of my vests, the back and front sewn together in the centre of the hemline, to provide just enough cover for my crotch. It wasn't the fashionable garment I wanted, but it had to do.

In those days we girls were not into skinny dipping, although the boys might have liked us to. Although we were maybe rough scruff, we were rather prudish rough scruff. None of our parents would have allowed us to wear a Bikini, which made its appearance first in 1947/48, and named after the Bikini atoll where Atom bombs were tested. On the odd occasion when Mum took me to Luton with her, I'd gaze at svelte like window dummies wearing clothes I could only dream of wearing. A proper elegant swimsuit came well down Mum's shopping list. Kath Wooding related to me that Miss Campbell, one of our new teachers when the school acquired the annexe, told some girls who had no swimsuit to take a jumper to school. She helped cut the jumper and sew it to shape, so I wasn't the only one with a home made effort.

We had no swimming pool in Flitwick. The nearest was Eversholt or Stewartby. The brook became our local lido. We congregated at a deeper stretch, on the west side of the big arch. As we reached 14 and 15, some boys and girls paired up. Going steady it was called. If the friendship deepened into love, perhaps there might be a baby on the way before a hastily arranged marriage took place. This was called a shotgun wedding, but at least the baby was born into a family unit. Not one of us owned a watch, but our stomachs told us when it was meal time. Movement of the sun across the heavens gave us another hint. 'It's dinnertime.'

The brook meandered under a tunnel, which was under the railway arch/bridge. It was cold under there.

Lizards were regular inhabitants of the brook at the point where we splashed around. Running up and down the brick supporting wall, little jerky movements, so fast, in and out of the water, here one minute gone the next. Although the bank was muddy, the water itself ran clear through the reeds, unpolluted.

When I see the brook today I despair at its poor condition. It is dirty, smelly, has yellow detergent infested gungy stretches, weed infested to the point of suffocation, rubbish strewn, absolutely lifeless, although Thelma Spavins (nee Stringer) told me a few years ago that there were fish in the brook as it flowed past the rear of Water Lane. I would not allow my dog to paddle in it, never mind allowing children to insert a toe.

We girls and boys changed on different sides of the big arch, but it didn't mean the boys were perfectly behaved. They liked to sneak a preview. Suddenly one of them would cry out, 'We can see yer tits Kathy.'

One day we caught Frankie Barnes and a couple of other boys creeping up on us as we changed. At 14 or so, we were unaware of the devastating affect our growing curves could be having on the boys, who were going through their own kind of pubescent changes. I was almost dressed when Frankie sidled up close and suggested we play Rabbits. 'Let me finish getting changed first,' I naively uttered, 'You don't get dressed to play Rabbits,' he said, expectantly. I had to burst his bubble poor chap. I am notoriously slow on the uptake, but as the penny dropped, as I realised what he expected of me, I told him not to be so daft. 'Just thought I'd ask,' he called, as we chased him off.

Another friend was Barry Jones, an outrageous flirt at the time. In the same class at school, he passed through the Alley daily from his home in Maulden Road. On our way home from school he always said, 'Wait for me in the morning,' and I often did. He'd come up the Alley with other schoolkids, and we all walked along together. He raced ahead, and demanded kisses from all the girls before letting us through the kissgates at the little arch. We girls climbed the wire fence beside the kissgate, ran up and down the embankment, ran through the arch to go through the same horseplay at the other kissgate, but he seldom got his kiss from me or any of the others.

He was a friend but never my boyfriend. One day, when we were walking to school on our own, he suddenly turned and took my hairgrips from my hair. Girls today let their hair fall all over their face, but I've never liked my hair over my eyes. He offered to give me my grips back if I went into the meadow with him.
'What for? We'll be late for school,' I said, rather naively,
'You know.' he laughed. Naïve I may have been, but I wasn't stupid.
I wasn't angry, just astonished that he had blurted it out, and I replied 'Not likely.' 'OK, but you might change your mind by dinnertime,' he laughed, putting his hands in his pockets and striding on ahead.

I was angry by playtime, and asked for my grips back, he replied, 'If you say you'll go in the field with me.'
The answer was still 'not likely.' At dinnertime I ran on ahead, upset, not speaking to him, but he caught up with me, said 'Sorry,' and gave me my grips back.

The kissgates and stile at the little arch, where we all enjoyed so much fun, have long ago disappeared, and all too shortly the few of us left from that generation will be gone too. Dust to dust.

What if I'd had access to the Pill, (available for the first time in the 1960s), or boys found it easier to obtain condoms? It wasn't any sense of morality that my refusal was based on. I simply didn't want to become pregnant, I knew that much. What if I had been told sex was the most enjoyable exercise on this planet? In today's more

liberal climate, the financial support given to one parent families, girls are left holding the baby while the blokes go off and father another child with another girl. I was on the bus one day a few years ago, and couldn't help overhearing some of the conversation between two girls in the seat behind me. One girl said to the other, 'Get yourself pregnant, and the council will have to give you a flat.'
A friend of mine became pregnant by a married man, she deliberately became pregnant a second time so that the older one had a sibling, and she could also enjoy greater increments from the Social Security. The council provided a house, she pays no rent or council tax, and hasn't worked for over ten years. If she went out to work, her income would drop dramatically.

Times have changed enormously since that day in 1935 when I was born, when girls found themselves thrown out of the family home, had to have babies adopted, or were considered so immoral and unhinged mentally they were incarcerated in a lunatic asylum.

Teenage sex did take place in the 1940s, but more discreetly. Girls did not brag about having sex with all and sundry. If a girl did get pregnant, the parents of both boy and girl expected them to marry. Double standards still prevailed. A girl was supposed to be a virgin until she wed, but the same wasn't demanded of boys, in fact, the opposite view was taken. Males were encouraged to have pre-marital sexual experiences.

The boys I knew were rough, not always well behaved, some might describe them as country bumkins, but they were decent, and would never force a girl to do anything she didn't want to do. It didn't stop them taking a chance, and hoping the answer would be yes, but if the answer was no, then no it was. Girls didn't say 'What's wrong, he doesn't want me, he never asks, is he gay or what?' If a girl refused a bloke's advances, he didn't accuse her of being lesbian, hoping she'd prove him wrong.

Sunny days often found me in the meadow, alone, lying in the long grass, gazing up at the azure sky, watching the white fluffy clouds drifting overhead, dreaming. Only country noises, the birds, the cows chomping nearby, bees buzzing as they flitted from clover to clover, perhaps the chkk chkk of a Moorhen could be heard, now and then a train passing.

A few weeks ago, at a boot sale near here, I saw a beaded necklace. It reminded me of the beaded necklaces we girls made with a small packet of plastic beads bought from Cousins shop for pennies. A bit of twine threaded through the beads, and hey presto!, I was sporting a colourful plastic necklace, as pleased with it as any rich girl dripping with gold. Around the same time, when I was maybe between 13 and 14, I began to take better care of myself. I'd started polishing my shoes almost daily. Washed myself properly, even bought a toothbrush and a tin of Gibbs Dentifrice powder. Even put curlers in my hair. I did feel somewhat shabby when I came into contact with better dressed girls and women, but I was learning. Learning how to be elegant, even without the cash to splash. By the time I was 16 there was massive improvement. I found a booklet at a jumble sale. Written by Jean Kent, then a famous actress in films and on stage, it gave me lots of make up tips which I have followed ever since. She was originally Jean Carr and on the same billing as Morecambe and Wise, comedians, when they were billed as Bartholomew and Wiseman. Change of name, change of fortune.

Throughout those years, I never felt lonely or unwanted. The only times I felt desperately unhappy was usually when Ernie was at home, making Mum upset, using foul language, hitting us. I had to go outside in the foulest of weather while my friends were warm and cosy indoors. I cannot recall being bullied at school or play. Teased yes, and we fell out with each other many times, saying such things as, 'I 'ate yer, I aint gooin ter speak ter yer agin, so there.' There were many scraps, but we always came around, and soon played in the yard as if no harsh words had been spoken.

I lost touch with all those friends, except Kathy Wooding (nee See), who had lovely dark hair worn in plaits. It is a little grey now, just like mine. Their memory lingers on. We had no Television, Computers, CDs, DVDs, no designer clothing, no personal   Stereos or Mobile Phones, no ballpoint pens, no Calculators, so you might ask, how on earth did we enjoy ourselves.

We did enjoy ourselves, the great outdoors was our playground. Central heating, double glazing, fitted kitchens, a family car, were just dreams for our elders. You name it, we couldn't afford it, were not allowed it, it had not been invented or designed, or we were not considered worthy enough. Improvements were on the horizon, but it was taking time.

Barry, Stanley, Frankie, lie in Flitwick Cemetery now, permanently asleep, victims of smoke related diseases, cut down before they reached the age of retirement. Richard suffered a stroke.

(Me) Kiss me Stanley, (Stanley) eh, what, are yer daft?

Chapter 56
EXCURSIONS and other EVENTS
Roll out the barrel, we'll have a barrel of fun

Oh I do like to be beside the seaside

Day trips, or excursions as we called them, to Southend, Clacton and other places were the highlight of our school holidays after the war. Package holidays to places like the Costa del Cheapo or Disneyland were for the future, and as for going on holiday to the Seychelles, I don't think any of us knew where it was on the map.

Today we can take a 7 day package tour to Barbados for less than a week's pay. That was well out of our reach in 1948. Those who did venture abroad found there were severe restrictions on how much currency they could take with them. Plane journey's took much longer than they do today. For example, a plane journey to New Zealand took two weeks, it is hard to believe it. Planes going to New York had to stop over in Newfoundland for re-fuelling. Holiday camps such as Butlin's and Pontin's were very popular, and cheap, but even they were beyond Mum's budget.

Around 1947/48, we began to take school trips away for the day. I believe we contributed a shilling or two towards the cost. One of Seamarks buses from Westoning came along, our class piled in, filling the bus up, and we headed for St Albans, carrying sandwiches and a bottle of pop. Some carried a school satchel, but I didn't own one, mine were carried in a paper carrier bag. Seamarks run Excursions everywhere after the war, as travel restrictions eased.

We arrived a little later at St Albans Cathedral, I had never seen such a magnificent, large and beautiful building. It is vast. Huge windows, tall spires, polished pews, little hidden corners, chancel, organ playing, the Angel Choir singing, it was so grand.

I watched a woman busy brass rubbing, as sunlight beamed through the windows. The teacher babbled on, I should have heeded her talk as we were to write an essay on our visit the next day.

After the Cathedral we headed for the Verulamium to look at the Roman remains. I soaked up the atmosphere on this lovely sunny day. This was an adventure to be savoured, however mundane it may seem to today's generation. At Verulamium we sat on the steps around the Roman theatre, which was excavated in the 1930s, eating our sandwiches and relaxing. Picturing the Gladiators fighting each other, and the local populace roaring and urging on the champions in a similar fashion to a football match, except it was real blood and gored guts they shouted for, (well, maybe it wasn't so different after all.) Perhaps there had been no Gladiators, maybe just a cock fight or two. We toured the ruins, examined artifacts in the Museum, marvelled at the Roman baths. All too soon we were on the bus and heading home. I was suitably impressed.

Seamarks had posters up everywhere, and notices in the Ampthill News, advertising their trips. Mum saw the advertisement for the excursion to Billings Aquadrome. Mum made sandwiches and packed a flask of tea. The bus had already picked up many families in Flitwick before it reached the Crown Inn. There were helloes, how are you? nice day, as we searched for an empty seat.

The Aquadrome had all the fun of the Fair, a boating park,

and plenty of things for us to do. Disneyland it wasn't, but we splashed in the paddling pool, ate Ice Cream, and enjoyed the many free activities.

There were no toilets on the bus, so after a few miles, on the way home, a chorus went up from the passengers to the driver for the bus to stop. The driver chose a suitable place, a dirt patch at the side of the road, but next to trees and bushes. One by one the passengers trooped off and went behind hedges and trees, did what was necessary. The men were all back on the bus quickly, they had only their flies to undo to do a pee, but the women had not only to look for a discreet place to take their pants down, they had to look after the children as well.

Back on the bus, the driver set off again, with the passengers relieved and singing popular songs. A few miles further on and the driver had to stop again. The beer the men had drunk, the tea the women had consumed, and the pop bottles emptied by the children was going through the system.

I was 13 before I enjoyed a trip to the seaside. The newly nationalised railways began to advertise cheap day excursions to Southend and other towns. Mum, me, Ernie, Joyce, and half the families in Ampthill, Flitwick, Harlington, Leagrave, Luton and Harpenden squeezed in to the cramped third class carriages.
Mum packed sandwiches. We could not afford to eat in cafes or restaurants. All during the war years, barbed wire, concrete pill boxes, and mines, had littered the beaches, so the seaside was more or less out of bounds for us inland children. We laughed, we were excited, we were impatient. 'when are we gittin' there?' Mum was a poor traveller, getting travel sick quickly. The journey started with her looking for a seat with her back to the engine and next to the window, she maintained she managed better that way. When she

felt sickly, she could lean out of the window for the cold air to cool her down as the train sped along.

Most of the trains were non-corridor, with bench seats in compartments the full width of the coach. Six seats with back to engine, six seats facing. Luggage rack overhead, but no toilets. On the wall behind each row of seats were displayed wonderful framed prints of famous castles and towns, or a country scene. Three pictures on each wall, one of the centre frames might hold a mirror instead. It was not unusual for people to hop off the train at a station down the line, use the toilet, and hop back on again just in time before the train moved on again. 'Hurry up, that's the whistle blowing, you can do a pee at the next stop,' Mum's yelled at children, as they reached the head of the queue.

The doors didn't open from the inside. The window was raised and lowered by a leather strap, it being yanked up taut, the window fell down into a void in the door. The window now open, the outside handle could be reached to open the door. The leather strap yanked upwards again brought the window up as far as needed or all the way. If the train was full, another 3 or 4 passengers squeezed into each individual compartment, standing down the centre, treading on seated passengers toes. Mum hated being squashed in, and it was all the worse if the weather was hot and humid. All I saw of London as we passed through were the mass of rail tracks at the junction where the train transferred on to the line for Southend. Steam wafted past the window, whistle blowing as we approached towns and village stations on the way, the train full of excited children. Believe me, kids in the car on a hot day can be tiring, but it is nothing to having to remember to take spare nappies, refreshments, spare knickers, towels, with two or three or more offspring all yelling 'Can I, or I want' on public transport.

Travelling light was not an option.

Mum was so glad to reach Southend, feeling rather faint and very anxious to alight from the confines of the warm carriage to breathe the fresh seaside air. The journey had been very uncomfortable for her. Several times she had leaned out of the window. The air cooled her down and she'd settle back in her seat until the next time. Adventure, new sights, we had arrived at our destination.

Ernie looked at his fob watch, which sat in the chest pocket of his suit's waistcoat, (westcut), mentioned the time, fixed his trilby firmly on his head, and promptly disappeared with other men to the pub. Mum wore a coat, I carried mine. Mum went to a little effort with her appearance, suffering curlers in her hair overnight, a splash of lipstick on her mouth. I wanted curls too, so I'd worn curlers overnight. We could not record that first visit, we had no camera.

Mum made a beeline to find a spot on the crowded beach. Southend beach was covered with hundreds of families down from London, as well as the excursions from inland. Deckchairs were like golddust, hard to find, but Mum had no money for deck chairs. She laid our coats on a small patch of sand behind a wall, and she sat down to rest.

I had no swimsuit, nor had Joyce, but paddling we girls went, hitching our dresses up above our knees and tucking it all into the elasticated legs of our knickers, squealing with delight as the cold water lapped our ankles. We were paddling in the sea, WOW!!
The sand between my toes, the sun shining down, what more was there? I went with others along the pier a short way, but not right to the end, we had little time on our side, and Southend Pier is the longest in Britain.

Mums wiped little children down with a towel, some children

329

getting sun burned and tired, bawling out to the very heavens in exasperation. Flasks of tea and sandwiches were brought out from shopping bags. The lids of flasks used as cups, (we had no paper cups). Bottles of Tizer, Corona, Lemonade, the shops along the promenade providing buckets, spades, hot water for flasks if needed. I had a few shillings to spend, most likely from money I earned at the Peasing or Bean nipping. Mum also had earned some cash at the Peasing. The Kurzaal beckoned. Mum reminded me to be back in time for the train before I went off with the other girls.

I was absolutely amazed at the Wall of Death. We stood around a platform structure at the top of the wall which surrounded the pit. Motor cyclists risking life and limb as slowly they started at the bottom, then faster and faster they came up the sheer sides to within inches of us. The Kurzaal was thrilling to this peasant country teenager, the fairground noises, the sideshows, the switchback, dodgems, Waltzer, and a big wheel where we were strapped in before it whirled round and round, up and up, up tilt twist turn. It was all over far too quickly for me. I didn't want to go home, but it was nearing time to go for the train. I did not have a watch, neither had any of my companions, but we kept an eye out for the time by clocks in the Kurzaal and by asking those who had a watch.

I'm not so sure I was interested in the opposite sex on that first trip, but by the next year I definitely was interested. We girls went talent spotting, and there was talent aplenty. It was like being in a Candy store, but not being allowed to taste anything. While working at Luton a couple of years later, I no longer went on family trips to the seaside. Perhaps the Kurzaal still exists in different format, with just as much excitement as I experienced. Maybe before I depart this mortal soil I will let some Southend sand warm my toes, and take a stroll along the longest pier in Britain.

The Manageress of the Luton store organised an annual outing to Southend in 1951, and Margate the following year. We travelled by bus to the Port of London, where we boarded Royal Sovereign pleasure boat for the trip down the Thames. That was the first time I had been on a boat. I've no photographs of my own, likely I'm in snapshots others took.

The first time I visited Whipsnade it was a School trip. Excited, noisy, we lined up behind the teacher to go through the entrance gates to be greeted with iffy smells. A very warm day as crocodile fashion we wound around the roads and paths. The teacher, it was either Miss Sharp or Miss Chatterton, droned on with all the information, we were to do an essay on the trip the next day. I did find it so interesting, the Tigers and Lions my favourites, the Seals playful, the Camels disgusting, the Zebras so bright, the Monkeys cheeky. Later on, Mum and Ernie took Joyce and I on trips to the Zoo, (now called Whipsnade Animal Park).

There is a movement intent on closing all Zoos. The campaigners insist that if we want to see wild animals we should go to their natural environment, as if there are unlimited funds in the Education budgets or pockets of parents, or even the time for such treks. If we were all to descend on those environments it would damage the very habitat they are trying to protect. Huge hotels, souvenir stores touting their goods, access roads built, food to import, and plastic bags floating up to join the Monkeys in the trees. Good Zoos and Animal parks do try their best, should be encouraged, registered, live up to a high standard, and mandated to look after their animals welfare properly, but not threatened with extinction. At the time of writing this, Zimbabwe is treating its wildlife appallingly. Poachers, ignored by police, and land grabbers are doing untold damage. A photo in one of the papers recently

331

upset me terribly. It was of a fine huge Elephant who had no trunk. Someone had savagely used the Elephant for target practice. So extremely barbaric. The Elephant died because it could no longer drink water. The Government of that country, and its dictator Mugabe, takes no heed to the pleas of conservationists who are trying desperately to look after the animals. To go to such a place to see the wild animals in the future, might be to see no wildlife at all, it will all be killed off either to feed the population, or killed by mindless individuals hellbent on destructive practices.

Computers give us images of wild animals, but a really decent animal park does it much better. Mum didn't like Whipsnade at all, preferring to sit on a bench near the entrance and wait for Ernie, Joyce and me to return. She perspired under the heat, felt faint, and had to remain sitting. I don't remember if Joyce had a ride on an Elephant, but I did, more than once. The Elephant was fitted with a seat rack, which could take six persons, three on one side, three on the other. Up and up I went on to the seat, the Elephant led by the Keeper. Swaying side by side, with me clinging to the strap across my tummy. Along a path, turn and come back. 6d a ride. As on other occasions, Mum packed sandwiches and a flask of tea. All too soon, it was time to go home. The first time we went to Whipsnade, I believe she was pregnant with Pat.

The excursions all took place on Sundays, it was the only day it could be because Ernie worked Monday to Friday all day, also Saturday mornings.

Chapter 57
VANDALISM

It was around the summer of 1948. The war was fading into history and people had turned their thoughts away from austerity to how it used to be before the conflict. Flowers and lawns appeared in gardens Our garden had no flowers. I'd pick wild flowers, to take home and plonk into a jam jar, to decorate the sideboard. As you already know, Mum had little income, so having vegetables grown in the garden wasn't only healthy for us, it saved money too. Cups, shoes, food, came before flowers. Scrumping apples was acceptable up to a point. Stealing turnips didn't bother the farmer as long as we didn't overdo it. Stealing flowers however, what was the point? Was there a need? We couldn't eat flowers. Stealing to eat, to provide warmth could be understood, even if not approved of, stealing because of envy wasn't acceptable at all. That was vandalism theft/unreasonable.

The Station Road allotments were heaving with vegetables to supplement many a family's dinner table. Some allotments were now sporting a few rows of colourful flowers. One day, idly ambling along the narrow paths, I noticed a patch of lovely double Asters. Colourful, standing in a row like Soldiers on parade. I went in to take a closer look. Avarice, envy, what made me take the next move? It wasn't need, unless you recognise need of the soul.

I pulled about 12 of the plants out of the ground, roots included. My first intention was to present them to Mum. Mum was poor, but she wasn't a thief, so I took cold feet before I reached the Alley. I panicked. Now what would I do with them? I decided to plant them somewhere, and chose a sandy spot in the orchard, near to the gable end of our houses.

Turning the corner of the houses on my way round to the yard, intending to get some water for the flowers, I saw P.C. Upchurch coming up the Alley on his bicycle. Oh Lordy!! was I in trouble? He was coming to arrest me. Take me to prison. What was I going to do. I hid behind the Watson's house for a minute or two before daring to take a peek out to see where he had gone, he was nowhere in sight. I took a drink of water to the Asters, pondered what to do. In the 1940s, Flitwick had a local Bobby living in the village. Upchurch lived at 32 Windmill Road.

Guilt, fear, the knowledge that I had committed a wrong act made me pluck those flowers out of their temporary place and take them back to where they belonged. I thought I was covering my tracks by replanting them, but knowing flowers as I do now, they would flop and die anyway. If anyone saw me, I never knew it. What the allotment holder thought of the vandal who had wrecked his flowers I shudder to think. In those days he could have beaten me up had he caught me, and be cheered for it.   The appearance of Upchurch that day sure prevented me from taking up a life of crime, I hadn't the stomach for more shennanigans like that. Somehow, taking a few turnips, or scrumping apples didn't rate the same anxiety. I've done a few daft things in my time, that was just another silly act.

I never found out why Upchurch was in the Alley that day. Ernie's older sister, who had been imprisoned for shoplifting, offered to show Mum how to do it. Her husband kept her short of money and at first she only stole food for her and her son, but gradually she added other things such as towels and cutlery etc. She said Mum could get lots of household things. Mum was poor enough, but said she was scared. Mum was downtrodden, had great difficulty paying her way, but she was no criminal and never did any shoplifting.

Chapter 58
GYPSIES

There are great differences between the Gypsies of old and the modern day travellers. This chapter relates to the true Romanies who encamped on the areas around Flitwick. Between Greenfield and Westoning, almost opposite a farm track to Worthy End farm, the roadside grass verges were a little wider than they are now, with a hedge of Hawthorn bounding the fields to the south. Gypsies encamped there in their old fashioned colourful curved roof, pony drawn wagons, (Vardos). Their strong sturdy piebald ponies could rest and graze, while the women went around the local villages and farms selling their wares. They built a communal fire of twigs and logs in a space between the wagons to cook their meals.

One day, the sun had been shining since early morning, it was warm as I made my way over the fields to Worthy End farm. I often went off that way for a solitary walk. Skirting the farm buildings, to a rise in the land overlooking the roadway, I sat down on the grass, from where I could see the small Romany encampment. I watched men and women making themselves useful. It was quiet, not a bird was singing, or at least I didn't hear them, they were all busy feeding. I seemed to be the only idle one, just enjoying the quiet moment, away from the anxieties of life in the Alley.

The women wore dark clothing except for a colourful scarf wrapped around a head or shoulder, their skin dark and swarthy, some said dirty, but they were as clean as any house dweller, and probably cleaner than myself. Wizened from ages of working out in the open, and cooking over the smoky outdoor fire. The men wore dark clothing, with a splash of colour from the a scarf. The Gypsies were self-sufficient then, they had to be, they did not receive state payouts. On the plus side, they were not hounded from place to place by the local Council, or the Police moving them on.

It seems they seldom overstayed their welcome at any one of their favourite stopping off places. Only long enough to do some trading, and get the laundry done. Clothing and linen draped over hedges to dry, nearby streams providing the water.

The Gypsies moved around from place to place as the seasons dictated how they would earn a crust, stopping at regular venues to rest the ponies, and to catch up on the chores. As well as selling their hand made products, the women also did a bit of fortune telling. 'Cross me palm with silver me dear,' had Mum handing over her last shilling, hoping to hear that good news was on the way. They were astute, very learned in their craft, and had little difficulty knowing exactly how Mum was situated, financially and emotionally.

The Gypsy, with traditional scarf over her head, drawn back and tied under her hair at the nape of her neck, told Mum no bad news, only that things would be better eventually, perhaps something significant for Mum to cling to, to hope for. Hope always springs eternal, hope for things to be better was all she had.

It was said that if a housewife refused to buy anything, or have her palm read, she'd be cursed, (a good ploy that was). Mum felt she had enough problems, she certainly did not want to invite a Gypsy curse, so would do everything she could to make sure the Gypsy went away satisfied, or as near satisfied as Mum could manage. Whether there was such a thing as a curse, and whether it worked or not, is debatable, but anything adverse happening to some people during the following period, a remark would be made, 'Well, gal, I did 'ear the Gypsies put a curse on 'er.'

If Mum had no money left, she borrowed a shilling or two from Millie or May, if only to buy a few clothes pegs or pot menders.

336

Pot menders are redundant now. If a pot springs a leak, we throw it out and buy a new one, but that wasn't always possible in the 1940s, when metal of any description was precious, and Mum's income did not stretch to replacing everything which wore out or was broken.

During the war, metal was needed by the armaments manufacturers, and after the war, it was needed to build up the export industry. I have seen Mum using a pot with several pot menders in it, to last a bit longer. A pot mender was two round pieces of tin, one placed on the outside of the pot, at the hole, and the other piece on the inside. A small nut and bolt was used to secure the mender in place. As you have read, Mum had to place her pots on the grill across the open flame in the black range. The pots became very sooty and hard to clean.

Copper bottom pots are sturdier and longer lasting, but Mum could never afford them. Pussy Cousins shop also sold pot menders, she had cards of them on a nail on the wall, along with cards of rubbers, hair nets, hair grips, shoe laces, et al.

The Gypsies made their pot menders from scrap metal, anything metal that was discarded and thrown away by others. They cut and shaped, using sharp tools which were often fashioned by themselves, very ingenious they were. It was always the women who sold the goods, the men stayed in camp to make things, or went out and about collecting the materials needed.

If Gypsies were in the neighbourhood when something was lost or stolen, such as a ring or a purse, maybe hens/eggs, even a pig being fattened up, they were blamed.

The Gypsies were also great basket weavers, good solid baskets, inexpensive, and I would not be surprised if some of them are still in use, handed down from mother to daughter, to grandchild. They obtained the wicker for making the baskets from the plentiful

Osier beds in and around the county. (Cane, if used, usually came from abroad, was expensive. Osier (Wicker) is lightweight, but strong, can be fashioned into furniture, called Wicker furniture, cradles, bird cages, eel traps, and garden riddles, as well as for baskets. It was cut in the autumn, peeled in Spring. The Gypsies cut, bundled, and stripped the Osier themselves.

In earlier times, a little into the 20th century, some poor women made baskets, the man of the house doing the cutting in the autumn, he was called the Wickerman. The women did the peeling, it was hard laborious work. The craft is still being carried on in some parts of the country. At the beginning of the 20th century, George Bunker, wheelwright of Flitwick's east end, had a daughter Lizzie, who was a basket weaver. George was father of the wheelwright who lived opposite the Dunstable Road school in the 1940s. There may be some of Lizzie's baskets still in existence.

From the early years, Romanies encamped in the orchard belonging to Millie Barnes father Albert Line, next to his little wooden bungalow at the end of Water Lane. (number 45). If you look in a little handbook in the library, "Flitwick A Vanishing Village," issued by Ampthill and District Archaeological History Society in 1992, you will see on page 68 a photograph of Joey, Craney, and Polly, dated 1905, regular visitors of the times. They sold hand made goods around the village, and helped with the annual harvest, being skilled to do such a job.

About 1948, Millie Barnes let some Gypsies have the use of the ground on the right hand side near the end of the Alley, just beyond number 20. Her sons had cultivated it for a few years, now it was growing only weeds. When a Gypsy and his wife wanted to rent the land, it provided Millie with a little extra income. Their names were Kate Loveridge, Thom, and Emma Smith. I believe Kate, was

338

either Emma's mother or Thom's mother. They built a small wooden chalet, which, as far as I can recall, had just one room, little more than a hut. After a week or two it began to take shape. Painted garden green, with two windows at the front and a central entry door.

We kids were invited in to have a look around. We'd been very curious as work progressed, forever asking, 'What's that fer? Why?' At one end of the room was a double bed, high off the ground with cupboards underneath, which was the traditional way of storage in their caravans, the wood painted and decorated in colourful patterns. Wall shelves around the room carried ornaments, delicate china vases, gold trimmed dishes and jugs. Just inside the door, to the left, stood a round wood burning stove, its tube shaped flue rising up through the roof. This was where Thom's wife did her cooking, as well as the stove keeping the little building snug and warm. To the right, just inside the door, a small table covered by a beautifully embroidered tablecloth. Two comfortable small armchairs nearby. There was another one or two chairs, or it may have been a bench, painted a pale colour. Outside was a smaller wooden hut, the lavatory, emptied same time as ours by the Council.

Now Thom and his wife had their own place to lay their head at night, they set to and started to construct a Vardo, the wooden caravan with curved roof. A cast iron chassis was delivered one day along with four wagon wheels. It was to be drawn by the traditional pony. He painted the wheels in strong shades of yellow, green and red. He fetched and carried materials for the job pushing his handcart up and down the Alley. Gradually the caravan took shape, just a box to begin with. Each time I came home from school he'd made more progress. It was fascinating to watch. One day, I saw him coming up the Alley pushing his handcart piled high with either Osier or Hazel cuttings. Next day, those strong flexible sticks rose

339

tall and straight from being fastened into the sides of the basic box.

Later, all was revealed. Thom bent each stick over in a curve, making the bare bones of the caravan roof, to be covered by tarpaulin which was sealed by tar. He made the tar up himself, using a large bucket over a fire on the ground. I love the smell of fresh tar. Then he painted the tarpaulin a strong green colour.

Every day he progressed, and every day he had an audience of us Alley kids hanging over the fence. A small window was formed in the rear of the caravan. Then came the stable like double doors, the top half opening independently of the bottom half. Each side of the entrance door, he put in narrow windows. A flue for the stove rose up through the roof. Steps were added. He sawed and carved, painted his bright colours, and when finished, his wife furnished it every bit as comfortable and traditional as she had the chalet. She let us look inside. I thought it beautifully done.

At the far end, a bed placed sideways to the window, lacy covers, high off the floor, cupboards below. She'd hand sewn pillow cases, cushions, lots of trimmings and colourful embroidery stitches. Cupboards, hooks and shelves lined the walls, carrying ornaments, brasses and crockery, all polished spanking clean. When she lifted the cover on the stove, coals and wood burning brightly were revealed. A kettle permanently kept hot.

When everything was complete, they moved in to the caravan, using the chalet hut only for workshop storage space. Thom became domesticated, planting vegetables on the patch of ground, unusual for a Gypsy. We moved out of the Alley shortly after that, so I am not sure when they moved on. Carrie's lino sellers took over the ground, then later, Frankie Barnes used the ground as a Scrap Dealers yard. He died from a heart attack, too young at only 63. I don't believe true Romany ways will ever be seen again in Flitwick.

Below: Handcart and Vardo

A fig for those by law protected
Liberty's a glorious feast
Courts for cowards were erected
Churches built to please the Priest

Here's to budgets, bags and wallets
Here's to all the wandering train
Here's to ragged brats and callets (camp-followers)
One and all cry out, Amen!

(Robert Burns 1759-1796)

Chapter 59
PRINCESS ELIZABETH WEDS
THAT GREEK CHAP

1947 and the wedding of the year between Princess Elizabeth and Philip Mountbatten filled the newspapers and magazines. The country went crazy over it, and much was made of the fact that she also had to find enough clothing coupons for her wedding finery. We wrote essays, and read through newspaper reports. The cinemas ran newsreels of the event. The teacher brought newspapers and magazines in to school. We couldn't see it on TV, we hadn't got one.

Church bells rang out on the day of the wedding, and one appropriate popular song that year was Let me call you Sweetheart, by Issy Brown. I saw the spectacle and colour at the cinema.

Ernie's cigarettes were up to half a crown per packet, making a dent in the household finances. The film Brighton Rock, shown that year, caused a stir, controversial, some local authorities banning it altogether because of the harrowing abortion scenes. Starring a young Dickie Attenborough, playing father of the unwanted child, with Hermoine Baddeley and William Hartnell, (late of Dr Who fame).

Local brides were not so lucky as the Princess. No new dress for them, they had to adapt one from pre-war, given to them by relative or friend. Many were marrying in a register office, short, quick, little ceremony, and much much cheaper than a church do.
Brides to be used their precious coupons to buy a good costume, (suit), of skirt and jacket, which they could wear to other events later.

There were stories of girls getting their hands on parachute silk, and the local seam-stress making the material into a lovely wedding dress.

I believe there was an air of jealousy over the goodies that were being heaped on the Princess, especially as for ordinary mortals, household articles had to be saved up for, ordered and waited for, often for over a year before delivery. Many items given to the Princess were in extremely short supply.

Those who were living in bad housing conditions as we were, spoke disparagingly of the Princess receiving a Hoover. They couldn't imagine the Princess whizzing along vacuuming all those Palace carpets.

'They should've give the 'oover to somebody 'ooh needed it.'

I heard women swooning over Philip, 'Ooh, aint 'ee 'andsome'

'She's a lucky sod' whilst others, mostly men, were a little more critical, saying such things as

'They say 'is dad were over friendly wi' 'itler,'

or 'Strikes me 'ees landed on 'is feet,'

or 'Jist another bloody Jerry aint 'ee.'

The wedding presents went on view to the public for the price of a small entrance fee. Mum and I could not afford to go to London, even had we wanted to. On the day of the Wedding, I think just about everyone was glued listening to the radio commentary, from the time the Princess left Buck House just after 11am to when she appeared on the balcony with Prince Philip later on.

It was a bit sad to recall that while Elizabeth and Philip enjoyed all this wealth and priviledge, Mum was struggling to feed us, and our lavatory was a bucket in a shed. Austerity and poverty were endemic, but it appeared to be only the lower echelons of society were suffering queues and shortages. Those with enough cash to splash, or those who could afford to command enough credit, could get almost anything they required. Young couples getting married were lucky if they could afford a honeymoon.

A fortnight in the Bahamas, or even Spain was an impossible dream. Bridegrooms wore their demob suits, or their service uniform. When the ceremony was over, it was back to a friend or relative's house to a small bedroom, or a double bed hastily arranged in a front parlour, their only little bit of private space. Some men married and promptly returned to work because they could not afford to lose a full day's pay. Receptions for ordinary mortals very often held in the family home, or a local hall, very few could afford to have a "DO" in a swanky hotel. Neighbours and friends helped out with the extra cutlery, glasses etc. Wedding presents to the couple were usually what could be called useful items, such as household linen, crockery, cheaper electrical items such as a toaster. Couples did not send out wedding lists. I dislike wedding lists. When Alvis and I married, the thought of sending out a list never occurred to us, and had we sent one, I am sure the guests would have felt offended.

However, it is fair to concede that we all push the boat out for special occasions, and what could be more special than a wedding, for rich or poor. We gasped at the lovely four tier wedding cake, especially as it was for real, and not just cardboard made to look like a cake. Mum's observation of the pomp, circumstance and opulence was, 'Well gal, they've got the money aint they.'

By 1958, when Alvis and I married, times were not as stringent as they were in the 1940s. We had a real 3 tier wedding cake, and over 100 guests to the reception in a large hall. We paid for our own wedding, although Alvis' mother and father paid for the cake and the cars. Ernie forbade Mum to come to Edinburgh, even though I was paying her fare. I was disappointed, but if Mum defied him, her life would have been hell for months on her return. I did not receive a wedding present from Mum and Ernie, I had not expected any different, so it was not too much of a disappointment.

Chapter 60
BLUEBELLS AND DAISIES

Spring and early summer is my favourite season. Daffodils in bloom, then Tulips, washing floating on the breeze on the washing line, trees greening up. During wartime, so many restrictions meant most gardens grew   vegetables only.   The war ended, lawns reappeared, with neat little borders of flowers.

The dirt yard we shared with numbers 26 and 30, at the end of the Alley, was a great playground for us kids, but no plants could survive there. Even the weeds gave up, except for a few persistent Dandelions. The blossom from the many orchards in Flitwick gave off a heady perfume, the sight of the pink and white flowers stunning in the Spring sunshine. Daffodils appeared by St David's Day, and that thought brings to mind a legend I heard of.

When Persephone, goddess of reviving crops was a young girl, she wandered through meadows gathering Daffodils, which were white. She made a garland of them for her hair, then became tired and fell asleep. Pluto, God of the underworld, found her and carried her away to be his wife, the Daffodils changing from white to yellow at his touch.

However beautiful the Daffodils are, also fruit tree blossom, what I looked forward to were Bluebells. On Good Friday, we went to the Wood, where there were masses and masses of them, along with Primroses. The Wood belonged to Colonel Lyall of the Manor, but every Good Friday people from the village were allowed to gather firewood there.

My memory could be wrong, but I can't recall it raining on any Good Friday during those years. The breathtaking sight was something I always do recall. Bluebells and Primroses spreading out way before our eyes, shafts of sunlight shining down through the branches. Mum and other women took sacks, and old prams, to fill with twigs and broken fallen branches. After the gales of the winter months there were plenty lying around. We children ran wild, climbing trees, chasing each other, playing hide and seek, before mothers, tired of wood gathering, stopped and opened shopping bags which held sandwiches and flasks of tea. The sandwiches wrapped in a cloth or tea towel, so no litter. No Tinfoil, plastic wrappings, ring pull cans.

The Wood still had red Squirrels darting from the undergrowth, scooping up anything edible they could scrounge, eating some and burying some. Before returning home I gathered armfuls of Bluebells and Primroses, to take home and plonk into jam jars to decorate the table. The Primroses lasted longer than the Bluebells. Mum was laden down with two or three sacks of wood, not too heavy, but bits of twigs protruded through the sacks, which must have made them a little uncomfortable to carry. As well as the flowers in Mum's shopping bag, I carried a sack of wood. Some boys had brought their home made wooden go-karts. To get there we trekked across the fields to Dunstable Road, on to the Stockings (short cut public way), until we reached the rutted track leading from Steppingly road to the Wood.

Nowadays children demand and are given Chocolate Easter Eggs in whatever size or shape they want. Favourite childrens characters on Television are copied into eggs. In the 40s Confectionary was rationed. I never had a chocolate egg.

Friends of mine tell me they had a hard boiled real egg, painted with vegetable dye, and rolled it down the nearest slope. Once, on visiting Gran Bland in Toddington, I do recall being given a plain boiled egg, and rolling it down the side of Conger hill, along with other children doing the same.

The Watsons next door kept hens, but I cannot imagine May letting her brood loose with her precious eggs to roll them around. Although Easter, including Good Friday is a religious festival, it wasn't significant to me in that way, except at school. We sang Easter hymns, including There is a Green Hill far away, Jesus Christ is risen today, and When I survey the wondrous cross.

Mum never went to church, although she was baptized in the Flitwick Parish Church in 1917. It is a pity she felt unable to go. I am sure she would have found friendship and kindness from some of the congregation, even if not from the holier than thou types.

I don't know if Mum thought much about Church, unless the subject arose, then she'd say she hadn't decent enough clothes. I cannot recall the Vicar ever visiting the Alley. Mum told me I had been christened a few days after I was born. It was either for me to be adopted into a Christian family, or perhaps it was the custom, St Faith's being a Christian home.

Mum loved flowers, the same as I do, but when Ernie grew them later on, he did it for showing off his skills to all and sundry, not for Mum to have the pleasure of a few indoors, displayed in vase on the table or sideboard.

On Good Friday, when the sun shone,
Off to the Woods went everyone,
Some to gather Bluebells, Primroses too,
Mum collected firewood, no need to queue,
We paused for a picnic,
Mum's work almost done,
And just for a change, she did have some fun.

In early summer, when I was younger, we girls congregated

347

in the meadow to pick the small white daisies, the leafless stems ideal for joining the flowers into delicate Daisy chains which we hung round our necks. They were our diamonds, and we spent hours making our necklaces, often competing to see who could make the longest before it broke. Picking the Daisy very close to the ground, we made a slit in the stem with our thumbnail, then poked another Daisy through that slit, making a slit in the stem of the second Daisy, repeating until a chain long enough was achieved. Throughout the summer months, Daisies were quickly followed by Buttercups, Kingcups, Clover pink and white, Tufted Vetch with its lovely delicate small blue flowers, and plenty of other wild flowers, such as little pink Campion flowers growing near the hedges. Lots of thick lush meadow grasses which the cows feasted on.

We always knew when a storm was brewing. The air become sultry, and cows gathered close together in a corner of the field. We'd make a dash for home as the raindrops started.

Chapter 61
ENTERTAINMENT

The wireless/radio, queueing at the cinema for cheap seats, rare visits to the theatre, I enjoyed them all.

Mum listened to the wireless during part of the day, usually Music While You Work, for the news, Workers Playtime, and then in the evening for the news and light entertainment programmes. One favourite was I.T.M.A. It's that man again Tommy Handley. Our wireless ran on a large battery and an accumulator, also 4 or 5 glass valves. Even those homes with electricity had a battery driven wireless because there were so few power points, perhaps only one which was not in a convenient place.

Many a time Ernie dismantled the wireless to fix something that had gone awry, to put new valves in, replace a battery. Ours was an old one, from the 1930s, but very important, especially during the war years. Television had not reached Flitwick. Started in 1936, it was shut down for the duration, and so few areas had a signal anyway that it hardly mattered. When it did reach Flitwick, the picture was black and white. No Breakfast TV, no overnight programmes, it didn't broadcast until around 5pm, and ended around 10pm. The test card came on, then it faded to a small dot. End of day

It was to be 1953, after we had moved to Dunstable Road, and the impending coronation of Queen Elizabeth before Ernie bought one. He paid a deposit at Wynne's Radio Shop on Station Square, and the rest was paid up in weekly instalments. It cost £54 plus interest. By the time Mum and Ernie acquired their TV I had left home, but watched the coronation on the TV in my lodgings. Those who had not yet acquired this new miracle were invited into homes which had one.

The accumulator for our old wireless was encased in heavy glass, with a wire carrying handle. I took it regularly to be recharged, sometimes to Sharpe's bicycle shop, sometimes to a small workshop at rear of Feazey's butcher shop. I took the accumulator along one day and collected it the next. Everything was hunky dory while the wireless worked, but some serious swearing was uttered when it didn't, as Ernie twiddled the dials this way and that, trying to get the sound right. It squeaked and crackled, crackled and squealed. The aerial was a length of wire led from the wireless out through the window and hooked on a nail high up the wall. One day, after collecting the accumulator from the workshop behind Feazey's, I was passing the old oil dump, coming towards the station.

Singing, feeling happy, swinging the accumulator by its wire handle this way and that. Turning, dancing, oblivious to whatever was happening around me, I was brought down to earth abruptly when suddenly the accumulator swung away from my hand, Crash!! It smashed into the corrugated metal fencing surrounding the quarry.

All the joy drowned away from me, down through my body to the broken glass and acid littering the verge. Oh God, what was I going to do now, was I in trouble?

I was filled with dread at the prospect of facing the music when I arrived home to report the accumulator lay shattered half way along the High Street. I sat down on the kerb, crying bitterly over my predicament. A middle aged woman stopped to ask me what was wrong. I told her of my fears, 'eeel thrash me, what'm I gooin' ter do' I wailed. She told me to go home and explain, and if my dad was bad to me, I was to tell her. That was easier said than done. She didn't know Ernie. He did hit me, rowed with Mum, told me I'd have to pay for it. I never did see that woman again.

Joyce and I were in bed early, before I.T.M.A. came on at

350

8.30 pm, but we could hear it. We listened to all the Churchill broadcasts, but the wireless was turned off when a broadcast, beamed from Germany began, 'Lord Haw Haw, speaking to you from Germany,' uttering Hitler's propaganda. His real name was William Joyce, of Anglo-American origin, and in 1946 he was hanged for treason. Other programmes of the time were Variety Bandbox, with comics and singers. Later in the evening Mum liked to listen to This is Henry Hall. The sound drifted upwards, so I heard plenty of programmes when I wasn't particularly tired.

Other artists Mum liked were Elsie and Doris Waters, who acted like a couple of women having a chat over the garden fence. Comedians Tommy Trinder and Arthur Askey who's catchphrase was Hello Playmates, and Bud Flannigan with the Crazy Gang. Band leader Billy Cotton gave us Cockney flavoured entertainment. Vera Lynn and Anne Shelton sang patriotic songs.

Records 78rpm, were made of Shellac, a hard material, before Vinyl came along. Bing Crosby sold more than a million records during the war, including his White Christmas, sung on the film Holiday Inn in 1942. Ernie ruined a lot of old shellac records by warming them up at the fire, the shellac softened and he shaped them into fluted bowls and vases, selling them for a few pennies each. He'd salvaged them from the village dump along the end of the Ridgeway. Ernie and Mum took me along a few times, for Ernie to see what others had thrown away, but the smell was awful, and not my idea of a fun day out.

The Watson's gramaphone was old fashioned with a winding up handle to side of the box, and a large horn to amplify the sound, (no loudspeakers). We learned the words of songs from the records played on it, such as Buttons and Bows, but one thing for sure, we did not worship teeny boy or girl groups. There weren't any.

351

One record in particular I do recall, it was played over and over again. Tip toe through the Tulips, from the film Gold Diggers of Broadway, a musical of the 1930s.

Compared to our daughter and granddaughters, who had posters all over their bedroom walls, I was very deprived. I was never in possession of a poster of a famous entertainer.

Wynne's radio shop on Station Square was the place to go in Flitwick for radios, repairs, and later on for Televisions. By 1948/49 business was booming for Wynne, with demand for new radios and televisions. He had a son same age as myself. To have a television was to be one up on your neighbours, and some thought it an extravagance they didn't need, but eventually as we know, almost every home in the land has one, or more, and the advances in technology mean the improvements on the original have been phenominal.

I read in a newspaper article recently, in one of those columns devoted to nothing in particular, that Scotsman John Logie Baird developed TV in the UK, and demonstrated it at the Royal Institution in London in 1926, but the very first programmes broadcast went out in America as early as 1928. The Yanks claimed that a 14 year old American named Filo Farnsworth invented Television. They didn't hang about did they?

Germany began broadcasting TV in 1935, but Britain's first TV programme, by the B.B.C, was broadcast from Olympia on August 26th 1936, Leslie Mitchell the first announcer.

1950, Ernie and Mum took Joyce and I to the Music hall in Luton, it was at one end of George Street. They met me at the end of my working day with M&S, about 6pm. I saw Max Wall, doing his famous disjointed walk, Max Millar, nicknamed Cheeky Chappie because of the risque double entendre jokes he told. He wore loud garish chequered suits. Jewel and Warriss, comedians, the Ink Spots, an American singing group, and a girl who twirled tassles from a small tab on her nipples. Wilson, Keppel, and Betty did their famous sand dance routine. The Crazy Gang, Bud Flannigan and Chesney Allan. Not all of the above on the same night I must add.

When I was a child, I travelled on the bus to Toddington on my own, where I was me at the Green by Aunt Betty, (Ernie's stepsister, by his Mum's second husband). We rushed down Gas Street to the little cinema for the Matinee. Sometimes I did not have enough money, but Grandad Gordon fidgeted in his pockets, teazed me he'd no money left, pretend to be annoyed, but always came up with the one or two pennies I was short of.

Betty, who was five years older than me, and I joined the queue with all the other noisy kids. It was 4d entrance fee, and for this we saw a short old silent movie, a main feature, such as a cowboy film, or it could be an old Fred Astaire and Ginger Rogers musical of the 1930s. Perhaps a Gangster movie starring James Cagney. I saw him in Angels with Dirty Faces with the Dead End Kids, and Pat O'Brien, who played the priest who persuaded Cagney not to be heroic when he went to the electric chair. They showed the Pathe, (or it might have been Movietone) Newsreels, a short serial, such as 'The Perils of Pauline, and a trailer for the next week's films.

Down in the pit, to the right of the screen, a woman played the organ, for the interval, and for the silent movies. Charlie Chaplin's little tramp, and the Keystone Kops were favourites, as was Bud Abbott and Lou Costello, and Laurel and Hardy. Ma and Pa Kettle films were old style hill billy. Whenever the film broke down, which was fairly frequent, we'd kick up a fuss, stomping our feet on the floor, it's a wonder the wooden floor didn't fall in, as we shouted and hollored, until at last, the projectionist got the reel turning again.

353

Turning our heads, we could see the little window through which the beam of light carrying the film came from.

At the Gas Street cinema I saw several Shirley Temple films of the 1930s, such as Rebecca of Sunnybrook Farm, and Heidi. Her co-star in many films was the actor W.G. Fields, who spoke very droll and smoked cigars. Other films I loved were the 1930s musicals, although they were in black and white, these included the famous marvellous Busby Berkeley choreographed spectaculars. Gene Kelly danced his way through Anchors Aweigh just after the war. Danny Kaye was a big star too, starring in a musical with the Goldwyn Girls in 1944. Lots of marching in it, a wartime movie to cheer us up. Although the matinees were for children, we did also see movies which could be described as adult. Whether they were classified or not I do not know, but we watched Casablanca, starring Humphrey Bogart and Ingrid Bergman. Bergman also starred with Bing Crosby in The Bells of St Mary's, Crosby sang the title song. The Marx Brothers Groucho, Chico, Harpo, and Zeppo made us laugh, although we didn't always understand the jokes. There was Old Mother Riley, played by Arthur Lucan, with his wife Kitty McShane as the daughter. The original King Kong had us clinging on to the end of our seats. Another very funny film was Charlie Chaplin's, The Piano Mover made in 1920. Claude Raines, The Invisible Man, made in 1933. We kids understood the film, pure fantasy and extremely funny in parts, as the Invisible Man made things move without his physical presence being seen. He wore bandages over his face and hands. It is still the best Invisible Man I've seen, (if you can say SEEN).

Robin Hood has been the hero of many films, but the first one I saw was made in 1938, starring Errol Flynn in all his dashing swashbuckling glory. Olivia de Haviland played Maid Marion.

Weepie films included an early silent movie Broken Blossoms starring Lilian Gish. Most films were in black and white, but gradually, colour films were being shown before I began going to the Zonita in Ampthill. I sat transfixed when I saw the film Bernadette, starring Jennifer Jones and Joseph Cotton. It was about the grotto at Lourdes, and Bernadette the girl who told everyone she had spoken with the Virgin Mary. I am not a Catholic, but it made a huge impression upon me.

In 1948 the Zonita extended their screening times to include Sundays. That was when Ernie decided he would take me to the cinema, saying he wanted to broaden my education. It did that alright. Mostly about fashion. The female stars beautifully made up and wearing fabulous clothes. The houses they lived in were wonderful, with long sweeping staircases, and furniture I'd never seen before. Perhaps that is where the materialistic streak I have came from.

The storyline was immaterial, as through the haze of cigarette smoke wafting overhead I watched every move of the stars. I wanted to look like Rita Hayworth one week, Ginger Rogers the next, or Elizabeth Taylor. I wanted to grow my hair longer and let it drape over one eyebrow in the same fashion as Veronica Lake.

There was Margaret Lockwood, Jane Russell, Joanne Fontaine, Joan Crawford, and Bette Davis, all wearing fabulous fashionable clothes. Betty Grable of the long legs had me looking at my own shortcomings. I imagined myself wafting down those long wide staircases, in my beautiful gown, all eyes on me as I neared the bottom, cigarette in long holder just like Bette Davis. For a magical hour or two I was swept away into fantasy land.

I may have seen Marilyn Monroe in her first screen role, age 21, in Dangerous Years, made in 1947. 1948 saw Doris Day, age 26, in the musical It's Magic.   Mum stayed at home with Joyce.

We went by bus from Station Square about 5.15pm in time to join the queue for the cheap seats, hoping to get in before the main feature began.

The Zonita was in the Art Deco style as were many picture houses built in the 20s and 30s.   We queued for the cheaper seats, which were at the front.   Ushered to the front row, you had to crane your neck upwards to see the film.   If two or three rows back, sitting behind someone wearing a large hat, I'd have to crane my neck this way and that to see around the hat. The auditorium filled with smoke from the many fags.   God Save the King played as the screen closed down, and most stood to attention before leaving.

There was no late bus, so we walked home. Along Arthur Street in Ampthill, on to the Maulden Road end of Flitwick.   We walked in silence.   I had nothing to say to Ernie, my head full of the scenes which had appeared on the silver screen.

I was the heroine, the glamorous leading lady, wafting down the grand staircase in a fabulous gown adorned with sparkling diamonds.   A staircase bigger than our whole house.   I was the heroine saving the hero from the baddies, I was the leading lady dancing in the chorus and going on to win the hearts and minds of the audience after being discovered and put in the lead.   I imagined growing up and living in a house with such a staircase, and going shopping for fabulous clothes as worn by Joan Crawford.   I was going to marry someone like my screen heroes.   One week it was Alan Ladd, another it was Gregory Peck, or Gene Kelly, perhaps Frank Sinatra or Joseph Cotton, Dana Andrews, Henry Fonda or Jimmy Stewart.   I was definitely not going to marry some horrible little man like Ernie and live in a hovel like our home in the Alley.

There was no harm in a little imagination. I did go on to

marry a loving man, who didn't smoke. We have lived all our married life in bungalows, so I never did get to waft down a huge grand staircase in my own elegant mansion. He doesn't bring flowers, or assail me with fancy words, his compliments are questionable. My family joke about my collection of old records, but there were a lot of good songs around in the 1940s.

This is a sample from 1948.

My Happiness by Pied Piper. On a Slow Boat to China, by Kay Kyser and Orchestra. Galway Bay by Bing Crosby. He recorded those Faraway Places and Now is the Hour. Lazy River by Mills Brothers. Lavender Blue, by Vera Lynn. Grandfather Clock by the Radio Revellers. All I want for Christmas is my two front teeth, by Spike Jones. Films were Joan of Arc, starring Ingrid Bergman, it had me gripping my seat as the Maid of Orleans fought, then was betrayed, and finally went up in flames. Zonita changed programmes two or three times each week to keep up with demand.

A childrens comic of the time was Film Fun. I can't remember all the characters. Abbot and Costello, Laurel and Hardy, George Formby getting into scrapes. Old Mother Riley with her long skirts and headscarf. I read it over and over again. My copies were bought at the jumble sales, maybe 5 or 6 copies for one penny. 1949 saw another batch of good songs, (and a few bad ones). Put your shoes on Lucy by the Five Smith Brothers, Cruising down the River, by Russ Morgan. Careless Hands by Bing Crosby, Confidentially by Reg Dixon and his organ. I'm a lonely little Petunia in an onion patch by Arthur Godfrey, (later of Dad's Army fame). Down in the Glen by Robert Wilson, I saw him later, in an Edinburgh theatre.

1950 had plenty of songs too, among them were Bewitched by Doris Day, Mule Train by Frankie Laine, If I knew you were coming I'd have baked a cake by Gracie Fields.

Films of 1950 were The Wooden Horse starring Anthony Steel, he was so handsome. Treasure Island starred Robert Newton as Long John Silver.

One day, after I started working for M&S, some of my workmates were talking of a film they wanted to see in the cinema across the road from the store. I declined their invitation to join them for lack of money. A few weeks later on they planned on seeing another film the following Saturday. I added up my funds and decided I could just about afford it. That evening I told Mum and Ernie where I was going and that I'd be late home, there was a train left Luton about 10.30pm or 10.45 pm. Normally I had to be in the house by 10 pm, as Ernie had to be up early, and I wasn't given a key.

I had a great deal of trouble trying to convince Mum and Ernie that if I got a train home before 10pm I would not see the end of the film. After much huffing and puffing, and warnings about boys, it was agreed I would go. I enjoyed the film and my friends company. When I emerged to go for the train, Ernie was waiting for me. He had came all the way from Flitwick hoping to catch me coming out of the cinema on a boy's arm. He'd forbidden boyfriends until I was 17, which edict was totally ignored by me. Another row, the girls could only look on in astonishment. I felt furious and humiliated. Ernie shouted and embarrassed me in front of those friends. Although the girls assured him I was with them all the time, he didn't believe it, 'They're all liars, the bloody lot of 'em, you're all the bloody same.' On the train home I was fuming.

Eventually, at the end of 1953, I was able to leave all that hassle behind, I left home, but have never regretted it. I was lucky, I had a good job, and was provided with a good clean home elsewhere.

Chapter 62
THEN and NOW

There was a time when wallpaper meant just that, paper for decorating walls. If you are unfamiliar with modern jargon, as I am, it can be very confusing. There was a time when Gay was a word for someone feeling glad, happy, and perhaps a little frivolous, not homosexuality. Text language, most vowels unused, oh dear, I'm even more confused. There was a time when desktop meant the top of a desk, not words and icons on a screen. 1940s, mobile phones, No. If we'd seen anyone walking along the street appearing to talk to himself while holding his ear, we'd have thought him quite daft. Most of us didn't have a telephone in the house, never mind the car, most of us didn't have a car either.

We couldn't 'phone for a chat, our friends had no 'phone. For emergencies we had the public call box beside the White Horse Inn. When we used that 'phone and got through, we didn't have to press numerous buttons before we spoke to someone, we didn't have to listen to a recorded message telling us we were in a queue. There were no phantom phone calls.

A queue, oh yes, we were well used to them. There were always queues at every shop, and if something which had been in short supply for a while, something very simple like Bananas, had been delivered, a queue quickly formed. A queue could form when it was only a rumour that someone's favourite cigarettes had been delivered to a shop.

The Post Office ran the Telephone service. A huge deposit was required to get a telephone installed. Television, Personal Stereo, DVD, Video, etc, how could we have those in the Alley, even had they been available to us, or affordable, we had no electricity.

Getting cash from a hole in the wall, what a laugh. Wages/salaries paid into a bank, what use was that. The only bank account most working folk had was a Post Office Savings book. They went to the Post Office on Saturday mornings to put a little money aside each week for a week or two annual holiday. Wages were paid in cash, weekly, or even daily for those on casual work.

A man or woman from the factory or shop wages department sat at a table in the workplace, or they went round the factory handing out the little brown envelopes, the worker signing their name in a ledger. My wages were paid out to me weekly in cash, by one of the cashiers from the office, in the canteen at dinnertime. Bills were paid in cash, or by remitting a Postal Order.

Cameras have been around for a long time, but we did not have one. I have no snaps of me as a child, no cine film of enjoying myself with friends. Anyone who was lucky enough to have one had a precious item.

Before the introduction of the National Health Service in 1948, many paid into private insurance for medical emergencies and Doctor's bills, but there were a lot, like my family, who could not afford it.

Boys comics illustrated stories of outer space, aliens, space ships etc, but few could have predicted the Yanks going to the moon, and all the other aviation advances. Concorde has been..................and gone.

Young people who emigrated to other shores did so in the belief that few would ever return, but today, we can travel between far distant countries at incredible speed. It is debatable if the coming of McDonald's and all the other instant eateries have been an improvement. We now have Asda, Tesco, Non-drip paint, Hatch back cars, Ballpoint pens, Plastic carrier bags, Home Computers, the

360

Internet, Supermarket Trolleys, Car seats for baby, Plastic pails, Loyalty cards, Credit cards, Satellite and Cable TV, wheely dustbins, Hair spray, Ring pull cans, Mobile 'phones, we take all those things for granted, can't do without them. That is to mention only a few of the innovations etc that have came our way in the last 70 years or more. We can use modern technology for all sorts of gadgets around the house, garden, work, on the road. My family gave me a Web cam gadget and a Digital camera. I'm just about getting to the stage where I can understand how to use them. Having a conversation with our daughter living in New Zealand is absolutely wonderful, but not something that could be enjoyed by families in the 1940s/50s

My first computer, bought in 1988 as a word processor to help me with my voluntary work, was out of date as soon as I got it home. My present computer, (the 3rd) has already been superseded by another more up to date model. In the attic I have the old typewriter I used before 1988, still useable but very primitive, at least it doesn't need an electricity supply, presuming of course I could still get the inking spools. I don't think Mum realised what an exciting time she lived in, she was too much weighed down with so many worries. Nuclear technology has brought benefits in medical treatments, life goes on, inventions to be invented, discoveries to be made, and we always hope good will triumph over evil, just as the world rid itself of Hitler and his cohorts.

For years, we older generation found it difficult to throw anything away. We were used to shortages. I still have a box of buttons. We never saw plastic bottles, plastic wrapped anything, childrens plastic toys, plastic bins.

Flitwick had no Sports Centre, Gymnasium, Swimming Pool.

To join a club somewhere with the facilities for indulging in various sports, was something only those with some spare cash could do, and in the Alley, we had no spare cash. I'd lean on the gate of the Tennis Club in Kings Road, balls flying over and back, scores being called out, wanted to join in, but it cost too much, Mum had little enough money to feed us. I could have beaten the pants off any of those players. (I'm sure of it). When paper was scarce, we didn't send or receive Christmas cards. We take it for granted that we can jet off to Spain, or anywhere else that takes our fancy, instead of settling for a day's excursion to Southend or Skegness. A week at Pontin's does not have the same attraction as a fortnight in Lanzarotte, or making it across the Atlantic to Disneyworld, that's another thing not there in the 1940s.

For those fortunate to have the use of a car as well as being able to pay the rent, mortgage, and eat, they had the freedom of the village, being able to stop and park up almost anywhere they chose without a Parkie slapping a ticket on the windscreen. You're nicked!! Traffic Lights, roundabouts, Traffic Wardens, multi-storey car parks, double yellow lines, car parking charges, motorways.

Some people say, and I have heard them say it, that we live in a commercial materialistic society, but it has always been that way, even as far back as in the iron age when those ancient peoples made brooches, and fancy pots, to barter with others for food and shelter.

I wish I could come back briefly for a few days in one hundred years time and look back on the inventions and discoveries of the 21st century. Will it be as amazing and exciting as last century. Unless someone cocks it all up by pressing the destruct button, or the Terrorists win and we revert to the middle ages, when anyone who disagreed with authority was killed, put to the rack, or made an outcast, when women had to kow tow to their menfolk, dress and behave how they were told to. Although I think the baring of the midriff is naff, not a pretty sight, I would not support a law to ban it.

Chapter 63
BLOOD SPORTS

During the last half century and more, we've seen public demonstrations for and against Fox Hunting, which evokes extreme emotions on both sides of the argument. My own view is that we once had Bear baiting. Only morons would demonstrate to bring it back. Badger baiting is illegal, and rightly so, so what makes Fox Hunting so different? Illegal Dog fighting, and Cock fighting, used to take place locally, regularly in Flitwick, possibly it still does, although I have no evidence to back up my guess. I know it did go on when I was a child, I heard adults talking about it, Ernie included. The venues and times spread by word of mouth. Had I been male, and a little older, I may have had lurid tales to tell.

Snares were set for Rabbits, Ferrets were sent into Rabbit burrows. A Fox tail was highly prized. Granny Bland used a Fox fur as a scarf, draped over her best coat. As did others.

In the 18th century, money was paid by the Parish for the destuction of foxes, badgers, hedgehogs, moles and polecats. Fox heads fetched one shilling each. We know now that Hedgehogs are very beneficial to a garden, eating up destructive slugs and snails.

Moleskin coats were fashionable once. Vicious gin traps are now illegal. Man has been hunting animals for sport since pre-history, but not only for that, the kill meant the community got fed that day. Foxes are not hunted to provide meat for the table.

One day, when wooding on the Moor behind Maulden Road, I was stopped in my tracks by a stranger on a bike who told me to go back. I heard exciting shouting from men in the distance, and found out later there had been a dog fight. 'I'm only gittin wood fer me Mum,' I replied, but his demeanor was not friendly.

I beat a hasty retreat.

For Christmas or Birthdays I was often given a Jigsaw, the pieces making up a picture of Fox hunting. As Oscar Wilde wrote, 'The unspeakable in pursuit of the uneatable.'

As a country bred girl, I'd like to see Fox hunting dumped in history's dustbin. It is out of date, cruel, and totally unnecessary. There are other ways of controlling the Fox population. As for the jobs and livelihoods of the people involved in Fox hunting, all I can say is, when the Lamplighters of old lost their jobs to Electric lighting, did the population demonstrate? When the combine harvester was developed, the men with Sycthes were given other jobs. Would we all do away with our central heating and go back to open coal fires, which heated just one room, in order for the miners to get their jobs back? I think not.

Chapter 64
AT SCHOOL and PLAY

I liked school, it was safe there, I knew what to do, it was the same faces, a familiar routine. I'd started school in 1940, now it was 1950 and I had to leave. Where would I go? what would I do? how could I cope?

Those last ten years had been filled with disappointments, violence, worry, nightmares, sleepless nights, all on the home front, but at school I could put all that to the back of my mind, I was comparitively happy. Plenty of friends, their parents being as poor, or almost as poor as my own Mum, so most of us were in the same boat. I did want, and need, to go off to work, to earn a living for myself, but leaving the group of schoolfriends I felt comfortable with was unsettling.

Since the school was built in the 19th century, many children from the east end of the village had trekked the same path as myself, over the fields, past the pond and smithy, to our place of education. A few names some a little older, some a little younger I recall.
Thelma and Hilda Stringer of Maulden Road, Barry Jones, also Maulden Road, June Stringer of Station Road, Denis Saunders of Water Lane, Thelma Beale of the Crown Inn, Angela Robinson of Station Road, Frank Woodcraft came from Maulden, Frank Barnes and Richard Thompson, Kathy Watson, Stanley Watson and Pearl Watson of the Alley, these all trekked to school over the fields.

Other school pupils from other parts of the village were Audrey O'Dell, Pauline Burrows, Alan Farmer, Jim Bonner, Carl England, pretty Mary Head, (of The Swan Inn), Denis Sharpe, Jim Wooding from Steppingly, and my best friend Kathy See, (who later married Jim Wooding). Kathy had lovely dark hair done up in plaits.

Classes were large, usually no less than 40 pupils to each classroom. Most of us never wore a uniform. Many of us wore hand me downs from older children. We all spoke with a thick Bedfordshire accent. I had no manners to speak of, except Mum had taught me how to say please and thank you. I didn't know what etiquette meant. Sadly, many I knew very well are now lying in the cemetery, gone too early.

Most of 1942 was spent in Kempston Childrens Home, but 1943 was interesting, when I left the infant school in Station Road to graduate to the Big School as we called the Dunstable Road establishment. First year or two to Miss Carr's class 4, then Miss Chatterton's class 3, followed by year or two in Miss Sharp's class 2. Usually the last classroom was Charlie Allan's classroom He was the Headmaster, but in 1947 the school leaving age was raised from 14 to 15. My last days at school were spent in the Annexe, in Mr Markham's classroom.

Miss Chatterton was strict, a martinet. Can't recall what the lesson's subject was, but I was sitting 3 or 4 rows from the front, perhaps having a hard time concentrating, maybe I was tired, but she took no prisoners, she waded right in at pupils if they seemed not to be paying attention. Perhaps I thought I was being picked on unfairly. I stood up from my desk and emotionally said,
' I'm gooin 'ome, I aint putting up wi' this' (or similar words), and to the amusement or astonishment of the other pupils I quickly marched out of school, with Miss Chatterton in pursuit. Mum wasn't pleased.

The School Inspector called personally to any child's home to find out the reason for absence, prosecutions did take place. Mum worried. Shamefacedly, the defiance muted, I had to return next day.

When we were around 13 years old, we children of Flitwick School were despatched to Stewartby Swimming Pool, getting there by Seamarks buses. The following year it was Eversholt Pool. Those swimming baths were pretty basic places compared to the first one which was opened in London in 1842 at Lemon St Goodman's Fields, for gentlemen only, the charge for a swim, one guinea.

It wasn't the fault of the Instructors that I never learned to swim, they did their best, but they had a very reluctant pupil, I was terrified I'd drown. I had to wear my adapted vest, for Mum could not afford to buy me a proper swimsuit. This did my confidence no good at all. I felt very embarrassed as I stripped down to this woolly thing. At that age, I was filling out around the bust, pubic hair appearing. The old sewn up vest was OK for the brook, but this was different. I felt uncomfortable with my towel too. Mum did her best, but the towels were poor quality, white became grey very quickly.

I did learn to swim a few years later, in Edinburgh, under pleasurable conditions, and wearing a smart fashionable swimsuit. But then, I had a motive. My fiance was a good swimmer, it was also great fun. At Stewartby and Eversholt, it was no fun at all.

One of my school reports says of my sports efforts, 'Maureen tries hard,' which about sums it up. The school had no Gym, so on wet days we missed out on physical exercise. On dry days, cold, freezing, or hot and sticky, we took the coire mats out from the boys cloakroom, took over the boys playground to spread the mats out, one mat to each girl. I'm not sure where the boys did their P. E. Road.Leap frog, aerobics, jumps, teamed up in twos or more for team efforts. I usually found our physical exercises lively.

I'm a grandmother now, but I can still touch my toes without bending my knees, exactly as Miss Chatterton, who took us for P.E, taught me to do. We went on country runs, along Hornes End, by the brook, through the big arch to Water Lane, up to the Station, down Dunstable road, exhausted. Or the route was shortened by cutting through the Alley and back to school over the fields and through the little arch. Some cheated and took that shorter route rather than stumble around by the Station bridge. There were nature rambles, gathering wild flowers and grasses, leaves, writing of them and pressing some in an exercise book. We did essays and illustrations on birds too. Although I was very interested in these nature studies, I was a hopeless artist. Still am, as you can see by the illustrations I've drawn in this book. Good ones were pinned on the classroom wall, it was a very rare one signed by me.

As I've mentioned earlier, we didn't get homework, all our school notebooks were kept in our desk, we sat in the same desk, in the same classroom throughout each term. Each teacher taught us all subjects except music and domestic science, (woodwork for the boys). The large blackboard sat neatly across a large easel, we had no rolling blackboards, no computers or televisions of course.

The wonders of nature are there for all to access by computer today, but in the 1940s we had to go out and have a look, recording it manually. However I do notice today that children have a wider curriculum than we ever had. Nature studies take place but children do not necessarily have to go out into the fields and byways to find out about it. Just as well, because so much of the beauty of nature in and around Flitwick has been lost under tarmac and brick. Older pupils today go out on work experience as part of their studies at the same age as we children of Flitwick School were leaving and starting on a career for real, earning a weekly wage, schooldays over.

We were independent, we did not expect our parents to subsidise us until we were in our 20s, they couldn't afford it. I am appalled to read that employers find many applicants for jobs cannot spell, or calculate without the aid of a calculator, and even then they get it wrong. Is it the fault of the teachers? or the teaching methods?

or is it the fault of parents who allow their children too much absence from school? Being unable to spell matters little to a Brickie, or labourer on a building site, or other jobs where they don't have to hold a pen, or tap a computer keyboard, but to anyone aiming for work in the commercial world, they should try a bit harder to spell correctly. Is it such a crime? Does it matter? It used to.

Girls played hockey. I was team captain a couple of times, tried my best. I think I was a better winger because I could dribble and run very well. These games were played on the sports field, which is now the Recreation ground behind the Community Hall in Dunstable Road. A Netball team was formed once, but I wasn't tall enough to be effective.

Boys played Rugby, Cricket, and Football. Considering we had little in the way of equipment, had no Sports clubs, and there were no Sports Centres locally in the 1940s, I reckon we were as fit, if not fitter, than many children today. Obesity wasn't a problem, and we'd never heard of anorexia. Rationing restricted our intake of sweet food, and our mothers fed us home cooking. Stodgy puddings and dumplings were balanced by healthy helpings of vegetables. Asthma wasn't such a big problem either. We had open fires with chimneys, we didn't have central heating or fitted carpets full of dust, we had draughty windows, we spent hours out of doors, all in all, we had plenty of air getting into our lungs.

Another activity was gardening. After the extra classrooms were added to the school in 1947/48 we older pupils were set the task of making the ground between the prefabs and the main building into a presentable garden with flowers and shrubs. We dug and planted, until at last, the piece of rough ground was transformed.

The school also had a larger plot of ground up Dunstable Road, opposite the Vicarage, where the older boys, Jim, Frankie,

369

Carl, Barry among them, grew vegetables. Potatoes, cabbages, leeks, carrots etc. All helped provide the school dinners. Flitwick Lower School later took over the site.

The School Gardening Club for the boys had been on the go for a very long time. In the edition of "Flitwick, A Vanishing Village" there are photographs of boys from an earlier generation. When the boys were sent off to do their groundwork, or to woodwork classes, we girls were instructed in the art of Domestic Science, Needlework, and Crafts, preparing us to be good little housewives.

After the war, women were expected to revert to being happy little subservient housewives, but there were rumblings of discontent. Plenty of younger women were unwilling to bury their own career ambitions in favour of marriage and numerous babies. They wanted more, they wanted a higher standard of living, and that required two incomes in a household.

It was usual for men to earn more than women doing the same job. Pity the woman trying to climb the career ladder, she found obstacles all the way, it needed guts to overcome them. When she got there eventually, she didn't enjoy the same increments as her male colleagues. Many working class women had been factory fodder, or went into domestic service before the war, but afterwards, things were different. No longer could the upper classes expect undivided devotion and loyalty while paying a pittance.

As well as our Sports and excercises at school, we did a lot of running around in the Alley. It was a good place for children from all over the place to gather, sometimes dallying there on the way home from school. We bounced balls against walls, we skipped, we splashed around in the brook, climbed trees, ran errands to the shops, helped around the house. We played ball, any ball we could lay our

370

hands on, juggled two or three at a time. We ran up and down the Alley, bouncing a ball on the ground as we ran. The boys kicked around any kind of ball they could find, using their coats on the ground as goalposts. A proper football was a treasure.

Boys and girls together formed teams to play Rounders, our version of American Baseball. We bundled our coats up and lay them on the ground for the corners, Any strong suitably shaped stick became a bat. A bit of squabbling often took place,
'I want to be in your team,' 'Why does he always have to be captain?' 'She's run out,' 'No I'm not,' 'Yes yer are.'

Home base was a few feet from Mum's back door, the corners at the edges of the yard. From 3 or 4 children upwards constituted a team, and runs were counted up without the aid of a referee or pencil and paper. Round the corners the players ran, the coats on the ground getting dustier and dustier. Sometimes the ball flew off into the distance, an outfielder sent to find it. We had no boundaries, if the ball went down the Alley, it had to be chased after while the player knocked up more runs. Boys played Marbles. They had names for variations of the game, and sat on the dusty ground totally immersed. Girls were not wanted, considered intruders. Another game usually the province only of the boys, was hitting cans off walls and fences with a home made catapult. Occasionally a window pane was broken when a stone flew off in the wrong direction.
If the culprit could be found, he was punished, physically by the parents, or often by the person who had suffered the damage.

TIG was an energetic game for both girls and boys. One of us would be IT, and the others ran hither and thither in all directions with IT trying to touch one of them, who would then take over as IT, the fun starting all over again. That game wore us out pretty quickly. We played hide and go seek, hiding in the orchard, behind hedges and doors. Our clothes became dirty when hiding in the coalhole.

Hopscotch was another lively activity. Squares were chalked on the tarmaced road beside our yard at the top end of the Alley. We always had plenty of chalk, either bought from the shop, or dug up from the railway embankment. The puck a small flat lump of stone.

Girls borrowed net curtains and dressed up as brides, we cycled, went scrumping for Apples, skated in winter, (no proper ice skates), icy slides in the Alley, threw snowballs. Our school playground games wouldn't have been the same without a skipping rope, whether it was one with wooden handles bought from the shop, or just a cut off section from our mother's clothes line. I once chopped a bit off Mum's washing line, and got slapped across my backside for it. She'd gone to hang the washing out to find the rope too short to stretch from house to barn. Skipping in a group became a skill. A long rope, girl at each end, other girls queueing to take their turn skipping through the long rope, moving all the time, girl who'd just taken a turn joins the end of the queue to have another go, and so on. Sometimes two ropes were used, turning in opposite directions, a girl at each end holding the rope, it needed co-ordination. Two girls could skip together using one rope. Bacwards skipping too. We spoke or sung rhymes and ditties as we skipped, not very politically correct even then. One such rhyme was Nebuchanezer King of the Jews, but he was actually King of Babylon, (Jeremiah chapters 32/33), however, we sang it like this,

Nebuchanezer King of the Jews, bought his wife a pair of shoes,
when the shoes began to wear, Nebuchanezer began to swear,
when the swearing had to stop, Nebuchanezer bought a shop,
when the shop began to sell, Nebuchanezer rang a bell,
when the bell began to ring, Nebuchanezer began to sing.

There were many other rhymes, most I have forgotten.

Boys wrote down train numbers and details in notebooks, exchanged and collected cards from cigarette and tea packets, some had go-karts adapted from old pram wheels and bits of planking, with no brakes, a length of string attached for steering.

When I took Sheila Barnes, and later my half sister Pat, out in their prams, I knew lots of nursery rhymes to sing to them, the words and tunes handed down from older people. Lack of space prevents me from mentioning them all. Those I have noted here are only the first line of each,

If All the World were paper, and all the sea was ink,
Old Mother Hubbard went to the cupboard
Who killed Cock Robin, I said the Sparrow.
The North wind doth blow and we shall have snow, what will poor Robin do then poor thing.
Doctor Foster went to Gloucester.
There was an old woman who lived in a shoe.
The Queen of Hearts, she made some tarts.
Jack Sprat could eat no fat, his wife could eat no lean.
Little boy blue, come blow up your horn.
Little Miss Muffet sat on a tuffet.
Little Polly Flinders, sat among the cinders.
Pat a Cake Pat a Cake, Baker's man.
Mary Mary quite contrary, how does your garden grow.
Twinkle Twinkle little star.
I had a little nut tree, nothing would it bear.
Sing a Song of Sixpence, pocketful of Rye.
Jack be nimble Jack be quick.
Hey diddle diddle, the cat and the fiddle.

The babies loved being tickled, laughing. This little piggy went to market, (then the next finger), this little piggy stayed at home, this little piggy had roast beef, this little piggy had none, (and then we get to the little finger, the pinkie), and this little piggy went wheee wheee wheee, (and I tickled them all the way up their arm and under the armpit, gently). Another tickling game was,

Round and round the Mulberry bush, (my finger going round and round their palm), up and down the garden, (my finger going up to elbow and back down to palm), one step two step, tickly under there, (and I tickled under the armpit). 'more, more,' they demanded.

Another old pastime, left over from Victorian times, and revived from time to time, were the wooden hoops, which we slapped with a short stick to keep them turning as we ran up and down the Alley. They were a forerunner of the plastic coated hula hoops children loved a decade or more later.

Stilts copied from those we'd seen at the circus, were fun to clatter up and down on. Some dads fixed up wooden foot rests on long poles for some children, but my stilts I devised myself using a couple of soup cans and lengths of string. The metal cans of the 1940s were thicker than those of today. We raced each other up and down the Alley.

In the Paddock, we did handstands against the oak tree, free handstands without support, did cartwheels. In the fields we played wheelbarrows, the game easy and cost nothing. One child was the barrow, walking on hands, while another child held their feet, the feet being the wheelbarrow handles.

It seemed so unfair when Mum called me in to go to bed before 8 oclock, especially when laying in bed, unable to sleep, I could hear my friends outside still enjoying themselves on those fine summer evenings

Spinning Tops, small ones, large ones, given to us as Christmas or Birthday presents, kept us busy too. Some were made of wood, some were metal. We whipped them up and down the Alley, trying to keep them spinning all the way there, turn, and back again. These games may seem rather tame by today's children, but we did enjoy getting out into the fresh air, letting off steam.

I can never remember being bored, we had no time. Idle hands did not stay idle for long. We read books, or we'd go to each others doors, 'Are yer comin' out to play?' we pleaded. We used coloured crayons in sketchbooks bought for a penny or two.

I did not receive pocket money, not many of us did. We did not get paid for doing chores around the house, or for running errands, unless it was for someone who was not family.

I've heard a lot of people say they did not like school milk. I loved the little bottle, one third of a pint, especially in the winter when it was warmed up on the radiators. Two or three boys carried the crates into the classrooms. By playtime, the milk was piping hot, so rolling down the sleeve of my jumper over my hands, I'd cuddle the bottle until the milk was cool enough to drink, sipping it slowly, enjoying it. (It was free). I needed the calories and calcium.

If we misbehaved in school time, the punishment was usually the cane, across the backsides of the boys, across the palm of the hand for the girls. Other forms of punishment were having to write "lines." To copy and learn off by heart either spelling words, or arithmetic problems. Too many mistakes and the teacher made us do it all over again and again. Boys wore flannel short trousers only to knee length until they were 12 or 13 years old. Towards the end of the 1940s, boys were going into longs at an earlier age.

The year I spent in the Headmaster's classroom wasn't as bad as I feared. The leaving age had been raised to 15 and some did not like that one little bit, they were impatient to leave and did not see the sense in staying on any longer. Jim Wooding was a chubby lad, a lively character, and one day he was playing up a bit, annoying Charlie Allen, the headmaster. When the headmaster left the room, Jim thought he could circumnavigate the expected punishment for his behaviour by breaking the dreaded cane in two. Charlie Allen got another from the storeroom, Jim broke that in two as well, right in front of the headmaster, but eventually Jim had to bend over and take his punishment, much to the amusement of the rest of us. Denis Saunders was also playing up one day, but escaped punishment. Denis had waggled his finger through the buttons on the flies of his trousers, rather crudely, and childish, but all innocent fun. I do try not to get too maudling, but in truth, if I had not enjoyed the companionship, friendship and support of my school pals, and other kind folk who knew of Mum's poverty, then I most suredly would have been the poorer in spirit for it. I was extremely fortunate to have them as friends and acquaintances. We read plays by Shakespeare and books by classic writers, sometimes acting parts.

I can recall one play, and I for once was the leading lady. It was in Miss Sharp's class. One of the boys was instructed to kiss me, and he did, very reluctantly, very quickly on my cheek, his face all screwed up, eyes closed, embarrassed.

One of my school reports has the teacher's remark, 'Good at acting.' I did work in films and television, later, much later, mostly on location, enjoying working in the company of leading actors.

On the week we were to break up for Christmas holidays, we had a party. We did the usual things, such as marching up and down to the Grand Old Duke of York. We stuck the tail on the donkey. One of the teachers played the piano for games which needed music accompaniment. Another lively game was Oranges and Lemons,

children lining up as in a queue,

Oranges and Lemons, say the bells of St Clement's, I owe you five farthings, say the bells of St Martin's, When will you pay me, say the bells of Old Bailey, When I grow rich, say the bells of Shoreditch,
(then slowly), Here comes a chopper to chop off your head, (down come the arms around whoever was passing under the arch formed by two standing opposite each other, arms raised and over to touch each other's hands). The pupil so caught was OUT. Rhyme repeated until all pupils were caught out.

We needed no expensive props to enjoy games. A skipping rope, a ball, some chalk, cost little. We made origami flexigons, fortune telling cubes as we called them. I'm bound to have forgotten a great deal of that which kept us amused and occupied.

'Do I 'ave ter kiss 'er?'   A double desk
'A Midsummer Night's Dream this ain't'
(more like a midsummer nightmare)

Chapter 65
DOMESTIC SCIENCE

I believe they call it Home Economics today. From young friends, I know most schools no longer teach Domestic Science, or if they do, it is nothing at all like the way we were taught in the 1940s.

Too many children are obese according to health reports. Is it that too many of them do not benefit from plain home cooking? Too many do not know what a vegetable tastes like as their mothers dish up another pasta dish? If they had eaten mashed vegetables when being weaned, they would eat vegetables later. Is it the childrens fault they are growing up with eating problems?

Originally we had no facility for teaching Domestic Science at Flitwick, so we boarded a bus at the start of the school day and travelled to Ampthill, to a building in Dunstable Road, near the Cedars. It had been a Food depot during the war.

The boys travelled to the same place, where they were taught woodwork. We girls donned white aprons, then each girl took up her place at a table. Cookers lined one wall, sinks another. We were told what we were to cook that day, issued with the ingredients, and the teacher then proceeded to tell us how to do it. At first we were given simple recipes, such as Victoria Sponge, later we progressed to making bread, pies, and biscuits. Must have been difficult for the teacher, meat was still rationed, so many dishes where meat was the main ingredient took some arranging. We made sausage rolls, and pies which included vegetables to pad them out. Swiss Rolls, and shown how to make Royal Icing, Chelsea buns, Bakewell tart, Steak and Kidney Pies, (some onion in it), stewing the meat, spending all morning making the pastry. Mum liked it when I went to the cookery classes because I always brought something tasty home.

We had to take either one or two shillings to help cover costs.

As well as showing us how to cook, the teacher sent 4 girls through to the attached flat to learn how to clean, cook a 2 or 3 course main meal, and make beds correctly. The flat had a bedroom, lounge, kitchen and bathroom. The kitchen was out of this world as far as I was concerned, coming from a house which had no kitchen sink or cooker. Everything was so new and clean. It had a gas cooker with three or four rings, a sink with hot and cold taps, cupboards for crockery and kitchen equipment, a larder for food, and a cupboard for cleaning materials. We had the use of a vacuum, a gas fired wash boiler, and everything was so easy to keep clean. Whites were washed in the boiler, colours by hand. It was then rinsed in the sink and put through the mangle which was not an old fashioned floor standing one like Mum's. It was a new mangle, the rollers driven by electricity, the mangle attached to a fitting at the side of the sink, so that as the water was squeezed out it dripped into the sink. I'd not seen such a wringer before. Simple to use. When the laundry was finished, we had to store the wringer away.

The washing was a few towels, teatowels, tablecloth. We had to learn to make a bed properly, with what the teacher called 'hospital corners,' tucking the sheets in correctly. The bathroom had the bath, a sink, lavatory, but no bidet, I'd never heard of a bidet. The bedroom held a single bed, a free standing wardrobe, chest of drawers, carpeted floor, dressing table.

I'd never used a vacuum before. Each week, it was a different 4 girls who were assigned to the duties in the flat. At midday, the four girls sat down with the teacher at the dining table, the meal prepared and served by two of the girls who had been given the kitchen duties as their assignment. Girls in the cookery classroom had school dinners delivered. The day we made a cottage loaf, I did

379

not get a slice for myself. I was a bit miffed about that. It was so soft, fresh and squashy and cut into a few slices. Mum sliced it, gave slice each to Joyce and Pat, two for Ernie, May Watson was in our house and was given a slice. 'Where's mine' I groaned, as I saw it all gone. When we made some buns, I ate one before I reached home.

I liked the cookery classes, not that I wanted to become a cook, but because we made things I didn't get at home.

When the annexe buildings were built to the rear of our own school, we stopped going to Ampthill and had cookery classes in one of the top classrooms, girls in one room, boys with their woodwork in the other room. We also had sewing tuition. How to use a sewing machine, make a button hole, put a placket in a skirt, yoke on a shirt.

We made our own sports outfits. For years we had tucked our skirts into our black elasticated leg knickers. Then we'd had a mismatch of skirts shorts/blouses. When we made our own, suddenly we looked more like a proper team. We sewed nightgowns, a lovely underslip, see chapter on clothing for more information. One term we were to take an old piece of lino to school, (the teacher gave me a piece). She taught us how to cut patterns in the lino, imprint the design on to a dirndle skirt we made, using fabric paint.

Oh yes! I was very conscientous, I was going to be a very practical and hardworking housewife, presuming of course I'd find someone who wanted to marry me. In the meantime I'd be expected to work in factory, shop, or work as a domestic servant.

I was eighteen before I sorted that out, when I enrolled at Boroughmuir School, (Edinburgh) for evening classes.

Chapter 66
FLITWICK IS DRAGGED
INTO THE 20th CENTURY

At last, half way through the 20th century, Flitwick began to show signs of throwing off Victoriana. It started with the new Council housing estate in the Avenue, when the roadmen with shovels and a steamroller laid out the roadways. Brickies, Joiners, Plumbers, Roofers, and all the other trades associated with housebuilding moved in. It all began to take shape, bringing hope to families living in overcrowded conditions or unsuitable accomodation. People like Renee Hymus, who slept with her children in our back bedroom.

Not for those new houses an outdoor privvy down the end of the garden, or attached to an outhouse. They were to have indoor bathrooms, hot and cold water taps for washing, electricity, all mod cons for growing families. Water and sewage pipes were laid, no more potties under the bed, no more cesspools, no more Wells.

In 1994, Flitwick Town Council published a book, "This History of Flitwick", and it says on page seven that real growth of Flitwick began in the 1970s. In my not so humble opinion, real growth began in the latter half of the 1940s, when that new Council housing estate was built, when mains water and sewerage services were laid down, when all homes were being supplied with electricity, when everyone who wanted a job was employed. Fowler and Chibnal began building private housing in Station Road and Oak Road. The rapid expansion of Flitwick began there and then, in those early years after the war, before 1950.

Workers commuted to Luton and Bedford, and the effects of larger pay packets began to show on the roads as cars appeared

381

outside the doors of working men.   Younger residents were not putting up with what their parents and grandparents had endured.

Television made its appearance, the World was opening up, the young wanted to be part of it.   The young of that era are all old and grey like me now, some are in the cemetery.

In the late 40s, a vision of better things was seen, and believed in.   I didn't take a lot of notice of all this modernising activity until the rest of the village roads began to be dug up.   We were all to benefit from flush lavatories and water on tap.

Around 1949, Dunstable Road was in the process of being dug up.   The workmen had an audience of schoolchildren every time school came out.   The smell of tar, the huge lumbering steamroller, the sound of shovels moving rubble around, the noise, we heard it all throughout the School.   At playtime we gawped through the railings as work progressed from the top of the slope, past the Vicarage, to the Fir Tree Inn.   Watching the Steamroller was fascinating.   Men dug trenches with pick and shovel, mixed tar in big barrels, pipes were laid, covered over with layers of stones, rubble, gravel, and tarmac.   Then the 'roller, rattling and puffing backwards and forwards finished it all off smoothly.   Now we were all going to be able to flush, WOW!!

Chapter 67
A NEW DECADE, A NEW BEGINNING

1950 and a new start for us. We moved out of the Alley early summer, and I left school on July 21st. Although I left with no paper qualifications, unemployment was low, and anyone fit and able to work found a job. Immigrants from the West Indies were here, they had no difficulty finding work, albeit much of it low paid. However, and this is something often forgotten today, the lower class natives of this island were also extremely low paid. Too many, like my family, still lived in hovels barely fit for habitation.

Our house move did not take us to one of those spanking new homes off the Avenue, or to Greenways where May Watson and her brood moved to. We moved to 13 Dunstable Road, a semi-detached council house built between the first and second world war. The rent was cheaper than the new houses on the estate. Our old house in the Alley was modernised with the addition of a bathroom next to the kitchen on the ground floor, and installation of electricity. The Well was made redundant. Claude and Eileen Barnes, who moved into number 30, did not have to go outside to the lavatory.

I began my career in the retail trade on the 14th August 1950 at Marks and Spencer in George Street Luton. I gave Mum half my wages each week. In return I had board and lodging, but had to pay my fares, dinners at M & S, buy my own clothes out of the other half.

Clothes rationing ended a year earlier. Mum could not afford to hit the shops and splurge on new clothes, but she did buy a new swagger coat from the Tally man, paying it up half a crown per week.

There were still long waiting lists for new cars. Even second-hand cars, mostly pre-war, cost a small fortune. Even if Ernie had known how to drive, we could not afford a car. Few families owned a telephone. Mum now had to pay for electricity and gas supply, but my money paid the rent, which was 13/6 per week, about 67p.

Lads who reached the age of 18 were called up for National Service, and many found themselves on their way to fight in the Korean War. Carl England, a former school friend, died in 1953, on National Service in Germany, when a tank overturned, trapping him.

I applied for positions as Junior Clerk, but I hadn't any qualifications for it. Someone came from the Education Authority, to find out what I'd like to do. When I said I'd like to be a Milliner, they pointed me in the direction of the hat factories, there were plenty in Luton. Luton's football team are called the Hatters.

I duly trotted along to the hat factories, got my name on the list of one, but they were not starting their new intake until the following January. I couldn't stay idle that long, Mum needed my money, so I had to find another job in the meantime. I scoured the papers, wrote a few letters. Sylvia Stringer, (or Hutchins) suggested I try Marks and Spencer as they always took on extra staff for Christmas. I spoke to a Supervisor, who arranged an appointment with the Manageress for me. Ernie insisted on accompanying me. I am sure the Manageress saw me squirming.

13 Dunstable Road had a square of garden at the front, laid to lawn surrounded by a border of Chrysanthemums left by the previous tenant. A hedge and small wooden gate finished the picture. The side access was then too narrow to let a car in, but it has been widened since Bowley's brush factory next door was demolished.

The house had no bathroom. Although the lavatory was outside, in a small brick extension to the barn, at least it flushed. Half way up the wall was the cistern, with a chain to pull as needed. No sink to wash our hands, and we still needed a Po under the bed.

We seldom used the front door, preferring instead to use the side door. The first kitchen held the mangle brought from the Alley and a Gas cooker. A window faced into the back garden. Through another door we entered a slightly larger kitchen housing a Belfast type sink, and a copper boiler in a corner. No furnishings. A door opened up into a cupboard under the stairs, the only cupboard in the kitchen. There was an old cast iron range, now unused. Window looking out to the gable end of the brush factory. Mum lit a fire under the copper boiler when she wanted to boil whites, the tub having to be physically filled with buckets of water. A tap near the bottom of the boiler emptied it. The sink had only a cold water tap. The floor of the kitchen was stone, the walls whitewashed brick.

Mum lit the old black range one day, but the chimney was blocked and smoke poured back into the room. There were no power points in the kitchen, only a single light bulb overhead. Mum still had to boil kettles and pots when needing hot water.

From the kitchen, we turned right into the living room, with two windows overlooking the rear garden. Ernie bought new utility furniture on hire purchase, a small sofa, two armchairs, dining table with four chairs, and sideboard. Mum sewed new curtains, strung on tapes hooked over nails, same as in the Alley. The previous tenant had left some decent lino on the floor, Mum made a new fireside rag rug. The room had a built in dresser, with shelves and cupboards handy for storage of crockery and our clothes, as we had no chests of drawers in the bedrooms.

The fireplace was what could be called 1930s style, small blue/green ceramic tiles, with a small grate and ceramic tiled hearth. Pat was only two years old, so a fireguard was permanently in place.

A new electric radio, (and later, the Television), was bought from Wynne's shop. In the whole house, there was but one power point, in the living room, just inside the door, next to Mum's chair.

The flex had to go under the fireside rug to the radio on the dresser.

At the front of the house was the parlour, no furniture to begin with, until Ernie managed to get a couple of second hand armchairs and a piano which badly needed tuning. In a corner of the room was a very fine Victorian style black cast iron fire surround with small dog grate. Never lit.

The stairs curved up to the bedrooms from the hall   just inside the front door, bare floorboards for the first year or two, until Mum acquired a carpet runner. Lino had been left on the hall floor by previous tenant. The only furniture brought with us from the Alley were beds, the rest put on a bonfire. Ernie said it had woodworm.

We had no vacuum, fridge, or other electrical gadgets.

I was appalled when Mum told me I was expected to do my courting in the parlour. Ernie had forbidden me to have boyfriends until I was 17. Naturally, this edict did not go down well with me, and was the cause of serious friction. The order banning me from fraternising with the opposite sex was totally ignored.

I took only one lad home to visit Mum, long after I had left home for good, and that was Alvis, who I eventually married. What was I supposed to do in that small room? hold hands and converse on the state of the Universe? Play the piano, with its out of tune keys? Any blossoming romance would have been over before it began. Joyce and I slept in the bedroom at the front of the house, Mum and Ernie slept in the back bedroom with Pat. Both bedrooms had a fireplace, small but very fine looking, we never used them. Mum could not afford the fuel. There was also an empty third bedroom. A few years later, the back bedroom and side bedroom were changed around a bit to provide enough room for the Council to fit a bathroom in, without losing a bedroom.

The previous tenant had left a small corner wardrobe in the

front bedroom, just big enough for five or six hangars, but enough for me, as I had not a lot of clothes anyway. My underwear, and Joyce's clothes, were kept in the cupboard of the dresser downstairs.

I was disappointed the house had no bathroom when we moved in. It was cold in the side bedroom as I washed myself down. Kettles of hot water had to be carried up, and the dirty water carried down. I couldn't afford bath oils, but a bar of soap and good scrub with the flannel and nail brush did wonders.

The back garden stretched up to the railway fence, until new homes were built there. Ernie soon had it productive.

Upstairs was very spartan, we had no carpets, no lino, just bare floorboards. Furniture was kitchen style chairs in front and back bedroom, and that tiny wardrobe in my bedroom, plus the washstand and basin with ewer in Mum's bedroom. We could not afford to furnish the bedrooms, or buy carpets for the floor.

Next door at number 11 lived Joy and Pam French, they heard many a row between Ernie and Mum, and a bit of screaming with rage from me, but they took it in good part, being sometimes annoyed, sometimes amused. Mum paid the electric when the bill came in, but the Gas slot meter had to be fed with single shillings. She'd give me a two bob bit, or 12 pennies and ask me to go along to Mrs Ellis at number 19 to ask if she'd got any shillings. Mrs Ellis must have got fed up with me, but I always found her very polite and obliging, a very nice woman.

The grass was growing on the front lawn. We had no mower, so one Sunday morning I took a pair of scissors and I cut that small patch of grass with those scissors. Sounds crazy!! Before it needed cut again, Ernie bought a pair of shears, they trimmed the hedge too.

One day, something happened which angered me, and embarrassed someone I hardly knew. It was a Sunday afternoon, and

I was in the front garden doing a bit of weeding, when a lad I had met through friends turned up at the gate and asked me if I'd like to go for a spin with him on his motor bike. It wasn't compulsory for riders to wear crash helmets in the early 1950s. I imagined myself astride that bike, the wind blowing in my hair, but it wasn't to be.

We were chatting, him astride his bike just outside the gate, me leaning on the gate. I was flattered that he had remembered me, and lapped up the obvious admiration, (and sexiness) in his blue eyes when all hell broke loose. Ernie must have seen me being chatted up, and suddenly he threw open one of the upstairs windows and yelled at me to get in the house. Then he yelled at the startled fellow to 'Bugger orf.' That was the end of that likely romance before it had even begun. The poor chap shot off as if the Devil himself were at his shoulder, and I never saw him again.

Any normal parents would have invited the chap in for a cup of tea, if only to give him the once over, even to be nosy to find out where he came from and what he did for a living. Inside the living room, a minute or so later, there was another fierce argument between Ernie and I, because I was furious. Mum wanted to 'keep the peace', What Peace? This was undignified war. According to Ernie, no decent girl had anything to do with fellows like that. 'Like what?' I demanded to know. Them that ride motor bikes came the reply. I wasn't to be out after 10 pm, which was difficult, because the train from Luton or Bedford did not comply with the timing, but he was unwilling to compromise. One night I arrived home off the train five minutes after 10 pm to find the door locked, and I had no key. Ernie would not give me a spare key. By this time I was nearly seventeen years old, getting very restless.

Once in the house, after knocking and knocking, and screaming, for nigh on twenty minutes, we had another fierce argument because of the few minutes I was late. I almost killed him. I hit him with one of the candlesticks from the mantleshelf. Fortunately for him, and for me, they were cheap tinny ones Mum had bought at a jumble sale, so they did no real damage. For my own sanity, and because I could not stand being in the same house as Ernie, I began making plans to leave home.

My first job at Marks and Spencer was on the Toy counter. For a kid who'd had little relationship with toys, you can imagine my delight as I demonstrated, smiled, laughed with the customers, it was exciting. When the manageress offered me a permanent job, I had no hesitation in accepting. I remained with M & S for another 11 years, moving from Luton to the Bedford store, then to Falkirk and finally Edinburgh. I never did become a Milliner.

Marks and Spencer staff had to adhere to certain high standards of dress and behaviour, which was good personal training for me. It taught me a lot, such as the use of deodorants, and good grooming. Except for the window dressers, female staff did not wear trousers. We wore an overall which had to have all the buttons done up. Cotton and hard to wash and press, they were replaced in 1951 with nylon overalls, much easier to launder, which we did ourselves.

Petrol rationing ended, we had no car, so no difference for us. The weather turned out terrible, with the Ouse bursting its banks, flooding Clapham and Kempston in May. Also in May, two men were killed by lightning, and crops were damaged. Flitwick had its share of storms. In May we experienced a snowstorm, but the summer turned out warm. Later, in November, an early icy winter set in, the buses were freezing. Who wants to give up their comfy car for a wet cold bus? Sewerage pipes were still being laid, but some vandals thought it a good idea to throw bricks on the pipes.

Income Tax was a whopping 40% (8/- to the £1), and coal

was 8 shillings per hundredweight, almost twice the 1946 price.
Pint of beer 1/4, (7p) pound of butter 1/6 (7.5p)

The Stone of Scone, (pronounced Scoon), was spirited away from Westminster Abbey on December 25th, to be returned the following year on 3rd February. Some said it wasn't the stolen stone. By the time I met Ian Hamilton, one of the conspirators, a number of years later at a conference I attended, he was a well respected member of the legal profession. A film is now in the making.

A letter cost tuppence halfpenny to send, a pair of shoes approximately £3, and Liz Taylor married her first husband Nicky Hilton. Her wedding gown costing £5000 was paid for by her studio, (over ten years wages for the ordinary mortal), but being wealthy didn't mean happiness for the couple, as they divorced just nine months later.

£35 would buy you a bedroom suite, a Swagger coat cost around 49/11, (£2.50), and 20 Woodbine cigarettes 2/7. (13p)
Soap came off ration in September.

Today, Flitwick is a thriving commuter town, many residents leaving early in the morning and not returning until evening. The town also boasts an industrial estate, providing work for some, but in 1950 for £10 assisted passage, those who were dissatisfied with living conditions here, and wanted to enjoy a better way of life, were being encouraged to emigrate to Canada, New Zealand, South Africa, Australia, where better paid jobs were going abegging.

Bricks and Tarmac now cover the fields of my youth, the old Rec is now a shopping centre. The brook is polluted, the Moor allotments are a paddock, but there have been vast improvements in the Alley. It is now a respectable place to live, we cannot call it the Alley any more.

Some changes in Flitwick I haven't liked, the worst change

I believe was the loss of the old Rec. The Council planners who decided future growth after the war, gave scant regard to the environmental impact of the changes to come. Flitwick had to grow, there was plenty of space, it desperately needed more local amenities, but why destroy that green space. Flitwick has no central park. The little patch of grass behind the Community Hall in Dunstable Road, cannot be called a park.

Flitwick couldn't remain static, buried in its pre-war status, but did they have to build over the old Rec? Where Cricketers, wearing crisp white shirts, white trousers with a smart crease, and woolly sweaters with a dark stripe at the V neck, batted with Willow, where clapping was heard as runs were made, or sighs and ohs when a player was bowled or run out.

From Church End to Steppingly Road to Running Waters to Maulden Road, Flitwick has no parkland. Is it any wonder that the Health Councils are very concerned because so many children are obese? Where in Fliwick can children play safely, but as importantly, can play without having to pay for the pleasure? Is it any wonder that many young teenagers hang about street corners? There was little chance of the 1940s child becoming obese. We had perhaps one or two pupils who it could be said were a bit heavy, but it was unlikely to be because of overeating or lack of exercise. Boys helped their dads in the garden, they ran around the school playground as energetically as any slimmer child. If any of us were unhealthy, it was usually because of one of the diseases endemic at the time, such as Polio, T.B. or attack of Measles, Mumps, 'Flu, weak heart.

Chapter 68
A BATH

A bath, a bath, my kingdom for a bath,but Hey!! where's the taps?

About a year after we moved into Dunstable Road, I came home from work to find we had been delivered a bath.

No ordinary bath this. It had no taps, no drainage plug, and on the small side. This was a cast iron hip bath, because only the hips get covered with water when sat in. The bath was sitting on the floor in the otherwise empty spare third bedroom. I had to traipse upstairs carrying kettles and pots of hot water in order to be able to sit in it and wash myself all over. Having a good long soak was impossible. The water became cold too quickly.

I tried it out, my legs dangling over the rim, and dreamt of the day when I could soak in a real bath full of bubbles and foam. My hair washed at the kitchen sink, water in the washing up bowl, kettle boiling on the stove, large jug to mix hot and cold at the ready. Amami or Drene shampoo in little sachets costing 9d each.

Friday night is Amami night used to be a slogan.

Eventually, as soon as I could afford it, I visited Marks and Spencer's resident hairdresser approximately every six weeks or so, but still washed my hair at home on Friday evenings. I can't believe I washed my hair and had a bath only once per week, but that was usual in most homes. Water had to be heated either by a back boiler in the fireplace, or an immersion heater in a water tank, or like me, the water had to be heated on the stove. This usually meant that only one member of the family could be bathed on any one day, unless they all dunked in the same water. Today I have central heating and endless hot water, which would have been a luxury for Mum.

She remarked to me one day, (I was about to have a rare second bath in one week),
'You'll wash yer self away if yer aint careful.'

Today, those homes that have escaped the demolition crews have been modernised, they have indoor bathrooms, but in the 1940s, a Po under the bed was a must, for no one wanted to go to the outside privvy in the middle of the night. Wealthy folk bathed as often as they cared to, they had bathrooms and servants. By the middle of the 19th century, bathrooms with hot and cold taps made their appearance in more prosperous households.

The middle classes usually bathed weekly, having fewer servants, but the millions of poor people in this country had to manage to keep clean as best they could, if they even bothered at all. Those living in large cities, in slums, lacking access to fresh water, must have experienced overwhelming difficulties. Public bath houses made an appearance, but the poor could not afford the fees. At a village near my present home, there is a swimming pool. At the side of the swimming pool is a bank of 6 or 7 baths. These were built to provide the Miners with a bath to wash the grime of their job off before they went home, to save the families from having to fill a tin bath in the house, because their homes had no bathrooms.

Unlike Edinburgh, which was one of the first cities to realise the significance of providing the populace with a supply of fresh water and good sewage system, Flitwick lagged far behind. The Parish Council were still arguing over the cost when the Second World War intervened. In the Victorian era, and right up to today in many places, the poor struggled on in appalling conditions, suffering economic insecurity, grinding poverty, with the continuous threat of illness and disease. A tin bath in front of the fire had to be sufficient for those who took personal hygiene seriously.

To their credit, those elected to office in Flitwick after the war, did do something about it. Those early new council houses on the new estate off the Avenue were well built of good quality for ordinary working class people to live in and enjoy, something only dreamt about previously Many of the tradesmen working on them had fought in the war, and were glad that it was all over and they could get on with constructive instead of destructive work.

13 Dunstable Road has a bathroom today, with hot and cold taps, and there is no longer any need for a Po under the bed. Where I sat in my hip bath, there now sits a modern bath, sink and w.c. Other older council houses, as at Hornes End, and Clophill Road Maulden, a small bathroom extension has been added on to the rear of the kitchen.

Andrew Cumming, an Edinburgh man, led the way in sanitary ware when he patented the first water closet in 1775. A man named Bramah was mentioned on TV as developing a water closet in 1778. 160 odd years later, we still waited in the Alley for ours.

394

Chapter 69
EPILOGUE

I strolled by the lake, looked at the Horsechestnut trees,
By the Manor, where we collected Conkers,
I walked by the Brook, no fish in it now, too dirty,
Childrens laughter, echoes from the past, I smile,
Remembering those that stepped this way with me,
Barry, Stanley, Angela, Kathy, June, Frankie, Hilda,
Thelma one and Thelma two, Carl, Dennis,
Dirty faces, skinned knees, climbing the embankment,
Paddling, Lizards frolicking, days full of fun,
In our dirt yard, by the house, coats bundled into heaps,
For rounders, we skipped, we threw a ball,
'Run to the shop,' a mother calls, to a child on stilts,
who pretends not to hear,
Gobstoppers, Sherbet, Skipping ropes, infectious laughter,
We've all grown old, some forever sleep,
but I remember them.

I was brought up in an era when Royalty, Politicians, and the Clergy were highly regarded and respected, when there were no graphic TV images of poverty and starvation in parts of the world where those that rule are corrupt, leading opulent lifestyles while their citizens starve and suffer appalling disease. Time will take care of Dictators, but how much can a country suffer before they go.

Electricity did not come to Flitwick and many other villages until 1930, and it was after the war before the village was provided with adequate mains sewage disposal. Why did we have to wait so long? Why is there still so much slum housing? Why do we need so many charities? Why do housing estates put up with all the graffiti and rubbish strewn everywhere? Why do landlords, public and private, allow their properties to deteriorate so very badly? And money doesn't matter? While I am writing this, the news on TV is all about what they call the Credit Crunch. We will see how it looks in a year or two. Will we be on the return to Victorian conditions, when the lower rungs of society had such a hard time just existing? When buying a pair of shoes meant starvation rations to pay for them? When living conditions were appalling? Will the National Health Service survive?

The Alley was not a pretty street, but it did have nature all around. The wild flowers in the meadow, Swallows ducking and diving, catching insects mid air, ripening corn in summer, green vegetables all year round.

It was a time of rumblings of discontent in distant lands ruled from Westminster, and that pink tinted map was about to undergo drastic change. I was part of history in the making.

A week or two at Butlin's was the height of a child's holiday ambition. Young people emigrated for a better life for themselves and their families. There were still too many people living in sub-standard accomodation, and being paid slave wages. Colour or ethnic origin, or religion, had little to do with it when I was growing up under those appalling conditions in the Alley.

Tempus Fugit, Goodnight.

Maureen Kerr, AMRSPH, on the day of her retirement,
age 60, from the Inland Revenue Stamping Office in Edinburgh.
Not a Celebrity, not famous.
An ordinary woman, wife, working mother who grew up in
a Bedfordshire village in the 1940s.
A village life that has disappeared.
The fields of Cabbages replaced by commuter land,
Tesco, tarmac, concrete, and bricks.
This is her memoirs of childhood, growing up in that village,
typical of rural villages of the time